The Casebook
of Sherlock Holmes

Arthur Conan Doyle

ALMA CLASSICS

ALMA CLASSICS
an imprint of

ALMA BOOKS LTD
Thornton House
Thornton Road
Wimbledon Village
London SW19 4NG
United Kingdom
www.almaclassics.com

The Casebook of Sherlock Holmes first published in 1927
This edition first published by Alma Classics in 2023

Cover image: Leo Nickolls Design

Edited text, notes and Extra Material © Alma Books Ltd

Printed in Great Britain by CPI Group (UK) Ltd, Croydon CR0 4YY

ISBN: 978-1-84749-882-3

Contents

Other books by ARTHUR CONAN DOYLE
published by Alma Classics

The Casebook
of Sherlock Holmes

PREFACE

I fear that Mr Sherlock Holmes may become like one of those popular tenors who, having outlived their time, are still tempted to make repeated farewell bows to their indulgent audiences. This must cease, and he must go the way of all flesh,* material or imaginary. One likes to think that there is some fantastic limbo for the children of imagination, some strange, impossible place where the beaux of Fielding may still make love to the belles of Richardson, where Scott's heroes still may strut, Dickens's delightful cockneys still raise a laugh, and Thackeray's worldlings continue to carry on their reprehensible careers.* Perhaps in some humble corner of such a Valhalla,* Sherlock and his Watson may for a time find a place, while some more astute sleuth with some even less astute comrade may fill the stage which they have vacated.

His career has been a long one – though it is possible to exaggerate it: decrepit gentlemen who approach me and declare that his adventures formed the reading of their boyhood do not meet the response from me which they seem to expect. One is not anxious to have one's personal dates handled so unkindly. As a matter of cold fact, Holmes made his debut in *A Study in Scarlet* and in *The Sign of Four*, two small booklets which appeared between 1887 and 1889.* It was in 1891 that 'A Scandal in Bohemia', the first of the long series of short stories, appeared in the *Strand Magazine*. The public seemed appreciative and desirous of more, so that from that date, thirty-six years ago, they have been produced in a broken series which now contains no fewer than fifty-six stories, republished in *The Adventures*, *The Memoirs*, *The Return* and *His*

Last Bow, and there remain these twelve published during the last few years which are here produced under the title of *The Casebook of Sherlock Holmes*. He began his adventures in the very heart of the later Victorian era, carried it through the all-too-short reign of Edward, and has managed to hold his own little niche even in these feverish days.* Thus it would be true to say that those who first read of him as young men have lived to see their own grown-up children following the same adventures in the same magazine. It is a striking example of the patience and loyalty of the British public.

I had fully determined at the conclusion of *The Memoirs* to bring Holmes to an end, as I felt that my literary energies should not be directed too much into one channel. That pale, clear-cut face and loose-limbed figure were taking up an undue share of my imagination. I did the deed, but, fortunately, no coroner had pronounced upon the remains, and so, after a long interval, it was not difficult for me to respond to the flattering demand and to explain my rash act away.* I have never regretted it, for I have not in actual practice found that these lighter sketches have prevented me from exploring and finding my limitations in such varied branches of literature as history, poetry, historical novels, psychic research and the drama.* Had Holmes never existed, I could not have done more, though he may perhaps have stood a little in the way of the recognition of my more serious literary work.

And so, reader, farewell to Sherlock Holmes! I thank you for your past constancy, and can but hope that some return has been made in the shape of that distraction from the worries of life and stimulating change of thought which can only be found in the fairy kingdom of romance.

ARTHUR CONAN DOYLE

THE ADVENTURE
OF THE ILLUSTRIOUS CLIENT

"I T CAN'T HURT NOW," was Mr Sherlock Holmes's comment when, for the tenth time in as many years, I asked his leave to reveal the following narrative. So it was that at last I obtained permission to put on record what was, in some ways, the supreme moment of my friend's career.

Both Holmes and I had a weakness for the Turkish bath. It was over a smoke in the pleasant lassitude of the drying room that I have found him less reticent and more human than anywhere else. On the upper floor of the Northumberland Avenue establishment there is an isolated corner where two couches lie side by side, and it was on these that we lay upon 3rd September 1902, the day when my narrative begins. I had asked him whether anything was stirring, and for answer he had shot his long, thin, nervous arm out of the sheets which enveloped him and had drawn an envelope from the inside pocket of the coat which hung beside him.

"It may be some fussy, self-important fool, it may be a matter of life or death," said he as he handed me the note. "I know no more than this message tells me."

It was from the Carlton Club,* and dated the evening before. This is what I read:

Sir James Damery presents his compliments to Mr Sherlock Holmes, and will call upon him at 4.30 tomorrow. Sir James begs to say that the matter upon which he desires to consult Mr Holmes is very delicate, and also very important. He trusts, therefore, that Mr Holmes will make every effort to grant this interview, and that he will confirm it over the telephone to the Carlton Club.

"I need not say that I have confirmed it, Watson," said Holmes as I returned the paper. "Do you know anything of this man Damery?"

"Only that his name is a household word in society."

"Well, I can tell you a little more than that. He has rather a reputation for arranging delicate matters which are to be kept out of the papers. You may remember his negotiations with Sir George Lewis over the Hammerford will case.* He is a man of the world with a natural turn for diplomacy. I am bound, therefore, to hope that it is not a false scent and that he has some real need for our assistance."

"Our?"

"Well, if you will be so good, Watson."

"I shall be honoured."

"Then you have the hour – four thirty. Until then we can put the matter out of our heads."

I was living in my own rooms in Queen Anne Street* at the time, but I was round at Baker Street before the time named. Sharp to the half-hour, Colonel Sir James Damery was announced. It is hardly necessary to describe him, for many will remember that large, bluff, honest personality, that broad, clean-shaven face – above all, that pleasant, mellow voice. Frankness shone from his grey Irish eyes, and good humour played round his mobile, smiling lips. His lucent top hat, his dark frock coat – indeed, every detail, from the pearl pin in the black satin cravat to the lavender spats over the varnished shoes – spoke of the meticulous care in dress for which he was famous. The big, masterful aristocrat dominated the little room.

"Of course, I was prepared to find Doctor Watson," he remarked with a courteous bow. "His collaboration may be very necessary, for we are dealing on this occasion, Mr Holmes, with a man to whom violence is familiar and who will, literally, stick at nothing. I should say that there is no more dangerous man in Europe."

"I have had several opponents to whom that flattering term has been applied," said Holmes with a smile. "Don't you smoke? Then you will excuse me if I light my pipe. If your man is more dangerous than the late Professor Moriarty, or than the living Colonel Sebastian Moran,* then he is indeed worth meeting. May I ask his name?"

"Have you ever heard of Baron Gruner?"

"You mean the Austrian murderer?"

Colonel Damery threw up his kid-gloved hands with a laugh. "There is no getting past you, Mr Holmes! Wonderful! So you have already sized him up as a murderer?"

"It is my business to follow the details of Continental crime. Who could possibly have read what happened at Prague and have any doubts as to the man's guilt? It was a purely technical legal point and the suspicious death of a witness that saved him! I am as sure that he killed his wife when the so-called 'accident' happened in the Splügen Pass* as if I had seen him do it. I knew, also, that he had come to England, and had a presentiment that sooner or later he would find me some work to do. Well, what has Baron Gruner been up to? I presume it is not this old tragedy which has come up again?"

"No, it is more serious than that. To revenge crime is important, but to prevent it is more so. It is a terrible thing, Mr Holmes, to see a dreadful event, an atrocious situation, preparing itself before your eyes, to clearly understand whither it will lead and yet to be utterly unable to avert it. Can a human being be placed in a more trying position?"

"Perhaps not."

"Then you will sympathize with the client in whose interests I am acting."

"I did not understand that you were merely an intermediary. Who is the principal?"

"Mr Holmes, I must beg you not to press that question. It is important that I should be able to assure him that his honoured name has been in no way dragged into the matter. His motives are, to the last degree, honourable and chivalrous, but he prefers to remain unknown. I need not say that your fees will be assured and that you will be given a perfectly free hand. Surely the actual name of your client is immaterial?"

"I am sorry," said Holmes. "I am accustomed to have mystery at one end of my cases, but to have it at both ends is too confusing. I fear, Sir James, that I must decline to act."

Our visitor was greatly disturbed. His large, sensitive face was darkened with emotion and disappointment.

"You hardly realize the effect of your own action, Mr Holmes," said he. "You place me in a most serious dilemma, for I am perfectly certain that you would be proud to take over the case if I could give you the facts, and yet a promise forbids me from revealing them all. May I, at least, lay all that I can before you?"

"By all means, so long as it is understood that I commit myself to nothing."

"That is understood. In the first place, you have no doubt heard of General de Merville?"

"De Merville of Khyber* fame? Yes, I have heard of him."

"He has a daughter, Violet de Merville – young, rich, beautiful, accomplished, a wonder-woman in every way. It is this daughter, this lovely, innocent girl, whom we are endeavouring to save from the clutches of a fiend."

"Baron Gruner has some hold over her, then?"

"The strongest of all holds where a woman is concerned – the hold of love. The fellow is, as you may have heard, extraordinarily handsome, with a most fascinating manner, a gentle voice and that air of romance and mystery which means so much to a woman. He is said to have the whole sex at his mercy and to have made ample use of the fact."

"But how came such a man to meet a lady of the standing of Miss Violet de Merville?"

"It was on a Mediterranean yachting voyage. The company, though select, paid their own passages. No doubt the promoters hardly realized the baron's true character until it was too late. The villain attached himself to the lady, and with such effect that he has completely and absolutely won her heart. To say that she loves him hardly expresses it. She dotes upon him, she is obsessed by him. Outside of him there is nothing on earth. She will not hear one word against him. Everything has been done to cure her of her madness, but in vain. To sum up, she proposes to marry him next month. As she is of age and has a will of iron, it is hard to know how to prevent her."

"Does she know about the Austrian episode?"

"The cunning devil has told her every unsavoury public scandal of his past life, but always in such a way as to make himself out to be an innocent martyr. She absolutely accepts his version and will listen to no other."

"Dear me! But surely you have inadvertently let out the name of your client? It is no doubt General de Merville."

Our visitor fidgeted in his chair.

"I could deceive you by saying so, Mr Holmes, but it would not be true. De Merville is a broken man. The strong soldier has been utterly demoralized by this incident. He has lost the nerve which never failed him on the battlefield and has become a weak, doddering old man, utterly incapable of contending with a brilliant, forceful rascal like this Austrian. My client, however, is an old friend, one who has known the general intimately for many years and taken a paternal interest in this young girl since she wore short frocks. He cannot see this tragedy consummated without some attempt to stop it. There is nothing in which Scotland Yard can act. It was his own suggestion that you should be called in, but it was, as I have said, on the express stipulation that he should not be personally involved in the matter. I have no doubt, Mr Holmes, with your great powers you could easily trace my client back through me, but I must ask you, as a point of honour, to refrain from doing so, and not to break in upon his incognito."

Holmes gave a whimsical smile.

"I think I may safely promise that," said he. "I may add that your problem interests me, and that I shall be prepared to look into it. How shall I keep in touch with you?"

"The Carlton Club will find me. But, in case of emergency, there is a private telephone call:* 'XX.31'."

Holmes noted it down and sat, still smiling, with the open memorandum book upon his knee.

"The baron's present address, please?"

"Vernon Lodge, near Kingston.* It is a large house. He has been fortunate in some rather shady speculations and is a rich man – which, naturally, makes him a more dangerous antagonist."

"Is he at home at present?"

"Yes."

"Apart from what you have told me, can you give me any further information about the man?"

"He has expensive tastes. He is a horse fancier. For a short time he played polo at Hurlingham,* but then this Prague affair got noised about and he had to leave. He collects books and pictures. He is a man with a considerable artistic side to his nature. He is, I believe, a recognized authority upon Chinese pottery, and has written a book upon the subject."

"A complex mind," said Holmes. "All great criminals have that. My old friend Charlie Peace was a violin virtuoso. Wainewright was no mean artist.* I could quote many more. Well, Sir James, you will inform your client that I am turning my mind upon Baron Gruner. I can say no more. I have some sources of information of my own, and I dare say we may find some means of opening the matter up."

When our visitor had left us, Holmes sat so long in deep thought that it seemed to me that he had forgotten my presence. At last, however, he came briskly back to earth.

"Well, Watson, any views?" he asked.

"I should think you had better see the young lady herself."

"My dear Watson, if her poor old broken father cannot move her, how shall I, a stranger, prevail? And yet there is something in the suggestion if all else fails. But I think we must begin from a different angle. I rather fancy that Shinwell Johnson might be a help."

I have not had occasion to mention Shinwell Johnson in these memoirs because I have seldom drawn my cases from the latter phases of my friend's career. During the first years of the century he became a valuable assistant. Johnson, I grieve to say, made his name first as a very dangerous villain and served two terms at Parkhurst.* Finally, he repented and allied himself to Holmes, acting as his agent in the huge criminal underworld of London, and obtaining information which often proved to be of vital importance. Had Johnson been a "nark"* of the police, he would soon have been exposed, but as he dealt with cases which never came directly into the courts, his activities were never realized by his companions. With the glamour of his two convictions upon him, he had the entrée* of every nightclub, dosshouse and gambling den in the town, and his quick observation and active brain made him an ideal agent for gaining information. It was to him that Sherlock Holmes now proposed to turn.

It was not possible for me to follow the immediate steps taken by my friend, for I had some pressing professional business of my own, but I met him by appointment that evening at Simpson's,* where, sitting at a small table in the front window and looking down at the rushing stream of life in the Strand, he told me something of what had passed.

"Johnson is on the prowl," said he. "He may pick up some garbage in the darker recesses of the underworld, for it is down there, amid the black roots of crime, that we must hunt for this man's secrets."

"But if the lady will not accept what is already known, why should any fresh discovery of yours turn her from her purpose?"

"Who knows, Watson? Woman's heart and mind are insoluble puzzles to the male. Murder might be condoned or explained, and yet some smaller offence might rankle. Baron Gruner remarked to me—"

"He remarked to you!"

"Oh, to be sure, I had not told you of my plans! Well, Watson, I love to come to close grips with my man. I like to meet him eye to eye and read for myself the stuff that he is made of. When I had given Johnson his instructions, I took a cab out to Kingston and found the baron in a most affable mood."

"Did he recognize you?"

"There was no difficulty about that, for I simply sent in my card. He is an excellent antagonist, cool as ice, silky-voiced and soothing as one of your fashionable consultants, and poisonous as a cobra. He has breed* in him, a real aristocrat of crime, with a superficial suggestion of afternoon tea and all the cruelty of the grave behind it. Yes, I am glad to have had my attention called to Baron Adelbert Gruner."

"You say he was affable?"

"A purring cat who thinks he sees prospective mice. Some people's affability is more deadly than the violence of coarser souls. His greeting was characteristic. 'I rather thought I should see you sooner or later, Mr Holmes,' said he. 'You have been engaged, no doubt, by General de Merville to endeavour to stop my marriage with his daughter, Violet. That is so, is it not?'

"I acquiesced.

"'My dear man,' said he, 'you will only ruin your own well-deserved reputation. It is not a case in which you can possibly succeed. You will have barren work, to say nothing of incurring some danger. Let me very strongly advise you to draw off at once.'

"'It is curious,' I answered, 'but that was the very advice which I had intended to give you. I have a respect for your brains, Baron, and the little which I have seen of your personality has not lessened it. Let me put it to you as man to man. No one wants to rake up your past and make you unduly uncomfortable. It is over, and you are now in smooth waters, but if you persist in this marriage, you will raise up a swarm of powerful enemies who will never leave you alone until they have made England too hot to hold you. Is the game worth it? Surely you would be wiser if you left the lady alone. It would not be pleasant for you if these facts of your past were brought to her notice.'

"The baron has little waxed tips of hair under his nose, like the short antennae of an insect. These quivered with amusement as he listened, and he finally broke into a gentle chuckle.

"'Excuse my amusement, Mr Holmes,' said he, 'but it is really funny to see you trying to play a hand with no cards in it. I don't think anyone could do it better, but it is rather pathetic, all the same. Not a colour card there, Mr Holmes – nothing but the smallest of the small.'

"'So you think.'

"'So I know. Let me make the thing clear to you, for my own hand is so strong that I can afford to show it. I have been fortunate enough to win the entire affection of this lady. This was given to me in spite of the fact that I told her very clearly of all the unhappy incidents in my past life. I also told her that certain wicked and designing persons – I hope you recognize yourself – would come to her and tell her these things, and I warned her how to treat them. You have heard of post-hypnotic suggestion, Mr Holmes? Well, you will see how it works, for a man of personality can use hypnotism without any vulgar passes or tomfoolery. So she is ready for you and, I have no doubt, would give you an appointment, for she is quite amenable to her father's will – save only in the one little matter.'

"Well, Watson, there seemed to be no more to say, so I took my leave with as much cold dignity as I could summon, but, as I had my hand on the door handle, he stopped me.

"'By the way, Mr Holmes,' said he, 'did you know Le Brun, the French agent?'

"'Yes,' said I.

"'Do you know what befell him?'

"'I heard that he was beaten by some Apaches* in the Montmartre district and crippled for life.'

"'Quite true, Mr Holmes. By a curious coincidence he had been enquiring into my affairs only a week before. Don't do it,

Mr Holmes – it's not a lucky thing to do. Several have found that out. My last word to you is: go your own way and let me go mine. Goodbye!'

"So there you are, Watson. You are up to date now."

"The fellow seems dangerous."

"Mighty dangerous. I disregard the blusterer, but this is the sort of man who says rather less than he means."*

"Must you interfere? Does it really matter if he marries the girl?"

"Considering that he undoubtedly murdered his last wife, I should say it mattered very much. Besides, the client! Well, well… we need not discuss that. When you have finished your coffee, you had best come home with me, for the blithe Shinwell will be there with his report."

We found him sure enough – a huge, coarse, red-faced, scorbutic* man with a pair of vivid black eyes which were the only external sign of the very cunning mind within. It seems that he had dived down into what was peculiarly his kingdom, and beside him on the settee was a brand which he had brought up* in the shape of a slim, flame-like young woman with a pale, intense face, youthful, and yet so worn with sin and sorrow that one read the terrible years which had left their leprous mark upon her.

"This is Miss Kitty Winter," said Shinwell Johnson, waving his fat hand as an introduction. "What she don't know – well, there, she'll speak for herself. Put my hand right on her, Mr Holmes, within an hour of your message."

"I'm easy to find," said the young woman. "Hell, London, gets me every time. Same address for Porky Shinwell. We're old mates, Porky, you and I. But – by cripes!* – there is another who ought to be down in a lower hell than we if there was any justice in the world! That is the man you are after, Mr Holmes."

Holmes smiled. "I gather we have your good wishes, Miss Winter."

"If I can help to put him where he belongs, I'm yours to the rattle,"* said our visitor with fierce energy. There was an intensity of hatred in her white, set face and her blazing eyes such as woman seldom and man never can attain. "You needn't go into my past, Mr Holmes. That's neither here nor there. But what I am, Adelbert Gruner made me. If I could pull him down!" She clutched frantically with her hands into the air. "Oh, if I could only pull him into the pit where he has pushed so many!"

"You know how the matter stands?"

"Porky Shinwell has been telling me. He's after some other poor fool and wants to marry her this time. You want to stop it. Well, you surely know enough about this devil to prevent any decent girl in her senses wanting to be in the same parish with him."

"She is not in her senses. She is madly in love. She has been told all about him. She cares nothing."

"Told about the murder?"

"Yes."

"My Lord, she must have a nerve!"

"She puts them all down as slanders."

"Couldn't you lay proofs before her silly eyes?"

"Well, can you help us do so?"

"Ain't I a proof myself? If I stood before her and told her how he used me…"

"Would you do this?"

"Would I? Would I not!"

"Well, it might be worth trying. But he has told her most of his sins and had pardon from her, and I understand she will not reopen the question."

"I'll lay he didn't tell her all," said Miss Winter. "I caught a glimpse of one or two murders besides the one that made such a fuss. He would speak of someone in his velvet way and then look at me with a steady eye and say: 'He died within a month.' It wasn't hot air, either. But I took little notice – you see, I loved him myself at that time. Whatever he did went with me, same as with this poor fool! There was just one thing that shook me. Yes – by cripes! – if it had not been for his poisonous, lying tongue that explains and soothes, I'd have left him that very night. It's a book he has – a brown-leather book with a lock, and his arms in gold on the outside. I think he was a bit drunk that night, or he would not have shown it to me."

"What was it, then?"

"I tell you, Mr Holmes, this man collects women, and takes a pride in his collection, as some men collect moths or butterflies. He had it all in that book. Snapshot photographs, names, details, everything about them. It was a beastly book – a book no man, even if he had come from the gutter, could have put together. But it was Adelbert Gruner's book all the same. 'Souls I have ruined.' He could have put that on the outside if he had been so minded. However, that's neither here nor there, for the book would not serve you, and, if it would, you can't get it."

"Where is it?"

"How can I tell you where it is now? It's more than a year since I left him. I know where he kept it then. He's a precise, tidy cat of a man in many of his ways, so maybe it is still in the pigeonhole of the old bureau in the inner study. Do you know his house?"

"I've been in the study," said Holmes.

"Have you, though? You haven't been slow on the job if you only started this morning. Maybe dear Adelbert has met his match this time. The outer study is the one with the Chinese crockery in it – big glass cupboard between the windows. Then behind his desk is the door that leads to the inner study – a small room where he keeps papers and things."

"Is he not afraid of burglars?"

"Adelbert is no coward. His worst enemy couldn't say that of him. He can look after himself. There's a burglar alarm at night. Besides, what is there for a burglar – unless they got away with all this fancy crockery?"

"No good," said Shinwell Johnson with the decided voice of the expert. "No fence wants stuff of that sort that you can neither melt nor sell."

"Quite so," said Holmes. "Well, now, Miss Winter, if you would call here tomorrow evening at five, I would consider in the mean while whether your suggestion of seeing this lady personally may not be arranged. I am exceedingly obliged to you for your coop-eration. I need not say that my clients will consider liberally—"

"None of that, Mr Holmes," cried the young woman. "I am not out for money. Let me see this man in the mud, and I've got all I worked for – in the mud with my foot on his cursed face. That's my price. I'm with you tomorrow or any other day so long as you are on his track. Porky here can tell you always where to find me."

I did not see Holmes again until the following evening, when we dined once more at our Strand restaurant. He shrugged his shoulders when I asked him what luck he had had in his interview. Then he told the story, which I would repeat in this way. His hard, dry statement needs some little editing to soften it into the terms of real life.

"There was no difficulty at all about the appointment," said Holmes, "for the girl glories in showing abject filial obedience in all secondary things in an attempt to atone for her flagrant breach of it in her engagement. The general phoned that all was ready, and the fiery Miss W. turned up according to schedule, so that at half-past five a cab deposited us outside 104 Berkeley Square, where the old soldier resides – one of those awful grey London castles which would make a church seem frivolous. A footman showed us into a great yellow-curtained drawing room, and there was the lady awaiting us – demure, pale, self-contained, as inflexible and remote as a snow image on a mountain.

"I don't quite know how to make her clear to you, Watson. Perhaps you may meet her before we are through, and you can use your own gift of words. She is beautiful, but with the ethereal other-world beauty of some fanatic whose thoughts are set on high. I have seen such faces in the pictures of the old masters of the Middle Ages. How a beast-man could have laid his vile paws upon such a being of the beyond I cannot imagine. You may have noticed how extremes call to each other – the spiritual to the animal, the caveman to the angel. You never saw a worse case than this.

"She knew what we had come for, of course – that villain had lost no time in poisoning her mind against us. Miss Winter's advent rather amazed her, I think, but she waved us into our respective chairs like a reverend abbess receiving two rather leprous mendicants. If your head is inclined to swell, my dear Watson, take a course of Miss Violet de Merville.

"'Well, sir,' said she in a voice like the wind from an iceberg, 'your name is familiar to me. You have called, as I understand, to malign my fiancé, Baron Gruner. It is only by my father's request that I see you at all, and I warn you in advance that anything you can say could not possibly have the slightest effect upon my mind.'

"I was sorry for her, Watson. I thought of her for the moment as I would have thought of a daughter of my own. I am not often eloquent. I use my head, not my heart. But I really did plead with her with all the warmth of words that I could find in my nature. I pictured to her the awful position of the woman who only wakes to a man's character after she is his wife – a woman who has to submit to be caressed by bloody hands and lecherous lips. I spared her nothing – the shame, the fear, the agony, the hopelessness of it all. All my hot words could not bring one tinge of colour to those ivory cheeks or one gleam of emotion to those abstracted eyes. I thought of what the rascal had said about a post-hypnotic influence. One could really believe that she was living above the earth in some ecstatic dream. Yet there was nothing indefinite in her replies.

"'I have listened to you with patience, Mr Holmes,' said she. 'The effect upon my mind is exactly as predicted. I am aware that Adelbert... that my fiancé has had a stormy life in which he has incurred bitter hatreds and most unjust aspersions. You are only the last of a series who have brought their slanders before me. Possibly you mean well, though I learn that you are a paid agent who would have been equally willing to act for the baron as against him. But in any case I wish you to understand once for all that I love him and that he loves me, and that the opinion of all the world is no more to me than the twitter of those birds outside the window. If his noble nature has ever for an instant fallen, it may be that I have been specially sent to raise it to its true and lofty level. I am not clear' – here she turned her eyes upon my companion – 'who this young lady may be.'

"I was about to answer when the girl broke in like a whirlwind. If ever you saw flame and ice face to face, it was those two women.

"'I'll tell you who I am,' she cried, springing out of her chair, her mouth all twisted with passion. 'I am his last mistress. I am one of a hundred that he has tempted and used and ruined and thrown into the refuse heap, as he will you also. *Your* refuse heap is more likely to be a grave, and maybe that's the best. I tell you, you foolish woman, if you marry this man he'll be the death of you. It may be a broken heart or it may be a broken neck, but he'll have you one way or the other. It's not out of love for you I'm speaking. I don't care a tinker's curse whether you live or die. It's out of hate for him and to spite him and to get back on him for what he did to me. But it's all the same, and you needn't look at me like that, my fine lady, for you may be lower than I am before you are through with it.'

"'I should prefer not to discuss such matters,' said Miss de Merville coldly. 'Let me say once for all that I am aware of three passages in my fiancé's life in which he became entangled with designing women, and that I am assured of his hearty repentance for any evil that he may have done.'

"'Three passages!' screamed my companion. 'You fool! You unutterable fool!'

"'Mr Holmes, I beg that you will bring this interview to an end,' said the icy voice. 'I have obeyed my father's wish in seeing you, but I am not compelled to listen to the ravings of this person.'

"With an oath Miss Winter darted forward, and if I had not caught her wrist, she would have clutched this maddening woman by the hair. I dragged her towards the door, and was lucky to get her back into the cab without a public scene, for she was beside herself with rage. In a cold way I felt pretty furious myself, Watson, for there was something indescribably annoying in the calm aloofness and supreme self-complaisance* of the woman whom we were trying to save. So now once again you know exactly how we stand, and it is clear that I must plan some fresh opening move, for this gambit won't work. I'll keep in touch with you, Watson, for it is more than likely that you will have your part to play, though it is just possible that the next move may lie with them rather than with us."

And it did. Their blow fell – or his blow rather, for never could I believe that the lady was privy to it. I think I could show you the very paving stone upon which I stood when my eyes fell upon the placard, and a pang of horror passed through my very soul. It was between the Grand Hotel and Charing Cross Station, where a one-legged newsvendor displayed his evening papers. The date was just two days after the last conversation. There, black upon yellow, was the terrible news sheet:

> MURDEROUS
> ATTACK
> UPON
> SHERLOCK
> HOLMES

I think I stood stunned for some moments. Then I have a confused recollection of snatching at a paper, of the remonstrance of the man, whom I had not paid, and, finally, of standing in the doorway of a chemist's shop while I turned up the fateful paragraph. This was how it ran:

We learn with regret that Mr Sherlock Holmes, the well-known private detective, was the victim this morning of a murderous assault which has left him in a precarious position. There are no exact details to hand, but the event seems to have occurred about twelve o'clock in Regent Street, outside the Café Royal.* The attack was made by two men armed with sticks, and Mr Holmes was beaten about the head and body, receiving injuries which the doctors describe as most serious. He was carried to Charing Cross Hospital, and afterwards insisted upon being taken to his rooms in Baker Street. The miscreants who attacked him appear to have been respectably dressed men, who escaped from the bystanders by passing through the Café Royal and out into Glasshouse Street behind it. No doubt they belonged to that criminal fraternity which has so often had occasion to bewail the activity and ingenuity of the injured man.

I need not say that my eyes had hardly glanced over the paragraph before I had sprung into a hansom and was on my way to Baker Street. I found Sir Leslie Oakshott, the famous surgeon, in the hall and his brougham* waiting at the kerb.

"No immediate danger," was his report. "Two lacerated scalp wounds and some considerable bruises. Several stitches have been necessary. Morphine has been injected, and quiet is essential, but an interview of a few minutes would not be absolutely forbidden."

With this permission I stole into the darkened room. The sufferer was wide awake, and I heard my name in a hoarse whisper. The blind was three quarters down, but one ray of sunlight slanted through and struck the bandaged head of the injured man. A crimson patch had soaked through the white linen compress. I sat beside him and bent my head.

"All right, Watson. Don't look so scared," he muttered in a very weak voice. "It's not as bad as it seems."

"Thank God for that!"

"I'm a bit of a singlestick* expert, as you know. I took most of them on my guard. It was the second man that was too much for me."

"What can I do, Holmes? Of course, it was that damned fellow who set them on. I'll go and thrash the hide off him if you give the word."

"Good old Watson! No, we can do nothing there unless the police lay their hands on the men. But their getaway had been well prepared. We may be sure of that. Wait a little. I have my plans. The first thing is to exaggerate my injuries. They'll come to you for news. Put it on thick, Watson. Lucky if I live the week out… concussion… delirium… what you like! You can't overdo it."

"But Sir Leslie Oakshott?"

"Oh, he's all right. He shall see the worst side of me. I'll look after that."

"Anything else?"

"Yes. Tell Shinwell Johnson to get that girl out of the way. Those beauties will be after her now. They know, of course, that she was with me in the case. If they dared to do me in, it is not likely they will neglect her. That is urgent. Do it tonight."

"I'll go now. Anything more?"

"Put my pipe on the table – and the tobacco slipper.* Right! Come in each morning, and we will plan our campaign."

I arranged with Johnson that evening to take Miss Winter to a quiet suburb and see that she lay low until the danger was past.

For six days the public were under the impression that Holmes was at the door of death. The bulletins were very grave, and there were sinister paragraphs in the papers. My continual visits assured me that it was not so bad as that. His wiry constitution and his determined will were working wonders. He was recovering fast, and I had suspicions at times that he was really finding himself faster than he pretended, even to me. There was a curious secretive streak in the man which led to many dramatic effects, but left even his closest friend guessing as to what his exact plans might be. He pushed to an extreme the axiom that the only safe plotter was he who plotted alone. I was nearer him than anyone else, and yet I was always conscious of the gap between.

On the seventh day, the stitches were taken out, in spite of which there was a report of erysipelas* in the evening papers. The same evening papers had an announcement which I was bound, sick or well, to carry to my friend. It was simply that among the passengers on the Cunard boat *Ruritania*,* starting from Liverpool on Friday, was the Baron Adelbert Gruner, who had some important financial business to settle in the States before his impending wedding to Miss Violet de Merville, only daughter of, etc., etc. Holmes listened to the news with a cold, concentrated look upon his pale face, which told me that it hit him hard.

"Friday!" he cried. "Only three clear days. I believe the rascal wants to put himself out of danger's way. But he won't, Watson! By the Lord Harry,* he won't! Now, Watson, I want you to do something for me."

"I am here to be used, Holmes."

"Well, then, spend the next twenty-four hours in an intensive study of Chinese pottery."

He gave no explanations, and I asked for none. By long experience I had learnt the wisdom of obedience. But when I had left his room, I walked down Baker Street, revolving in my head how on earth I was to carry out so strange an order. Finally I drove to the London Library* in St James's Square, put the matter to my friend Lomax, the sub-librarian, and departed to my rooms with a goodly volume under my arm.

It is said that the barrister who crams up a case with such care that he can examine an expert witness upon the Monday has forgotten all his forced knowledge before the Saturday. Certainly I should not like now to pose as an authority upon ceramics. And yet all that evening and all that night, with a short interval for rest, and all next morning I was sucking in knowledge and committing names to memory. There I learnt of the hallmarks of the great artist-decorators, of the mystery of cyclical dates,* the marks of the Hung-wu and the beauties of the Yung-lo, the writings of Tang-ying and the glories of the primitive period of the Sung and the Yuan.* I was charged with all this information when I called upon Holmes next evening. He was out of bed now, though you would not have guessed it from the published reports, and he sat with his much-bandaged head resting upon his hand in the depth of his favourite armchair.

"Why, Holmes," I said, "if one believed the papers, you are dying."

"That," said he, "is the very impression which I intended to convey. And now, Watson, have you learnt your lessons?"

"At least I have tried to."

"Good. You could keep up an intelligent conversation on the subject?"

"I believe I could."

"Then hand me that little box from the mantelpiece."

He opened the lid and took out a small object most carefully wrapped in some fine Eastern silk. This he unfolded, and disclosed a delicate little saucer of the most beautiful deep-blue colour.

"It needs careful handling, Watson. This is the real eggshell pottery of the Ming dynasty. No finer piece ever passed through Christie's.* A complete set of this would be worth a king's ransom – in fact, it is doubtful if there is a complete set outside the imperial palace of Peking. The sight of this would drive a real connoisseur wild."

"What am I to do with it?"

Holmes handed me a card upon which was printed: "Doctor Hill Barton, 369 Half Moon Street."

"That is your name for the evening, Watson. You will call upon Baron Gruner. I know something of his habits, and at half-past eight he would probably be disengaged. A note will tell him in advance that you are about to call, and you will say that you are bringing him a specimen of an absolutely unique set of Ming china. You may as well be a medical man, since that is a part which you can play without duplicity. You are a collector, this set has come your way, you have heard of the baron's interest in the subject, and you are not averse to selling at a price."

"What price?"

"Well asked, Watson. You would certainly fall down badly if you did not know the value of your own wares. This saucer was got for me by Sir James, and comes, I understand, from the collection of his client. You will not exaggerate if you say that it could hardly be matched in the world."

"I could perhaps suggest that the set should be valued by an expert."

"Excellent, Watson! You scintillate today. Suggest Christie or Sotheby.* Your delicacy prevents your putting a price for yourself."

"But if he won't see me?"

"Oh, yes, he will see you. He has the collection mania in its most acute form – and especially on this subject, on which he is an acknowledged authority. Sit down, Watson, and I will dictate the letter. No answer needed. You will merely say that you are coming, and why."

It was an admirable document – short, courteous and stimulating to the curiosity of the connoisseur. A district messenger was duly dispatched with it. On the same evening, with the precious saucer in my hand and the card of Doctor Hill Barton in my pocket, I set off on my own adventure.

The beautiful house and grounds indicated that Baron Gruner was, as Sir James had said, a man of considerable wealth. A long winding drive, with banks of rare shrubs on either side, opened out into a great gravelled square adorned with statues. The place had been built by a South African gold king in the days of the great boom,* and the long, low house with the turrets at the corners, though an architectural nightmare, was imposing in its size and solidity. A butler who would have adorned a bench of bishops showed me in, and handed me over to a plush-clad footman, who ushered me into the baron's presence.

He was standing at the open front of a great case which stood between the windows, and which contained part of his Chinese collection. He turned as I entered with a small brown vase in his hand.

"Pray sit down, doctor," said he. "I was looking over my own treasures and wondering whether I could really afford to add to them. This little Tang* specimen, which dates from the seventh century, would probably interest you. I am sure you never saw finer workmanship or a richer glaze. Have you the Ming saucer with you of which you spoke?"

I carefully unpacked it and handed it to him. He seated himself at his desk, pulled over the lamp, for it was growing dark, and set himself to examine it. As he did so, the yellow light beat upon his own features, and I was able to study them at my ease.

He was certainly a remarkably handsome man. His European reputation for beauty was fully deserved. In figure he was not more than of middle size, but was built upon graceful and active lines. His face was swarthy, almost Oriental, with large, dark, languorous eyes which might easily hold an irresistible fascination for women. His hair and moustache were raven-black, the latter short, pointed and carefully waxed. His features were regular and pleasing, save only his straight, thin-lipped mouth. If ever I saw a murderer's mouth, it was there – a cruel, hard gash in the face, compressed, inexorable and terrible. He was ill-advised to train his moustache away from it, for it was Nature's danger signal, set as a warning to his victims. His voice was engaging, and his manners perfect. In age I should have put him at little over thirty, though his record afterwards showed that he was forty-two.

"Very fine – very fine indeed!" he said at last. "And you say you have a set of six to correspond. What puzzles me is that I should not have heard of such magnificent specimens. I only know of one in England to match this, and it is certainly not likely to be in the market. Would it be indiscreet if I were to ask you, Doctor Hill Barton, how you obtained this?"

"Does it really matter?" I asked, with as careless an air as I could muster. "You can see that the piece is genuine, and, as to the value, I am content to take an expert's valuation."

"Very mysterious," said he, with a quick, suspicious flash of his dark eyes. "In dealing with objects of such value, one naturally wishes to know all about the transaction. That the piece is genuine is certain. I have no doubts at all about that. But suppose – I am bound to take every possibility into account – that it should prove afterwards that you had no right to sell?"

"I would guarantee you against any claim of the sort."

"That, of course, would open up the question as to what your guarantee was worth."

"My bankers would answer that."

"Quite so. And yet the whole transaction strikes me as rather unusual."

"You can do business or not," said I with indifference. "I have given you the first offer as I understood that you were a connoisseur, but I shall have no difficulty in other quarters."

"Who told you I was a connoisseur?"

"I was aware that you had written a book upon the subject."

"Have you read the book?"

"No."

"Dear me, this becomes more and more difficult for me to understand! You are a connoisseur and collector with a very valuable piece in your collection, and yet you have never troubled to consult the one book which would have told you of the real meaning and value of what you held. How do you explain that?"

"I am a very busy man. I am a doctor in practice."

"That is no answer. If a man has a hobby, he follows it up, whatever his other pursuits may be. You said in your note that you were a connoisseur."

"So I am."

"Might I ask you a few questions to test you? I am obliged to tell you, doctor – if you are indeed a doctor – that the incident becomes more and more suspicious. I would ask you what do you know of the Emperor Shomu, and how do you associate him with the Shoso-in near Nara? Dear me, does that puzzle you? Tell me a little about the Northern Wei dynasty and its place in the history of ceramics."*

I sprang from my chair in simulated anger.

"This is intolerable, sir," said I. "I came here to do you a favour, and not to be examined as if I were a schoolboy. My knowledge on these subjects may be second only to your own, but I certainly shall not answer questions which have been put in so offensive a way."

He looked at me steadily. The languor had gone from his eyes. They suddenly glared. There was a gleam of teeth from between those cruel lips.

"What is the game? You are here as a spy. You are an emissary of Holmes. This is a trick that you are playing upon me. The fellow is dying, I hear, so he sends his tools to keep watch upon me. You've made your way in here without leave, and – by God! – you may find it harder to get out than to get in."

He had sprung to his feet, and I stepped back, bracing myself for an attack, for the man was beside himself with rage. He may have suspected me from the first – certainly this cross-examination had shown him the truth – but it was clear that I could not hope to deceive him. He dived his hand into a side drawer and rummaged furiously. Then something struck upon his ear, for he stood listening intently.

"Ah," he cried, "ah!" – and dashed into the room behind him.

Two steps took me to the open door, and my mind will ever carry a clear picture of the scene within. The window leading out to the garden was wide open. Beside it, looking like some terrible ghost, his head girt with bloody bandages, his face drawn and white, stood Sherlock Holmes. The next instant he was through the gap, and I heard the crash of his body among the laurel bushes outside. With a howl of rage the master of the house rushed after him to the open window.

And then! It was done in an instant, and yet I clearly saw it. An arm – a woman's arm – shot out from among the leaves. At the same instant the baron uttered a horrible cry – a yell which will always ring in my memory. He clapped his two hands to his face and rushed round the room, beating his head horribly against the walls. Then he fell upon the carpet, rolling and writhing, while scream after scream resounded through the house.

"Water! For God's sake, water!" was his cry.

I seized a carafe from a side table and rushed to his aid. At the same moment the butler and several footmen ran in from the hall. I remember that one of them fainted as I knelt by the injured man and turned that awful face to the light of the lamp. The vitriol* was eating into it everywhere and dripping from the ears and the chin. One eye was already white and glazed. The other was red and inflamed. The features which I had admired a few minutes before were now like some beautiful painting over which the artist has passed a wet and foul sponge. They were blurred, discoloured, inhuman, terrible.

In a few words I explained exactly what had occurred, so far as the vitriol attack was concerned. Some had climbed through the window and others had rushed out onto the lawn, but it was dark and it had begun to rain. Between his screams the victim raged and raved against the avenger. "It was that hellcat, Kitty Winter!" he cried. "Oh, the she-devil! She shall pay for it! She shall pay! Oh, God in heaven, this pain is more than I can bear!"

I bathed his face in oil, put cotton wadding on the raw surfaces and administered a hypodermic of morphia. All suspicion of me had passed from his mind in the presence of this shock, and he clung to my hands as if I might have the power even yet to clear those dead-fish eyes which gazed up at me. I could have wept over the ruin had I not remembered very clearly the vile life which had led up to so hideous a change. It was loathsome to feel the pawing of his burning hands, and I was relieved when his family surgeon, closely followed by a specialist, came to relieve me of my charge. An inspector of police had also arrived, and to him I handed my real card. It would have been useless as well as foolish to do otherwise, for I was nearly as well known by sight at the Yard as Holmes himself. Then I left that house of gloom and terror. Within an hour I was at Baker Street.

Holmes was seated in his familiar chair, looking very pale and exhausted. Apart from his injuries, even his iron nerves had been shocked by the events of the evening, and he listened with horror to my account of the baron's transformation.

"The wages of sin,* Watson – the wages of sin!" said he. "Sooner or later it will always come. God knows, there was sin enough," he added, taking up a brown volume from the table. "Here is the book the woman talked of. If this will not break off the marriage, nothing ever could. But it will, Watson. It must. No self-respecting woman could stand it."

"It is his love diary?"

"Or his lust diary. Call it what you will. The moment the woman told us of it, I realized what a tremendous weapon was there, if we could but lay our hands on it. I said nothing at the time to indicate my thoughts, for this woman might have given it away. But I brooded over it. Then this assault upon me gave me the chance of letting the baron think that no precautions need be taken against me. That was all to the good. I would have waited a little longer, but his visit to America forced my hand. He would never have left so compromising a document behind him. Therefore we had to act at once. Burglary at night is impossible. He takes precautions. But there was a chance in the evening if I could only be sure that his attention was engaged. That was where you and your blue saucer came in. But I had to be sure of the position of the book, and I knew I had only a few minutes in which to act, for my time was limited by your knowledge of Chinese pottery. Therefore I gathered the girl up at the last moment. How could I guess what the little packet was that she carried so carefully under her cloak? I thought she had come altogether on my business, but it seems she had some of her own."

"He guessed I came from you."

"I feared he would. But you held him in play just long enough for me to get the book, though not long enough for an unobserved escape. Ah, Sir James, I am very glad you have come!"

Our courtly friend had appeared in answer to a previous summons. He listened with the deepest attention to Holmes's account of what had occurred.

"You have done wonders – wonders!" he cried when he had heard the narrative. "But if these injuries are as terrible as Doctor Watson describes, then surely our purpose of thwarting the marriage is sufficiently gained without the use of this horrible book."

Holmes shook his head.

"Women of the de Merville type do not act like that. She would love him the more as a disfigured martyr. No, no. It is his moral side, not his physical, which we have to destroy. That book will bring her back to earth – and I know nothing else that could. It is in his own writing. She cannot get past it."

Sir James carried away both it and the precious saucer. As I was myself overdue, I went down with him into the street. A brougham was waiting for him. He sprang in, gave a hurried order to the cockaded coachman* and drove swiftly away. He flung his overcoat half out of the window to cover the armorial bearings upon the panel, but I had seen them in the glare of our fanlight nonetheless. I gasped with surprise. Then I turned back and ascended the stair to Holmes's room.

"I have found out who our client is," I cried, bursting with my great news. "Why, Holmes, it is—"

"It is a loyal friend and a chivalrous gentleman,"* said Holmes, holding up a restraining hand. "Let that now and for ever be enough for us."

I do not know how the incriminating book was used. Sir James may have managed it. Or it is more probable that so delicate a task was entrusted to the young lady's father. The effect, at any rate, was all that could be desired. Three days later appeared a paragraph in the *Morning Post* to say that the marriage between Baron Adelbert Gruner and Miss Violet de Merville would not take place. The same paper had the first police-court hearing of the proceedings against Miss Kitty Winter on the grave charge of vitriol-throwing. Such extenuating circumstances came out in the trial that the sentence, as will be remembered, was the lowest that was possible for such an offence. Sherlock Holmes was threatened with a prosecution for burglary, but when an object is good and a client is sufficiently illustrious, even the rigid British law becomes human and elastic. My friend has not yet stood in the dock.

THE ADVENTURE
OF THE BLANCHED SOLDIER

T HE IDEAS OF MY FRIEND WATSON, though limited, are
   exceedingly pertinacious. For a long time he has worried* me
to write an experience of my own.* Perhaps I have rather invited
this persecution, since I have often had occasion to point out to
him how superficial are his own accounts and to accuse him of
pandering to popular taste instead of confining himself rigidly to
facts and figures. "Try it yourself, Holmes!" he has retorted, and
I am compelled to admit that, having taken my pen in my hand,
I do begin to realize that the matter must be presented in such a
way as may interest the reader. The following case can hardly fail
to do so, as it is among the strangest happenings in my collection,
though it chanced that Watson had no note of it in his collection.
Speaking of my old friend and biographer, I would take this opportunity to remark that if I burden myself with a companion in my
various little inquiries it is not done out of sentiment or caprice,
but it is that Watson has some remarkable characteristics of his
own, to which in his modesty he has given small attention amid
his exaggerated estimates of my own performances. A confederate who foresees your conclusions and course of action is always
dangerous, but one to whom each development comes as a per-
petual surprise, and to whom the future is always a closed book,
is indeed an ideal helpmate.

I find from my notebook that it was in January 1903, just after
the conclusion of the Boer War,* that I had my visit from Mr James
M. Dodd – a big, fresh, sunburnt, upstanding Briton. The good

Watson had at that time deserted me for a wife,* the only selfish action which I can recall in our association. I was alone.

It is my habit to sit with my back to the window and to place my visitors in the opposite chair, where the light falls full upon them. Mr James M. Dodd seemed somewhat at a loss how to begin the interview. I did not attempt to help him, for his silence gave me more time for observation. I have found it wise to impress clients with a sense of power, and so I gave him some of my conclusions.

"From South Africa, sir, I perceive."

"Yes, sir," he answered with some surprise.

"Imperial Yeomanry, I fancy."

"Exactly."

"Middlesex Corps, no doubt."

"That is so. Mr Holmes, you are a wizard."

I smiled at his bewildered expression.

"When a gentleman of virile appearance enters my room with such tan upon his face as an English sun could never give, and with his handkerchief in his sleeve instead of in his pocket, it is not difficult to place him. You wear a short beard, which shows that you were not a regular. You have the cut of a riding man. As to Middlesex, your card has already shown me that you are a stockbroker from Throgmorton Street.* What other regiment would you join?"

"You see everything."

"I see no more than you, but I have trained myself to notice what I see. However, Mr Dodd, it was not to discuss the science of observation that you called upon me this morning. What has been happening at Tuxbury Old Park?"

"Mr Holmes!..."

"My dear sir, there is no mystery. Your letter came with that heading, and as you fixed this appointment in very pressing terms, it was clear that something sudden and important had occurred."

"Yes, indeed. But the letter was written in the afternoon, and a good deal has happened since then. If Colonel Emsworth had not kicked me out—"

"Kicked you out!"

"Well, that was what it amounted to. He is a hard nail, is Colonel Emsworth. The greatest martinet* in the army in his day, and it was a day of rough language, too. I couldn't have stuck the colonel if it had not been for Godfrey's sake."

I lit my pipe and leant back in my chair.

"Perhaps you will explain what you are talking about."

My client grinned mischievously.

"I had got into the way of supposing that you knew everything without being told," said he. "But I will give you the facts, and I hope to God that you will be able to tell me what they mean. I've been awake all night puzzling my brain, and the more I think, the more incredible does it become.

"When I joined up in January 1901 – just two years ago – young Godfrey Emsworth had joined the same squadron. He was Colonel Emsworth's only son – Emsworth, the Crimean VC* – and he had the fighting blood in him, so it is no wonder he volunteered. There was not a finer lad in the regiment. We formed a friendship – the sort of friendship which can only be made when one lives the same life and shares the same joys and sorrows. He was my mate – and that means a good deal in the army. We took the rough and the smooth together for a year of hard fighting. Then he was hit with a bullet from an elephant gun in the action near Diamond Hill outside Pretoria.* I got one letter from the hospital at Cape Town and one from Southampton. Since then not a word – not one word, Mr Holmes, for six months and more, and he my closest pal.

"Well, when the war was over and we all got back, I wrote to his father and asked where Godfrey was. No answer. I waited a bit and then I wrote again. This time I had a reply, short and gruff. Godfrey had gone on a voyage round the world, and it was not likely that he would be back for a year. That was all.

"I wasn't satisfied, Mr Holmes. The whole thing seemed to me so damned unnatural. He was a good lad, and he would not drop a pal like that. It was not like him. Then, again, I happened to know that he was heir to a lot of money, and also that his father and he did not always hit it off too well. The old man was sometimes a bully, and young Godfrey had too much spirit to stand it. No, I wasn't satisfied, and I determined that I would get to the root of the matter. It happened, however, that my own affairs needed a lot of straightening out, after two years' absence, and so it is only this week that I have been able to take up Godfrey's case again. But since I have taken it up, I mean to drop everything in order to see it through."

Mr James M. Dodd appeared to be the sort of person whom it would be better to have as a friend than as an enemy. His blue eyes were stern, and his square jaw had set hard as he spoke.

"Well, what have you done?" I asked.

"My first move was to get down to his home, Tuxbury Old Park, near Bedford, and to see for myself how the ground lay. I wrote to the mother, therefore – I had had quite enough of the curmudgeon of a father – and I made a clean frontal attack: Godfrey was my chum, I had a great deal of interest which I might tell her of our common experiences, I should be in the neighbourhood – would there be any objection, et cetera? In reply I had quite an amiable answer from her and an offer to put me up for the night. That was what took me down on Monday.

"Tuxbury Old Hall is inaccessible – five miles from anywhere. There was no trap* at the station, so I had to walk, carrying my suitcase, and it was nearly dark before I arrived. It is a great wandering house, standing in a considerable park. I should judge it was of all sorts of ages and styles, starting on a half-timbered Elizabethan foundation and ending in a Victorian portico. Inside it was all panelling and tapestry and half-effaced old pictures – a house of shadows and mystery. There was a butler, old Ralph, who seemed about the same age as the house, and there was his wife, who might have been older. She had been Godfrey's nurse, and I had heard him speak of her as second only to his mother in his affections, so I was drawn to her in spite of her queer appearance. The mother I liked also – a gentle little white mouse of a woman. It was only the colonel himself whom I barred.

"We had a bit of a barney right away, and I should have walked back to the station if I had not felt that it might be playing his game for me to do so. I was shown straight into his study, and there I found him – a huge, bow-backed man with a smoky skin and a straggling grey beard, seated behind his littered desk. A red-veined nose jutted out like a vulture's beak, and two fierce grey eyes glared at me from under tufted brows. I could understand now why Godfrey seldom spoke of his father.

"'Well, sir,' said he in a rasping voice. 'I should be interested to know the real reasons for this visit.'

"I answered that I had explained them in my letter to his wife.

"'Yes, yes – you said that you had known Godfrey in Africa. We have, of course, only your word for that.'

"'I have his letters to me in my pocket.'

"'Kindly let me see them.'

"He glanced at the two which I handed him, and then he tossed them back.

"'Well, what then?' he asked.

"'I was fond of your son Godfrey, sir. Many ties and memories united us. Is it not natural that I should wonder at his sudden silence and should wish to know what has become of him?'

"'I have some recollection, sir, that I had already corresponded with you and had told you what had become of him. He has gone upon a voyage round the world. His health was in a poor way after his African experiences, and both his mother and I were of opinion that complete rest and change were needed. Kindly pass that explanation on to any other friends who may be interested in the matter.'

"'Certainly,' I answered. 'But perhaps you would have the goodness to let me have the name of the steamer and of the line by which he sailed, together with the date. I have no doubt that I should be able to get a letter through to him.'

"My request seemed both to puzzle and to irritate my host. His great eyebrows came down over his eyes, and he tapped his fingers impatiently on the table. He looked up at last with the expression of one who has seen his adversary make a dangerous move at chess, and has decided how to meet it.

"'Many people, Mr Dodd,' said he, 'would take offence at your infernal pertinacity and would think that this insistence had reached the point of damned impertinence.'

"'You must put it down, sir, to my real love for your son.'

"'Exactly. I have already made every allowance upon that score. I must ask you, however, to drop these enquiries. Every family has its own inner knowledge and its own motives, which cannot always be made clear to outsiders, however well intentioned. My wife is anxious to hear something of Godfrey's past which you are in a position to tell her, but I would ask you to let the present and the future alone. Such enquiries serve no useful purpose, sir, and place us in a delicate and difficult position.'

"So I came to a dead end, Mr Holmes. There was no getting past it. I could only pretend to accept the situation and register a vow inwardly that I would never rest until my friend's fate had been cleared up. It was a dull evening. We dined quietly, the three of us, in a gloomy, faded old room. The lady questioned me eagerly about her son, but the old man seemed morose and depressed. I was so bored by the whole proceeding that I made an excuse as soon as I decently could and retired to my bedroom. It was a large, bare room on the ground floor, as gloomy as the rest of the house, but after a year of sleeping upon the veldt, Mr Holmes, one is not too particular about one's quarters. I opened the curtains and looked out into the garden, remarking that it was a fine night with a bright half-moon. Then I sat down by the roaring fire with the lamp on a table beside me, and endeavoured to distract my mind with a novel. I was interrupted, however, by Ralph, the old butler, who came in with a fresh supply of coals.

"'I thought you might run short in the night-time, sir. It is bitter weather, and these rooms are cold.'

"He hesitated before leaving the room, and when I looked round, he was standing facing me with a wistful look upon his wrinkled face.

"'Beg your pardon, sir, but I could not help hearing what you said of young Master Godfrey at dinner. You know, sir, that my wife nursed him, and so I may say I am his foster-father. It's natural we should take an interest. And you say he carried himself well, sir?'

"'There was no braver man in the regiment. He pulled me out once from under the rifles of the Boers, or maybe I should not be here.'

"The old butler rubbed his skinny hands.

"'Yes, sir, yes, that is Master Godfrey all over. He was always courageous. There's not a tree in the park, sir, that he has not climbed. Nothing would stop him. He was a fine boy – and oh, sir, he was a fine man.'

"I sprang to my feet.

"'Look here!' I cried. 'You say he *was*. You speak as if he were dead. What is all this mystery? What has become of Godfrey Emsworth?'

"I gripped the old man by the shoulder, but he shrank away.

"'I don't know what you mean, sir. Ask the master about Master Godfrey. He knows. It is not for me to interfere.'

"He was leaving the room, but I held his arm.

"'Listen,' I said. 'You are going to answer one question before you leave if I have to hold you all night. Is Godfrey dead?'

"He could not face my eyes. He was like a man hypnotized. The answer was dragged from his lips. It was a terrible and unexpected one.

"'I wish to God he was!' he cried, and, tearing himself free, he dashed from the room.

"You will think, Mr Holmes, that I returned to my chair in no very happy state of mind. The old man's words seemed to me to bear only one interpretation. Clearly my poor friend had become involved in some criminal or, at the least, disreputable transaction which touched the family honour. That stern old man had sent his son away and hidden him from the world lest some scandal should come to light. Godfrey was a reckless fellow. He was easily influenced by those around him. No doubt he had fallen into bad hands and been misled to his ruin. It was a piteous business, if it was indeed so, but even now it was my duty to hunt him out and see if I could aid him. I was anxiously pondering the matter when I looked up, and there was Godfrey Emsworth standing before me."

My client had paused as one in deep emotion.

"Pray continue," I said. "Your problem presents some very unusual features."

"He was outside the window, Mr Holmes, with his face pressed against the glass. I have told you that I looked out at the night. When I did so, I left the curtains partly open. His figure was framed in this gap. The window came down to the ground, and I could see the whole length of it, but it was his face which held my gaze. He was deadly pale – never have I seen a man so white. I reckon ghosts may look like that – but his eyes met mine, and they were the eyes of a living man. He sprang back when he saw that I was looking at him, and he vanished into the darkness.

"There was something shocking about the man, Mr Holmes. It wasn't merely that ghastly face glimmering as white as cheese in the darkness. It was more subtle than that: something slinking, something furtive, something guilty – something very unlike the frank, manly lad that I had known. It left a feeling of horror in my mind.

"But when a man has been soldiering for a year or two with brother Boer as a playmate, he keeps his nerve and acts quickly. Godfrey had hardly vanished before I was at the window. There was an awkward catch, and it was some little time before I could throw it up. Then I nipped through and ran down the garden path in the direction that I thought he might have taken.

"It was a long path, and the light was not very good, but it seemed to me something was moving ahead of me. I ran on and called his name, but it was no use. When I got to the end of the path, there were several others branching in different directions to various outhouses. I stood hesitating, and as I did so I heard distinctly the sound of a closing door. It was not behind me in the house, but ahead of me, somewhere in the darkness. That was enough,

Mr Holmes, to assure me that what I had seen was not a vision. Godfrey had run away from me, and he had shut a door behind him. Of that I was certain.

"There was nothing more I could do, and I spent an uneasy night turning the matter over in my mind and trying to find some theory which would cover the facts. Next day I found the colonel rather more conciliatory, and as his wife remarked that there were some places of interest in the neighbourhood, it gave me an opening to ask whether my presence for one more night would incommode them. A somewhat grudging acquiescence from the old man gave me a clear day in which to make my observations. I was already perfectly convinced that Godfrey was in hiding somewhere near, but where and why remained to be solved.

"The house was so large and so rambling that a regiment might be hid away in it and no one the wiser. If the secret lay there, it was difficult for me to penetrate it. But the door which I had heard close was certainly not in the house. I must explore the garden and see what I could find. There was no difficulty in the way, for the old people were busy in their own fashion and left me to my own devices.

"There were several small outhouses, but at the end of the garden there was a detached building of some size – large enough for a gardener's or a gamekeeper's residence. Could this be the place whence the sound of that shutting door had come? I approached it in a careless fashion, as though I were strolling aimlessly round the grounds. As I did so, a small, brisk, bearded man in a black coat and bowler hat – not at all the gardener type – came out of the door. To my surprise, he locked it after him and put the key in his pocket. Then he looked at me with some surprise on his face.

"'Are you a visitor here?' he asked.

"I explained that I was and that I was a friend of Godfrey's.

"'What a pity that he should be away on his travels, for he would have so liked to see me,' I continued.

"'Quite so. Exactly,' said he with a rather guilty air. 'No doubt you will renew your visit at some more propitious time.' He passed on, but when I turned I observed that he was standing watching me, half concealed by the laurels at the far end of the garden.

"I had a good look at the little house as I passed it, but the windows were heavily curtained, and, so far as one could see, it was empty. I might spoil my own game, and even be ordered off the premises, if I were too audacious, for I was still conscious that I was being watched. Therefore I strolled back to the house and waited for night before I went on with my enquiry. When all was dark and quiet, I slipped out of my window and made my way as silently as possible to the mysterious lodge.

"I have said that it was heavily curtained, but now I found that the windows were shuttered as well. Some light, however, was breaking through one of them, so I concentrated my attention upon this. I was in luck, for the curtain had not been quite closed, and there was a crack in the shutter so that I could see the inside of the room. It was a cheery place enough, a bright lamp and a blazing fire. Opposite to me was seated the little man whom I had seen in the morning. He was smoking a pipe and reading a paper."

"What paper?" I asked.

My client seemed annoyed at the interruption of his narrative.

"Can it matter?" he asked.

"It is most essential."

"I really took no notice."

"Possibly you observed whether it was a broad-leafed paper or of that smaller type which one associates with weeklies."

"Now that you mention it, it was not large. It might have been the *Spectator*. However, I had little thought to spare upon such details, for a second man was seated with his back to the window, and I could swear that this second man was Godfrey. I could not see his face, but I knew the familiar slope of his shoulders. He was leaning upon his elbow in an attitude of great melancholy, his body turned towards the fire. I was hesitating as to what I should do when there was a sharp tap on my shoulder, and there was Colonel Emsworth beside me.

"'This way, sir!' said he in a low voice. He walked in silence to the house, and I followed him into my own bedroom. He had picked up a timetable in the hall.

"'There is a train to London at eight thirty,' said he. 'The trap will be at the door at eight.'

"He was white with rage, and, indeed, I felt myself in so difficult a position that I could only stammer out a few incoherent apologies, in which I tried to excuse myself by urging my anxiety for my friend.

"'The matter will not bear discussion,' said he abruptly. 'You have made a most damnable intrusion into the privacy of our family. You were here as a guest, and you have become a spy. I have nothing more to say, sir, save that I have no wish ever to see you again.'

"At this I lost my temper, Mr Holmes, and I spoke with some warmth.

"'I have seen your son, and I am convinced that for some reason of your own you are concealing him from the world. I have no idea what your motives are in cutting him off in this fashion, but I am sure that he is no longer a free agent. I warn you, Colonel Emsworth, that until I am assured as to the safety and well-being of my friend, I shall never desist in my efforts to get to the bottom of the mystery, and I shall certainly not allow myself to be intimidated by anything which you may say or do.'

"The old fellow looked diabolical, and I really thought he was about to attack me. I have said that he was a gaunt, fierce old giant, and though I am no weakling I might have been hard put to it to hold my own against him. However, after a long glare of rage he turned upon his heel and walked out of the room. For my part, I took the appointed train in the morning, with the full intention of coming straight to you and asking for your advice and assistance at the appointment for which I had already written."

Such was the problem which my visitor laid before me. It presented, as the astute reader will have already perceived, few difficulties in its solution, for a very limited choice of alternatives must get to the root of the matter. Still, elementary as it was, there were points of interest and novelty about it which may excuse my placing it upon record. I now proceeded, using my familiar method of logical analysis, to narrow down the possible solutions.

"The servants…" I asked. "How many were in the house?"

"To the best of my belief there were only the old butler and his wife. They seemed to live in the simplest fashion."

"There was no servant, then, in the detached house?"

"None, unless the little man with the beard acted as such. He seemed, however, to be quite a superior person."

"That seems very suggestive. Had you any indication that food was conveyed from the one house to the other?"

"Now that you mention it, I did see old Ralph carrying a basket down the garden walk and going in the direction of this house. The idea of food did not occur to me at the moment."

"Did you make any local enquiries?"

"Yes, I did. I spoke to the stationmaster and also to the innkeeper in the village. I simply asked if they knew anything of my old comrade, Godfrey Emsworth. Both of them assured me that he had gone for a voyage round the world. He had come home and then had almost at once started off again. The story was evidently universally accepted."

"You said nothing of your suspicions?"

"Nothing."

"That was very wise. The matter should certainly be enquired into. I will go back with you to Tuxbury Old Park."

"Today?"

It happened that at the moment I was clearing up the case which my friend Watson has described as that of the Abbey School, in which the Duke of Greyminster was so deeply involved.* I had also a commission from the Sultan of Turkey which called for immediate action, as political consequences of the gravest kind might arise from its neglect. Therefore it was not until the beginning of the next week, as my diary records, that I was able to start forth on my mission to Bedfordshire in company with Mr James M. Dodd. As we drove to Euston, we picked up a grave and taciturn

gentleman of iron-grey aspect, with whom I had made the necessary arrangements.

"This is an old friend," said I to Dodd. "It is possible that his
presence may be entirely unnecessary, and, on the other hand,
it may be essential. It is not necessary at the present stage to go
further into the matter."

The narratives of Watson have accustomed the reader, no doubt,
to the fact that I do not waste words or disclose my thoughts while
a case is actually under consideration. Dodd seemed surprised, but
nothing more was said, and the three of us continued our journey
together. In the train I asked Dodd one more question which I
wished our companion to hear.

"You say that you saw your friend's face quite clearly at the
window, so clearly that you are sure of his identity?"

"I have no doubt about it whatever. His nose was pressed against
the glass. The lamplight shone full upon him."

"It could not have been someone resembling him?"

"No, no – it was he."

"But you say he was changed?"

"Only in colour. His face was – how shall I describe it? – it was
of a fish-belly whiteness. It was bleached."

"Was it equally pale all over?"

"I think not. It was his brow which I saw so clearly as it was
pressed against the window."

"Did you call to him?"

"I was too startled and horrified for the moment. Then I pursued
him, as I have told you, but without result."

My case was practically complete, and there was only one small
incident needed to round it off. When, after a considerable drive,
we arrived at the strange old rambling house which my client
had described, it was Ralph, the elderly butler, who opened the
door. I had requisitioned the carriage for the day and had asked
my elderly friend to remain within it unless we should summon
him. Ralph, a little wrinkled old fellow, was in the conventional
costume of black coat and pepper-and-salt trousers, with only one

curious variant. He wore brown-leather gloves, which at sight of us he instantly shuffled off, laying them down on the hall table as we passed in. I have, as my friend Watson may have remarked, an abnormally acute set of senses, and a faint but incisive scent was apparent. It seemed to centre on the hall table. I turned, placed my hat there, knocked it off, stooped to pick it up, and contrived to bring my nose within a foot of the gloves. Yes, it was undoubtedly from them that the curious tarry odour was oozing. I passed on into the study with my case complete. Alas, that I should have to show my hand so when I tell my own story! It was by concealing such links in the chain that Watson was enabled to produce his meretricious finales.

Colonel Emsworth was not in his room, but he came quickly enough on receipt of Ralph's message. We heard his quick, heavy step in the passage. The door was flung open, and he rushed in with bristling beard and twisted features, as terrible an old man as ever I have seen. He held our cards in his hand, and he tore them up and stamped on the fragments.

"Have I not told you, you infernal busybody, that you are warned off the premises? Never dare to show your damned face here again. If you enter again without my leave, I shall be within my rights if I use violence. I'll shoot you, sir! By God, I will! As to you, sir" – turning upon me – "I extend the same warning to you. I am familiar with your ignoble profession, but you must take your reputed talents to some other field. There is no opening for them here."

"I cannot leave here," said my client firmly, "until I hear from Godfrey's own lips that he is under no restraint."

Our involuntary host rang the bell.

"Ralph," he said, "telephone down to the county police and ask the inspector to send up two constables. Tell him there are burglars in the house."

"One moment," said I. "You must be aware, Mr Dodd, that Colonel Emsworth is within his rights and that we have no legal status within his house. On the other hand, he should recognize that your action is prompted entirely by solicitude for his son. I venture to hope that, if I were allowed to have five minutes' conversation with Colonel Emsworth, I could certainly alter his view of the matter."

"I am not so easily altered," said the old soldier. "Ralph, do what I have told you. What the devil are you waiting for? Ring up the police!"

"Nothing of the sort," I said, putting my back to the door. "Any police interference would bring about the very catastrophe which you dread." I took out my notebook and scribbled one word upon a loose sheet. "That," said I as I handed it to Colonel Emsworth, "is what has brought us here."

He stared at the writing with a face from which every expression save amazement had vanished.

"How do you know?" he gasped, sitting down heavily in his chair.

"It is my business to know things. That is my trade."

He sat in deep thought, his gaunt hand tugging at his straggling beard. Then he made a gesture of resignation.

"Well, if you wish to see Godfrey, you shall. It is no doing of mine, but you have forced my hand. Ralph, tell Mr Godfrey and Mr Kent that in five minutes we shall be with them."

At the end of that time we passed down the garden path and found ourselves in front of the mystery house at the end. A small bearded man stood at the door with a look of considerable astonishment upon his face.

"This is very sudden, Colonel Emsworth," said he. "This will disarrange all our plans."

"I can't help it, Mr Kent. Our hands have been forced. Can Mr Godfrey see us?"

"Yes – he is waiting inside." He turned and led us into a large, plainly furnished front room. A man was standing with his back to the fire, and at the sight of him my client sprang forward with outstretched hand.

"Why, Godfrey, old man, this is fine!"

But the other waved him back.

47

"Don't touch me, Jimmie. Keep your distance. Yes, you may well stare! I don't quite look the smart Lance Corporal Emsworth, of B Squadron, do I?"

His appearance was certainly extraordinary. One could see that he had indeed been a handsome man with clear-cut features sunburnt by an African sun, but mottled in patches over this darker surface were curious whitish patches which had bleached his skin.

"That's why I don't court visitors," said he. "I don't mind you, Jimmie, but I could have done without your friend. I suppose there is some good reason for it, but you have me at a disadvantage."

"I wanted to be sure that all was well with you, Godfrey. I saw you that night when you looked into my window, and I could not let the matter rest till I had cleared things up."

"Old Ralph told me you were there, and I couldn't help taking a peep at you. I hoped you would not have seen me, and I had to run to my burrow when I heard the window go up."

"But what in Heaven's name is the matter?"

"Well, it's not a long story to tell," said he, lighting a cigarette. "You remember that morning fight at Buffelspruit, outside Pretoria,* on the eastern railway line? You heard I was hit?"

"Yes, I heard that, but I never got particulars."

"Three of us got separated from the others. It was very broken country, you may remember. There was Simpson – the fellow we called Baldy Simpson – and Anderson, and I. We were clearing brother Boer, but he lay low and got the three of us. The other two were killed. I got an elephant bullet through my shoulder. I stuck on to my horse, however, and he galloped several miles before I fainted and rolled off the saddle.

"When I came to myself, it was nightfall, and I raised myself up, feeling very weak and ill. To my surprise there was a house close beside me, a fairly large house with a broad stoep* and many windows. It was deadly cold. You remember the kind of numb cold which used to come at evening – a deadly, sickening sort of cold, very different from a crisp, healthy frost. Well, I was chilled to the bone, and my only hope seemed to lie in reaching that house. I staggered to my feet and dragged myself along, hardly conscious of what I did. I have a dim memory of slowly ascending the steps, entering a wide-opened door, passing into a large room which contained several beds, and throwing myself down with a gasp of satisfaction upon one of them. It was unmade, but that troubled me not at all. I drew the clothes over my shivering body, and in a moment I was in a deep sleep.

"It was morning when I wakened, and it seemed to me that instead of coming out into a world of sanity I had emerged into some extraordinary nightmare. The African sun flooded through the big, curtainless windows, and every detail of the great, bare, whitewashed dormitory stood out hard and clear. In front of me was standing a small, dwarf-like man with a huge, bulbous head, who was jabbering excitedly in Dutch, waving two horrible hands which looked to me like brown sponges. Behind him stood a group of people who seemed to be intensely amused by the situation, but a chill came over me as I looked at them. Not one of them was a normal human being. Every one was twisted or swollen or disfigured in some strange way. The laughter of these strange monstrosities was a dreadful thing to hear.

"It seemed that none of them could speak English, but the situation wanted clearing up, for the creature with the big head was growing furiously angry, and, uttering wild-beast cries, he had laid his deformed hands upon me and was dragging me out of bed, regardless of the fresh flow of blood from my wound. The little monster was as strong as a bull, and I don't know what he might have done to me had not an elderly man who was clearly in authority been attracted to the room by the hubbub. He said a few stern words in Dutch, and my persecutor shrank away. Then he turned upon me, gazing at me in the utmost amazement.

"'How in the world did you come here?' he asked in amazement. 'Wait a bit! I see that you are tired out, and that wounded shoulder of yours wants looking after. I am a doctor, and I'll soon have you tied up. But – man alive! – you are in far greater danger here than ever you were on the battlefield. You are in the Leper Hospital, and you have slept in a leper's bed.'

"Need I tell you more, Jimmie? It seems that in view of the approaching battle all these poor creatures had been evacuated the day before. Then, as the British advanced, they had been brought back by this, their medical superintendent, who assured me that, though he believed he was immune to the disease, he would nonetheless never have dared to do what I had done. He put me in a private room, treated me kindly, and within a week or so I was removed to the general hospital at Pretoria.

"So there you have my tragedy. I hoped against hope, but it was not until I had reached home that the terrible signs which you see upon my face told me that I had not escaped. What was I to do? I was in this lonely house. We had two servants whom we could utterly trust. There was a house where I could live. Under pledge of secrecy, Mr Kent, who is a surgeon, was prepared to stay with me. It seemed simple enough on those lines. The alternative was a dreadful one – segregation for life among strangers with never a hope of release. But absolute secrecy was necessary, or even in this quiet countryside there would have been an outcry, and I should have been dragged to my horrible doom. Even you, Jimmie – even you had to be kept in the dark. Why my father has relented I cannot imagine."

Colonel Emsworth pointed to me.

"This is the gentleman who forced my hand." He unfolded the scrap of paper on which I had written the word "leprosy". "It seemed to me that if he knew so much as that, it was safer that he should know all."

"And so it was," said I. "Who knows but good may come of it? I understand that only Mr Kent has seen the patient. May I ask, sir, if you are an authority on such complaints, which are, I understand, tropical or semi-tropical in their nature?"

"I have the ordinary knowledge of the educated medical man," he observed with some stiffness.

"I have no doubt, sir, that you are fully competent, but I am sure that you will agree that in such a case a second opinion is valuable. You have avoided this, I understand, for fear that pressure should be put upon you to segregate the patient."

"That is so," said Colonel Emsworth.

"I foresaw this situation," I explained, "and I have brought with me a friend whose discretion may absolutely be trusted. I was able once to do him a professional service, and he is ready to advise as a friend rather than as a specialist. His name is Sir James Saunders."

The prospect of an interview with Lord Roberts* would not have excited greater wonder and pleasure in a raw subaltern than was now reflected upon the face of Mr Kent.

"I shall indeed be proud," he murmured.

"Then I will ask Sir James to step this way. He is at present in the carriage outside the door. Meanwhile, Colonel Emsworth, we may perhaps assemble in your study, where I could give the necessary explanations."

And here it is that I miss my Watson. By cunning questions and ejaculations of wonder he could elevate my simple art, which is but systematized common sense, into a prodigy. When I tell my own story, I have no such aid. And yet I will give my process of thought even as I gave it to my small audience, which included Godfrey's mother, in the study of Colonel Emsworth.

"That process," said I, "starts upon the supposition that when you have eliminated all which is impossible, then whatever remains, however improbable, must be the truth. It may well be that several explanations remain, in which case one tries test after test until one or other of them has a convincing amount of support. We will now apply this principle to the case in point. As it was first presented to me, there were three possible explanations of the seclusion or incarceration of this gentleman in an outhouse of his father's mansion. There was the explanation that he was in hiding for a crime, or that he was mad and that they wished to avoid an asylum, or that he had some disease which caused his segregation. I could think of no other adequate solutions. These, then, had to be sifted and balanced against each other.

"The criminal solution would not bear inspection. No unsolved crime had been reported from that district. I was sure of that. If it were some crime not yet discovered, then clearly it would be to the interest of the family to get rid of the delinquent and send him abroad rather than keep him concealed at home. I could see no explanation for such a line of conduct.

"Insanity was more plausible. The presence of the second person in the outhouse suggested a keeper. The fact that he locked the door when he came out strengthened the supposition and gave the idea of constraint. On the other hand, this constraint could not be severe, or the young man could not have got loose and come down to have a look at his friend. You will remember, Mr Dodd, that I felt round for points, asking you, for example, about the paper which Mr Kent was reading. Had it been the *Lancet* or the *British Medical Journal* it would have helped me. It is not illegal, however, to keep a lunatic upon private premises so long as there is a qualified person in attendance and that the authorities have been duly notified. Why, then, all this desperate desire for secrecy? Once again I could not get the theory to fit the facts.

"There remained the third possibility, into which, rare and unlikely as it was, everything seemed to fit. Leprosy is not uncommon in South Africa. By some extraordinary chance this youth might have contracted it. His people would be placed in a very dreadful position, since they would desire to save him from segregation. Great secrecy would be needed to prevent rumours from getting about and subsequent interference by the authorities. A devoted medical man, if sufficiently paid, would easily be found to take charge of the sufferer. There would be no reason why the latter should not be allowed freedom after dark. Bleaching of the skin is a common result of the disease. The case was a strong one – so strong that I determined to act as if it were actually proved. When on arriving here I noticed that Ralph, who carries out the meals, had gloves which are impregnated with disinfectants, my last doubts were removed. A single word showed you, sir, that your secret was discovered, and if I wrote rather than said it, it was to prove to you that my discretion was to be trusted."

I was finishing this little analysis of the case when the door was opened and the austere figure of the great dermatologist was ushered in. But for once his sphinx-like features had relaxed and there was a warm humanity in his eyes. He strode up to Colonel Emsworth and shook him by the hand.

"It is often my lot to bring ill tidings, and seldom good," said he. "This occasion is the more welcome. It is not leprosy."

"What?"

"A well-marked case of pseudo-leprosy or ichthyosis, a scale-like affection of the skin – unsightly, obstinate, but possibly curable, and certainly non-infective. Yes, Mr Holmes, the coincidence is a remarkable one. But is it coincidence? Are there not subtle forces at work of which we know little? Are we assured that the apprehension from which this young man has no doubt suffered terribly since his exposure to its contagion may not produce a physical effect which simulates that which it fears? At any rate, I pledge my professional reputation... But the lady has fainted! I think that Mr Kent had better be with her until she recovers from this joyous shock."

THE ADVENTURE
OF THE MAZARIN STONE[*]

I T WAS PLEASANT TO DOCTOR WATSON to find himself once
more in the untidy room of the first floor in Baker Street which
had been the starting point of so many remarkable adventures. He
looked round him at the scientific charts upon the wall, the acid-
charred bench of chemicals, the violin case leaning in the corner,
the coal scuttle, which contained of old the pipes and tobacco.
Finally, his eyes came round to the fresh and smiling face of Billy,
the young but very wise and tactful page who had helped a little
to fill up the gap of loneliness and isolation which surrounded the
saturnine figure of the great detective.

"It all seems very unchanged, Billy. You don't change, either.
I hope the same can be said of him?"

Billy glanced, with some solicitude, at the closed door of the
bedroom.

"I think he's in bed and asleep," he said.

It was seven in the evening of a lovely summer's day, but Doctor
Watson was sufficiently familiar with the irregularity of his old
friend's hours to feel no surprise at the idea.

"That means a case, I suppose?"

"Yes, sir – he is very hard at it just now. I'm frightened for his
health. He gets paler and thinner, and he eats nothing. 'When will
you be pleased to dine, Mr Holmes?' Mrs Hudson asked. 'Seven
thirty, the day after tomorrow,' said he. You know his way when
he is keen on a case."

"Yes, Billy, I know."

"He's following someone. Yesterday he was out as a workman looking for a job. Today he was an old woman. Fairly took me in, he did, and I ought to know his ways by now." Billy pointed with a grin to a very baggy parasol which leant against the sofa. "That's part of the old woman's outfit," he said.

"But what is it all about, Billy?"

Billy sank his voice, as one who discusses great secrets of state. "I don't mind telling you, sir, but it should go no farther. It's this case of the Crown diamond."

"What – the hundred-thousand-pound burglary?"

"Yes, sir. They must get it back, sir. Why, we had the prime minister and the home secretary both sitting on that very sofa. Mr Holmes was very nice to them. He soon put them at their ease and promised he would do all he could. Then there is Lord Cantlemere—"

"Ah!"

"Yes, sir – you know what that means. He's a stiff 'un, sir, if I may say so. I can get along with the prime minister, and I've nothing against the home secretary, who seemed a civil, obliging sort of man, but I can't stand His Lordship. Neither can Mr Holmes, sir. You see, he don't believe in Mr Holmes, and he was against employing him. He'd *rather* he failed."

"And Mr Holmes knows it?"

"Mr Holmes always knows whatever there is to know."

"Well, we'll hope he won't fail, and that Lord Cantlemere will be confounded. But I say, Billy, what is that curtain for across the window?"

"Mr Holmes had it put up there three days ago. We've got something funny behind it."

Billy advanced and drew away the drapery which screened the alcove of the bow window.

Doctor Watson could not restrain a cry of amazement. There was a facsimile of his old friend, dressing gown and all, the face turned three quarters towards the window and downwards, as though reading an invisible book, while the body was sunk deep in an armchair. Billy detached the head and held it in the air.

"We put it at different angles, so that it may seem more lifelike. I wouldn't dare touch it if the blind were not down. But when it's up you can see this from across the way."

"We used something of the sort once before."*

"Before my time," said Billy. He drew the window curtains apart and looked out into the street. "There are folk who watch us from over yonder. I can see a fellow now at the window. Have a look for yourself."

Watson had taken a step forward when the bedroom door opened, and the long, thin form of Holmes emerged, his face pale and drawn, but his step and bearing as active as ever. With a single spring he was at the window, and had drawn the blind once more.

"That will do, Billy," said he. "You were in danger of your life then, my boy, and I can't do without you just yet. Well, Watson, it is good to see you in your old quarters once again. You come at a critical moment."

"So I gather."

"You can go, Billy. That boy is a problem, Watson. How far am I justified in allowing him to be in danger?"

"Danger of what, Holmes?"

"Of sudden death. I'm expecting something this evening."

"Expecting what?"

"To be murdered, Watson."

"No, no – you are joking, Holmes!"

"Even my limited sense of humour could evolve a better joke than that. But we may be comfortable in the mean time, may we not? Is alcohol permitted? The gasogene* and cigars are in the old place. Let me see you once more in the customary armchair. You have not, I hope, learnt to despise my pipe and my lamentable tobacco? It has to take the place of food these days."

"But why not eat?"

"Because the faculties become refined when you starve them. Why, surely, as a doctor, my dear Watson, you must admit that what your digestion gains in the way of blood supply is so much lost to the brain. I am a brain, Watson. The rest of me is a mere appendix. Therefore, it is the brain I must consider."

"But this danger, Holmes?"

"Ah, yes – in case it should come off, it would perhaps be as well that you should burden your memory with the name and address of the murderer. You can give it to Scotland Yard, with my love and a parting blessing. Sylvius is the name – Count Negretto Sylvius.* Write it down, man, write it down! 136 Moorside Gardens, NW. Got it?"

Watson's honest face was twitching with anxiety. He knew only too well the immense risks taken by Holmes, and was well aware that what he said was more likely to be understatement than exaggeration. Watson was always the man of action, and he rose to the occasion.

"Count me in, Holmes. I have nothing to do for a day or two."

"Your morals don't improve, Watson. You have added fibbing to your other vices. You bear every sign of the busy medical man, with calls on him every hour."

"Not such important ones. But can't you have this fellow arrested?"

"Yes, Watson, I could. That's what worries him so."

"But why don't you?"

"Because I don't know where the diamond is."

"Ah! Billy told me – the missing Crown jewel!"

"Yes, the great yellow Mazarin stone.* I've cast my net and I have my fish. But I have not got the stone. What is the use of taking *them*? We can make the world a better place by laying them by the heels. But that is not what I am out for. It's the stone I want."

"And is this Count Sylvius one of your fish?"

"Yes, and he's a shark. He bites. The other is Sam Merton, the boxer. Not a bad fellow, Sam, but the count has used him. Sam's not a shark. He is a great big silly bull-headed gudgeon.* But he is flopping about in my net all the same."

"Where is this Count Sylvius?"

"I've been at his very elbow all the morning. You've seen me as an old lady, Watson. I was never more convincing. He actually picked up my parasol for me once. 'By your leave, madam,' said he – half-Italian, you know, and with the southern graces of manner when in the mood, but a devil incarnate in the other mood. Life is full of whimsical happenings, Watson."

"It might have been tragedy."

"Well, perhaps it might. I followed him to old Straubenzee's workshop in the Minories.* Straubenzee made the airgun – a very pretty bit of work, as I understand, and I rather fancy it is in the opposite window at the present moment. Have you seen the dummy? Of course, Billy showed it to you. Well, it may get a bullet through its beautiful head at any moment. Ah, Billy, what is it?"

The boy had reappeared in the room with a card upon a tray. Holmes glanced at it with raised eyebrows and an amused smile.

"The man himself. I had hardly expected this. Grasp the nettle, Watson! A man of nerve. Possibly you have heard of his reputation as a shooter of big game. It would indeed be a triumphant ending to his excellent sporting record if he added me to his bag. This is a proof that he feels my toe very close behind his heel."

"Send for the police."

"I probably shall. But not just yet. Would you glance carefully out of the window, Watson, and see if anyone is hanging about in the street?"

Watson looked warily round the edge of the curtain.

"Yes, there is one rough fellow near the door."

"That will be Sam Merton – the faithful but rather fatuous Sam. Where is this gentleman, Billy?"

"In the waiting room, sir."

"Show him up when I ring."

"Yes, sir."

"If I am not in the room, show him in all the same."

"Yes, sir."

Watson waited until the door was closed, and then he turned earnestly to his companion.

"Look here, Holmes, this is simply impossible. This is a desperate man who sticks at nothing. He may have come to murder you."

"I should not be surprised."

"I insist upon staying with you."

"You would be horribly in the way."

"In *his* way?"

"No, my dear fellow – in my way."

"Well, I can't possibly leave you."

"Yes, you can, Watson. And you will, for you have never failed to play the game. I am sure you will play it to the end. This man has come for his own purpose, but he may stay for mine." Holmes took out his notebook and scribbled a few lines. "Take a cab to Scotland Yard and give this to Youghal of the CID. Come back with the police. The fellow's arrest will follow."

"I'll do that with joy."

"Before you return, I may have just time enough to find out where the stone is." He touched the bell. "I think we will go out through the bedroom. This second exit is exceedingly useful. I rather want to see my shark without his seeing me, and I have, as you will remember, my own way of doing it."

It was, therefore, an empty room into which Billy, a minute later, ushered Count Sylvius. The famous game shot, sportsman and man about town was a big, swarthy fellow, with a formidable dark moustache shading a cruel, thin-lipped mouth, and surmounted by a long, curved nose, like the beak of an eagle. He was well dressed, but his brilliant necktie, shining pin and glittering rings were flamboyant in their effect. As the door closed behind him, he looked round him with fierce, startled eyes, like one who suspects a trap at every turn. Then he gave a violent start as he saw the impassive head and the collar of the dressing gown which projected above the armchair in the window. At first his expression was one of pure amazement. Then the light of a horrible hope gleamed in his dark, murderous eyes. He took one more glance round to see that there were no witnesses, and then, on tiptoe, his thick stick half raised, he approached the silent figure. He was crouching for his final spring and blow when a cool, sardonic voice greeted him from the open bedroom door:

"Don't break it, Count! Don't break it!"

The assassin staggered back, amazement in his convulsed face. For an instant he half-raised his loaded cane once more, as if he would turn his violence from the effigy to the original, but there was something in that steady grey eye and mocking smile which caused his hand to sink to his side.

"It's a pretty little thing," said Holmes, advancing towards the image. "Tavernier, the French modeller, made it. He is as good at waxworks as your friend Straubenzee is at airguns."

"Airguns, sir! What do you mean?"

"Put your hat and stick on the side table. Thank you! Pray take a seat. Would you care to put your revolver out also? Oh, very good, if you prefer to sit upon it. Your visit is really most opportune, for I wanted badly to have a few minutes' chat with you."

The count scowled, with heavy, threatening eyebrows.

"I, too, wished to have some words with you, Holmes. That is why I am here. I won't deny that I intended to assault you just now."

Holmes swung his leg on the edge of the table.

"I rather gathered that you had some idea of the sort in your head," said he. "But why these personal attentions?"

"Because you have gone out of your way to annoy me. Because you have put your creatures upon my track."

"My creatures! I assure you no!"

"Nonsense! I have had them followed. Two can play at that game, Holmes."

"It is a small point, Count Sylvius, but perhaps you would kindly give me my prefix when you address me. You can understand that, with my routine of work, I should find myself on familiar terms with half the rogues' gallery, and you will agree that exceptions are invidious."

"Well, *Mr* Holmes, then."

"Excellent! But I assure you you are mistaken about my alleged agents."

Count Sylvius laughed contemptuously.

"Other people can observe as well as you. Yesterday there was an old sporting man. Today it was an elderly woman. They held me in view all day."

"Really, sir, you compliment me. Old Baron Dowson said the night before he was hanged that in my case what the law had gained the stage had lost. And now you give my little impersonations your kindly praise!"

"It was you – you yourself?"

Holmes shrugged his shoulders. "You can see in the corner the parasol which you so politely handed to me in the Minories before you began to suspect."

"If I had known, you might never—"

"Have seen this humble home again. I was well aware of it. We all have neglected opportunities to deplore. As it happens, you did not know, so here we are!"

The count's knotted brows gathered more heavily over his menacing eyes. "What you say only makes the matter worse. It was not your agents, but your play-acting, busybody self! You admit that you have dogged me. Why?"

"Come now, Count. You used to shoot lions in Algeria."

"Well?"

"But why?"

"Why? The sport… the excitement… the danger!"

"And, no doubt, to free the country from a pest?"

"Exactly!"

"My reasons in a nutshell!"

The count sprang to his feet, and his hand involuntarily moved back to his hip pocket.

"Sit down, sir, sit down! There was another, more practical, reason. I want that yellow diamond!"

Count Sylvius lay back in his chair with an evil smile.

"Upon my word!" said he.

"You knew that I was after you for that. The real reason why you are here tonight is to find out how much I know about the matter and how far my removal is absolutely essential. Well, I should say that, from your point of view, it *is* absolutely essential, for I know all about it, save only one thing, which you are about to tell me."

"Oh, indeed! And, pray, what is this missing fact?"

"Where the Crown diamond now is."

The count looked sharply at his companion. "Oh, you want to know that, do you? How the devil should I be able to tell you where it is?"

"You can, and you will."

"Indeed!"

"You can't bluff me, Count Sylvius." Holmes's eyes, as he gazed at him, contracted and lightened until they were like two menacing points of steel. "You are absolute plate glass. I see to the very back of your mind."

"Then, of course, you see where the diamond is!"

Holmes clapped his hands with amusement, and then pointed a derisive finger. "Then you do know. You have admitted it!"

"I admit nothing."

"Now, Count, if you will be reasonable, we can do business. If not, you will get hurt."

Count Sylvius threw up his eyes to the ceiling. "And you talk about bluff!" said he.

Holmes looked at him thoughtfully, like a master chess player who meditates his crowning move. Then he threw open the table drawer and drew out a squat notebook.

"Do you know what I keep in this book?"

"No, sir, I do not!"

"You!"

"Me?"

"Yes, sir, *you*! You are all here – every action of your vile and dangerous life."

"Damn you, Holmes!" cried the count with blazing eyes. "There are limits to my patience!"

"It's all here, Count. The real facts as to the death of old Mrs Harold, who left you the Blymer estate, which you so rapidly gambled away."

"You are dreaming!"

"And the complete life history of Miss Minnie Warrender."

"Tut! You will make nothing of that!"

"Plenty more here, Count. Here is the robbery in the train-de-luxe* to the Riviera on 13th February 1892. Here is the forged cheque in the same year on the Crédit Lyonnais."*

"No – you're wrong there."

"Then I am right on the others! Now, Count, you are a card player. When the other fellow has all the trumps, it saves time to throw down your hand."

"What has all this talk to do with the jewel of which you spoke?"

"Gently, Count. Restrain that eager mind! Let me get to the points in my own humdrum fashion. I have all this against you – but, above all, I have a clear case against both you and your fighting bully in the case of the Crown diamond."

"Indeed!"

"I have the cabman who took you to Whitehall and the cabman who brought you away. I have the commissionaire* who saw you near the case. I have Ikey Sanders, who refused to cut it up for you. Ikey has peached,* and the game is up."

The veins stood out on the count's forehead. His dark, hairy hands were clenched in a convulsion of restrained emotion. He tried to speak, but the words would not shape themselves.

"That's the hand I play from," said Holmes. "I put it all upon the table. But one card is missing. It's the King of Diamonds. I don't know where the stone is."

"You never shall know."

"No? Now, be reasonable, Count. Consider the situation. You are going to be locked up for twenty years. So is Sam Merton. What good are you to get out of your diamond? None in the world. But if you hand it over – well, I'll compound a felony.* We don't want you or Sam. We want the stone. Give that up, and so far as I am concerned you can go free so long as you behave yourself in the future. If you make another slip – well, it will be the last. But this time my commission is to get the stone, not you."

"But if I refuse?"

"Why, then – alas! – it must be you and not the stone."

Billy had appeared in answer to a ring.

"I think, Count, that it would be as well to have your friend Sam at this conference. After all, his interests should be represented. Billy, you will see a large and ugly gentleman outside the front door. Ask him to come up."

"If he won't come, sir?"

"No violence, Billy. Don't be rough with him. If you tell him that Count Sylvius wants him, he will certainly come."

"What are you going to do now?" asked the count as Billy disappeared.

"My friend Watson was with me just now. I told him that I had a shark and a gudgeon in my net – now I am drawing the net and up they come together."

The count had risen from his chair, and his hand was behind his back. Holmes held something half protruding from the pocket of his dressing gown.

"You won't die in your bed, Holmes."

"I have often had the same idea. Does it matter very much? After all, Count, your own exit is more likely to be perpendicular than horizontal. But these anticipations of the future are morbid. Why not give ourselves up to the unrestrained enjoyment of the present?"

A sudden wild-beast light sprang up in the dark, menacing eyes of the master criminal. Holmes's figure seemed to grow taller as he grew tense and ready.

"It is no use your fingering your revolver, my friend," he said in a quiet voice. "You know perfectly well that you dare not use it, even if I gave you time to draw it. Nasty, noisy things, revolvers, Count. Better stick to airguns. Ah! I think I hear the fairy footstep of your estimable partner. Good day, Mr Merton. Rather dull in the street, is it not?"

The prizefighter, a heavily built young man with a stupid, obstinate, slab-sided face, stood awkwardly at the door, looking about him with a puzzled expression. Holmes's debonair manner was a new experience, and though he vaguely felt that it was hostile, he did not know how to counter it. He turned to his more astute comrade for help.

"What's the game now, Count? What's this fellow want? What's up?" His voice was deep and raucous.

The count shrugged his shoulders, and it was Holmes who answered.

"If I may put it in a nutshell, Mr Merton, I should say it was *all* up."

The boxer still addressed his remarks to his associate.

"Is this cove* trying to be funny, or what? I'm not in the funny mood myself."

"No, I expect not," said Holmes. "I think I can promise you that you will feel even less humorous as the evening advances. Now, look here, Count Sylvius. I'm a busy man and I can't waste time. I'm going into that bedroom. Pray make yourselves quite at home in my absence. You can explain to your friend how the matter lies without the restraint of my presence. I shall try over the *Hoffmann* 'Barcarolle'* upon my violin. In five minutes I shall return for your final answer. You quite grasp the alternative, do you not? Shall we take you, or shall we have the stone?"

Holmes withdrew, picking up his violin from the corner as he passed. A few moments later the long-drawn, wailing notes of that most haunting of tunes came faintly through the closed door of the bedroom.

"What is it, then?" asked Merton anxiously as his companion turned to him. "Does he know about the stone?"

"He knows a damned sight too much about it. I'm not sure that he doesn't know all about it."

"Good Lord!" The boxer's sallow face turned a shade whiter.

"Ikey Sanders has split* on us."

"He has, has he? I'll do him down a thick 'un for that if I swing for it."*

"That won't help us much. We've got to make up our minds what to do."

"Half a mo'," said the boxer, looking suspiciously at the bed-room door. "He's a leery* cove that wants watching. I suppose he's not listening?"

"How can he be listening with that music going?"

"That's right. Maybe somebody's behind a curtain. Too many curtains in this room." As he looked round, he suddenly saw for the first time the effigy in the window, and stood staring and pointing, too amazed for words.

"Tut! It's only a dummy," said the count.

"A fake, is it? Well, strike me! Madame Tussaud* ain't in it. It's the living spit of him, gown and all. But them curtains, Count!"

"Oh, confound the curtains! We are wasting our time, and there is none too much. He can lag us over this stone."

"The deuce he can!"

"But he'll let us slip if we only tell him where the swag is."

"What! Give it up? Give up a hundred thousand quid?"

"It's one or the other."

Merton scratched his short-cropped pate.

"He's alone in there. Let's do him in. If his light were out, we should have nothing to fear."

The count shook his head.

"He is armed and ready. If we shot him we could hardly get away in a place like this. Besides, it's likely enough that the police know whatever evidence he has got. Hallo! What was that?"

There was a vague sound which seemed to come from the window. Both men sprang round, but all was quiet. Save for the one strange figure seated in the chair, the room was certainly empty.

"Something in the street," said Merton. "Now look here, guv'nor, you've got the brains. Surely you can think a way out of it. If slug-ging is no use, then it's up to you."

"I've fooled better men than he," the count answered. "The stone is here in my secret pocket. I take no chances leaving it about. It can be out of England tonight and cut into four pieces in Amsterdam before Sunday. He knows nothing of Van Seddar."

"I thought Van Seddar was going next week."

"He *was*. But now he must get off by the next boat. One or other of us must slip round with the stone to Lime Street and tell him."

"But the false bottom ain't ready."

"Well, he must take it as it is and chance it. There's not a moment to lose." Again, with the sense of danger which becomes an instinct with the sportsman, he paused and looked hard at the window. Yes, it was surely from the street that the faint sound had come.

"As to Holmes," he continued, "we can fool him easily enough. You see, the damned fool won't arrest us if he can get the stone. Well, we'll promise him the stone. We'll put him on the wrong track about it, and before he finds that it *is* the wrong track, it will be in Holland and we out of the country."

"That sounds good to me!" cried Sam Merton with a grin.

"You go on and tell the Dutchman to get a move on him. I'll see this sucker and fill him up with a bogus confession. I'll tell him that the stone is in Liverpool. Confound that whining music – it gets on my nerves! By the time he finds it isn't in Liverpool, it will be in quarters and we on the blue water. Come back here, out of a line with that keyhole. Here is the stone."

"I wonder you dare carry it."

"Where could I have it safer? If we could take it out of Whitehall, someone else could surely take it out of my lodgings."

"Let's have a look at it."

Count Sylvius cast a somewhat unflattering glance at his associate, and disregarded the unwashed hand which was extended towards him.

"What – d'ye think I'm going to snatch it off you? See here, mister, I'm getting a bit tired of your ways."

"Well, well... no offence, Sam. We can't afford to quarrel. Come over to the window if you want to see the beauty properly. Now hold it to the light! Here!"

"Thank you!"

With a single spring Holmes had leapt from the dummy's chair and had grasped the precious jewel. He held it now in one hand, while his other pointed a revolver at the count's head. The two villains staggered back in utter amazement. Before they had recovered, Holmes had pressed the electric bell.

"No violence, gentlemen – no violence, I beg of you! Consider the furniture! It must be very clear to you that your position is an impossible one. The police are waiting below."

The count's bewilderment overmastered his rage and fear.

"But how the deuce…" he gasped.

"Your surprise is very natural. You are not aware that a second door from my bedroom leads behind that curtain. I fancied that you must have heard me when I displaced the figure, but luck was on my side. It gave me a chance of listening to your racy conversation, which would have been painfully constrained, had you been aware of my presence."

The count gave a gesture of resignation.

"We give you best, Holmes. I believe you are the Devil himself."

"Not far from him, at any rate," Holmes answered with a polite smile.

Sam Merton's slow intellect had only gradually appreciated the situation. Now, as the sound of heavy steps came from the stairs outside, he broke silence at last.

"A fair cop!" said he. "But, I say, what about that bloomin' fiddle! I hear it yet."

"Tut-tut!" Holmes answered. "You are perfectly right. Let it play! These modern gramophones are a remarkable invention."

There was an inrush of police, the handcuffs clicked and the criminals were led to the waiting cab. Watson lingered with Holmes, congratulating him upon this fresh leaf added to his laurels. Once more their conversation was interrupted by the imperturbable Billy with his card tray.

"Lord Cantlemere, sir."

"Show him up, Billy. This is the eminent peer who represents the very highest interests," said Holmes. "He is an excellent and loyal person, but rather of the old regime. Shall we make him unbend? Dare we venture upon a slight liberty? He knows, we may conjecture, nothing of what has occurred."

The door opened to admit a thin, austere figure with a hatchet face and drooping mid-Victorian whiskers of a glossy blackness which hardly corresponded with the rounded shoulders and feeble gait. Holmes advanced affably, and shook an unresponsive hand.

"How do you do, Lord Cantlemere? It is chilly for the time of year, but rather warm indoors. May I take your overcoat?"

"No, I thank you – I will not take it off."

Holmes laid his hand insistently upon the sleeve.

"Pray allow me! My friend Doctor Watson would assure you that these changes of temperature are most insidious."

His Lordship shook himself free with some impatience.

"I am quite comfortable, sir. I have no need to stay. I have simply looked in to know how your self-appointed task was progressing."

"It is difficult – very difficult."

"I feared that you would find it so."

There was a distinct sneer in the old courtier's words and manner.

"Every man finds his limitations, Mr Holmes, but at least it cures us of the weakness of self-satisfaction."

"Yes, sir, I have been much perplexed."

"No doubt."

"Especially upon one point. Possibly you could help me upon it?"

"You apply for my advice rather late in the day. I thought that you had your own all-sufficient methods. Still, I am ready to help you."

"You see, Lord Cantlemere, we can no doubt frame a case against the actual thieves."

"When you have caught them."

"Exactly. But the question is: how shall we proceed against the receiver?"

"Is this not rather premature?"

"It is as well to have our plans ready. Now, what would you regard as final evidence against the receiver?"

"The actual possession of the stone."

"You would arrest him upon that?"

"Most undoubtedly."

Holmes seldom laughed, but he got as near it as his old friend Watson could remember.

"In that case, my dear sir, I shall be under the painful necessity of advising your arrest."

Lord Cantlemere was very angry. Some of the ancient fires flickered up into his sallow cheeks.

"You take a great liberty, Mr Holmes. In fifty years of official life I cannot recall such a case. I am a busy man, sir, engaged upon important affairs, and I have no time or taste for foolish jokes. I may tell you frankly, sir, that I have never been a believer in your powers, and that I have always been of the opinion that the matter was far safer in the hands of the regular police force. Your conduct confirms all my conclusions. I have the honour, sir, to wish you good evening."

Holmes had swiftly changed his position and was between the peer and the door.

"One moment, sir," said he. "To actually go off with the Mazarin stone would be a more serious offence than to be found in temporary possession of it."

"Sir, this is intolerable! Let me pass."

"Put your hand in the right-hand pocket of your overcoat."

"What do you mean, sir?"

"Come, come – do what I ask."

An instant later the amazed peer was standing, blinking and stammering, with the great yellow stone on his shaking palm.

"What? What? How is this, Mr Holmes?"

"Too bad, Lord Cantlemere, too bad!" cried Holmes. "My old friend here will tell you that I have an impish habit of practical joking. Also, that I can never resist a dramatic situation. I took the liberty – the very great liberty, I admit – of putting the stone into your pocket at the beginning of our interview."

The old peer stared from the stone to the smiling face before him.

"Sir, I am bewildered. But – yes – it is indeed the Mazarin stone. We are greatly your debtors, Mr Holmes. Your sense of humour may, as you admit, be somewhat perverted, and its exhibition remarkably untimely, but at least I withdraw any reflection I have made upon your amazing professional powers. But how—"

"The case is but half finished – the details can wait. No doubt, Lord Cantlemere, your pleasure in telling of this successful result in the exalted circle to which you return will be some small atonement for my practical joke. Billy, you will show His Lordship out, and tell Mrs Hudson that I should be glad if she would send up dinner for two as soon as possible."

THE ADVENTURE
OF THE THREE GABLES

I DON'T THINK THAT any of my adventures with Mr Sherlock Holmes opened quite so abruptly, or so dramatically, as that which I associate with the Three Gables. I had not seen Holmes for some days, and had no idea of the new channel into which his activities had been directed. He was in a chatty mood that morning, however, and had just settled me into the well-worn low armchair on one side of the fire, while he had curled down with his pipe in his mouth upon the opposite chair, when our visitor arrived. If I had said that a mad bull had arrived, it would give a clearer impression of what occurred.

The door had flown open, and a huge Negro had burst into the room. He would have been a comic figure if he had not been terrific, for he was dressed in a very loud grey check suit with a flowing salmon-coloured tie. His broad face and flattened nose were thrust forward, as his sullen dark eyes, with a smouldering gleam of malice in them, turned from one of us to the other.

"Which of you genelmen is Masser Holmes?" he asked.

Holmes raised his pipe with a languid smile.

"Oh! It's you, is it?" said our visitor, coming with an unpleasant, stealthy step round the angle of the table. "See here, Masser Holmes, you keep your hands out of other folks' business. Leave folks to manage their own affairs. Got that, Masser Holmes?"

"Keep on talking," said Holmes. "It's fine."

"Oh! It's fine, is it?" growled the savage. "It won't be so damn fine if I have to trim you up a bit. I've handled your kind before now, and they didn't look fine when I was through with them. Look at that, Masser Holmes!"

He swung a huge knotted lump of a fist under my friend's nose. Holmes examined it closely with an air of great interest. "Were you born so?" he asked. "Or did it come by degrees?"

It may have been the icy coolness of my friend, or it may have been the slight clatter which I made as I picked up the poker. In any case, our visitor's manner became less flamboyant.

"Well, I've given you fair warnin'," said he. "I've a friend that's interested out Harrow* way – you know what I'm meaning – and he don't intend to have no buttin' in by you. Got that? You ain't the law, and I ain't the law either, and if you come in, I'll be on hand also. Don't you forget it."

"I've wanted to meet you for some time," said Holmes. "I won't ask you to sit down, for I don't like the smell of you,* but aren't you Steve Dixie, the bruiser?"

"That's my name, Masser Holmes, and you'll get put through it for sure if you give me any lip."

"It is certainly the last thing you need," said Holmes, staring at our visitor's hideous mouth. "But it was the killing of young Perkins outside the Holborn Bar... What? You're not going?"

The Negro had sprung back, and his face was leaden. "I won't listen to no such talk," said he. "What have I to do with this 'ere Perkins, Masser Holmes? I was trainin' at the Bull Ring in Birmingham* when this boy done gone get into trouble."

"Yes, you'll tell the magistrate about it, Steve," said Holmes. "I've been watching you and Barney Stockdale—"

"So help me the Lord! Masser Holmes—"

"That's enough. Get out of it. I'll pick you up when I want you."

"Good mornin', Masser Holmes. I hope there ain't no hard feelin's about this 'ere visit?"

"There will be unless you tell me who sent you."

"Why, there ain't no secret about that, Masser Holmes. It was that same genelman that you have just done gone mention."

"And who set him on to it?"

"S'elp me. I don't know, Masser Holmes. He just say, 'Steve, you go see Mr Holmes, and tell him his life ain't safe if he go down Harrow way.' That's the whole truth."

Without waiting for any further questioning, our visitor bolted out of the room almost as precipitately as he had entered. Holmes knocked out the ashes of his pipe with a quiet chuckle.

"I am glad you were not forced to break his woolly head, Watson. I observed your manoeuvres with the poker. But he is really rather a harmless fellow – a great muscular, foolish, blustering baby, and easily cowed, as you have seen. He is one of the Spencer John gang, and has taken part in some dirty work of late which I may clear up when I have time. His immediate principal, Barney, is a more astute person. They specialize in assaults, intimidation and the like. What I want to know is: who is at the back of them on this particular occasion?"

"But why do they want to intimidate you?"

"It is this Harrow Weald* case. It decides me to look into the matter, for if it is worth anyone's while to take so much trouble, there must be something in it."

"But what is it?"

"I was going to tell you when we had this comic interlude. Here is Mrs Maberley's note. If you care to come with me, we will wire her and go out at once."

DEAR MR SHERLOCK HOLMES (I read),
I have had a succession of strange incidents occur to me in con-nection with this house, and I should much value your advice. You would find me at home any time tomorrow. The house is within a short walk of the Weald station.* I believe that my late husband, Mortimer Maberley, was one of your early clients.
Yours faithfully,
MARY MABERLEY

The address was "The Three Gables, Harrow Weald".

"So that's that!" said Holmes. "And now, if you can spare the time, Watson, we will get upon our way."

A short railway journey, and a shorter drive, brought us to the house, a brick-and-timber villa standing in its own acre of undeveloped grassland. Three small projections above the upper windows made a feeble attempt to justify its name. Behind was a grove of melancholy, half-grown pines, and the whole aspect of the place was poor and depressing. Nonetheless, we found the house to be well furnished, and the lady who received us was a most engaging elderly person, who bore every mark of refinement and culture.

"I remember your husband well, madam," said Holmes, "though it is some years since he used my services in some trifling matter."

"Probably you would be more familiar with the name of my son Douglas."

Holmes looked at her with great interest.

"Dear me! Are you the mother of Douglas Maberley? I knew him slightly. But, of course, all London knew him. What a magnificent creature he was! Where is he now?"

"Dead, Mr Holmes, dead! He was attaché at Rome,* and he died there of pneumonia last month."

"I am sorry. One could not connect death with such a man. I have never known anyone so vitally alive. He lived intensely – every fibre of him!"

"Too intensely, Mr Holmes. That was the ruin of him. You remember him as he was – debonair and splendid. You did not see the moody, morose, brooding creature into which he developed. His heart was broken. In a single month I seemed to see my gallant boy turn into a worn-out, cynical man."

"A love affair – a woman?"

"Or a fiend. Well, it was not to talk of my poor lad that I asked you to come, Mr Holmes."

"Doctor Watson and I are at your service."

"There have been some very strange happenings. I have been in this house more than a year now, and as I wished to lead a retired life I have seen little of my neighbours. Three days ago I had a call from a man who said that he was a house agent. He said that this house would exactly suit a client of his, and that if I would part with it money would be no object. It seemed to me very strange, as there are several empty houses on the market which appear to be equally eligible, but naturally I was interested in what he said. I therefore named a price which was five hundred pounds more than I gave. He at once closed with the offer, but added that his client desired to buy the furniture as well, and would I put a price upon it. Some of this furniture is from my old home, and it is, as you see, very good, so that I named a good round sum. To this also he at once agreed. I had always wanted to travel, and the bargain was so good a one that it really seemed that I should be my own mistress for the rest of my life.

"Yesterday the man arrived with the agreement all drawn out. Luckily I showed it to Mr Sutro, my lawyer, who lives in Harrow. He said to me, 'This is a very strange document. Are you aware that if you sign it you could not legally take *anything* out of the house – not even your own private possessions?' When the man came again in the evening, I pointed this out, and I said that I meant only to sell the furniture.

"'No, no – everything,' said he.

"'But my clothes? My jewels?'

"'Well, well… some concession might be made for your personal effects. But nothing shall go out of the house unchecked. My client is a very liberal man, but he has his fads and his own way of doing things. It is everything or nothing with him.'

"'Then it must be nothing,' said I. And there the matter was left, but the whole thing seemed to me to be so unusual that I thought—"

Here we had a very extraordinary interruption.

Holmes raised his hand for silence. Then he strode across the room, flung open the door and dragged in a great gaunt woman whom he had seized by the shoulder. She entered with ungainly struggles, like some huge awkward chicken torn squawking out of its coop.

"Leave me alone! What are you a-doin' of?" she screeched.

"Why, Susan, what is this?"

"Well, ma'am, I was comin' in to ask if the visitors was stayin' for lunch when this man jumped out at me."

"I have been listening to her for the last five minutes, but did not wish to interrupt your most interesting narrative. Just a little wheezy, Susan, are you not? You breathe too heavily for that kind of work."

Susan turned a sulky but amazed face upon her captor. "Who be you, anyhow, and what right have you a-pullin' me about like this?"

"It was merely that I wished to ask a question in your presence. Did you, Mrs Maberley, mention to anyone that you were going to write to me and consult me?"

"No, Mr Holmes, I did not."

"Who posted your letter?"

"Susan did."

"Exactly. Now, Susan, to whom was it that you wrote or sent a message to say that your mistress was asking advice from me?"

"It's a lie. I sent no message."

"Now, Susan, wheezy people may not live long, you know. It's a wicked thing to tell fibs. Whom did you tell?"

"Susan!" cried her mistress. "I believe you are a bad, treacherous woman. I remember now that I saw you speaking to someone over the hedge."

"That was my own business," said the woman sullenly.

"Suppose I tell you that it was Barney Stockdale to whom you spoke?" said Holmes.

"Well, if you know, what do you want to ask for?"

"I was not sure, but I know now. Well now, Susan, it will be worth ten pounds to you if you will tell me who is at the back of Barney."

"Someone that could lay down a thousand pounds for every ten you have in the world."

"So, a rich man? No – you smiled… a rich woman. Now we have got so far, you may as well give the name and earn the tenner."

"I'll see you in hell first."

"Oh, Susan! Language!"

"I am clearing out of here. I've had enough of you all. I'll send for my box tomorrow." She flounced for the door.

"Goodbye, Susan. Paregoric* is the stuff... Now," he continued, turning suddenly from lively to severe when the door had closed behind the flushed and angry woman, "this gang means business. Look how close they play the game. Your letter to me had the 10 p.m. postmark. And yet Susan passes the word to Barney. Barney has time to go to his employer and get instructions; he or she – I incline to the latter from Susan's grin when she thought I had blundered – forms a plan. Black Steve is called in, and I am warned off by eleven o'clock next morning. That's quick work, you know."

"But what do they want?"

"Yes, that's the question. Who had the house before you?"

"A retired sea captain called Ferguson."

"Anything remarkable about him?"

"Not that ever I heard of."

"I was wondering whether he could have buried something. Of course, when people bury treasure nowadays they do it in the Post Office bank. But there are always some lunatics about. It would be a dull world without them. At first I thought of some buried valuable. But why, in that case, should they want your furniture? You don't happen to have a Raphael* or a first folio Shakespeare* without knowing it?"

"No, I don't think I have anything rarer than a Crown Derby tea set."*

"That would hardly justify all this mystery. Besides, why should they not openly state what they want? If they covet your tea set, they can surely offer a price for it without buying you out lock, stock and barrel. No, as I read it, there is something which you do not know that you have, and which you would not give up if you did know."

"That is how I read it," said I.

"Doctor Watson agrees, so that settles it."

"Well, Mr Holmes, what can it be?"

"Let us see whether by this purely mental analysis we can get it to a finer point. You have been in this house a year."

"Nearly two."

"All the better. During this long period no one wants anything from you. Now suddenly within three or four days you have urgent demands. What would you gather from that?"

"It can only mean," said I, "that the object, whatever it may be, has only just come into the house."

"Settled once again," said Holmes. "Now, Mrs Maberley, has any object just arrived?"

"No – I have bought nothing new this year."

"Indeed! That is very remarkable. Well, I think we had best let matters develop a little further until we have clearer data. Is that lawyer of yours a capable man?"

"Mr Sutro is most capable."

"Have you another maid, or was the fair Susan, who has just banged your front door, alone?"

"I have a young girl."

"Try and get Sutro to spend a night or two in the house. You might possibly want protection."

"Against whom?"

"Who knows? The matter is certainly obscure. If I can't find what they are after, I must approach the matter from the other end, and try to get at the principal. Did this house-agent man give any address?"

"Simply his card and occupation. Haines-Johnson, auctioneer and valuer."

"I don't think we shall find him in the directory. Honest business-men don't conceal their place of business. Well, you will let me know any fresh development. I have taken up your case, and you may rely upon it that I shall see it through."

As we passed through the hall, Holmes's eyes, which missed nothing, lighted upon several trunks and cases which were piled in the corner. The labels shone out upon them.

"'Milano'. 'Lucerne'. These are from Italy."*

"They are poor Douglas's things."

"You have not unpacked them? How long have you had them?"

"They arrived last week."

"But you said… Why, surely this might be the missing link. How do we know that there is not something of value there?"

"There could not possibly be, Mr Holmes. Poor Douglas had only his pay and a small annuity. What could he have of value?"

Holmes was lost in thought.

"Delay no longer, Mrs Maberley," he said at last. "Have these things taken upstairs to your bedroom. Examine them as soon as possible and see what they contain. I will come tomorrow and hear your report."

It was quite evident that the Three Gables was under very close surveillance, for as we came round the high hedge at the end of the lane there was the Negro prizefighter standing in the shadow. We came on him quite suddenly, and a grim and menacing figure he looked in that lonely place. Holmes clapped his hand to his pocket.

"Lookin' for your gun, Masser Holmes?"

"No – for my scent bottle, Steve."

"You are funny, Masser Holmes, ain't you?"

"It won't be funny for you, Steve, if I get after you. I gave you fair warning this morning."

"Well, Masser Holmes, I done gone think over what you said, and I don't want no more talk about that affair of Masser Perkins. S'pose I can help you, Masser Holmes, I will."

"Well, then, tell me who is behind you on this job?"

"So help me the Lord! Masser Holmes, I told you the truth before. I don't know. My boss Barney gives me orders, and that's all."

"Well, just bear in mind, Steve, that the lady in that house, and everything under that roof, is under my protection. Don't you forget it."

"All right, Masser Holmes. I'll remember."

"I've got him thoroughly frightened for his own skin, Watson," Holmes remarked as we walked on. "I think he would double-cross his employer if he knew who he was. It was lucky I had some knowledge of the Spencer John crowd, and that Steve was one of them. Now, Watson, this is a case for Langdale Pike,* and I am going to see him now. When I get back, I may be clearer in the matter."

I saw no more of Holmes during the day, but I could well imagine how he spent it, for Langdale Pike was his human book of reference upon all matters of social scandal. This strange, languid creature spent his waking hours in the bow window of a St James's Street club, and was the receiving station, as well as the transmitter, for all the gossip of the metropolis. He made, it was said, a four-figure income by the paragraphs which he contributed every week to the garbage papers which cater for an inquisitive public. If ever, far down in the turbid depths of London life, there was some strange swirl or eddy, it was marked with automatic exactness by this human dial upon the surface. Holmes discreetly helped Langdale to knowledge, and on occasion was helped in turn.

When I met my friend in his room early next morning, I was conscious from his bearing that all was well, but nonetheless a most unpleasant surprise was awaiting us. It took the shape of the following telegram:

PLEASE COME OUT AT ONCE. CLIENT'S HOUSE BURGLED IN THE NIGHT. POLICE IN POSSESSION.

SUTRO

Holmes whistled. "The drama has come to a crisis, and quicker than I had expected. There is a great driving power at the back of this business, Watson, which does not surprise me after what I have heard. This Sutro, of course, is her lawyer. I made a mistake, I fear, in not asking you to spend the night on guard. This fellow has clearly proved a broken reed.* Well, there is nothing for it but another journey to Harrow Weald."

We found the Three Gables a very different establishment to the orderly household of the previous day. A small group of idlers had assembled at the garden gate, while a couple of constables were examining the windows and the geranium beds. Within we met a grey old gentleman, who introduced himself as the lawyer, together with a bustling, rubicund inspector, who greeted Holmes as an old friend.

"Well, Mr Holmes, no chance for you in this case, I'm afraid. Just a common, ordinary burglary, and well within the capacity of the poor old police. No experts need apply."

"I am sure the case is in very good hands," said Holmes. "Merely a common burglary, you say?"

"Quite so. We know pretty well who the men are and where to find them. It is that gang of Barney Stockdale, with the big nigger in it – they've been seen about here."

"Excellent! What did they get?"

"Well, they don't seem to have got much. Mrs Maberley was chloroformed and the house was... Ah! Here is the lady herself."

Our friend of yesterday, looking very pale and ill, had entered the room, leaning upon a little maidservant.

"You gave me good advice, Mr Holmes," said she, smiling ruefully. "Alas, I did not take it! I did not wish to trouble Mr Sutro, and so I was unprotected."

"I only heard of it this morning," the lawyer explained.

"Mr Holmes advised me to have some friend in the house. I neglected his advice, and I have paid for it."

"You look wretchedly ill," said Holmes. "Perhaps you are hardly equal to telling me what occurred."

"It is all here," said the inspector, tapping a bulky notebook.

"Still, if the lady is not too exhausted..."

"There is really so little to tell. I have no doubt that wicked Susan had planned an entrance for them. They must have known the house to an inch. I was conscious for a moment of the chloroform rag which was thrust over my mouth, but I have no notion how long I may have been senseless. When I woke, one man was at the bedside and another was rising with a bundle in his hand from among my son's baggage, which was partially opened and littered over the floor. Before he could get away, I sprang up and seized him."

"You took a big risk," said the inspector.

"I clung to him, but he shook me off, and the other may have struck me, for I can remember no more. Mary the maid heard the noise and began screaming out of the window. That brought the police, but the rascals had got away."

"What did they take?"

"Well, I don't think there is anything of value missing. I am sure there was nothing in my son's trunks."

"Did the men leave no clue?"

"There was one sheet of paper which I may have torn from the man that I grasped. It was lying all crumpled on the floor. It is in my son's handwriting."

"Which means that it is not of much use," said the inspector. "Now, if it had been in the burglar's—"

"Exactly," said Holmes. "What rugged common sense! Nonetheless, I should be curious to see it."

The inspector drew a folded sheet of foolscap from his pocketbook.

"I never pass anything, however trifling," said he with some pomposity. "That is my advice to you, Mr Holmes. In twenty-five years' experience I have learnt my lesson. There is always the chance of fingermarks or something."

Holmes inspected the sheet of paper.

"What do you make of it, Inspector?"

"Seems to be the end of some queer novel, so far as I can see."

"It may certainly prove to be the end of a queer tale," said Holmes. "You have noticed the number on the top of the page. It is two hundred and forty-five. Where are the odd two hundred and forty-four pages?"

"Well, I suppose the burglars got those. Much good may it do them!"

"It seems a queer thing to break into a house in order to steal such papers as that. Does it suggest anything to you, Inspector?"

"Yes, sir – it suggests that in their hurry the rascals just grabbed at what came first to hand. I wish them joy of what they got."

"Why should they go to my son's things?" asked Mrs Maberley.

"Well, they found nothing valuable downstairs, so they tried their luck upstairs. That is how I read it. What do you make of it, Mr Holmes?"

"I must think it over, Inspector. Come to the window, Watson." Then, as we stood together, he read over the fragment of paper. It began in the middle of a sentence and ran like this:

...face bled considerably from the cuts and blows, but it was nothing to the bleeding of his heart as he saw that lovely face, the face for which he had been prepared to sacrifice his very life, looking out at his agony and humiliation. She smiled – yes, by Heaven! – she smiled, like the heartless fiend she was, as he looked up at her. It was at that moment that love died and hate was born. Man must live for something. If it is not for your embrace, my lady, then it shall surely be for your undoing and my complete revenge.

"Queer grammar!" said Holmes with a smile as he handed the paper back to the inspector. "Did you notice how the 'he' suddenly changed to 'my'? The writer was so carried away by his own story that he imagined himself at the supreme moment to be the hero."

"It seemed mighty poor stuff," said the inspector as he replaced it in his book. "What? Are you off, Mr Holmes?"

"I don't think there is anything more for me to do now that the case is in such capable hands. By the way, Mrs Maberley, did you say you wished to travel?"

"It has always been my dream, Mr Holmes."

"Where would you like to go – Cairo, Madeira, the Riviera?"

"Oh! If I had the money, I would go round the world."

"Quite so. Round the world. Well, good morning. I may drop you a line in the evening." As we passed the window, I caught a glimpse of the inspector's smile and shake of the head. "These clever fellows have always a touch of madness." That was what I read in the inspector's smile.

"Now, Watson, we are at the last lap of our little journey," said Holmes when we were back in the roar of central London once more. "I think we had best clear the matter up at once, and it would be well that you should come with me, for it is safer to have a witness when you are dealing with such a lady as Isadora Klein."

We had taken a cab and were speeding to some address in Grosvenor Square. Holmes had been sunk in thought, but he roused himself suddenly.

"By the way, Watson, I suppose you see it all clearly?"

"No, I can't say that I do. I only gather that we are going to see the lady who is behind all this mischief."

"Exactly! But does the name Isadora Klein convey nothing to you? She was, of course, *the* celebrated beauty. There was never a woman to touch her. She is pure Spanish, the real blood of the masterful conquistadors,* and her people have been leaders in Pernambuco* for generations. She married the aged German sugar king, Klein, and presently found herself the richest as well as the most lovely widow upon earth. Then there was an interval of adventure when she pleased her own tastes. She had several lovers, and Douglas Maberley, one of the most striking men in London, was one of them. It was by all accounts more than an adventure with him. He was not a society butterfly, but a strong, proud man who gave and expected all. But she is the '*belle dame sans merci*'* of fiction. When her caprice is satisfied, the matter is ended, and if the other party in the matter can't take her word for it, she knows how to bring it home to him."

"Then that was his own story—"

"Ah! You are piecing it together now. I hear that she is about to marry the young Duke of Lomond, who might almost be her son. His Grace's ma might overlook the age, but a big scandal would be a different matter, so it is imperative… Ah! Here we are."

It was one of the finest corner houses of the West End. A machine-like footman took up our cards and returned with word that the lady was not at home. "Then we shall wait until she is," said Holmes cheerfully.

The machine broke down.

"Not at home means not at home to *you*," said the footman.

"Good," Holmes answered. "That means that we shall not have to wait. Kindly give this note to your mistress."

He scribbled three or four words upon a sheet of his notebook, folded it, and handed it to the man.

"What did you say, Holmes?" I asked.

"I simply wrote: 'Shall it be the police, then?' I think that should pass us in."

It did – with amazing celerity. A minute later we were in an *Arabian Nights** drawing room, vast and wonderful, in a half-gloom, picked out with an occasional pink electric light. The lady had come, I felt, to that time of life when even the proudest beauty finds the half-light more welcome. She rose from a settee as we entered: tall, queenly, a perfect figure, a lovely mask-like face, with two wonderful Spanish eyes which looked murder at us both.

"What is this intrusion – and this insulting message?" she asked, holding up the slip of paper.

"I need not explain, madam. I have too much respect for your intelligence to do so – though I confess that intelligence has been surprisingly at fault of late."

"How so, sir?"

"By supposing that your hired bullies could frighten me from my work. Surely no man would take up my profession if it were not that danger attracts him. It was you, then, who forced me to examine the case of young Maberley."

"I have no idea what you are talking about. What have I to do with hired bullies?"

Holmes turned away wearily.

"Yes, I have overrated* your intelligence. Well, good afternoon!"

"Stop! Where are you going?"

"To Scotland Yard."

We had not got halfway to the door before she had overtaken us and was holding his arm. She had turned in a moment from steel to velvet.

"Come and sit down, gentlemen. Let us talk this matter over. I feel that I may be frank with you, Mr Holmes. You have the feelings of a gentleman. How quick a woman's instinct is to find it out. I will treat you as a friend."

"I cannot promise to reciprocate, madam. I am not the law, but I represent justice so far as my feeble powers go. I am ready to listen, and then I will tell you how I will act."

"No doubt it was foolish of me to threaten a brave man like yourself."

"What was really foolish, madam, is that you have placed yourself in the power of a band of rascals who may blackmail or give you away."

"No, no! I am not so simple. Since I have promised to be frank, I may say that no one, save Barney Stockdale and Susan, his wife, have the least idea who their employer is. As to them, well, it is not the first..." She smiled and nodded, with a charming coquettish intimacy.

"I see. You've tested them before."

"They are good hounds who run silent."

"Such hounds have a way sooner or later of biting the hand that feeds them. They will be arrested for this burglary. The police are already after them."

"They will take what comes to them. That is what they are paid for. I shall not appear in the matter."

"Unless I bring you into it."

"No, no – you would not. You are a gentleman. It is a woman's secret."

"In the first place you must give back this manuscript."

She broke into a ripple of laughter, and walked to the fireplace. There was a calcined* mass which she broke up with the poker. "Shall I give this back?" she asked. So roguish and exquisite did she look as she stood before us with a challenging smile that I felt of all Holmes's criminals this was the one whom he would find it hardest to face. However, he was immune from sentiment.

"That seals your fate," he said coldly. "You are very prompt in your actions, madam, but you have overdone it on this occasion."

She threw the poker down with a clatter.

"How hard you are!" she cried. "May I tell you the whole story?"

"I fancy I could tell it to you."

"But you must look at it with my eyes, Mr Holmes. You must realize it from the point of view of a woman who sees all her life's ambition about to be ruined at the last moment. Is such a woman to be blamed if she protects herself?"

"The original sin was yours."

"Yes, yes! I admit it. He was a dear boy, Douglas, but it so chanced that he could not fit into my plans. He wanted marriage – marriage, Mr Holmes – with a penniless commoner. Nothing less would serve him. Then he became pertinacious. Because I had given he seemed to think that I still must give, and to him only. It was intolerable. At last I had to make him realize it."

"By hiring ruffians to beat him under your own window."

"You do indeed seem to know everything. Well, it is true. Barney and the boys drove him away, and were, I admit, a little rough in doing so. But what did he do then? Could I have believed that a gentleman would do such an act? He wrote a book in which he described his own story. I, of course, was the wolf – he the lamb. It was all there, under different names, of course, but who in all London would have failed to recognize it? What do you say to that, Mr Holmes?"

"Well, he was within his rights."

"It was as if the air of Italy had got into his blood and brought with it the old cruel Italian spirit. He wrote to me and sent me a copy of his book that I might have the torture of anticipation. There were two copies, he said – one for me, one for his publisher."

"How did you know the publisher's had not reached him?"

"I knew who his publisher was. It is not his only novel, you know. I found out that he had not heard from Italy. Then came Douglas's sudden death. So long as that other manuscript was in the world, there was no safety for me. Of course, it must be among his effects, and these would be returned to his mother. I set the gang at work. One of them got into the house as serv-ant. I wanted to do the thing honestly. I really and truly did. I was ready to buy the house and everything in it. I offered any price she cared to ask. I only tried the other way when everything else had failed. Now, Mr Holmes, granting that I was too hard on Douglas – and, God knows, I am sorry for it! – what else could I do with my whole future at stake?"

Sherlock Holmes shrugged his shoulders.

"Well, well…" said he. "I suppose I shall have to compound a felony* as usual. How much does it cost to go round the world in first-class style?"

The lady stared in amazement.

"Could it be done on five thousand pounds?"

"Well, I should think so, indeed!"

"Very good. I think you will sign me a cheque for that, and I will see that it comes to Mrs Maberley. You owe her a little change of air. Meantime, lady" – he wagged a cautionary forefinger – "have a care! Have a care! You can't play with edged tools for ever without cutting those dainty hands."

THE ADVENTURE
OF THE SUSSEX VAMPIRE

HOLMES HAD READ CAREFULLY a note which the last post had brought him. Then, with the dry chuckle which was his nearest approach to a laugh, he tossed it over to me.

"For a mixture of the modern and the medieval, of the practical and of the wildly fanciful, I think this is surely the limit," said he. "What do you make of it, Watson?"

I read as follows:

46 Old Jewry,*
19th Nov.

Re Vampires

SIR,

Our client, Mr Robert Ferguson, of Ferguson & Muirhead, tea brokers, of Mincing Lane,* has made some enquiry from us in a communication of even date,* concerning vampires. As our firm specializes entirely upon the assessment of machinery, the matter hardly comes within our purview, and we have therefore recommended Mr Ferguson to call upon you and lay the matter before you. We have not forgotten your successful action in the case of Matilda Briggs.

We are, sir, faithfully yours,
MORRISON, MORRISON & DODD

per E.J.C.*

"Matilda Briggs was not the name of a young woman, Watson," said Holmes in a reminiscent voice. "It was a ship which is associated with the giant rat of Sumatra, a story for which the world is not yet prepared.* But what do we know about vampires? Does it come within our purview either? Anything is better than stagnation, but really we seem to have been switched on to a Grimms' fairy tale.* Make a long arm, Watson, and see what V has to say."

I leant back and took down the great index volume to which he referred. Holmes balanced it on his knee and his eyes moved slowly and lovingly over the record of old cases, mixed with the accumulated information of a lifetime.

"'Voyage of the *Gloria Scott*'," he read. "That was a bad business. I have some recollection that you made a record of it, Watson, though I was unable to congratulate you upon the result. 'Victor Lynch, the forger'. 'Venomous lizard or Gila'. Remarkable case, that! 'Vittoria, the circus belle'. 'Vanderbilt and the yeggman'. 'Vipers'. 'Vigor, the Hammersmith wonder'.* Hullo! Hullo! Good old index. You can't beat it. Listen to this, Watson. 'Vampirism in Hungary'. And again, 'Vampires in Transylvania'."* He turned over the pages with eagerness, but after a short, intent perusal he threw down the great book with a snarl of disappointment.

"Rubbish, Watson, rubbish! What have we to do with walking corpses who can only be held in their grave by stakes driven through their hearts? It's pure lunacy."

"But surely," said I, "the vampire was not necessarily a dead man? A living person might have the habit. I have read, for example, of the old sucking the blood of the young in order to retain their youth."

"You are right, Watson. It mentions the legend in one of these references. But are we to give serious attention to such things? This agency stands flat-footed upon the ground, and there it must remain. The world is big enough for us. No ghosts need apply. I fear that we cannot take Mr Robert Ferguson very seriously. Possibly this note may be from him, and may throw some light upon what is worrying him."

He took up a second letter which had lain unnoticed upon the table whilst he had been absorbed with the first. This he began to read with a smile of amusement upon his face which gradually faded away into an expression of intense interest and concentration. When he had finished, he sat for some little time lost in thought with the letter dangling from his fingers. Finally, with a start, he aroused himself from his reverie.

"Cheeseman's, Lamberley. Where is Lamberley, Watson?"

"It is in Sussex, south of Horsham."

"Not very far, eh? And Cheeseman's?"

"I know that country, Holmes. It is full of old houses which are named after the men who built them centuries ago. You get Odley's and Harvey's and Carriton's – the folk are forgotten, but their names live in their houses."

"Precisely," said Holmes coldly. It was one of the peculiarities of his proud, self-contained nature that, though he docketed any fresh information very quickly and accurately in his brain, he seldom made any acknowledgement to the giver. "I rather fancy we shall know a good deal more about Cheeseman's, Lamberley, before we are through. The letter is, as I had hoped, from Robert Ferguson. By the way, he claims acquaintance with you."

"With me!"

"You had better read it."

He handed the letter across. It was headed with the address quoted.

DEAR MR HOLMES (it said) – I have been recommended to you by my lawyers, but indeed the matter is so extraordinarily delicate that it is most difficult to discuss. It concerns a friend for whom I am acting. This gentleman married some five years ago a Peruvian lady, the daughter of a Peruvian merchant, whom he had met in connection with the importation of nitrates. The lady was very beautiful, but the fact of her foreign birth and of her alien religion* always caused a separation of interests and of feelings between husband and wife, so that after a time his love may have cooled towards her and he may have come to regard their union as a mistake. He felt there were sides of her character which he could never explore or understand. This was the more painful as she was as loving a wife as a man could have – to all appearance absolutely devoted.

Now for the point which I will make more plain when we meet. Indeed, this note is merely to give you a general idea of the situation and to ascertain whether you would care to interest yourself in the matter. The lady began to show some curious traits quite alien to her ordinarily sweet and gentle disposition. The gentleman had been married twice, and he had one son by the first wife. This boy was now fifteen, a very charming and affectionate youth, though unhappily injured through an accident in childhood. Twice the wife was caught in the act of assaulting this poor lad in the most unprovoked way. Once she struck him with a stick and left a great weal on his arm.

This was a small matter, however, compared with her conduct to her own child, a dear boy just under one year of age. On one occasion about a month ago, this child had been left by its nurse for a few minutes. A loud cry from the baby, as of pain, called the nurse back. As she ran into the room, she saw her employer, the lady, leaning over the baby and apparently biting his neck. There was a small wound in the neck, from which a stream of blood had escaped. The nurse was so horrified that she wished to call the husband, but the lady implored her not to do so, and actually gave her five pounds as a price for her silence. No explanation was ever given, and for the moment the matter was passed over.

It left, however, a terrible impression upon the nurse's mind, and from that time she began to watch her mistress closely, and to keep a closer guard upon the baby, whom she tenderly loved. It seemed to her that even as she watched the mother, so the mother watched her, and that every time she was compelled to leave the baby alone the mother was waiting to get at it. Day and night the nurse covered the child, and day and night the silent, watchful mother seemed to be lying in wait as a wolf waits for a lamb. It must read most incredible to you, and yet I beg you to take it seriously, for a child's life and a man's sanity may depend upon it.

At last there came one dreadful day when the facts could no longer be concealed from the husband. The nurse's nerve had given way – she could stand the strain no longer, and she made a clean breast of it all to the man. To him it seemed as wild a tale as it may now seem to you. He knew his wife to be a loving wife, and, save for the assaults upon her stepson, a loving mother. Why, then, should she wound her own dear little baby? He told the nurse that she was dreaming, that her suspicions were those of a lunatic, and that such libels upon her mistress were not to be tolerated. Whilst they were talking, a sudden cry of pain was heard. Nurse and master rushed together to the nursery. Imagine his feelings, Mr Holmes, as he saw his wife rise from a kneeling position beside the cot, and saw blood upon the child's exposed neck and upon the sheet. With a cry of horror, he turned his wife's face to the light and saw blood all round her lips. It was she – she beyond all question – who had drunk the poor baby's blood.

So the matter stands. She is now confined to her room. There has been no explanation. The husband is half demented. He knows, and I know, little of vampirism beyond the name. We had thought it was some wild tale of foreign parts. And yet here in the very heart of the English Sussex... well, all this can be discussed with you in the morning. Will you see me? Will you use your great powers in aiding a distracted man? If so, kindly wire to Ferguson, Cheeseman's, Lamberley, and I will be at your rooms by ten o'clock.

Yours faithfully,
ROBERT FERGUSON

P.S. I believe your friend Watson played rugby for Blackheath when I was three-quarter for Richmond.* It is the only personal introduction which I can give.

"Of course I remember him," said I as I laid down the letter. "Big Bob Ferguson, the finest three-quarter Richmond ever had. He was always a good-natured chap. It's like him to be so concerned over a friend's case."

Holmes looked at me thoughtfully and shook his head.

"I never get your limits, Watson," said he. "There are unexplored possibilities about you. Take a wire down,* like a good fellow. 'Will examine your case with pleasure.'"

"*Your* case!"

"We must not let him think that this agency is a home for the weak-minded. Of course it is his case. Send him that wire and let the matter rest till morning."

Promptly at ten o'clock next morning Ferguson strode into our room. I had remembered him as a long, slab-sided man with loose limbs and a fine turn of speed, which had carried him round many an opposing back. There is surely nothing in life more painful than to meet the wreck of a fine athlete whom one has known in his prime. His great frame had fallen in, his flaxen hair was scanty and his shoulders were bowed. I fear that I roused corresponding emotions in him.

"Hullo, Watson," said he, and his voice was still deep and hearty. "You don't look quite the man you did when I threw you over the ropes into the crowd at the Old Deer Park.* I expect I have changed a bit also. But it's this last day or two that has aged me. I see by your telegram, Mr Holmes, that it is no use my pretending to be anyone's deputy."

"It is simpler to deal direct," said Holmes.

"Of course it is. But you can imagine how difficult it is when you are speaking of the one woman whom you are bound to protect and help. What can I do? How am I to go to the police with such a story? And yet the kiddies have got to be protected. Is it madness, Mr Holmes? Is it something in the blood? Have you any similar case in your experience? For God's sake, give me some advice, for I am at my wits' end."

"Very naturally, Mr Ferguson. Now sit here and pull yourself together and give me a few clear answers. I can assure you that I am very far from being at my wits' end, and that I am confident we shall find some solution. First of all, tell me what steps you have taken. Is your wife still near the children?"

"We had a dreadful scene. She is a most loving woman, Mr Holmes. If ever a woman loved a man with all her heart and soul, she loves me. She was cut to the heart that I should have discovered this horrible, this incredible secret. She would not even speak. She gave no answer to my reproaches, save to gaze at me with a sort of wild, despairing look in her eyes. Then she rushed to her room and locked herself in. Since then she has refused to see me. She has a maid who was with her before her marriage, Dolores by name – a friend rather than a servant. She takes her food to her."

"Then the child is in no immediate danger?"

"Mrs Mason, the nurse, has sworn that she will not leave it night or day. I can absolutely trust her. I am more uneasy about poor little Jack, for, as I told you in my note, he has twice been assaulted by her."

"But never wounded?"

"No – she struck him savagely. It is the more terrible as he is a poor little inoffensive cripple." Ferguson's gaunt features softened as he spoke of his boy. "You would think that the dear lad's condition would soften anyone's heart. A fall in childhood and a twisted spine, Mr Holmes. But the dearest, most loving heart within."

Holmes had picked up the letter of yesterday and was reading it over. "What other inmates are there in your house, Mr Ferguson?"

"Two servants who have not been long with us. One stablehand, Michael, who sleeps in the house. My wife, myself, my boy Jack, baby, Dolores and Mrs Mason. That is all."

"I gather that you did not know your wife well at the time of your marriage?"

"I had only known her a few weeks."

"How long had this maid Dolores been with her?"

"Some years."

"Then your wife's character would really be better known by Dolores than by you?"

"Yes, you may say so."

Holmes made a note.

"I fancy," said he, "that I may be of more use at Lamberley than here. It is eminently a case for personal investigation. If the lady remains in her room, our presence could not annoy or inconvenience her. Of course, we would stay at the inn."

Ferguson gave a gesture of relief.

"It is what I hoped, Mr Holmes. There is an excellent train at two from Victoria, if you could come."

"Of course we could come. There is a lull at present. I can give you my undivided energies. Watson, of course, comes with us. But there are one or two points upon which I wish to be very sure before I start. This unhappy lady, as I understand it, has appeared to assault both the children, her own baby and your little son?"

"That is so."

"But the assaults take different forms, do they not? She has beaten your son."

"Once with a stick and once very savagely with her hands."

"Did she give no explanation why she struck him?"

"None, save that she hated him. Again and again she said so."

"Well, that is not unknown among stepmothers. A posthumous jealousy, we will say. Is the lady jealous by nature?"

"Yes, she is very jealous – jealous with all the strength of her fiery tropical love."

"But the boy – he is fifteen, I understand, and probably very developed in mind, since his body has been circumscribed in action. Did he give you no explanation of these assaults?"

"No – he declared there was no reason."

"Were they good friends at other times?"

"No – there was never any love between them."

"Yet you say he is affectionate?"

"Never in the world could there be so devoted a son. My life is his life. He is absorbed in what I say or do."

Once again Holmes made a note. For some time he sat lost in thought.

"No doubt you and the boy were great comrades before this second marriage. You were thrown very close together, were you not?"

"Very much so."

"And the boy, having so affectionate a nature, was devoted, no doubt, to the memory of his mother?"

"Most devoted."

"He would certainly seem to be a most interesting lad. There is one other point about these assaults. Were the strange attacks upon the baby and the assaults upon your son at the same period?"

"In the first case it was so. It was as if some frenzy had seized her, and she had vented her rage upon both. In the second case it was only Jack who suffered. Mrs Mason had no complaint to make about the baby."

"That certainly complicates matters."

"I don't quite follow you, Mr Holmes."

"Possibly not. One forms provisional theories and waits for time or fuller knowledge to explode them. A bad habit, Mr Ferguson – but human nature is weak. I fear that your old friend here has given an exaggerated view of my scientific methods. However, I will only say at the present stage that your problem does not appear to me to be insoluble, and that you may expect to find us at Victoria at two o'clock."

It was evening of a dull, foggy November day when, having left our bags at the Chequers, Lamberley, we drove through the Sussex clay of a long winding lane, and finally reached the isolated and ancient farmhouse in which Ferguson dwelt. It was a large, straggling building, very old in the centre, very new at the wings, with towering Tudor chimneys and a lichen-spotted, high-pitched roof of Horsham slabs. The doorsteps were worn into curves, and the ancient tiles which lined the porch were marked with the rebus* of a cheese and a man, after the original builder. Within, the ceilings were corrugated with heavy oaken beams, and the uneven floors sagged into sharp curves. An odour of age and decay pervaded the whole crumbling building.

There was one very large central room, into which Ferguson led us. Here, in a huge old-fashioned fireplace with an iron screen behind it dated 1670, there blazed and spluttered a splendid log fire.

The room, as I gazed round, was a most singular mixture of dates and of places. The half-panelled walls may well have belonged to the original yeoman farmer of the seventeenth century. They were ornamented, however, on the lower part by a line of well-chosen modern watercolours, while above, where yellow plaster took the place of oak, there was hung a fine collection of South American utensils and weapons, which had been brought, no doubt, by the Peruvian lady upstairs. Holmes rose with that quick curiosity which sprang from his eager mind, and examined them with some care. He returned with his eyes full of thought.

"Hullo!" he cried. "Hullo!"

A spaniel had lain in a basket in the corner. It came slowly forward towards its master, walking with difficulty. Its hind legs moved irregularly, and its tail was on the ground. It licked Ferguson's hand.

"What is it, Mr Holmes?"

"The dog. What's the matter with it?"

"That's what puzzled the vet. A sort of paralysis. Spinal meningitis, he thought. But it is passing. He'll be all right soon – won't you, Carlo?"

A shiver of assent passed through the drooping tail. The dog's mournful eyes passed from one of us to the other. He knew that we were discussing his case.

"Did it come on suddenly?"

"In a single night."

"How long ago?"

"It may have been four months ago."

"Very remarkable. Very suggestive."

"What do you see in it, Mr Holmes?"

"A confirmation of what I had already thought."

"For God's sake, what *do* you think, Mr Holmes? It may be a mere intellectual puzzle to you, but it is life and death to me! My wife a would-be murderer – my child in constant danger! Don't play with me, Mr Holmes. It is too terribly serious."

The big rugby three-quarter was trembling all over. Holmes put his hand soothingly upon his arm.

"I fear that there is pain for you, Mr Ferguson, whatever the solution may be," said he. "I would spare you all I can. I cannot say more for the instant, but before I leave this house I hope I may have something definite."

"Please God you may! If you will excuse me, gentlemen, I will go up to my wife's room and see if there has been any change."

He was away some minutes, during which Holmes resumed his examination of the curiosities upon the wall. When our host returned, it was clear from his downcast face that he had made no progress. He brought with him a tall, slim, brown-faced girl.

"The tea is ready, Dolores," said Ferguson. "See that your mistress has everything she can wish."

"She verra ill," cried the girl, looking with indignant eyes at her master. "She no ask for food. She verra ill. She need doctor. I frightened stay alone with her without doctor."

Ferguson looked at me with a question in his eyes.

"I should be so glad if I could be of use."

"Would your mistress see Doctor Watson?"

"I take him. I no ask leave. She needs doctor."

"Then I'll come with you at once."

I followed the girl, who was quivering with strong emotion, up the staircase and down an ancient corridor. At the end was an iron-clamped and massive door. It struck me as I looked at it that if Ferguson tried to force his way to his wife, he would find it no easy matter. The girl drew a key from her pocket, and the heavy oaken planks creaked upon their old hinges. I passed in, and she swiftly followed, fastening the door behind her.

On the bed a woman was lying who was clearly in a high fever. She was only half conscious, but as I entered she raised a pair of frightened but beautiful eyes and glared at me in apprehension. Seeing a stranger, she appeared to be relieved, and sank back with a sigh upon the pillow. I stepped up to her with a few reassuring words, and she lay still while I took her pulse and temperature. Both were high, and yet my impression was that the condition was rather that of mental and nervous excitement than of any actual seizure.

"She lie like that one day, two day. I 'fraid she die," said the girl.

The woman turned her flushed and handsome face towards me. "Where is my husband?"

"He is below, and would wish to see you."

"I will not see him. I will not see him." Then she seemed to wander off into delirium. "A fiend! A fiend! Oh, what shall I do with this devil?"

"Can I help you in any way?"

"No. No one can help. It is finished. All is destroyed. Do what I will, all is destroyed."

The woman must have some strange delusion. I could not see honest Bob Ferguson in the character of fiend or devil.

"Madam," I said, "your husband loves you dearly. He is deeply grieved at this happening."

Again she turned on me those glorious eyes.

"He loves me. Yes. But do I not love him? Do I not love him even to sacrifice myself rather than break his dear heart? That is how I love him. And yet he could think of me – he could speak of me so."

"He is full of grief, but he cannot understand."

"No, he cannot understand. But he should trust."

"Will you not see him?" I suggested.

"No, no – I cannot forget those terrible words nor the look upon his face. I will not see him. Go now. You can do nothing for me. Tell him only one thing. I want my child. I have a right to my child. That is the only message I can send him." She turned her face to the wall and would say no more.

I returned to the room downstairs, where Ferguson and Holmes still sat by the fire. Ferguson listened moodily to my account of the interview.

"How can I send her the child?" he said. "How do I know what strange impulse might come upon her? How can I ever forget how she rose from beside it with its blood upon her lips?" He shuddered at the recollection. "The child is safe with Mrs Mason, and there he must remain."

A smart maid, the only modern thing which we had seen in the house, had brought in some tea. As she was serving it, the door opened and a youth entered the room. He was a remarkable lad, pale-faced and fair-haired, with excitable light-blue eyes which blazed into a sudden flame of emotion and joy as they rested upon his father. He rushed forward and threw his arms round his neck with the abandon of a loving girl.

"Oh, Daddy," he cried, "I did not know that you were due yet. I should have been here to meet you. Oh, I am so glad to see you!"

Ferguson gently disengaged himself from the embrace with some little show of embarrassment.

"Dear old chap," said he, patting the flaxen head with a very tender hand, "I came early because my friends, Mr Holmes and Doctor Watson, have been persuaded to come down and spend an evening with us."

"Is that Mr Holmes, the detective?"

"Yes."

The youth looked at us with a very penetrating and, as it seemed to me, unfriendly gaze.

"What about your other child, Mr Ferguson?" asked Holmes. "Might we make the acquaintance of the baby?"

"Ask Mrs Mason to bring baby down," said Ferguson. The boy went off with a curious, shambling gait which told my surgical eyes that he was suffering from a weak spine. Presently he returned, and behind him came a tall, gaunt woman bearing in her arms a very beautiful child, dark-eyed, golden-haired, a wonderful mixture of the Saxon and the Latin. Ferguson was evidently devoted to it, for he took it into his arms and fondled it most tenderly.

"Fancy anyone having the heart to hurt him," he muttered as he glanced down at the small, angry red pucker upon the cherub throat.

It was at this moment that I chanced to glance at Holmes, and saw a most singular intentness in his expression. His face was as set as if it had been carved out of old ivory, and his eyes, which had glanced for a moment at father and child, were now fixed with eager curiosity upon something at the other side of the room. Following his gaze I could only guess that he was looking out through the window at the melancholy, dripping garden. It is true that a shutter had half closed outside and obstructed the view, but nonetheless it was certainly at the window that Holmes was fixing his concentrated attention. Then he smiled, and his eyes came back to the baby. On its chubby neck there was this small puckered mark. Without speaking, Holmes examined it with care. Finally he shook one of the dimpled fists which waved in front of him.

"Goodbye, little man. You have made a strange start in life. Nurse, I should wish to have a word with you in private."

He took her aside and spoke earnestly for a few minutes. I only heard the last words, which were: "Your anxiety will soon, I hope, be set at rest." The woman, who seemed to be a sour, silent kind of creature, withdrew with the child.

"What is Mrs Mason like?" asked Holmes.

"Not very prepossessing externally, as you can see, but a heart of gold, and devoted to the child."

"Do you like her, Jack?" Holmes turned suddenly upon the boy. His expressive mobile face shadowed over, and he shook his head.

"Jacky has very strong likes and dislikes," said Ferguson, putting his arm round the boy. "Luckily I am one of his likes."

The boy cooed and nestled his head upon his father's breast. Ferguson gently disengaged him.

"Run away, little Jacky," said he, and he watched his son with loving eyes until he disappeared. "Now, Mr Holmes," he continued, when the boy was gone, "I really feel that I have brought you on a fool's errand, for what can you possibly do, save give me your sympathy? It must be an exceedingly delicate and complex affair from your point of view."

"It is certainly delicate," said my friend with an amused smile, "but I have not been struck up to now with its complexity. It has been a case for intellectual deduction, but when this original intellectual deduction is confirmed point by point by quite a number of independent incidents, then the subjective becomes objective and we can say confidently that we have reached our goal. I had, in fact, reached it before we left Baker Street, and the rest has merely been observation and confirmation."

Ferguson put his big hand to his furrowed forehead.

"For Heaven's sake, Holmes," he said hoarsely, "if you can see the truth in this matter, do not keep me in suspense. How do I stand? What shall I do? I care nothing as to how you have found your facts, so long as you have really got them."

"Certainly I owe you an explanation, and you shall have it. But you will permit me to handle the matter in my own way? Is the lady capable of seeing us, Watson?"

"She is ill, but she is quite rational."

"Very good. It is only in her presence that we can clear the matter up. Let us go up to her."

"She will not see me," cried Ferguson.

"Oh, yes, she will," said Holmes. He scribbled a few lines upon a sheet of paper. "You at least have the entrée, Watson. Will you have the goodness to give the lady this note?"

I ascended again and handed the note to Dolores, who cautiously opened the door. A minute later I heard a cry from within, a cry in which joy and surprise seemed to be blended. Dolores looked out.

"She will see them. She will leesten," said she.

At my summons Ferguson and Holmes came up. As we entered the room, Ferguson took a step or two towards his wife, who had raised herself in the bed, but she held out her hand to repulse him. He sank into an armchair, while Holmes seated himself beside him, after bowing to the lady, who looked at him with wide-eyed amazement.

"I think we can dispense with Dolores," said Holmes. "Oh, very well, madam, if you would rather she stayed I can see no objection. Now, Mr Ferguson, I am a busy man with many calls, and my methods have to be short and direct. The swiftest surgery is the least painful. Let me first say what will ease your mind. Your wife is a very good, a very loving and a very ill-used woman."

Ferguson sat up with a cry of joy.

"Prove that, Mr Holmes, and I am your debtor for ever."

"I will do so, but in doing so I must wound you deeply in another direction."

"I care nothing so long as you clear my wife. Everything on earth is insignificant compared to that."

"Let me tell you, then, the train of reasoning which passed through my mind in Baker Street. The idea of a vampire was to me absurd. Such things do not happen in criminal practice in England. And yet your observation was precise. You had seen the lady rise from beside the child's cot with the blood upon her lips."

"I did."

"Did it not occur to you that a bleeding wound may be sucked for some other purpose than to draw the blood from it? Was there not a queen in English history who sucked such a wound to draw poison from it?"*

"Poison!"

"A South American household. My instinct felt the presence of those weapons upon the wall before my eyes ever saw them. It might have been other poison, but that was what occurred to me. When I saw that little empty quiver beside the small bird bow,* it was just what I expected to see. If the child were pricked with one of those arrows dipped in curare* or some other devilish drug, it would mean death if the venom were not sucked out.

"And the dog! If one were to use such a poison, would one not try it first in order to see that it had not lost its power? I did not foresee the dog, but at least I understood him and he fitted into my reconstruction.

"Now do you understand? Your wife feared such an attack. She saw it made and saved the child's life, and yet she shrank from telling you all the truth, for she knew how you loved the boy and feared lest it break your heart."

"Jacky!"

"I watched him as you fondled the child just now. His face was clearly reflected in the glass of the window where the shutter formed a background. I saw such jealousy, such cruel hatred, as I have seldom seen in a human face."

"My Jacky!"

"You have to face it, Mr Ferguson. It is the more painful because it is a distorted love, a maniacal exaggerated love for you, and possibly for his dead mother, which has prompted his action. His very soul is consumed with hatred for this splendid child, whose health and beauty are a contrast to his own weakness."

"Good God! It is incredible!"

"Have I spoken the truth, madam?"

The lady was sobbing, with her face buried in the pillows. Now she turned to her husband.

"How could I tell you, Bob? I felt the blow it would be to you. It was better that I should wait and that it should come from some other lips than mine. When this gentleman, who seems to have powers of magic, wrote that he knew all, I was glad."

"I think a year at sea would be my prescription for Master Jacky," said Holmes, rising from his chair. "Only one thing is still clouded, madam. We can quite understand your attacks upon Master Jacky. There is a limit to a mother's patience. But how did you dare to leave the child these last two days?"

"I had told Mrs Mason. She knew."

"Exactly. So I imagined."

Ferguson was standing by the bed, choking, his hands outstretched and quivering.

"This, I fancy, is the time for our exit, Watson," said Holmes in a whisper. "If you will take one elbow of the too-faithful Dolores, I will take the other. There, now," he added as he closed the door behind him. "I think we may leave them to settle the rest among themselves."

I have only one further note of this case. It is the letter which Holmes wrote in final answer to that with which the narrative begins. It ran thus:

Baker Street,
21st Nov.

Re Vampires

SIR,

Referring to your letter of the 19th, I beg to state that I have looked into the enquiry of your client, Mr Robert Ferguson, of Ferguson & Muirhead, tea brokers, of Mincing Lane, and that the matter has been brought to a satisfactory conclusion. With thanks for your recommendation,

I am, sir,

Faithfully yours,

SHERLOCK HOLMES

THE ADVENTURE
OF THE THREE GARRIDEBS

I T MAY HAVE BEEN A COMEDY, or it may have been a tragedy. It cost one man his reason, it cost me a bloodletting, and it cost yet another man the penalties of the law. Yet there was certainly an element of comedy. Well, you shall judge for yourselves.

I remember the date very well, for it was in the same month that Holmes refused a knighthood* for services which may perhaps some day be described. I only refer to the matter in passing, for in my position of partner and confidant I am obliged to be particularly careful to avoid any indiscretion. I repeat, however, that this enables me to fix the date, which was the latter end of June 1902, shortly after the conclusion of the South African War.* Holmes had spent several days in bed, as was his habit from time to time, but he emerged that morning with a long foolscap document in his hand and a twinkle of amusement in his austere grey eyes.

"There is a chance for you to make some money, friend Watson," said he. "Have you ever heard the name of Garrideb?"

I admitted that I had not.

"Well, if you can lay your hand upon a Garrideb, there's money in it."

"Why?"

"Ah, that's a long story – rather a whimsical one, too. I don't think in all our explorations of human complexities we have ever come upon anything more singular. The fellow will be here presently for cross-examination, so I won't open the matter up till he comes. But meanwhile, that's the name we want."

The telephone directory lay on the table beside me, and I turned over the pages in a rather hopeless quest. But to my amazement there was this strange name in its due place. I gave a cry of triumph.

"Here you are, Holmes! Here it is!"

Holmes took the book from my hand.

"'Garrideb, N.,'" he read, "'136 Little Ryder Street, W.' Sorry to disappoint you, my dear Watson, but this is the man himself. That is the address upon his letter. We want another to match him."

Mrs Hudson had come in with a card upon a tray. I took it up and glanced at it.

"Why, here it is!" I cried in amazement. "This is a different initial. John Garrideb, Counsellor at Law, Moorville, Kansas, USA."

Holmes smiled as he looked at the card. "I am afraid you must make yet another effort, Watson," said he. "This gentleman is also in the plot already, though I certainly did not expect to see him this morning. However, he is in a position to tell us a good deal which I want to know."

A moment later he was in the room. Mr John Garrideb, Counsellor at Law, was a short, powerful man with the round, fresh, clean-shaven face characteristic of so many American men of affairs. The general effect was chubby and rather childlike, so that one received the impression of quite a young man with a broad, set smile upon his face. His eyes, however, were arresting. Seldom in any human head have I seen a pair which bespoke a more intense inward life, so bright were they, so alert, so responsive to every change of thought. His accent was American, but was not accompanied by any eccentricity of speech.

"Mr Holmes?" he asked, glancing from one to the other. "Ah, yes! Your pictures are not unlike you, sir, if I may say so. I believe you have had a letter from my namesake, Mr Nathan Garrideb, have you not?"

"Pray sit down," said Sherlock Holmes. "We shall, I fancy, have a good deal to discuss." He took up his sheets of foolscap. "You are, of course, the Mr John Garrideb mentioned in this document. But surely you have been in England some time?"

"Why do you say that, Mr Holmes?" I seemed to read sudden suspicion in those expressive eyes.

"Your whole outfit is English."

Mr Garrideb forced a laugh. "I've read of your tricks, Mr Holmes, but I never thought I would be the subject of them. Where do you read that?"

"The shoulder cut of your coat, the toes of your boots – could anyone doubt it?"

"Well, well… I had no idea I was so obvious a Britisher. But business brought me over here some time ago, and so, as you say, my outfit is nearly all London. However, I guess your time is of value, and we did not meet to talk about the cut of my socks. What about getting down to that paper you hold in your hand?"

Holmes had in some way ruffled our visitor, whose chubby face had assumed a far less amiable expression.

"Patience! Patience, Mr Garrideb!" said my friend in a soothing voice. "Doctor Watson would tell you that these little digressions of mine sometimes prove in the end to have some bearing on the matter. But why did Mr Nathan Garrideb not come with you?"

"Why did he ever drag you into it at all?" asked our visitor, with a sudden outflame of anger. "What in thunder had you to do with it? Here was a bit of professional business between two gentlemen, and one of them must needs call in a detective! I saw him this morning, and he told me this fool trick he had played me, and that's why I am here. But I feel bad about it, all the same."

"There was no reflection upon you, Mr Garrideb. It was simply zeal upon his part to gain your end – an end which is, I understand, equally vital for both of you. He knew that I had means of getting information, and, therefore, it was very natural that he should apply to me."

Our visitor's angry face gradually cleared.

"Well, that puts it different," said he. "When I went to see him this morning and he told me he had sent to a detective, I just asked for your address and came right away. I don't want police butting into a private matter. But if you are content just to help us find the man, there can be no harm in that."

"Well, that is just how it stands," said Holmes. "And now, sir, since you are here, we had best have a clear account from your own lips. My friend here knows nothing of the details."

Mr Garrideb surveyed me with not too friendly a gaze.

"Need he know?" he asked.

"We usually work together."

"Well, there's no reason it should be kept a secret. I'll give you the facts as short as I can make them. If you came from Kansas, I would not need to explain to you who Alexander Hamilton Garrideb* was. He made his money in real estate, and afterwards in the wheat pit* at Chicago, but he spent it in buying up as much land as would make one of your counties, lying along the Arkansas River, west of Fort Dodge.* It's grazing land and lumber land and arable land and mineralized land, and just every sort of land that brings dollars to the man that owns it.

"He had no kith nor kin – or, if he had, I never heard of it. But he took a kind of pride in the queerness of his name. That was what brought us together. I was in the law at Topeka,* and one day I had a visit from the old man, and he was tickled to death to meet another man with his own name. It was his pet fad, and he was dead set to find out if there were any more Garridebs in the world. 'Find me another!' said he. I told him I was a busy man and could not spend my life hiking round the world in search of Garridebs. 'Nonetheless,' said he, 'that is just what you will do if things pan out as I planned them.' I thought he was joking, but there was a powerful lot of meaning in the words, as I was soon to discover.

"For he died within a year of saying them, and he left a will behind him. It was the queerest will that has ever been filed in the state of Kansas. His property was divided into three parts, and I was to have one on condition that I found two Garridebs who would share the remainder. It's five million dollars for each if it is a cent, but we can't lay a finger on it until we all three stand in a row.

"It was so big a chance that I just let my legal practice slide and I set forth looking for Garridebs. There is not one in the United States. I went through it, sir, with a fine-toothed comb and never a Garrideb could I catch. Then I tried the old country. Sure enough there was the name in the London telephone directory. I went after him two days ago and explained the whole matter to him. But he is a lone man, like myself, with some women relations, but no men. It says three adult men in the will. So you see we still have a vacancy, and if you can help to fill it, we will be very ready to pay your charges."

"Well, Watson," said Holmes with a smile, "I said it was rather whimsical, did I not? I should have thought, sir, that your obvious way was to advertise in the agony columns of the papers."

"I have done that, Mr Holmes. No replies."

"Dear me! Well, it is certainly a most curious little problem. I may take a glance at it in my leisure. By the way, it is curious that you should have come from Topeka. I used to have a correspondent – he is dead now – old Dr Lysander Starr, who was mayor in 1890."

"Good old Dr Starr!" said our visitor. "His name is still honoured. Well, Mr Holmes, I suppose all we can do is to report to you and let you know how we progress. I reckon you will hear within a day or two." With this assurance our American bowed and departed.

Holmes had lit his pipe, and he sat for some time with a curious smile upon his face.

"Well?" I asked at last.

"I am wondering, Watson – just wondering!"

"At what?"

Holmes took his pipe from his lips.

"I was wondering, Watson, what on earth could be the object of this man in telling us such a rigmarole of lies. I nearly asked him so – for there are times when a brutal frontal attack is the best policy – but I judged it better to let him think he had fooled us. Here is a man with an English coat frayed at the elbow and trousers bagged at the knee with a year's wear, and yet by this document and by his own account he is a provincial American lately landed in London. There have been no advertisements in the agony columns. You know that I miss nothing there. They are my favourite covert for putting up a bird,* and I would never have overlooked such a cock pheasant as that. I never knew a Dr Lysander Starr of Topeka.* Touch him where you would, he was false. I think the fellow is really an American, but he has worn his accent smooth with years of London. What is his game, then, and what motive lies behind this preposterous search for Garridebs? It's worth our attention, for, granting that the man is a rascal, he is certainly a complex and ingenious one. We must now find out if our other correspondent is a fraud also. Just ring him up, Watson."

I did so, and heard a thin, quavering voice at the other end of the line.

"Yes, yes, I am Mr Nathan Garrideb. Is Mr Holmes there? I should very much like to have a word with Mr Holmes."

My friend took the instrument, and I heard the usual syncopated dialogue.

"Yes, he has been here. I understand that you don't know him… How long?… Only two days!… Yes, yes, of course, it is a most captivating prospect. Will you be at home this evening? I suppose your namesake will not be there?… Very good, we will come then, for I would rather have a chat without him… Doctor Watson will come with me… I understood from your note that you did not go out often… Well, we shall be round about six. You need not mention it to the American lawyer… Very good. Goodbye!"

It was twilight of a lovely spring evening, and even Little Ryder Street, one of the smaller offshoots from the Edgware Road, within a stone-cast of old Tyburn Tree* of evil memory, looked golden and wonderful in the slanting rays of the setting sun. The particular house to which we were directed was a large, old-fashioned, early-Georgian edifice with a flat brick face broken only by two deep bay windows on the ground floor. It was on this ground floor that our client lived, and, indeed, the low windows proved to be the front of the huge room in which he spent his waking hours. Holmes pointed as we passed to the small brass plate which bore the curious name.

"Up some years, Watson," he remarked, indicating its discoloured surface. "It's *his* real name, anyhow, and that is something to note."

The house had a common stair, and there were a number of names painted in the hall, some indicating offices and some private chambers. It was not a collection of residential flats, but rather the abode of bohemian bachelors. Our client opened the door for us himself and apologized by saying that the woman in charge left at four o'clock. Mr Nathan Garrideb proved to be a very tall, loose-jointed, round-backed person, gaunt and bald, some sixty-odd years of age. He had a cadaverous face, with the dull dead skin of a man to whom exercise was unknown. Large round spectacles and a small projecting goat's beard combined with his stooping attitude to give him an expression of peering curiosity. The general effect, however, was amiable, though eccentric.

The room was as curious as its occupant. It looked like a small museum. It was both broad and deep, with cupboards and cabinets all round, crowded with specimens, geological and anatomical. Cases of butterflies and moths flanked each side of the entrance. A large table in the centre was littered with all sorts of debris, while the tall brass tube of a powerful microscope bristled up amongst them. As I glanced round, I was surprised at the universality of the man's interests. Here was a case of ancient coins. There was a cabinet of flint instruments. Behind his central table was a large cupboard of fossil bones. Above was a line of plaster skulls with such names as "Neanderthal", "Heidelberg", "Cro-Magnon"* printed beneath them. It was clear that he was a student of many subjects. As he stood in front of us now, he held a piece of chamois leather in his right hand with which he was polishing a coin.

"Syracusan* – of the best period," he explained, holding it up. "They degenerated greatly towards the end. At their best I hold them supreme, though some prefer the Alexandrian school.* You will find a chair here, Mr Holmes. Pray allow me to clear these bones. And you, sir – ah, yes, Doctor Watson – if you would have the goodness to put the Japanese vase to one side... You see round me my little interests in life. My doctor lectures me about never going out, but why should I go out when I have so much to hold me here? I can assure you that the adequate cataloguing of one of those cabinets would take me three good months."

Holmes looked round him with curiosity.

"But do you tell me that you *never* go out?" he said.

"Now and again I drive down to Sotheby's or Christie's. Otherwise I very seldom leave my room. I am not too strong, and my researches are very absorbing. But you can imagine, Mr Holmes, what a terrific shock – pleasant but terrific – it was for me when I heard of this unparalleled good fortune. It only needs one more Garrideb to complete the matter, and surely we can find one. I had a brother, but he is dead, and female relatives are disqualified. But there must surely be others in the world. I had heard that you handled strange cases, and that was why I sent to you. Of course, this American gentleman is quite right, and I should have taken his advice first, but I acted for the best."

"I think you acted very wisely indeed," said Holmes. "But are you really anxious to acquire an estate in America?"

"Certainly not, sir. Nothing would induce me to leave my collection. But this gentleman has assured me that he will buy me out as soon as we have established our claim. Five million dollars was the sum named. There are a dozen specimens in the market at the present moment which fill gaps in my collection, and which I am unable to purchase for want of a few hundred pounds. Just think what I could do with five million dollars. Why, I have the nucleus of a national collection. I shall be the Hans Sloane* of my age."

His eyes gleamed behind his great spectacles. It was very clear that no pains would be spared by Mr Nathan Garrideb in finding a namesake.

"I merely called to make your acquaintance, and there is no reason why I should interrupt your studies," said Holmes. "I prefer to establish personal touch with those with whom I do business. There are few questions I need ask, for I have your very clear narrative in my pocket, and I filled up the blanks when this American gentleman called. I understand that up to this week you were unaware of his existence."

"That is so. He called last Tuesday."

"Did he tell you of our interview today?"

"Yes, he came straight back to me. He had been very angry."

"Why should he be angry?"

"He seemed to think it was some reflection on his honour. But he was quite cheerful again when he returned."

"Did he suggest any course of action?"

"No, sir, he did not."

"Has he had, or asked for, any money from you?"

"No, sir, never!"

"You see no possible object he has in view?"

"None, except what he states."

"Did you tell him of our telephone appointment?"

"Yes, sir, I did."

Holmes was lost in thought. I could see that he was puzzled.

"Have you any articles of great value in your collection?"

"No, sir. I am not a rich man. It is a good collection, but not a very valuable one."

"You have no fear of burglars?"

"Not the least."

"How long have you been in these rooms?"

"Nearly five years."

Holmes's cross-examination was interrupted by an imperative knocking at the door. No sooner had our client unlatched it than the American lawyer burst excitedly into the room.

"Here you are!" he cried, waving a paper over his head. "I thought I should be in time to get you. Mr Nathan Garrideb, my congratulations! You are a rich man, sir. Our business is happily finished, and all is well. As to you, Mr Holmes, we can only say we are sorry if we have given you any useless trouble."

He handed over the paper to our client, who stood staring at a marked advertisement. Holmes and I leant forward and read it over his shoulder. This is how it ran:

HOWARD GARRIDEB

Constructor of Agricultural Machinery.

Binders, reapers, steam and hand plows, drills,* harrows, farmers' carts, buckboards* and all other appliances.

Estimates for Artesian Wells.*
Apply Grosvenor Buildings, Aston.*

"Glorious!" gasped our host. "That makes our third man."

"I had opened up enquiries in Birmingham," said the American, "and my agent there has sent me this advertisement from a local paper. We must hustle and put the thing through. I have written to this man and told him that you will see him in his office tomorrow afternoon at four o'clock."

"You want *me* to see him?"

"What do you say, Mr Holmes? Don't you think it would be wiser? Here am I, a wandering American with a wonderful tale. Why should he believe what I tell him? But you are a Britisher with solid references, and he is bound to take notice of what you say. I would go with you if you wished, but I have a very busy day tomorrow, and I could always follow you if you are in any trouble."

"Well, I have not made such a journey for years."

"It is nothing, Mr Garrideb. I have figured out your connections. You leave at twelve and should be there soon after two. Then you can be back the same night. All you have to do is to see this man, explain the matter and get an affidavit of his existence. By the Lord!" he added hotly. "Considering I've come all the way from the centre of America, it is surely little enough if you go a hundred miles in order to put this matter through."

"Quite so," said Holmes. "I think what this gentleman says is very true."

Mr Nathan Garrideb shrugged his shoulders with a disconsolate air. "Well, if you insist, I shall go," said he. "It is certainly hard for me to refuse you anything, considering the glory of hope that you have brought into my life."

"Then that is agreed," said Holmes, "and no doubt you will let me have a report as soon as you can."

"I'll see to that," said the American. "Well," he added, looking at his watch, "I'll have to get on. I'll call tomorrow, Mr Nathan, and see you off to Birmingham. Coming my way, Mr Holmes? Well, then, goodbye, and we may have good news for you tomorrow night."

I noticed that my friend's face cleared when the American left the room, and the look of thoughtful perplexity had vanished.

"I wish I could look over your collection, Mr Garrideb," said he. "In my profession all sorts of odd knowledge comes useful, and this room of yours is a storehouse of it."

Our client shone with pleasure, and his eyes gleamed from behind his big glasses.

"I had always heard, sir, that you were a very intelligent man," said he. "I could take you round now, if you have the time."

"Unfortunately, I have not. But these specimens are so well labelled and classified that they hardly need your personal explanation. If I should be able to look in tomorrow, I presume that there would be no objection to my glancing over them?"

"None at all. You are most welcome. The place will, of course, be shut up, but Mrs Saunders is in the basement up to four o'clock and would let you in with her key."

"Well, I happen to be clear tomorrow afternoon. If you would say a word to Mrs Saunders it would be quite in order. By the way, who is your house agent?"

Our client was amazed at the sudden question.

"Holloway & Steele, in the Edgware Road. But why?"

"I am a bit of an archaeologist myself when it comes to houses," said Holmes, laughing. "I was wondering if this was Queen Anne or Georgian."

"Georgian, beyond doubt."

"Really. I should have thought a little earlier. However, it is easily ascertained. Well, goodbye, Mr Garrideb, and may you have every success in your Birmingham journey."

The house agent's was close by, but we found that it was closed for the day, so we made our way back to Baker Street. It was not till after dinner that Holmes reverted to the subject.

"Our little problem draws to a close," said he. "No doubt you have outlined the solution in your own mind."

"I can make neither head nor tail of it."

"The head is surely clear enough, and the tail we should see tomorrow. Did you notice nothing curious about that advertisement?"

"I saw that the word 'plough' was misspelt."

"Oh, you did notice that, did you? Come, Watson, you improve all the time. Yes, it was bad English, but good American. The printer had set it up as received. Then the buckboards. That is American also. And artesian wells are commoner with them than with us. It was a typical American advertisement, but purporting to be from an English firm. What do you make of that?"

"I can only suppose that this American lawyer put it in himself. What his object was I fail to understand."

"Well, there are alternative explanations. Anyhow, he wanted to get this good old fossil up to Birmingham. That is very clear. I might have told him that he was clearly going on a wild-goose chase, but, on second thoughts, it seemed better to clear the stage by letting him go. Tomorrow, Watson... well, tomorrow will speak for itself."

Holmes was up and out early. When he returned at lunchtime, I noticed that his face was very grave.

"This is a more serious matter than I had expected, Watson," said he. "It is fair to tell you so, though I know it will only be an additional reason to you for running your head into danger. I should know my Watson by now. But there *is* danger, and you should know it."

"Well, it is not the first we have shared, Holmes. I hope it may not be the last. What is the particular danger this time?"

"We are up against a very hard case. I have identified Mr John Garrideb, Counsellor at Law. He is none other than 'Killer' Evans, of sinister and murderous reputation."

"I fear I am none the wiser."

"Ah, it is not part of your profession to carry about a portable *Newgate Calendar** in your memory. I have been down to see friend Lestrade at the Yard. There may be an occasional want of imaginative intuition down there, but they lead the world for thoroughness and method. I had an idea that we might get on the track of our American friend in their records. Sure enough, I found his chubby face smiling up at me from the rogues' portrait gallery.* 'James Winter, alias Morecroft, alias Killer Evans' was the inscription below." Holmes drew an envelope from his pocket. "I scribbled down a few points from his dossier. Aged forty-four. Native of Chicago. Known to have shot three men in the States. Escaped from penitentiary through political influence. Came to London in 1893. Shot a man over cards in a nightclub in the Waterloo Road in January 1895. Man died, but he was shown to have been the aggressor in the row. Dead man was identified as Rodger Prescott, famous as forger and coiner in Chicago. Killer Evans released in 1901. Has been under police supervision since, but so far as known has led an honest life. Very dangerous man, usually carries arms and is prepared to use them. That is our bird, Watson – a sporting bird, as you must admit."

"But what is his game?"

"Well, it begins to define itself. I have been to the house agent's. Our client, as he told us, has been there five years. It was unlet for a year before then. The previous tenant was a gentleman at large named Waldron. Waldron's appearance was well remembered at the office. He had suddenly vanished, and nothing more been heard of him. He was a tall, bearded man with very dark features. Now, Prescott, the man whom Killer Evans had shot, was, according to Scotland Yard, a tall, dark man with a beard. As a working hypothesis, I think we may take it that Prescott, the American criminal, used to live in the very room which our innocent friend now devotes to his museum. So at last we get a link, you see."

"And the next link?"

"Well, we must go now and look for that."

He took a revolver from the drawer and handed it to me.

"I have my old favourite with me. If our Wild West friend tries to live up to his nickname, we must be ready for him. I'll give you an hour for a siesta, Watson, and then I think it will be time for our Ryder Street adventure."

It was just four o'clock when we reached the curious apartment of Nathan Garrideb. Mrs Saunders, the caretaker, was about to leave, but she had no hesitation in admitting us, for the door shut with a spring lock, and Holmes promised to see that all was safe before we left. Shortly afterwards the outer door closed, her bonnet passed the bow window, and we knew that we were alone in the lower floor of the house. Holmes made a rapid examination of the premises. There was one cupboard in a dark corner which stood out a little from the wall. It was behind this that we eventually crouched, while Holmes in a whisper outlined his intentions.

"He wanted to get our amiable friend out of his room – that is very clear, and, as the collector never went out, it took some planning to do it. The whole of this Garrideb invention was apparently for no other end. I must say, Watson, that there is a certain devilish ingenuity about it even if the queer name of the tenant did give him an opening which he could hardly have expected. He wove his plot with remarkable cunning."

"But what did he want?"

"Well, that is what we are here to find out. It has nothing whatever to do with our client, so far as I can read the situation. It is something connected with the man he murdered – the man who may have been his confederate in crime. There is some guilty secret in the room. That is how I read it. At first I thought our friend might have something in his collection more valuable than he knew – something worth the attention of a big criminal. But the fact that Rodger Prescott of evil memory inhabited these rooms points to some deeper reason. Well, Watson, we can but possess our souls in patience* and see what the hour may bring."

That hour was not long in striking. We crouched closer in the shadow as we heard the outer door open and shut. Then came the sharp, metallic snap of a key, and the American was in the room. He closed the door softly behind him, took a sharp glance around him to see that all was safe, threw off his overcoat and walked up to the central table with the brisk manner of one who knows exactly what he has to do and how to do it. He pushed the table to one side, tore up the square of carpet on which it rested, rolled it completely back, and then, drawing a jemmy* from his inside pocket, he knelt down and worked vigorously upon the floor. Presently we heard the sound of sliding boards, and an instant later a square had opened in the planks. Killer Evans struck a match, lit a stump of candle and vanished from our view.

Clearly our moment had come. Holmes touched my wrist as a signal, and together we stole across to the open trapdoor. Gently as we moved, however, the old floor must have creaked under our feet, for the head of our American, peering anxiously round, emerged suddenly from the open space. His face turned upon us with a glare of baffled rage, which gradually softened into a rather shamefaced grin as he realized that two pistols were pointed at his head.

"Well, well!" said he coolly as he scrambled to the surface. "I guess you have been one too many for me, Mr Holmes. Saw through my game, I suppose, and played me for a sucker from the first. Well, sir, I hand it to you – you have me beat and—"

In an instant he had whisked out a revolver from his breast and had fired two shots. I felt a sudden hot sear as if a red-hot iron had been pressed to my thigh. There was a crash as Holmes's pistol came down on the man's head. I had a vision of him sprawling upon the floor with blood running down his face while Holmes rummaged him for weapons. Then my friend's wiry arms were round me, and he was leading me to a chair.

"You're not hurt, Watson? For God's sake, say that you are not hurt!"

It was worth a wound – it was worth many wounds – to know the depth of loyalty and love which lay behind that cold mask. The clear, hard eyes were dimmed for a moment, and the firm lips were shaking. For the one and only time I caught a glimpse of a great heart as well as of a great brain. All my years of humble but single-minded service culminated in that moment of revelation.

"It's nothing, Holmes. It's a mere scratch."

He had ripped up my trousers with his pocket knife.

"You are right," he cried, with an immense sigh of relief. "It is quite superficial." His face set like flint as he glared at our prisoner, who was sitting up with a dazed face. "By the Lord, it is as well for you. If you had killed Watson, you would not have got out of this room alive. Now, sir, what have you to say for yourself?"

He had nothing to say for himself. He only lay and scowled. I leant on Holmes's arm, and together we looked down into the small cellar which had been disclosed by the secret flap. It was still illuminated by the candle which Evans had taken down with him. Our eyes fell upon a mass of rusted machinery, great rolls of paper, a litter of bottles and, neatly arranged upon a small table, a number of neat little bundles.

"A printing press – a counterfeiter's outfit," said Holmes.

"Yes, sir," said our prisoner, staggering slowly to his feet and then sinking into the chair. "The greatest counterfeiter London ever saw. That's Prescott's machine, and those bundles on the table are two thousand of Prescott's notes, worth a hundred each and fit to pass anywhere. Help yourselves, gentlemen. Call it a deal and let me beat it."

Holmes laughed.

"We don't do things like that, Mr Evans. There is no bolthole for you in this country. You shot this man Prescott, did you not?"

"Yes, sir, and got five years for it, though it was he who pulled on me – five years, when I should have had a medal the size of a soup plate. No living man could tell a Prescott from a Bank of England, and if I hadn't put him out, he would have flooded London with them. I was the only one in the world who knew where he made them. Can you wonder that I wanted to get to the place? And can you wonder that when I found this crazy boob of a bug-hunter with the queer name squatting right on the top of it, and never quitting his room, I had to do the best I could to shift him? Maybe

I would have been wiser if I had put him away. It would have been easy enough, but I'm a soft-hearted guy that can't begin shooting unless the other man has a gun also. But say, Mr Holmes, what have I done wrong, anyhow? I've not used this plant. I've not hurt this old stiff. Where do you get me?"

"Only attempted murder, so far as I can see," said Holmes. "But that's not our job. They take that at the next stage. What we wanted at present was just your sweet self. Please give the Yard a call, Watson. It won't be entirely unexpected."

So those were the facts about Killer Evans and his remarkable invention of the three Garridebs. We heard later that our poor old friend never got over the shock of his dissipated dreams. When his castle in the air fell down, it buried him beneath the ruins. He was last heard of at a nursing home in Brixton. It was a glad day at the Yard when the Prescott outfit was discovered, for, though they knew that it existed, they had never been able, after the death of the man, to find out where it was. Evans had indeed done great service and caused several worthy CID men to sleep the sounder, for the counterfeiter stands in a class by himself as a public danger. They would willingly have subscribed to that soup-plate medal of which the criminal had spoken, but an unappreciative bench* took a less favourable view, and the Killer returned to those shades from which he had just emerged.

THE PROBLEM
OF THOR BRIDGE

S OMEWHERE IN THE VAULTS of the bank of Cox & Co.,* at
Charing Cross, there is a travel-worn and battered tin dispatch
box with my name, "John H. Watson, MD, Late Indian Army",*
painted upon the lid. It is crammed with papers, nearly all of
which are records of cases to illustrate the curious problems which
Mr Sherlock Holmes had at various times to examine. Some, and
not the least interesting, were complete failures, and as such will
hardly bear narrating, since no final explanation is forthcoming.
A problem without a solution may interest the student, but can
hardly fail to annoy the casual reader. Among these unfinished
tales is that of Mr James Phillimore, who, stepping back into his
own house to get his umbrella, was never more seen in this world.
No less remarkable is that of the cutter* *Alicia*, which sailed one
spring morning into a small patch of mist from where she never
again emerged, nor was anything further ever heard of herself and
her crew. A third case worthy of note is that of Isadora Persano,
the well-known journalist and duellist, who was found stark
staring mad with a matchbox in front of him which contained
a remarkable worm, said to be unknown to science. Apart from
these unfathomed cases, there are some which involve the secrets
of private families to an extent which would mean consternation
in many exalted quarters if it were thought possible that they
might find their way into print. I need not say that such a breach of
confidence is unthinkable, and that these records will be separated
and destroyed now that my friend has time to turn his energies to

the matter. There remain a considerable residue of cases of greater or less interest which I might have edited before had I not feared to give the public a surfeit which might react upon the reputation of the man whom above all others I revere. In some I was myself concerned and can speak as an eyewitness, while in others I was either not present or played so small a part that they could only be told as by a third person.* The following narrative is drawn from my own experience.

It was a wild morning in October, and I observed as I was dressing how the last remaining leaves were being whirled from the solitary plane tree which graces the yard behind our house. I descended to breakfast prepared to find my companion in depressed spirits, for, like all great artists, he was easily impressed by his surroundings. On the contrary, I found that he had nearly finished his meal, and that his mood was particularly bright and joyous, with that somewhat sinister cheerfulness which was characteristic of his lighter moments.

"You have a case, Holmes?" I remarked.

"The faculty of deduction is certainly contagious, Watson," he answered. "It has enabled you to probe my secret. Yes, I have a case. After a month of trivialities and stagnation, the wheels move once more."

"Might I share it?"

"There is little to share, but we may discuss it when you have consumed the two hard-boiled eggs with which our new cook has favoured us. Their condition may not be unconnected with the copy of the *Family Herald** which I observed yesterday upon the hall table. Even so trivial a matter as cooking an egg demands an attention which is conscious of the passage of time, and incompatible with the love romance in that excellent periodical."

A quarter of an hour later the table had been cleared, and we were face to face. He had drawn a letter from his pocket.

"You have heard of Neil Gibson, the Gold King?" he said.

"You mean the American senator?"

"Well, he was once senator for some western state, but is better known as the greatest gold-mining magnate in the world."*

"Yes, I know of him. He has surely lived in England for some time. His name is very familiar."

"Yes – he bought a considerable estate in Hampshire some five years ago. Possibly you have already heard of the tragic end of his wife?"

"Of course. I remember it now. That is why the name is familiar. But I really know nothing of the details."

Holmes waved his hand towards some papers on a chair. "I had no idea that the case was coming my way, or I should have had my extracts ready," said he. "The fact is that the problem, though exceedingly sensational, appeared to present no difficulty. The interesting personality of the accused does not obscure the clearness of the evidence. That was the view taken by the coroner's jury and also in the police-court proceedings. It is now referred to the assizes* at Winchester. I fear it is a thankless business. I can discover facts, Watson, but I cannot change them. Unless some entirely new and unexpected ones come to light, I do not see what my client can hope for."

"Your client?"

"Ah, I forgot I had not told you. I am getting into your involved habit, Watson, of telling a story backwards. You had best read this first."

The letter which he handed to me, written in a bold, masterful hand, ran as follows:

CLARIDGE'S HOTEL, 3rd October

DEAR MR SHERLOCK HOLMES,

I can't see the best woman God ever made go to her death without doing all that is possible to save her. I can't explain things – I can't even try to explain them, but I know beyond all doubt that Miss Dunbar is innocent. You know the facts – who doesn't? It has been the gossip of the country. And never a voice raised for her! It's the damned injustice of it all that makes me crazy. That woman has a heart that wouldn't let her kill a fly. Well, I'll come at eleven tomorrow and see if you can get some ray of light in the dark. Maybe I have a clue and don't know it. Anyhow, all I know and all I have and all I am are for your use if only you can save her. If ever in your life you showed your powers, put them now into this case.

Yours faithfully,

J. NEIL GIBSON

"There you have it," said Sherlock Holmes, knocking out the ashes of his after-breakfast pipe and slowly refilling it. "That is the gentleman I await. As to the story, you have hardly time to master all these papers, so I must give it to you in a nutshell if you are to take an intelligent interest in the proceedings. This man is the greatest financial power in the world, and a man, as I understand, of most violent and formidable character. He married a wife, the victim of this tragedy, of whom I know nothing save that she was past her prime, which was the more unfortunate as a very attractive governess superintended the education of two young children. These are the three people concerned, and the scene is a grand old manor house, the centre of an historical English estate. Then as to the tragedy. The wife was found in the grounds nearly half a mile from the house, late at night, clad in her dinner dress, with a shawl over her shoulders and a revolver bullet through her brain. No weapon was found near her, and there was no local clue as to the murder. No weapon near her, Watson – mark that! The crime seems to have been committed late in the evening, and the body was found by a gamekeeper about eleven o'clock, when it was examined by the police and by a doctor before being carried up to the house. Is this too condensed, or can you follow it clearly?"

"It is all very clear. But why suspect the governess?"

"Well, in the first place there is some very direct evidence. A revolver with one discharged chamber and a calibre which corresponded with the bullet was found on the floor of her wardrobe."

His eyes fixed, and he repeated in broken words, "On–the–floor–of–her–wardrobe." Then he sank into silence, and I saw that some train of thought had been set moving which I should be foolish to interrupt. Suddenly with a start he emerged into brisk life once more. "Yes, Watson, it was found. Pretty damning, eh? So the two juries thought. Then the dead woman had a note upon her making an appointment at that very place and signed by the governess. How's that? Finally, there is the motive. Senator Gibson is an attractive person. If his wife dies, who more likely to succeed her than the young lady who had already by all accounts received pressing attentions from her employer? Love, fortune, power, all depending upon one middle-aged life. Ugly, Watson – very ugly!"

"Yes, indeed, Holmes."

"Nor could she prove an alibi. On the contrary, she had to admit that she was down near Thor Bridge – that was the scene of the tragedy – about that hour. She couldn't deny it, for some passing villager had seen her there."

"That really seems final."

"And yet, Watson... and yet! This bridge – a single broad span of stone with balustraded sides – carries the drive over the narrowest part of a long, deep, reed-girt* sheet of water. Thor Mere it is called. In the mouth of the bridge lay the dead woman. Such are the main facts. But here, if I mistake not, is our client, considerably before his time."

Billy had opened the door, but the name which he announced was an unexpected one. Mr Marlow Bates was a stranger to both of us. He was a thin, nervous wisp of a man with frightened eyes and a twitching, hesitating manner – a man whom my own professional eye would judge to be on the brink of an absolute nervous breakdown.

"You seem agitated, Mr Bates," said Holmes. "Pray sit down. I fear I can only give you a short time, for I have an appointment at eleven."

"I know you have," our visitor gasped, shooting out short sentences like a man who is out of breath. "Mr Gibson is coming.

Mr Gibson is my employer. I am manager of his estate. Mr Holmes, he is a villain – an infernal villain."

"Strong language, Mr Bates."

"I have to be emphatic, Mr Holmes, for the time is so limited. I would not have him find me here for the world. He is almost due now. But I was so situated that I could not come earlier. His secretary, Mr Ferguson, only told me this morning of his appointment with you."

"And you are his manager?"

"I have given him notice. In a couple of weeks I shall have shaken off his accursed slavery. A hard man, Mr Holmes, hard to all about him. Those public charities are a screen to cover his private iniquities. But his wife was his chief victim. He was brutal to her – yes, sir, brutal! How she came by her death I do not know, but I am sure that he had made her life a misery to her. She was a creature of the tropics, a Brazilian by birth, as no doubt you know?"

"No – it had escaped me."

"Tropical by birth and tropical by nature. A child of the sun and of passion. She had loved him as such women can love, but when her own physical charms had faded – I am told that they once were great – there was nothing to hold him. We all liked her and felt for her and hated him for the way that he treated her. But he is plausible and cunning. That is all I have to say to you. Don't take him at his face value. There is more behind. Now I'll go. No, no, don't detain me! He is almost due."

With a frightened look at the clock our strange visitor literally ran to the door and disappeared.

"Well! Well!" said Holmes after an interval of silence. "Mr Gibson seems to have a nice loyal household. But the warning is a useful one, and now we can only wait till the man himself appears."

Sharp at the hour we heard a heavy step upon the stairs, and the famous millionaire was shown into the room. As I looked upon him, I understood not only the fears and dislike of his manager, but also the execrations which so many business rivals have heaped upon his head. If I were a sculptor and desired to idealize the successful man of affairs, iron of nerve and leathery of conscience, I should choose Mr Neil Gibson as my model. His tall, gaunt, craggy figure had a suggestion of hunger and rapacity. An Abraham Lincoln keyed to base uses instead of high ones would give some idea of the man. His face might have been chiselled in granite, hard-set, craggy, remorseless, with deep lines upon it, the scars of many a crisis. Cold grey eyes, looking shrewdly out from under bristling brows, surveyed us each in turn. He bowed in perfunctory fashion as Holmes mentioned my name, and then with a masterful air of possession he drew a chair up to my companion and seated himself with his bony knees almost touching him.

"Let me say right here, Mr Holmes," he began, "that money is nothing to me in this case. You can burn it if it's any use in lighting you to the truth. This woman is innocent, and this woman has to be cleared, and it's up to you to do it. Name your figure!"

"My professional charges are upon a fixed scale," said Holmes coldly. "I do not vary them, save when I remit them altogether."

"Well, if dollars make no difference to you, think of the reputation. If you pull this off, every paper in England and America will be booming* you. You'll be the talk of two continents."

"Thank you, Mr Gibson, I do not think that I am in need of booming. It may surprise you to know that I prefer to work anonymously, and that it is the problem itself which attracts me. But we are wasting time. Let us get down to the facts."

"I think that you will find all the main ones in the press reports. I don't know that I can add anything which will help you. But if there is anything you would wish more light upon – well, I am here to give it."

"Well, there is just one point."

"What is it?"

"What were the exact relations between you and Miss Dunbar?"

The Gold King gave a violent start, and half-rose from his chair. Then his massive calm came back to him.

"I suppose you are within your rights – and maybe doing your duty – in asking such a question, Mr Holmes."

"We will agree to suppose so," said Holmes.

"Then I can assure you that our relations were entirely and always those of an employer towards a young lady whom he never conversed with, or ever saw, save when she was in the company of his children."

Holmes rose from his chair.

"I am a rather busy man, Mr Gibson," said he, "and I have no time or taste for aimless conversations. I wish you good morning."

Our visitor had risen also, and his great loose figure towered above Holmes. There was an angry gleam from under those bristling brows and a tinge of colour in the sallow cheeks.

"What the devil do you mean by this, Mr Holmes? Do you dismiss my case?"

"Well, Mr Gibson, at least I dismiss you. I should have thought my words were plain."

"Plain enough, but what's at the back of it? Raising the price on me, or afraid to tackle it, or what? I've a right to a plain answer."

"Well, perhaps you have," said Holmes. "I'll give you one. This case is quite sufficiently complicated to start with, without the further difficulty of false information."

"Meaning that I lie."

"Well, I was trying to express it as delicately as I could, but if you insist upon the word, I will not contradict you."

I sprang to my feet, for the expression upon the millionaire's face was fiendish in its intensity, and he had raised his great knotted fist. Holmes smiled languidly and reached his hand out for his pipe.

"Don't be noisy, Mr Gibson. I find that after breakfast even the smallest argument is unsettling. I suggest that a stroll in the morning air and a little quiet thought will be greatly to your advantage."

With an effort the Gold King mastered his fury. I could not but admire him, for by a supreme self-command he had turned in a minute from a hot flame of anger to a frigid and contemptuous indifference.

"Well, it's your choice. I guess you know how to run your own business. I can't make you touch the case against your will. You've done yourself no good this morning, Mr Holmes, for I have broken stronger men than you. No man ever crossed me and was the better for it."

"So many have said so, and yet here I am," said Holmes, smiling. "Well, good morning, Mr Gibson. You have a good deal yet to learn."

Our visitor made a noisy exit, but Holmes smoked in imperturbable silence with dreamy eyes fixed upon the ceiling.

"Any views, Watson?" he asked at last.

"Well, Holmes, I must confess that when I consider that this is a man who would certainly brush any obstacle from his path, and when I remember that his wife may have been an obstacle and an object of dislike, as that man Bates plainly told us, it seems to me—"

"Exactly. And to me also."

"But what were his relations with the governess, and how did you discover them?"

"Bluff, Watson, bluff! When I considered the passionate, unconventional, unbusinesslike tone of his letter, and contrasted it with his self-contained manner and appearance, it was pretty clear that there was some deep emotion which centred upon the accused woman rather than upon the victim. We've got to understand the exact relations of those three people if we are to reach the truth. You saw the frontal attack which I made upon him and how imperturbably he received it. Then I bluffed him by giving him the impression that I was absolutely certain, when in reality I was only extremely suspicious."

"Perhaps he will come back?"

"He is sure to come back. He *must* come back. He can't leave it where it is. Ha! Isn't that a ring? Yes, there is his footstep. Well, Mr Gibson, I was just saying to Doctor Watson that you were somewhat overdue."

The Gold King had re-entered the room in a more chastened mood than he had left it. His wounded pride still showed in his resentful eyes, but his common sense had shown him that he must yield if he would attain his end.

"I've been thinking it over, Mr Holmes, and I feel that I have been hasty in taking your remarks amiss. You are justified in getting down to the facts, whatever they may be, and I think the more of you for it. I can assure you, however, that the relations between Miss Dunbar and me don't really touch this case."

"That is for me to decide, is it not?"

"Yes, I guess that is so. You're like a surgeon who wants every symptom before he can give his diagnosis."

"Exactly. That expresses it. And it is only a patient who has an object in deceiving his surgeon who would conceal the facts of his case."

"That may be so, but you will admit, Mr Holmes, that most men would shy off a bit when they are asked point-blank what their relations with a woman may be – if there is really some serious feeling in the case. I guess most men have a little private reserve of their own in some corner of their souls where they don't welcome intruders. And you burst suddenly into it. But the object excuses you, since it was to try and save her. Well, the stakes are down and the reserve open, and you can explore where you will. What is it you want?"

"The truth."

The Gold King paused for a moment as one who marshals his thoughts. His grim, deep-lined face had become even sadder and more grave.

"I can give it to you in a very few words, Mr Holmes," said he at last. "There are some things that are painful as well as difficult to say, so I won't go deeper than is needful. I met my wife when I was gold-hunting in Brazil. Maria Pinto was the daughter of a government official at Manaos,* and she was very beautiful. I was young and ardent in those days, but even now, as I look back with colder blood and a more critical eye, I can see that she was rare and wonderful in her beauty. It was a deep, rich nature, too, passionate, wholehearted, tropical, ill-balanced, very different from the American women whom I had known. Well, to make a long story short, I loved her and I married her. It was only when the romance had passed – and it lingered for years – that I realized that we had nothing, absolutely nothing, in common. My love faded. If hers had faded also, it might have been easier. But you know the wonderful way of women! Do what I might, nothing could turn her from me. If I have been harsh to her, even brutal as some have said, it has been because I knew that if I could kill her love, or if it turned to hate, it would be easier for both of us. But nothing changed her. She adored me in those English woods as she had adored me twenty years ago on the banks of the Amazon. Do what I might, she was as devoted as ever.

"Then came Miss Grace Dunbar. She answered our advertisement and became governess to our two children. Perhaps you have seen her portrait in the papers. The whole world has proclaimed that she also is a very beautiful woman. Now, I make no pretence to be more moral than my neighbours, and I will admit to you that I could not live under the same roof with such a woman and in daily contact with her without feeling a passionate regard for her. Do you blame me, Mr Holmes?"

"I do not blame you for feeling it. I should blame you if you expressed it, since this young lady was in a sense under your protection."

"Well, maybe so," said the millionaire, though for a moment the reproof had brought the old angry gleam into his eyes. "I'm not pretending to be any better than I am. I guess all my life I've been a man that reached out his hand for what he wanted, and I never wanted anything more than the love and possession of that woman. I told her so."

"Oh, you did, did you?"

Holmes could look very formidable when he was moved.

"I said to her that if I could marry her I would, but that it was out of my power. I said that money was no object, and that all I could do to make her happy and comfortable would be done."

"Very generous, I am sure," said Holmes with a sneer.

"See here, Mr Holmes. I came to you on a question of evidence, not on a question of morals. I'm not asking for your criticism."

"It is only for the young lady's sake that I touch your case at all," said Holmes sternly. "I don't know that anything she is accused of is really worse than what you have yourself admitted, that you have tried to ruin a defenceless girl who was under your roof. Some of you rich men have to be taught that all the world cannot be bribed into condoning your offences."

To my surprise, the Gold King took the reproof with equanimity.

"That's how I feel myself about it now. I thank God that my plans did not work out as I intended. She would have none of it, and she wanted to leave the house instantly."

"Why did she not?"

"Well, in the first place, others were dependent upon her, and it was no light matter for her to let them all down by sacrificing her living. When I had sworn – as I did – that she should never be molested again, she consented to remain. But there was another reason. She knew the influence she had over me, and that it was stronger than any other influence in the world. She wanted to use it for good."

"How?"

"Well, she knew something of my affairs. They are large, Mr Holmes – large beyond the belief of an ordinary man. I can make or break – and it is usually break. It wasn't individuals only. It was communities, cities, even nations. Business is a hard game, and the weak go to the wall. I played the game for all it was worth. I never squealed myself, and I never cared if the other fellow squealed. But she saw it different. I guess she was right. She believed and said that a fortune for one man that was more than he needed should not be built on ten thousand ruined men who were left without the means of life. That was how she saw it, and I guess she could see past the dollars to something that was more lasting. She found that I listened to what she said, and she believed she was serving the world by influencing my actions. So she stayed – and then this came along."

"Can you throw any light upon that?"

The Gold King paused for a minute or more, his head sunk in his hands, lost in deep thought.

"It's very black against her. I can't deny that. And women lead an inward life and may do things beyond the judgement of a man. At first I was so rattled and taken aback that I was ready to think she had been led away in some extraordinary fashion that was clean against her usual nature. One explanation came into my head. I give it to you, Mr Holmes, for what it is worth. There is no doubt that my wife was bitterly jealous. There is a soul-jealousy that can be as frantic as any body-jealousy, and though my wife had no cause – and I think she understood this – for the latter, she was aware that this English girl exerted an influence upon my mind and my acts that she herself never had. It was an influence for good, but that did not mend the matter. She was crazy with hatred, and the heat of the Amazon was always in her blood. She might have planned to murder Miss Dunbar – or we will say to threaten her with a gun and so frighten her into leaving us. Then there might have been a scuffle and the gun gone off and shot the woman who held it."

"That possibility had already occurred to me," said Holmes. "Indeed, it is the only obvious alternative to deliberate murder."

"But she utterly denies it."

"Well, that is not final – is it? One can understand that a woman placed in so awful a position might hurry home still in her bewilderment holding the revolver. She might even throw it down among her clothes, hardly knowing what she was doing, and when it was found she might try to lie her way out by a total denial, since all explanation was impossible. What is against such a supposition?"

"Miss Dunbar herself."

"Well, perhaps."

Holmes looked at his watch. "I have no doubt we can get the necessary permits this morning and reach Winchester by the evening train. When I have seen this young lady, it is very possible that I may be of more use to you in the matter, though I cannot promise that my conclusions will necessarily be such as you desire."

There was some delay in the official pass, and instead of reaching Winchester that day we went down to Thor Place, the Hampshire estate of Mr Neil Gibson. He did not accompany us himself, but we had the address of Sergeant Coventry, of the local police, who had first examined into the affair. He was a tall, thin, cadaverous man with a secretive and mysterious manner, which conveyed the idea that he knew or suspected a very great deal more than he dared say. He had a trick, too, of suddenly sinking his voice to a whisper as if he had come upon something of vital importance, though the information was usually commonplace enough. Behind these tricks of manner he soon showed himself to be a decent, honest fellow who was not too proud to admit that he was out of his depth and would welcome any help.

"Anyhow, I'd rather have you than Scotland Yard, Mr Holmes," said he. "If the Yard gets called into a case, then the local loses all credit for success and may be blamed for failure. Now, you play straight, so I've heard."

"I need not appear in the matter at all," said Holmes, to the evident relief of our melancholy acquaintance. "If I can clear it up, I don't ask to have my name mentioned."

"Well, it's very handsome of you, I am sure. And your friend, Doctor Watson, can be trusted, I know. Now, Mr Holmes, as we walk down to the place, there is one question I should like to ask you. I'd breathe it to no soul but you." He looked round as though he hardly dare utter the words. "Don't you think there might be a case against Mr Neil Gibson himself?"

"I have been considering that."

"You've not seen Miss Dunbar. She is a wonderful fine woman in every way. He may well have wished his wife out of the road. And these Americans are readier with pistols than our folk are. It was *his* pistol, you know."

"Was that clearly made out?"

"Yes, sir. It was one of a pair that he had."

"One of a pair? Where is the other?"

"Well, the gentleman has a lot of firearms of one sort and another. We never quite matched that particular pistol – but the box was made for two."

"If it was one of a pair, you should surely be able to match it."

"Well, we have them all laid out at the house, if you would care to look them over."

"Later, perhaps. I think we will walk down together and have a look at the scene of the tragedy."

This conversation had taken place in the little front room of Sergeant Coventry's humble cottage, which served as the local police station. A walk of half a mile or so across a windswept heath, all gold and bronze with the fading ferns, brought us to a side gate opening into the grounds of the Thor Place estate. A path led us through the pheasant preserves, and then from a clearing we saw the widespread, half-timbered house, half Tudor and half Georgian, upon the crest of the hill. Beside us there was a long, reedy pool, constricted in the centre where the main carriage drive passed over a stone bridge, but swelling into small lakes on either side. Our guide paused at the mouth of this bridge, and he pointed to the ground.

"That was where Mrs Gibson's body lay. I marked it by that stone."

"I understand that you were there before it was moved?"

"Yes – they sent for me at once."

"Who did?"

"Mr Gibson himself. The moment the alarm was given and he had rushed down with others from the house, he insisted that nothing should be moved until the police should arrive."

"That was sensible. I gathered from the newspaper report that the shot was fired from close quarters."

"Yes, sir, very close."

"Near the right temple?"

"Just behind it, sir."

"How did the body lie?"

"On the back, sir. No trace of a struggle. No marks. No weapon. The short note from Miss Dunbar was clutched in her left hand."

"Clutched, you say?"

"Yes, sir – we could hardly open the fingers."

"That is of great importance. It excludes the idea that anyone could have placed the note there after death in order to furnish a false clue. Dear me! The note, as I remember, was quite short. 'I will be at Thor Bridge at nine o'clock – G. Dunbar.' Was that not so?"

"Yes, sir."

"Did Miss Dunbar admit writing it?"

"Yes, sir."

"What was her explanation?"

"Her defence was reserved for the assizes. She would say nothing."

"The problem is certainly a very interesting one. The point of the letter is very obscure, is it not?"

"Well, sir," said the guide, "it seemed, if I may be so bold as to say so, the only really clear point in the whole case."

Holmes shook his head.

"Granting that the letter is genuine and was really written, it was certainly received some time before – say one hour or two. Why, then, was this lady still clasping it in her left hand? Why should she carry it so carefully? She did not need to refer to it in the interview. Does it not seem remarkable?"

"Well, sir, as you put it, perhaps it does."

"I think I should like to sit quietly for a few minutes and think it out." He seated himself upon the stone ledge of the bridge, and I could see his quick grey eyes darting their questioning glances in every direction. Suddenly he sprang up again and ran across to the opposite parapet, whipped his lens from his pocket and began to examine the stonework.

"This is curious," said he.

"Yes, sir – we saw the chip on the ledge. I expect it's been done by some passer-by."

The stonework was grey, but at this one point it showed white for a space not larger than a sixpence. When examined closely, one could see that the surface was chipped as by a sharp blow.

"It took some violence to do that," said Holmes thoughtfully. With his cane he struck the ledge several times without leaving a mark. "Yes, it was a hard knock. In a curious place, too. It was not from above, but from below, for you see that it is on the *lower* edge of the parapet."

"But it is at least fifteen feet from the body."

"Yes, it is fifteen feet from the body. It may have nothing to do with the matter, but it is a point worth noting. I do not think that we have anything more to learn here. There were no footsteps, you say?"

"The ground was iron-hard, sir. There were no traces at all."

"Then we can go. We will go up to the house first and look over these weapons of which you speak. Then we shall get on to Winchester, for I should desire to see Miss Dunbar before we go further."

Mr Neil Gibson had not returned from town, but we saw in the house the neurotic Mr Bates who had called upon us in the morning. He showed us with a sinister relish the formidable array of firearms of various shapes and sizes which his employer had accumulated in the course of an adventurous life.

"Mr Gibson has his enemies, as anyone would expect who knew him and his methods," said he. "He sleeps with a loaded revolver in the drawer beside his bed. He is a man of violence, sir, and there are times when all of us are afraid of him. I am sure that the poor lady who has passed was often terrified."

"Did you ever witness physical violence towards her?"

"No, I cannot say that. But I have heard words which were nearly as bad – words of cold, cutting contempt, even before the servants."

"Our millionaire does not seem to shine in private life," remarked Holmes as we made our way to the station. "Well, Watson, we have come on a good many facts, some of them new ones, and yet I seem some way from my conclusion. In spite of the very evident dislike which Mr Bates has to his employer, I gather from him that when the alarm came he was undoubtedly in his library. Dinner was over at eight thirty, and all was normal up to then. It is true that the alarm was somewhat late in the evening, but the tragedy certainly occurred about the hour named in the note. There is no evidence at all that Mr Gibson had been out of doors since his return from town at five o'clock. On the other hand, Miss Dunbar, as I understand it, admits that she had made an appointment to meet Mrs Gibson at the bridge. Beyond this she would say nothing, as her lawyer had advised her to reserve her defence. We have several very vital questions to ask that young lady, and my mind will not be easy until we have seen her. I must confess that the case would seem to me to be very black against her if it were not for one thing."

"And what is that, Holmes?"

"The finding of the pistol in her wardrobe."

"Dear me, Holmes!" I cried. "That seemed to me to be the most damning incident of all."

"Not so, Watson. It had struck me even at my first perfunctory reading as very strange, and now that I am in closer touch with the case it is my only firm ground for hope. We must look for consistency. Where there is a want of it, we must suspect deception."

"I hardly follow you."

"Well now, Watson, suppose for a moment that we visualize you in the character of a woman who, in a cold, premeditated fashion, is about to get rid of a rival. You have planned it. A note has been written. The victim has come. You have your weapon. The crime is done. It has been workmanlike and complete. Do you tell me that after carrying out so crafty a crime you would now ruin your reputation as a criminal by forgetting to fling your weapon into those adjacent reed beds which would for ever cover it, but you must needs carry it carefully home and put it in your own wardrobe, the very first place that would be searched? Your best friends would hardly call you a schemer, Watson, and yet I could not picture you doing anything so crude as that."

"In the excitement of the moment—"

"No, no, Watson, I will not admit that it is possible. Where a crime is coolly premeditated, then the means of covering it are coolly premeditated also. I hope, therefore, that we are in the presence of a serious misconception."

"But there is so much to explain."

"Well, we shall set about explaining it. When once your point of view is changed, the very thing which was so damning becomes a clue to the truth. For example, there is this revolver. Miss Dunbar disclaims all knowledge of it. On our new theory she is speaking truth when she says so. Therefore, it was placed in her wardrobe. Who placed it there? Someone who wished to incriminate her. Was not that person the actual criminal? You see how we come at once upon a most fruitful line of enquiry."

We were compelled to spend the night at Winchester, as the formalities had not yet been completed, but next morning, in the company of Mr Joyce Cummings, the rising barrister who was entrusted with the defence, we were allowed to see the young lady in her cell. I had expected from all that we had heard to see a beautiful woman, but I can never forget the effect which Miss Dunbar produced upon me. It was no wonder that even the masterful millionaire had found in her something more powerful than himself – something which could control and guide him. One felt, too, as one looked at that strong, clear-cut and yet sensitive face, that even should she be capable of some impetuous deed, nonetheless there was an innate nobility of character which would make her influence always for the good. She was a brunette, tall, with a noble figure and commanding presence, but her dark eyes had in them the appealing, helpless expression of the hunted creature who feels the nets around it, but can see no way out from the toils. Now, as she realized the presence and the help of my famous friend, there came a touch of colour in her wan cheeks, and a light of hope began to glimmer in the glance which she turned upon us.

"Perhaps Mr Neil Gibson has told you something of what occurred between us?" she asked in a low, agitated voice.

"Yes," Holmes answered. "You need not pain yourself by entering into that part of the story. After seeing you, I am prepared to accept Mr Gibson's statement both as to the influence which you had over him and as to the innocence of your relations with him. But why was the whole situation not brought out in court?"

"It seemed to me incredible that such a charge could be sustained. I thought that if we waited the whole thing must clear itself up without our being compelled to enter into painful details of the inner life of the family. But I understand that far from clearing it has become even more serious."

"My dear young lady," cried Holmes earnestly, "I beg you to have no illusions upon the point. Mr Cummings here would assure you that all the cards are at present against us, and that we must do everything that is possible if we are to win clear. It would be a cruel deception to pretend that you are not in very great danger. Give me all the help you can, then, to get at the truth."

"I will conceal nothing."

"Tell us, then, of your true relations with Mr Gibson's wife."

"She hated me, Mr Holmes. She hated me with all the fervour of her tropical nature. She was a woman who would do nothing by halves, and the measure of her love for her husband was the measure also of her hatred for me. It is probable that she misunderstood our relations. I would not wish to wrong her, but she loved so vividly in a physical sense that she could hardly understand the mental, and even spiritual, tie which held her husband to me, or imagine that it was only my desire to influence his power to good ends which kept me under his roof. I can see now that I was wrong. Nothing could justify me in remaining where I was a cause of unhappiness, and yet it is certain that the unhappiness would have remained even if I had left the house."

"Now, Miss Dunbar," said Holmes, "I beg you to tell us exactly what occurred that evening."

"I can tell you the truth so far as I know it, Mr Holmes, but I am in a position to prove nothing, and there are points – the most vital points – which I can neither explain nor can I imagine any explanation."

"If you will find the facts, perhaps others may find the explanation."

"With regard, then, to my presence at Thor Bridge that night, I received a note from Mrs Gibson in the morning. It lay on the table of the schoolroom, and it may have been left there by her own hand. It implored me to see her there after dinner, said she had something important to say to me, and asked me to leave an answer on the sundial in the garden, as she desired no one to be in our confidence. I saw no reason for such secrecy, but I did as she asked, accepting the appointment. She asked me to destroy her note, and I burned it in the schoolroom grate. She was very much afraid of her husband, who treated her with a harshness for which I frequently reproached him, and I could only imagine that she acted in this way because she did not wish him to know of our interview."

"Yet she kept your reply very carefully?"

"Yes. I was surprised to hear that she had it in her hand when she died."

"Well, what happened then?"

"I went down as I had promised. When I reached the bridge, she was waiting for me. Never did I realize till that moment how this poor creature hated me. She was like a madwoman – indeed, I think she *was* a madwoman, subtly mad with the deep power of deception which insane people may have. How else could she have met me with unconcern every day and yet had so raging a hatred of me in her heart? I will not say what she said. She poured her whole wild fury out in burning and horrible words. I did not even answer – I could not. It was dreadful to see her. I put my hands to my ears and rushed away. When I left her, she was standing still shrieking out her curses at me, in the mouth of the bridge."

"Where she was afterwards found?"

"Within a few yards from the spot."

"And yet, presuming that she met her death shortly after you left her, you heard no shot?"

"No, I heard nothing. But, indeed, Mr Holmes, I was so agitated and horrified by this terrible outbreak that I rushed to get back to the peace of my own room, and I was incapable of noticing anything which happened."

"You say that you returned to your room. Did you leave it again before next morning?"

"Yes – when the alarm came that the poor creature had met her death, I ran out with the others."

"Did you see Mr Gibson?"

"Yes – he had just returned from the bridge when I saw him. He had sent for the doctor and the police."

"Did he seem to you much perturbed?"

"Mr Gibson is a very strong, self-contained man. I do not think that he would ever show his emotions on the surface. But I, who knew him so well, could see that he was deeply concerned."

"Then we come to the all-important point. This pistol that was found in your room. Had you ever seen it before?"

"Never, I swear it."

"When was it found?"

"Next morning, when the police made their search."

"Among your clothes?"

"Yes – on the floor of my wardrobe, under my dresses."

"You could not guess how long it had been there?"

"It had not been there the morning before."

"How do you know?"

"Because I tidied out the wardrobe."

"That is final. Then someone came into your room and placed the pistol there in order to inculpate you."

"It must have been so."

"And when?"

"It could only have been at mealtime, or else at the hours when I would be in the schoolroom with the children."

"As you were when you got the note?"

"Yes – from that time onwards for the whole morning."

"Thank you, Miss Dunbar. Is there any other point which could help me in the investigation?"

"I can think of none."

"There was some sign of violence on the stonework of the bridge – a perfectly fresh chip just opposite the body. Could you suggest any possible explanation of that?"

"Surely it must be a mere coincidence."

"Curious, Miss Dunbar, very curious. Why should it appear at the very time of the tragedy, and why at the very place?"

"But what could have caused it? Only great violence could have such an effect."

Holmes did not answer. His pale, eager face had suddenly assumed that tense, faraway expression which I had learnt to associate with the supreme manifestations of his genius. So evident was the crisis in his mind that none of us dared to speak, and we sat, barrister, prisoner and myself, watching him in a concentrated and absorbed silence. Suddenly he sprang from his chair, vibrating with nervous energy and the pressing need for action.

"Come, Watson, come!" he cried.

"What is it, Mr Holmes?"

"Never mind, my dear lady. You will hear from me, Mr Cummings. With the help of the God of justice I will give you a case which will make England ring. You will get news by tomorrow, Miss Dunbar, and meanwhile take my assurance that the clouds are lifting and that I have every hope that the light of truth is breaking through."

It was not a long journey from Winchester to Thor Place, but it was long to me in my impatience, while for Holmes it was evident that it seemed endless – for, in his nervous restlessness, he could not sit still, but paced the carriage or drummed with his long, sensitive fingers upon the cushions beside him. Suddenly, however, as we neared our destination, he seated himself opposite to me – we had a first-class carriage to ourselves – and, laying a hand upon each of my knees, he looked into my eyes with the peculiarly mischievous gaze which was characteristic of his more imp-like moods.

"Watson," said he, "I have some recollection that you go armed upon these excursions of ours."

It was as well for him that I did so, for he took little care for his own safety when his mind was once absorbed by a problem, so that more than once my revolver had been a good friend in need. I reminded him of the fact.

"Yes, yes, I am a little absent-minded in such matters. But have you your revolver on you?"

I produced it from my hip pocket – a short, handy but very serviceable little weapon. He undid the catch, shook out the cartridges, and examined it with care.

"It's heavy – remarkably heavy," said he.

"Yes, it is a solid bit of work."

He mused over it for a minute.

"Do you know, Watson," said he, "I believe your revolver is going to have a very intimate connection with the mystery which we are investigating."

"My dear Holmes, you are joking."

"No, Watson, I am very serious. There is a test before us. If the test comes off, all will be clear. And the test will depend upon the conduct of this little weapon. One cartridge out. Now we will replace the other five and put on the safety catch. So! That increases the weight and makes it a better reproduction."

I had no glimmer of what was in his mind, nor did he enlighten me, but sat lost in thought until we pulled up in the little Hampshire station. We secured a ramshackle trap, and in a quarter of an hour were at the house of our confidential friend, the sergeant.

"A clue, Mr Holmes? What is it?"

"It all depends upon the behaviour of Doctor Watson's revolver," said my friend. "Here it is. Now, officer, can you give me ten yards of string?"

The village shop provided a ball of stout twine.

"I think that this is all we will need," said Holmes. "Now, if you please, we will get off on what I hope is the last stage of our journey."

The sun was setting, and turning the rolling Hampshire moor into a wonderful autumnal panorama. The sergeant, with many critical and incredulous glances, which showed his deep doubts of the sanity of my companion, lurched along beside us. As we approached the scene of the crime, I could see that my friend under all his habitual coolness was in truth deeply agitated.

"Yes," he said in answer to my remark, "you have seen me miss my mark before, Watson. I have an instinct for such things, and yet it has sometimes played me false. It seemed a certainty when first it flashed across my mind in the cell at Winchester, but one drawback of an active mind is that one can always conceive alternative explanations which would make our scent a false one. And yet... and yet... Well, Watson, we can but try."

As he walked, he had firmly tied one end of the string to the handle of the revolver. We had now reached the scene of the tragedy. With great care he marked out under the guidance of the policeman the exact spot where the body had been stretched. He then hunted among the heather and the ferns until he found a considerable stone. This he secured to the other end of his line of string, and he hung it over the parapet of the bridge so that it swung clear above the water. He then stood on the fatal spot, some distance from the edge of the bridge, with my revolver in his hand, the string being taut between the weapon and the heavy stone on the farther side.

"Now for it!" he cried.

At the words he raised the pistol to his head, and then let go his grip. In an instant it had been whisked away by the weight of the stone, had struck with a sharp crack against the parapet, and had vanished over the side into the water.* It had hardly gone before Holmes was kneeling beside the stonework, and a joyous cry showed that he had found what he expected.

"Was there ever a more exact demonstration?" he cried. "See, Watson, your revolver has solved the problem!" As he spoke, he pointed to a second chip of the exact size and shape of the first which had appeared on the under edge of the stone balustrade.

"We'll stay at the inn tonight," he continued as he rose and faced the astonished sergeant. "You will, of course, get a grappling hook and you will easily restore my friend's revolver. You will also find beside it the revolver, string and weight with which this vindictive woman attempted to disguise her own crime and to fasten a charge of murder upon an innocent victim. You can let Mr Gibson know that I will see him in the morning, when steps can be taken for Miss Dunbar's vindication."

Late that evening, as we sat together smoking our pipes in the village inn, Holmes gave me a brief review of what had passed.

"I fear, Watson," said he, "that you will not improve any reputation which I may have acquired by adding 'The Case of the Thor Bridge Mystery' to your annals. I have been sluggish in mind and wanting in that mixture of imagination and reality which is the basis of my art. I confess that the chip in the stonework was a sufficient clue to suggest the true solution, and that I blame myself for not having attained it sooner.

"It must be admitted that the workings of this unhappy woman's mind were deep and subtle, so that it was no very simple matter to unravel her plot. I do not think that in our adventures we have ever come across a stranger example of what perverted love can bring about. Whether Miss Dunbar was her rival in a physical or in a merely mental sense seems to have been equally unforgivable in her eyes. No doubt she blamed this innocent lady for all those harsh dealings and unkind words with which her husband tried to repel her too demonstrative affection. Her first resolution was to end her own life. Her second was to do it in such a way as to involve her victim in a fate which was worse far than any sudden death could be.

"We can follow the various steps quite clearly, and they show a remarkable subtlety of mind. A note was extracted very cleverly from Miss Dunbar which would make it appear that she had chosen the scene of the crime. In her anxiety that it should be discovered she somewhat overdid it, by holding it in her hand to the last. This alone should have excited my suspicions earlier than it did.

"Then she took one of her husband's revolvers – there was, as you saw, an arsenal in the house – and kept it for her own use. A similar one she concealed that morning in Miss Dunbar's wardrobe after discharging one barrel, which she could easily do in the woods without attracting attention. She then went down to the bridge, where she had contrived this exceedingly ingenious method for getting rid of her weapon. When Miss Dunbar appeared, she used her last breath in pouring out her hatred, and then, when she was out of hearing, carried out her terrible purpose. Every link is now in its place, and the chain is complete. The papers may ask why the mere was not dragged in the first instance, but it is easy to be wise after the event, and in any case the expanse of a reed-filled lake is no easy matter to drag unless you have a clear perception of what you are looking for and where. Well, Watson, we have helped a remarkable woman, and also a formidable man. Should they in the future join their forces, as seems not unlikely, the financial world may find that Mr Neil Gibson has learnt something in that schoolroom of Sorrow where our earthly lessons are taught."

THE ADVENTURE
OF THE CREEPING MAN

M R SHERLOCK HOLMES was always of opinion that I should publish the singular facts connected with Professor Presbury, if only to dispel once for all the ugly rumours which some twenty years ago agitated the university and were echoed in the learned societies of London. There were, however, certain obstacles in the way, and the true history of this curious case remained entombed in the tin box which contains so many records of my friend's adventures. Now we have at last obtained permission to ventilate the facts which formed one of the very last cases handled by Holmes before his retirement from practice. Even now a certain reticence and discretion have to be observed in laying the matter before the public.

It was one Sunday evening early in September of the year 1903 that I received one of Holmes's laconic messages: "Come at once if convenient – if inconvenient come all the same – s.h." The relations between us in those latter days were peculiar. He was a man of habits, narrow and concentrated habits, and I had become one of them. As an institution I was like the violin, the shag tobacco, the old black pipe, the index books, and others perhaps less excusable.* When it was a case of active work and a comrade was needed upon whose nerve he could place some reliance, my role was obvious. But apart from this I had uses. I was a whetstone for his mind. I stimulated him. He liked to think aloud in my presence. His remarks could hardly be said to be made to me – many of them would have been as appropriately addressed to his bedstead – but nonetheless, having formed the habit, it had become in some way helpful that I should register and interject. If I irritated him by a certain methodical slowness in my mentality, that irritation served only to make his own flame-like intuitions and impressions flash up the more vividly and swiftly. Such was my humble role in our alliance.

When I arrived at Baker Street, I found him huddled up in his armchair with updrawn knees, his pipe in his mouth and his brow furrowed with thought. It was clear that he was in the throes of some vexatious problem. With a wave of his hand he indicated my old armchair, but otherwise for half an hour he gave no sign that he was aware of my presence. Then with a start he seemed to come from his reverie, and, with his usual whimsical smile, he greeted me back to what had once been my home.

"You will excuse a certain abstraction of mind, my dear Watson," said he. "Some curious facts have been submitted to me within the last twenty-four hours, and they in turn have given rise to some speculations of a more general character. I have serious thoughts of writing a small monograph upon the uses of dogs in the work of the detective."

"But surely, Holmes, this has been explored," said I. "Bloodhounds – sleuth-hounds…"

"No, no, Watson – that side of the matter is, of course, obvious. But there is another which is far more subtle. You may recollect that in the case which you, in your sensational way, coupled with the Copper Beeches, I was able, by watching the mind of the child, to form a deduction as to the criminal habits of the very smug and respectable father."*

"Yes, I remember it well."

"My line of thoughts about dogs is analogous. A dog reflects the family life. Whoever saw a frisky dog in a gloomy family, or a sad dog in a happy one? Snarling people have snarling dogs – dangerous people have dangerous ones. And their passing moods may reflect the passing moods of others."

I shook my head. "Surely, Holmes, this is a little far-fetched," said I.

He had refilled his pipe and resumed his seat, taking no notice of my comment.

"The practical application of what I have said is very close to the problem which I am investigating. It is a tangled skein, you understand, and I am looking for a loose end. One possible loose end lies in the question: why does Professor Presbury's faithful wolfhound, Roy, endeavour to bite him?"

I sank back in my chair in some disappointment. Was it for so trivial a question as this that I had been summoned from my work? Holmes glanced across at me.

"The same old Watson!" said he. "You never learn that the gravest issues may depend upon the smallest things. But is it not on the face of it strange that a staid, elderly philosopher – you've heard of Presbury, of course, the famous Camford* physiologist? – that such a man, whose friend has been his devoted wolfhound, should now have been twice attacked by his own dog? What do you make of it?"

"The dog is ill."

"Well, that has to be considered. But he attacks no one else, nor does he apparently molest his master, save on very special occasions. Curious, Watson – very curious. But young Mr Bennett is before his time, if that is his ring. I had hoped to have a longer chat with you before he came."

There was a quick step on the stairs, a sharp tap at the door, and a moment later the new client presented himself. He was a tall, handsome youth about thirty, well dressed and elegant, but with something in his bearing which suggested the shyness of the student rather than the self-possession of the man of the world. He shook hands with Holmes, and then looked with some surprise at me.

"This matter is very delicate, Mr Holmes." he said. "Consider the relation in which I stand to Professor Presbury, both privately and publicly. I really can hardly justify myself if I speak before any third person."

"Have no fear, Mr Bennett. Doctor Watson is the very soul of discretion, and I can assure you that this is a matter in which I am very likely to need an assistant."

"As you like, Mr Holmes. You will, I am sure, understand my having some reserves in the matter."

"You will appreciate it, Watson, when I tell you that this gentleman, Mr Trevor Bennett, is professional assistant to the great scientist, lives under his roof and is engaged to his only daughter. Certainly we must agree that the professor has every claim upon his loyalty and devotion. But it may best be shown by taking the necessary steps to clear up this strange mystery."

"I hope so, Mr Holmes. That is my one object. Does Doctor Watson know the situation?"

"I have not had time to explain it."

"Then perhaps I had better go over the ground again before explaining some fresh developments."

"I will do so myself," said Holmes, "in order to show that I have the events in their due order. The professor, Watson, is a man of European reputation. His life has been academic. There has never been a breath of scandal. He is a widower with one daughter, Edith. He is, I gather, a man of very virile and positive – one might almost say combative – character. So the matter stood until a very few months ago.

"Then the current of his life was broken. He is sixty-one years of age, but he became engaged to the daughter of Professor Morphy, his colleague in the chair of Comparative Anatomy. It was not, as I understand, the reasoned courting of an elderly man, but rather the passionate frenzy of youth, for no one could have shown himself a more devoted lover. The lady, Alice Morphy, was a very perfect girl both in mind and body, so that there was every excuse for the professor's infatuation. Nonetheless, it did not meet with full approval in his own family."

"We thought it rather excessive," said our visitor.

"Exactly. Excessive and a little violent and unnatural. Professor Presbury was rich, however, and there was no objection upon the part of the father. The daughter, however, had other views, and there were already several candidates for her hand, who, if they were less eligible from a worldly point of view, were at least more of an age. The girl seemed to like the professor in spite of his eccentricities. It was only age which stood in the way.

"About this time a little mystery suddenly clouded the normal routine of the professor's life. He did what he had never done before. He left home and gave no indication where he was going. He was away a fortnight, and returned looking rather travel-worn. He made no allusion to where he had been, although he was usually the frankest of men. It chanced, however, that our client here, Mr Bennett, received a letter from a fellow student in Prague, who said that he was glad to have seen Professor Presbury there, although he had not been able to talk to him. Only in this way did his own household learn where he had been.

"Now comes the point. From that time onwards a curious change came over the professor. He became furtive and sly. Those around him had always the feeling that he was not the man that they had known, but that he was under some shadow which had darkened his higher qualities. His intellect was not affected. His lectures were as brilliant as ever. But always there was something new, something sinister and unexpected. His daughter, who was devoted to him, tried again and again to resume the old relations and to penetrate this mask which her father seemed to have put on. You, sir, as I understand, did the same – but all was in vain. And now, Mr Bennett, tell in your own words the incident of the letters."

"You must understand, Doctor Watson, that the professor had no secrets from me. If I were his son or his younger brother, I could not have more completely enjoyed his confidence. As his secretary I handled every paper which came to him, and I opened and sub-divided his letters. Shortly after his return, all this was changed. He told me that certain letters might come to him from London which would be marked by a cross under the stamp. These were to be set aside for his own eyes only. I may say that several of these did pass through my hands, that they had the EC* mark and were in an illiterate handwriting. If he answered them at all, the answers did not pass through my hands, nor into the letter basket in which our correspondence was collected."

"And the box," said Holmes.

"Ah, yes, the box. The professor brought back a little wooden box from his travels. It was the one thing which suggested a Continental tour, for it was one of those quaint carved things which one associates with Germany. This he placed in his instrument cupboard. One day, in looking for a cannula, I took up the box. To my surprise he was very angry, and reproved me in words which were quite savage for my curiosity. It was the first time such a thing had happened, and I was deeply hurt. I endeavoured to explain that it was a mere accident that I had touched the box, but all the evening I was conscious that he looked at me harshly and that the incident was rankling in his mind." Mr Bennett drew a little diary book from his pocket. "That was on 2nd July," said he.

"You are certainly an admirable witness," said Holmes. "I may need some of these dates which you have noted."

"I learnt method among other things from my great teacher. From the time that I observed abnormality in his behaviour, I felt that it was my duty to study his case. Thus I have it here that it was on that very day, 2nd July, that Roy attacked the professor, as he came from his study into the hall. Again on 11th July there was a scene of the same sort, and then I have a note of yet another upon 20th July. After that, we had to banish Roy to the stables. He was a dear, affectionate animal – but I fear I weary you."

Mr Bennett spoke in a tone of reproach, for it was very clear that Holmes was not listening. His face was rigid and his eyes gazed abstractedly at the ceiling. With an effort he recovered himself.

"Singular! Most singular!" he murmured. "These details were new to me, Mr Bennett. I think we have now fairly gone over the old ground, have we not? But you spoke of some fresh developments."

The pleasant, open face of our visitor clouded over, shadowed by some grim remembrance. "What I speak of occurred the night before last," said he. "I was lying awake about two in the morning, when I was aware of a dull, muffled sound coming from the passage. I opened my door and peeped out. I should explain that the professor sleeps at the end of the passage—"

"The date being?..." asked Holmes.

Our visitor was clearly annoyed at so irrelevant an interruption.

"I have said, sir, that it was the night before last – that is, 4th September."

Holmes nodded and smiled.

"Pray continue," said he.

"He sleeps at the end of the passage, and would have to pass my door in order to reach the staircase. It was a really terrifying experience, Mr Holmes. I think that I am as strong-nerved as my neighbours, but I was shaken by what I saw. The passage was dark, save that one window halfway along it threw a patch of light. I could see that something was coming along the passage, something dark and crouching. Then suddenly it emerged into the light, and I saw that it was he. He was crawling, Mr Holmes – crawling! He was not quite on his hands and knees. I should rather say on his hands and feet, with his face sunk between his hands. Yet he seemed to move with ease. I was so paralysed by the sight that it was not until he had reached my door that I was able to step forward and ask if I could assist him. His answer was extraordinary. He sprang up, spat out some atrocious word at me and hurried on past me and down the staircase. I waited about for an hour, but he did not come back. It must have been daylight before he regained his room."

"Well, Watson, what make you of that?" asked Holmes, with the air of the pathologist who presents a rare specimen.

"Lumbago,* possibly. I have known a severe attack make a man walk in just such a way, and nothing would be more trying to the temper."

"Good, Watson! You always keep us flat-footed on the ground. But we can hardly accept lumbago, since he was able to stand erect in a moment."

"He was never better in health," said Bennett. "In fact, he is stronger than I have known him for years. But there are the facts,

Mr Holmes. It is not a case in which we can consult the police, and yet we are utterly at our wits' end as to what to do, and we feel in some strange way that we are drifting towards disaster. Edith – Miss Presbury – feels as I do, that we cannot wait passively any longer."

"It is certainly a very curious and suggestive case. What do you think, Watson?"

"Speaking as a medical man," said I, "it appears to be a case for an alienist.* The old gentleman's cerebral processes were disturbed by the love affair. He made a journey abroad in the hope of breaking himself of the passion. His letters and the box may be connected with some other private transaction – a loan, perhaps, or share certificates, which are in the box."

"And the wolfhound no doubt disapproved of the financial bargain. No, no, Watson, there is more in it than this. Now, I can only suggest—"

What Sherlock Holmes was about to suggest will never be known, for at this moment the door opened and a young lady was shown into the room. As she appeared, Mr Bennett sprang up with a cry and ran forward with his hands out to meet those which she had herself outstretched.

"Edith, dear! Nothing the matter, I hope?"

"I felt I must follow you. Oh, Jack,* I have been so dreadfully frightened! It is awful to be there alone."

"Mr Holmes, this is the young lady I spoke of. This is my fiancée."

"We were gradually coming to that conclusion, were we not, Watson?" Holmes answered with a smile. "I take it, Miss Presbury, that there is some fresh development in the case, and that you thought we should know?"

Our new visitor – a bright, handsome girl of a conventional English type – smiled back at Holmes as she seated herself beside Mr Bennett.

"When I found Mr Bennett had left his hotel, I thought I should probably find him here. Of course, he had told me that he would consult you. But oh, Mr Holmes, can you do nothing for my poor father?"

"I have hopes, Miss Presbury, but the case is still obscure. Perhaps what you have to say may throw some fresh light upon it."

"It was last night, Mr Holmes. He had been very strange all day. I am sure that there are times when he has no recollection of what he does. He lives as in a strange dream. Yesterday was such a day. It was not my father with whom I lived. His outward shell was there, but it was not really he."

"Tell me what happened."

"I was awakened in the night by the dog barking most furiously. Poor Roy, he is chained now near the stable. I may say that I always sleep with my door locked, for, as Jack – as Mr Bennett – will tell you, we all have a feeling of impending danger. My room is on the second floor. It happened that the blind was up in my window, and there was bright moonlight outside. As I lay with my eyes fixed upon the square of light, listening to the frenzied barkings of the dog, I was amazed to see my father's face looking in at me. Mr Holmes, I nearly died of surprise and horror. There it was, pressed against the window pane, and one hand seemed to be raised as if to push up the window. If that window had opened, I think I should have gone mad. It was no delusion, Mr Holmes. Don't deceive yourself by thinking so. I dare say it was twenty seconds or so that I lay paralysed and watched the face. Then it vanished, but I could not – I could not spring out of bed and look out after it. I lay cold and shivering till morning. At breakfast he was sharp and fierce in manner, and made no allusion to the adventure of the night. Neither did I, but I gave an excuse for coming to town – and here I am."

Holmes looked thoroughly surprised at Miss Presbury's narrative.

"My dear young lady, you say that your room is on the second floor. Is there a long ladder in the garden?"

"No, Mr Holmes – that is the amazing part of it. There is no possible way of reaching the window – and yet he was there."

"The date being 5th September," said Holmes. "That certainly complicates matters."

It was the young lady's turn to look surprised. "This is the second time that you have alluded to the date, Mr Holmes," said Bennett. "Is it possible that it has any bearing upon the case?"

"It is possible – very possible – and yet I have not my full material at present."

"Possibly you are thinking of the connection between insanity and phases of the moon?"

"No, I assure you. It was quite a different line of thought. Possibly you can leave your notebook with me and I will check the dates. Now I think, Watson, that our line of action is perfectly clear. This young lady has informed us – and I have the greatest confidence in her intuition – that her father remembers little or nothing which occurs upon certain dates. We will therefore call upon him as if he had given us an appointment upon such a date. He will put it down to his own lack of memory. Thus we will open our campaign by having a good close view of him."

"That is excellent," said Mr Bennett. "I warn you, however, that the professor is irascible and violent at times."

Holmes smiled. "There are reasons why we should come at once – very cogent reasons if my theories hold good. Tomorrow, Mr Bennett, will certainly see us in Camford. There is, if I remember right, an inn called the Chequers, where the port used to be above mediocrity and the linen was above reproach. I think, Watson, that our lot for the next few days might lie in less pleasant places."

Monday morning found us on our way to the famous university town – an easy effort on the part of Holmes, who had no roots to pull up, but one which involved frantic planning and hurrying on my part, as my practice was by this time not inconsiderable. Holmes made no allusion to the case until after we had deposited our suitcases at the ancient hostel of which he had spoken.

"I think, Watson, that we can catch the professor just before lunch. He lectures at eleven, and should have an interval at home."

"What possible excuse have we for calling?"

Holmes glanced at his notebook.

"There was a period of excitement upon 25th August.* We will assume that he is a little hazy as to what he does at such times. If we insist that we are there by appointment, I think he will hardly venture to contradict us. Have you the effrontery necessary to put it through?"

"We can but try."

"Excellent, Watson! Compound of the Busy Bee and Excelsior.* We can but try – the motto of the firm. A friendly native will surely guide us."

Such a one on the back of a smart hansom swept us past a row of ancient colleges, and finally turning into a tree-lined drive pulled up at the door of a charming house, girt round with lawns and covered with purple wisteria. Professor Presbury was certainly surrounded with every sign not only of comfort but of luxury. Even as we pulled up, a grizzled head appeared at the front window, and we were aware of a pair of keen eyes from under shaggy brows which surveyed us through large horn glasses. A moment later we were actually in his sanctum, and the mysterious scientist, whose vagaries had brought us from London, was standing before us. There was certainly no sign of eccentricity either in his manner or appearance, for he was a portly, large-featured man – grave, tall and frock-coated, with the dignity of bearing which a lecturer needs. His eyes were his most remarkable feature: keen, observant and clever to the verge of cunning.

He looked at our cards. "Pray sit down, gentlemen. What can I do for you?"

Mr Holmes smiled amiably.

"It was the question which I was about to put to you, Professor."

"To me, sir!"

"Possibly there is some mistake. I heard through a second person that Professor Presbury of Camford had need of my services."

"Oh, indeed!" It seemed to me that there was a malicious sparkle in the intense grey eyes. "You heard that, did you? May I ask the name of your informant?"

"I am sorry, Professor, but the matter was rather confidential. If I have made a mistake, there is no harm done. I can only express my regret."

"Not at all. I should wish to go further into this matter. It interests me. Have you any scrap of writing, any letter or telegram, to bear out your assertion?"

"No, I have not."

"I presume that you do not go so far as to assert that I summoned you?"

"I would rather answer no questions," said Holmes.

"No, I dare say not," said the professor with asperity. "However, that particular one can be answered very easily without your aid."

He walked across the room to the bell. Our London friend, Mr Bennett, answered the call.

"Come in, Mr Bennett. These two gentlemen have come from London under the impression that they have been summoned. You handle all my correspondence. Have you a note of anything going to a person named Holmes?"

"No, sir," Bennett answered with a flush.

"That is conclusive," said the professor, glaring angrily at my companion. "Now, sir" – he leant forward with his two hands upon the table – "it seems to me that your position is a very questionable one."

Holmes shrugged his shoulders.

"I can only repeat that I am sorry that we have made a needless intrusion."

"Hardly enough, Mr Holmes!" the old man cried in a high screaming voice, with extraordinary malignancy upon his face. He got between us and the door as he spoke, and he shook his two hands at us with furious passion. "You can hardly get out of it so easily as that." His face was convulsed, and he grinned and gibbered at us in his senseless rage. I am convinced that we should have had to fight our way out of the room if Mr Bennett had not intervened.

"My dear Professor," he cried, "consider your position! Consider the scandal at the university! Mr Holmes is a well-known man. You cannot possibly treat him with such discourtesy."

Sulkily our host – if I may call him so – cleared the path to the door. We were glad to find ourselves outside the house and in the quiet of the tree-lined drive. Holmes seemed greatly amused by the episode.

"Our learned friend's nerves are somewhat out of order," said he. "Perhaps our intrusion was a little crude, and yet we have gained that personal contact which I desired. But, dear me, Watson, he is surely at our heels. The villain still pursues us."

There were the sounds of running feet behind, but it was, to my relief, not the formidable professor but his assistant who appeared round the curve of the drive. He came panting up to us.

"I am so sorry, Mr Holmes. I wished to apologize."

"My dear sir, there is no need. It is all in the way of professional experience."

"I have never seen him in a more dangerous mood. But he grows more sinister. You can understand now why his daughter and I are alarmed. And yet his mind is perfectly clear."

"Too clear!" said Holmes. "That was my miscalculation. It is evident that his memory is much more reliable than I had thought. By the way, can we, before we go, see the window of Miss Presbury's room?"

Mr Bennett pushed his way through some shrubs, and we had a view of the side of the house.

"It is there. The second on the left."

"Dear me, it seems hardly accessible. And yet you will observe that there is a creeper below and a water pipe above which give some foothold."

"I could not climb it myself," said Mr Bennett.

"Very likely. It would certainly be a dangerous exploit for any normal man."

"There was one other thing I wished to tell you, Mr Holmes. I have the address of the man in London to whom the professor writes. He seems to have written this morning, and I got it from his blotting paper. It is an ignoble position for a trusted secretary, but what else can I do?"

Holmes glanced at the paper and put it into his pocket.

"Dorak – a curious name. Slavonic,* I imagine. Well, it is an important link in the chain. We return to London this afternoon, Mr Bennett. I see no good purpose to be served by our remaining. We cannot arrest the professor, because he has done no crime, nor can we place him under constraint, for he cannot be proved to be mad. No action is as yet possible."

"Then what on earth are we to do?"

"A little patience, Mr Bennett. Things will soon develop. Unless I am mistaken, next Tuesday may mark a crisis. Certainly we shall be in Camford on that day. Meanwhile, the general position is undeniably unpleasant, and if Miss Presbury can prolong her visit…"

"That is easy."

"Then let her stay till we can assure her that all danger is past. Meanwhile, let him have his way and do not cross him. So long as he is in a good humour, all is well."

"There he is!" said Bennett in a startled whisper. Looking between the branches, we saw the tall, erect figure emerge from the hall door and look around him. He stood leaning forward, his hands swinging straight before him, his head turning from side to side. The secretary with a last wave slipped off among the trees, and we saw him presently rejoin his employer, the two entering the house together in what seemed to be animated and even excited conversation.

"I expect the old gentleman has been putting two and two together," said Holmes as we walked hotelwards. "He struck me as having a particularly clear and logical brain, from the little I saw of him. Explosive, no doubt, but then from his point of view he has something to explode about if detectives are put on his track and he suspects his own household of doing it. I rather fancy that friend Bennett is in for an uncomfortable time."

Holmes stopped at a post office and sent off a telegram on our way. The answer reached us in the evening, and he tossed it across to me.

HAVE VISITED THE COMMERCIAL ROAD AND SEEN DORAK. SUAVE PERSON, BOHEMIAN,* ELDERLY. KEEPS LARGE GENERAL STORE

MERCER

"Mercer is since your time," said Holmes. "He is my general utility man who looks up routine business. It was important to know something of the man with whom our professor was so secretly corresponding. His nationality connects up with the Prague visit."

"Thank goodness that something connects with something," said I. "At present we seem to be faced by a long series of inexplicable incidents with no bearing upon each other. For example, what possible connection can there be between an angry wolfhound and a visit to Bohemia, or either of them with a man crawling down a passage at night? As to your dates, that is the biggest mystification of all."

Holmes smiled and rubbed his hands. We were, I may say, seated in the old sitting room of the ancient hotel, with a bottle of the famous vintage of which Holmes had spoken on the table between us.

"Well, now, let us take the dates first," said he, his fingertips together and his manner as if he were addressing a class. "This excellent young man's diary shows that there was trouble upon 2nd July, and from then onwards it seems to have been at nine-day intervals, with, so far as I remember, only one exception. Thus the last outbreak upon Friday was on 3rd September, which also falls into the series, as did 25th August, which preceded it. The thing is beyond coincidence."

I was forced to agree.

"Let us, then, form the provisional theory that every nine days the professor takes some strong drug which has a passing but highly poisonous effect. His naturally violent nature is intensified by it. He learnt to take this drug while he was in Prague, and is now supplied with it by a Bohemian intermediary in London. This all hangs together, Watson!"

"But the dog, the face at the window, the creeping man in the passage?"

"Well, well, we have made a beginning. I should not expect any fresh developments until next Tuesday. In the mean time, we can only keep in touch with friend Bennett and enjoy the amenities of this charming town."

In the morning Mr Bennett slipped round to bring us the latest report. As Holmes had imagined, times had not been easy with him. Without exactly accusing him of being responsible for our presence, the professor had been very rough and rude in his speech, and evidently felt some strong grievance. This morning he was quite himself again, however, and had delivered his usual brilliant lecture to a crowded class. "Apart from his queer fits," said Bennett, "he has actually more energy and vitality than I can ever remember, nor was his brain ever clearer. But it's not he – it's never the man whom we have known."

"I don't think you have anything to fear now for a week at least," Holmes answered. "I am a busy man, and Doctor Watson has his patients to attend to. Let us agree that we meet here at this hour next Tuesday, and I shall be surprised if before we leave you again we are not able to explain, even if we cannot perhaps put an end to, your troubles. Meanwhile, keep us posted in what occurs."

I saw nothing of my friend for the next few days, but on the following Monday evening I had a short note asking me to meet him next day at the train. From what he told me as we travelled up to Camford, all was well: the peace of the professor's house had been unruffled, and his own conduct perfectly normal. This also was the report which was given us by Mr Bennett himself when he called upon us that evening at our old quarters in the Chequers. "He heard from his London correspondent today. There was a letter and there was a small packet, each with the cross under the stamp which warned me not to touch them. There has been nothing else."

"That may prove quite enough," said Holmes grimly. "Now, Mr Bennett, we shall, I think, come to some conclusion tonight. If my deductions are correct, we should have an opportunity of bringing matters to a head. In order to do so, it is necessary to hold the professor under observation. I would suggest, therefore, that you remain awake and on the lookout. Should you hear him pass your door, do not interrupt him, but follow him as discreetly as you can. Doctor Watson and I will not be far off. By the way, where is the key of that little box of which you spoke?"

"Upon his watch chain."

"I fancy our researches must lie in that direction. At the worst the lock should not be very formidable. Have you any other able-bodied man on the premises?"

"There is the coachman, Macphail."

"Where does he sleep?"

"Over the stables."

"We might possibly want him. Well, we can do no more until we see how things develop. Goodbye – but I expect that we shall see you before morning."

It was nearly midnight before we took our station among some bushes immediately opposite the hall door of the professor. It was a fine night, but chilly, and we were glad of our warm overcoats. There was a breeze, and clouds were scudding across the sky, obscuring from time to time the half-moon. It would have been a dismal vigil were it not for the expectation and excitement which carried us along, and the assurance of my comrade that we had probably reached the end of the strange sequence of events which had engaged our attention.

"If the cycle of nine days holds good, then we shall have the professor at his worst tonight," said Holmes. "The fact that these strange symptoms began after his visit to Prague, that he is in secret correspondence with a Bohemian dealer in London, who presumably represents someone in Prague, and that he received a packet from him this very day, all point in one direction. What he takes and why he takes it are still beyond our ken, but that it emanates in some way from Prague is clear enough. He takes it under definite directions which regulate this ninth-day system, which was the first point which attracted my attention. But his symptoms are most remarkable. Did you observe his knuckles?"

I had to confess that I did not.

"Thick and horny in a way which is quite new in my experience. Always look at the hands first, Watson. Then cuffs, trouser knees and boots. Very curious knuckles which can only be explained by the mode of progression observed by…" Holmes paused, and suddenly clapped his hand to his forehead. "Oh, Watson, Watson, what a fool I have been! It seems incredible, and yet it must be true. All points in one direction. How could I miss seeing the connection of ideas? Those knuckles – how could I have passed those knuckles? And the dog! And the ivy! It's surely time that I disappeared into that little farm of my dreams. Look out, Watson! Here he is! We shall have the chance of seeing for ourselves."

The hall door had slowly opened, and against the lamplit background we saw the tall figure of Professor Presbury. He was clad in his dressing gown. As he stood outlined in the doorway, he was erect but leaning forward with dangling arms, as when we saw him last.

Now he stepped forward into the drive, and an extraordinary change came over him. He sank down into a crouching position, and moved along upon his hands and feet, skipping every now and then as if he were overflowing with energy and vitality. He moved along the face of the house and then round the corner. As he disappeared, Bennett slipped through the hall door and softly followed him.

"Come, Watson, come!" cried Holmes, and we stole as softly as we could through the bushes until we had gained a spot whence we could see the other side of the house, which was bathed in the light of the half-moon. The professor was clearly visible crouching at the foot of the ivy-covered wall. As we watched him, he suddenly began with incredible agility to ascend it. From branch to branch he sprang, sure of foot and firm of grasp, climbing apparently in mere joy at his own powers, with no definite object in view. With his dressing gown flapping on each side of him, he looked like some huge bat glued against the side of his own house, a great square dark patch upon the moonlit wall. Presently he tired of this amusement, and, dropping from branch to branch, he squatted down into the old attitude and moved towards the stables, creeping along in the same strange way as before. The wolfhound was out now, barking furiously, and more excited than ever when it actually caught sight of its master. It was straining on its chain, and quivering with eagerness and rage. The professor squatted down very deliberately just out of reach of the hound, and began to provoke it in every possible way. He took handfuls of pebbles from the drive and threw them in the dog's face, prodded him with a stick which he had picked up, flicked his hands about only a few inches from the gaping mouth and endeavoured in every way to increase the animal's fury, which was already beyond all control. In all our adventures I do not know that I have ever seen a more strange sight than this impassive and still dignified figure crouching frog-like upon the ground and goading to a wilder exhibition of passion the maddened hound, which ramped and raged in front of him, by all manner of ingenious and calculated cruelty.

And then in a moment it happened! It was not the chain that broke, but it was the collar that slipped, for it had been made for a thick-necked Newfoundland.* We heard the rattle of falling metal, and the next instant dog and man were rolling on the ground together, the one roaring in rage, the other screaming in a strange shrill falsetto of terror. It was a very narrow thing for the professor's life. The savage creature had him fairly by the throat, its fangs had bitten deep, and he was senseless before we could reach them and drag the two apart. It might have been a dangerous task for us, but Bennett's voice and presence brought the great wolfhound instantly to reason. The uproar had brought the sleepy and astonished coachman from his room above the stables. "I'm not surprised," said he, shaking his head. "I've seen him at it before. I knew the dog would get him sooner or later."

The hound was secured, and together we carried the professor up to his room, where Bennett, who had a medical degree, helped me to dress his torn throat. The sharp teeth had passed danger-ously near the carotid artery, and the haemorrhage was serious. In half an hour the danger was past: I had given the patient an injection of morphia, and he had sunk into deep sleep. Then, and only then, were we able to look at each other and to take stock of the situation.

"I think a first-class surgeon should see him," said I.

"For God's sake, no!" cried Bennett. "At present the scandal is confined to our own household. It is safe with us. If it gets beyond these walls, it will never stop. Consider his position at the university, his European reputation, the feelings of his daughter."

"Quite so," said Holmes. "I think it may be quite possible to keep the matter to ourselves, and also to prevent its recurrence now that we have a free hand. The key from the watch chain, Mr Bennett. Macphail will guard the patient and let us know if there is any change. Let us see what we can find in the professor's mysterious box."

There was not much, but there was enough: an empty phial, another nearly full, a hypodermic syringe, several letters in a crabbed, foreign hand. The marks on the envelopes showed that they were those which had disturbed the routine of the secretary, and each was dated from the Commercial Road and signed "A. Dorak". They were mere invoices to say that a fresh bottle was being sent to Professor Presbury, or receipts to acknowledge money. There was one other envelope, however, in a more educated hand and bearing the Austrian stamp* with the postmark of Prague. "Here we have our material!" cried Holmes as he tore out the enclosure.

HONOURED COLLEAGUE (it ran). Since your esteemed visit I have thought much of your case, and though in your circum-stances there are some special reasons for the treatment, I would nonetheless enjoin caution, as my results have shown that it is not without danger of a kind.

It is possible that the serum of anthropoid* would have been better. I have, as I explained to you, used black-faced langur because a specimen was accessible. Langur is, of course, a crawler and climber, while anthropoid walks erect, and is in all ways nearer.

I beg you to take every possible precaution that there be no premature revelation of the process. I have one other client in England, and Dorak is my agent for both.

Weekly reports will oblige.

Yours with high esteem,

H. LOWENSTEIN

Lowenstein! The name brought back to me the memory of some snippet from a newspaper which spoke of an obscure scientist who was striving in some unknown way for the secret of rejuvenescence and the elixir of life. Lowenstein of Prague! Lowenstein with the wondrous strength-giving serum, tabooed by the profession because he refused to reveal its source. In a few words I said what I remembered. Bennett had taken a manual of zoology from the shelves. "'Langur,'" he read, "'the great black-faced monkey of the Himalayan slopes, biggest and most human of climbing monkeys.' Many details are added. Well, thanks to you, Mr Holmes, it is very clear that we have traced the evil to its source."

"The real source," said Holmes, "lies, of course, in that untimely love affair which gave our impetuous professor the idea that he could only gain his wish by turning himself into a younger man. When one tries to rise above Nature one is liable to fall below it. The highest type of man may revert to the animal if he leaves the straight road of destiny." He sat musing for a little with the phial in his hand, looking at the clear liquid within. "When I have written to this man and told him that I hold him criminally responsible for the poisons which he circulates, we will have no more trouble. But it may recur. Others may find a better way. There is danger there – a very real danger to humanity. Consider, Watson, that the material, the sensual, the worldly would all prolong their worthless lives. The spiritual would not avoid the call to something higher. It would be the survival of the least fit. What sort of cesspool may not our poor world become?" Suddenly the dreamer disappeared, and Holmes, the man of action, sprang from his chair. "I think there is nothing more to be said, Mr Bennett. The various incidents will now fit themselves easily into the general scheme. The dog, of course, was aware of the change far more quickly than you. His smell would ensure that. It was the monkey, not the professor, whom Roy attacked, just as it was the monkey who teased Roy. Climbing was a joy to the creature, and it was a mere chance, I take it, that the pastime brought him to the young lady's window. There is an early train to town, Watson, but I think we shall just have time for a cup of tea at the Chequers before we catch it."

THE ADVENTURE
OF THE LION'S MANE

I T IS A MOST SINGULAR THING that a problem which was
certainly as abstruse and unusual as any which I have faced
in my long professional career should have come to me after my
retirement – and be brought, as it were, to my very door. It occurred
after my withdrawal to my little Sussex home, when I had given
myself up entirely to that soothing life of nature for which I had
so often yearned during the long years spent amid the gloom of
London.* At this period of my life the good Watson had passed
almost beyond my ken. An occasional weekend visit was the most
that I ever saw of him. Thus I must act as my own chronicler. Ah!
Had he but been with me, how much he might have made of so
wonderful a happening and of my eventual triumph against every
difficulty! As it is, however, I must needs tell my tale in my own plain
way, showing by my words each step upon the difficult road which
lay before me as I searched for the mystery of the Lion's Mane.

My villa is situated upon the southern slope of the Downs,* commanding a great view of the Channel. At this point the coastline
is entirely of chalk cliffs, which can only be descended by a single,
long, tortuous path, which is steep and slippery. At the bottom of
the path lie a hundred yards of pebbles and shingle, even when
the tide is at full. Here and there, however, there are curves and
hollows which make splendid swimming pools filled afresh with
each flow. This admirable beach extends for some miles in each
direction, save only at one point where the little cove and village
of Fulworth break the line.

My house is lonely. I, my old housekeeper and my bees have the estate all to ourselves. Half a mile off, however, is Harold Stackhurst's well-known coaching establishment, the Gables – quite a large place, which contains some score of young fellows preparing for various professions, with a staff of several masters. Stackhurst himself was a well-known rowing Blue* in his day, and an excellent all-round scholar. He and I were always friendly from the day I came to the coast, and he was the one man who was on such terms with me that we could drop in on each other in the evenings without an invitation.

Towards the end of July 1907, there was a severe gale, the wind blowing up-Channel, heaping the seas to the base of the cliffs and leaving a lagoon at the turn of the tide. On the morning of which I speak, the wind had abated, and all nature was newly washed and fresh. It was impossible to work upon so delightful a day, and I strolled out before breakfast to enjoy the exquisite air. I walked along the cliff path which led to the steep descent to the beach. As I walked, I heard a shout behind me, and there was Harold Stackhurst waving his hand in cheery greeting.

"What a morning, Mr Holmes! I thought I should see you out."

"Going for a swim, I see."

"At your old tricks again," he laughed, patting his bulging pocket. "Yes. McPherson started early, and I expect I may find him there."

Fitzroy McPherson was the science master – a fine upstanding young fellow whose life had been crippled by heart trouble following rheumatic fever. He was a natural athlete, however, and excelled in every game which did not throw too great a strain upon him. Summer and winter he went for his swim, and, as I am a swimmer myself, I have often joined him.

At this moment we saw the man himself. His head showed above the edge of the cliff where the path ends. Then his whole figure appeared at the top, staggering like a drunken man. The next instant he threw up his hands, and, with a terrible cry, fell upon his face. Stackhurst and I rushed forward – it may have been fifty yards – and turned him on his back. He was obviously dying. Those glazed sunken eyes and dreadful livid cheeks could mean nothing else. One glimmer of life came into his face for an instant, and he uttered two or three words with an eager air of warning. They were slurred and indistinct, but to my ear the last of them, which burst in a shriek from his lips, were "the lion's mane". It was utterly irrelevant and unintelligible, and yet I could twist the sound into no other sense. Then he half-raised himself from the ground, threw his arms into the air and fell forward on his side. He was dead.

My companion was paralysed by the sudden horror of it, but I, as may well be imagined, had every sense on the alert. And I had need, for it was speedily evident that we were in the presence of an extraordinary case. The man was dressed only in his Burberry overcoat, his trousers and an unlaced pair of canvas shoes. As he fell over, his Burberry, which had been simply thrown round his shoulders, slipped off, exposing his trunk. We stared at it in amazement. His back was covered with dark red lines as though he had been terribly flogged by a thin wire scourge. The instrument with which this punishment had been inflicted was clearly flexible, for the long, angry weals curved round his shoulders and ribs. There was blood dripping down his chin, for he had bitten through his lower lip in the paroxysm of his agony. His drawn and distorted face told how terrible that agony had been.

I was kneeling and Stackhurst standing by the body when a shadow fell across us, and we found that Ian Murdoch was by our side. Murdoch was the mathematical coach at the establishment – a tall, dark, thin man, so taciturn and aloof that none can be said to have been his friend. He seemed to live in some high, abstract region of surds and conic sections* with little to connect him with ordinary life. He was looked upon as an oddity by the students, and would have been their butt, but there was some strange, outlandish blood in the man, which showed itself not only in his coal-black eyes and swarthy face, but also in occasional outbreaks of temper, which could only be described as ferocious. On one occasion, being plagued by a little dog belonging to McPherson, he had caught the creature up and hurled it through the plate-glass window, an action for which Stackhurst would certainly have given him his dismissal had he not been a very valuable teacher. Such was the strange, complex man who now appeared beside us. He seemed to be honestly shocked at the sight before him, though the incident of the dog may show that there was no great sympathy between the dead man and himself.

"Poor fellow! Poor fellow! What can I do? How can I help?"

"Were you with him? Can you tell us what has happened?"

"No, no, I was late this morning. I was not on the beach at all. I have come straight from the Gables. What can I do?"

"You can hurry to the police station at Fulworth. Report the matter at once."

Without a word he made off at top speed, and I proceeded to take the matter in hand, while Stackhurst, dazed at this tragedy, remained by the body. My first task naturally was to note who was on the beach. From the top of the path I could see the whole sweep of it, and it was absolutely deserted save that two or three dark figures could be seen far away moving towards the village of Fulworth. Having satisfied myself upon this point, I walked slowly down the path. There was clay or soft marl mixed with the chalk, and every here and there I saw the same footstep, both ascending and descending. No one else had gone down to the beach by this track that morning. At one place I observed the print of an open hand with the fingers towards the incline. This could only mean that poor McPherson had fallen as he ascended. There were rounded depressions, too, which suggested that he had come down upon his knees more than once. At the bottom of the path was the considerable lagoon left by the retreating tide. At the side of it McPherson had undressed, for there lay his towel on a rock. It was folded and dry, so that it would seem that after all he had never entered the water. Once or twice, as I hunted round amid the hard shingle, I came on little patches of sand where the print of his canvas shoe, and also of his naked foot, could be seen. The latter fact proved that he had made all ready to bathe, though the towel indicated that he had not actually done so.

And here was the problem clearly defined – as strange a one as had ever confronted me. The man had not been on the beach more than a quarter of an hour at the most. Stackhurst had followed him from the Gables, so there could be no doubt about that. He had gone to bathe and had stripped, as the naked footsteps showed. Then he had suddenly huddled on his clothes again – they were all dishevelled and unfastened – and he had returned without bathing, or at any rate without drying himself. And the reason for his change of purpose had been that he had been scourged in some savage, inhuman fashion, tortured until he bit his lip through in his agony, and was left with only strength enough to crawl away and to die. Who had done this barbarous deed? There were, it is true, small grottoes and caves in the base of the cliffs, but the low sun shone directly into them, and there was no place for concealment. Then, again, there were those distant figures on the beach. They seemed too far away to have been connected with the crime, and the broad lagoon in which McPherson had intended to bathe lay between him and them, lapping up to the rocks. On the sea two or three fishing boats were at no great distance. Their occupants might be examined at our leisure. There were several roads for enquiry, but none which led to any very obvious goal.

When I at last returned to the body, I found that a little group of wandering folk had gathered round it. Stackhurst was, of course, still there, and Ian Murdoch had just arrived with Anderson, the village constable, a big, ginger-moustached man of the slow solid Sussex breed – a breed which covers much good sense under a heavy, silent exterior. He listened to everything, took note of all we said, and finally drew me aside.

"I'd be glad of your advice, Mr Holmes. This is a big thing for me to handle, and I'll hear of it from Lewes* if I go wrong."

I advised him to send for his immediate superior, and for a doctor – also to allow nothing to be moved, and as few fresh footmarks as possible to be made, until they came. In the mean time I searched the dead man's pockets. There were his handkerchief, a large knife and a small folding card case. From this projected a slip of paper, which I unfolded and handed to the constable. There was written on it in a scrawling, feminine hand: "I will be there, you may be sure – Maudie." It read like a love affair, an assignation, though when and where were a blank. The constable replaced it in the card case and returned it with the other things to the pockets of the Burberry. Then, as nothing more suggested itself, I walked back to my house for breakfast, having first arranged that the base of the cliffs should be thoroughly searched.

Stackhurst was round in an hour or two to tell me that the body had been removed to the Gables, where the inquest would be held. He brought with him some serious and definite news. As I expected, nothing had been found in the small caves below the cliff, but he had examined the papers in McPherson's desk, and there were several which showed an intimate correspondence with a certain Miss Maud Bellamy, of Fulworth. We had then established the identity of the writer of the note.

"The police have the letters," he explained. "I could not bring them. But there is no doubt that it was a serious love affair. I see no reason, however, to connect it with that horrible happening save, indeed, that the lady had made an appointment with him."

"But hardly at a bathing pool which all of you were in the habit of using," I remarked.

"It is mere chance," said he, "that several of the students were not with McPherson."

"Was it mere chance?"

Stackhurst knit his brows in thought.

"Ian Murdoch held them back," said he. "He would insist upon some algebraic demonstration before breakfast. Poor chap, he is dreadfully cut up about it all."

"And yet I gather that they were not friends."

"At one time they were not. But for a year or more Murdoch has been as near to McPherson as he ever could be to anyone. He is not of a very sympathetic disposition by nature."

"So I understand. I seem to remember your telling me once about a quarrel over the ill usage of a dog."

"That blew over all right."

"But left some vindictive feeling, perhaps."

"No, no – I am sure they were real friends."

"Well, then, we must explore the matter of the girl. Do you know her?"

"Everyone knows her. She is the beauty of the neighbourhood – a real beauty, Holmes, who would draw attention everywhere. I knew that McPherson was attracted by her, but I had no notion that it had gone so far as these letters would seem to indicate."

"But who is she?"

"She is the daughter of old Tom Bellamy, who owns all the boats and bathing cots* at Fulworth. He was a fisherman to start with, but is now a man of some substance. He and his son William run the business."

"Shall we walk into Fulworth and see them?"

"On what pretext?"

"Oh, we can easily find a pretext. After all, this poor man did not ill-use himself in this outrageous way. Some human hand was on the handle of that scourge, if indeed it was a scourge which inflicted the injuries. His circle of acquaintances in this lonely place was surely limited. Let us follow it up in every direction, and we can hardly fail to come upon the motive, which in turn should lead us to the criminal."

It would have been a pleasant walk across the thyme-scented Downs had our minds not been poisoned by the tragedy we had witnessed. The village of Fulworth lies in a hollow curving in a semicircle round the bay. Behind the old-fashioned hamlet several modern houses have been built upon the rising ground. It was to one of these that Stackhurst guided me.

"That's the Haven, as Bellamy called it. The one with the corner tower and slate roof. Not bad for a man who started with nothing but... By Jove, look at that!"

The garden gate of the Haven had opened, and a man had emerged. There was no mistaking that tall, angular, straggling figure. It was Ian Murdoch, the mathematician. A moment later we confronted him upon the road.

"Hullo!" said Stackhurst. The man nodded, gave us a sideways glance from his curious dark eyes, and would have passed us, but his principal pulled him up.

"What were you doing there?" he asked.

Murdoch's face flushed with anger. "I am your subordinate, sir, under your roof. I am not aware that I owe you any account of my private actions."

Stackhurst's nerves were near the surface after all he had endured. Otherwise, perhaps, he would have waited. Now he lost his temper completely.

"In the circumstances your answer is pure impertinence, Mr Murdoch."

"Your own question might perhaps come under the same heading."

"This is not the first time that I have had to overlook your insubordinate ways. It will certainly be the last. You will kindly make fresh arrangements for your future as speedily as you can."

"I had intended to do so. I have lost today the only person who made the Gables habitable."

He strode off upon his way, while Stackhurst, with angry eyes, stood glaring after him. "Is he not an impossible, intolerable man?" he cried.

The one thing that impressed itself forcibly upon my mind was that Mr Ian Murdoch was taking the first chance to open a path of escape from the scene of the crime. Suspicion, vague and nebulous, was now beginning to take outline in my mind. Perhaps the visit to the Bellamys might throw some further light upon the matter. Stackhurst pulled himself together, and we went forward to the house.

Mr Bellamy proved to be a middle-aged man with a flaming-red beard. He seemed to be in a very angry mood, and his face was soon as florid as his hair.

"No, sir, I do not desire any particulars. My son here" – indicating a powerful young man, with a heavy, sullen face, in the corner of the sitting room – "is of one mind with me that Mr McPherson's attentions to Maud were insulting. Yes, sir, the word 'marriage' was never mentioned, and yet there were letters and meetings, and a great deal more of which neither of us could approve. She has no mother, and we are her only guardians. We are determined—"

But the words were taken from his mouth by the appearance of the lady herself. There was no gainsaying that she would have graced any assembly in the world. Who could have imagined that so rare a flower would grow from such a root and in such an atmosphere? Women have seldom been an attraction to me, for my brain has always governed my heart, but I could not look upon her perfect, clear-cut face, with all the soft freshness of the Downlands in her delicate colouring, without realizing that no young man would cross her path unscathed. Such was the girl who had pushed open the door and stood now, wide-eyed and intense, in front of Harold Stackhurst.

"I know already that Fitzroy is dead," she said. "Do not be afraid to tell me the particulars."

"This other gentleman of yours let us know the news," explained the father.

"There is no reason why my sister should be brought into the matter," growled the younger man.

The sister turned a sharp, fierce look upon him.

"This is my business, William. Kindly leave me to manage it in my own way. By all accounts there has been a crime committed. If I can help to show who did it, it is the least I can do for him who is gone."

She listened to a short account from my companion, with a composed concentration which showed me that she possessed strong character as well as great beauty. Maud Bellamy will always remain in my memory as a most complete and remarkable woman. It seems that she already knew me by sight, for she turned to me at the end.

"Bring them to justice, Mr Holmes. You have my sympathy and my help, whoever they may be." It seemed to me that she glanced defiantly at her father and brother as she spoke.

"Thank you," said I. "I value a woman's instinct in such matters. You use the word 'they'. You think that more than one was concerned?"

"I knew Mr McPherson well enough to be aware that he was a brave and a strong man. No single person could ever have inflicted such an outrage upon him."

"Might I have one word with you alone?"

"I tell you, Maud, not to mix yourself up in the matter," cried her father angrily.

She looked at me helplessly. "What can I do?"

"The whole world will know the facts presently, so there can be no harm if I discuss them here," said I. "I should have preferred privacy, but if your father will not allow it, he must share the deliberations." Then I spoke of the note which had been found in the dead man's pocket. "It is sure to be produced at the inquest. May I ask you to throw any light upon it that you can?"

"I see no reason for mystery," she answered. "We were engaged to be married, and we only kept it secret because Fitzroy's uncle, who is very old and said to be dying, might have disinherited him if he had married against his wish. There was no other reason."

"You could have told us," growled Mr Bellamy.

"So I would, Father, if you had ever shown sympathy."

"I object to my girl picking up with men outside her own station."

"It was your prejudice against him which prevented us from telling you. As to this appointment" – she fumbled in her dress and produced a crumpled note – "it was in answer to this."

DEAREST (ran the message), The old place on the beach just after sunset on Tuesday. It is the only time I can get away – F.M.

"Tuesday was today, and I had meant to meet him tonight."

I turned over the paper. "This never came by post. How did you get it?"

"I would rather not answer that question. It has really nothing to do with the matter which you are investigating. But anything which bears upon that I will most freely answer."

She was as good as her word, but there was nothing which was helpful in our investigation. She had no reason to think that her fiancé had any hidden enemy, but she admitted that she had had several warm admirers.

"May I ask if Mr Ian Murdoch was one of them?"

She blushed and seemed confused.

"There was a time when I thought he was. But that was all changed when he understood the relations between Fitzroy and myself."

Again the shadow round this strange man seemed to me to be taking more definite shape. His record must be examined. His rooms must be privately searched. Stackhurst was a willing collaborator, for in his mind also suspicions were forming. We returned from our visit to the Haven with the hope that one free end of this tangled skein was already in our hands.

A week passed. The inquest had thrown no light upon the matter and had been adjourned for further evidence. Stackhurst had made discreet enquiry about his subordinate, and there had been a superficial search of his room, but without result. Personally, I had gone over the whole ground again, both physically and mentally, but with no new conclusions. In all my chronicles the reader will find no case which brought me so completely to the limit of my powers. Even my imagination could conceive no solution to the mystery. And then there came the incident of the dog.

It was my old housekeeper who heard of it first by that strange wireless by which such people collect the news of the countryside.

"Sad story this, sir, about Mr McPherson's dog," said she one evening.

I do not encourage such conversations, but the words arrested my attention.

"What of Mr McPherson's dog?"

"Dead, sir. Died of grief for its master."

"Who told you this?"

"Why, sir, everyone is talking of it. It took on terrible, and has eaten nothing for a week. Then today two of the young gentlemen from the Gables found it dead – down on the beach, sir, at the very place where its master met his end."

"At the very place." The words stood out clear in my memory. Some dim perception that the matter was vital rose in my mind. That the dog should die was after the beautiful, faithful nature of dogs. But 'in the very place'! Why should this lonely beach be fatal to it? Was it possible that it, also, had been sacrificed to some revengeful feud? Was it possible?... Yes, the perception was dim, but already something was building up in my mind. In a few minutes I was on my way to the Gables, where I found Stackhurst in his study. At my request he sent for Sudbury and Blount, the two students who had found the dog.

"Yes, it lay on the very edge of the pool," said one of them. "It must have followed the trail of its dead master."

I saw the faithful little creature, an Airedale terrier,* laid out upon the mat in the hall. The body was stiff and rigid, the eyes projecting and the limbs contorted. There was agony in every line of it.

From the Gables I walked down to the bathing pool. The sun had sunk, and the shadow of the great cliff lay black across the water, which glimmered dully like a sheet of lead. The place was deserted, and there was no sign of life save for two seabirds circling and screaming overhead. In the fading light I could dimly make out the little dog's spoor upon the sand round the very rock on which his master's towel had been laid. For a long time I stood in deep meditation while the shadows grew darker around me. My mind was filled with racing thoughts. You have known what it was to be in a nightmare in which you feel that there is some all-important thing for which you search and which you know is there, though it remains forever just beyond your reach. That was how I felt that evening as I stood alone by that place of death. Then at last I turned and walked slowly homewards.

I had just reached the top of the path when it came to me. Like a flash, I remembered the thing for which I had so eagerly and vainly grasped. You will know, or Watson has written in vain, that I hold a vast store of out-of-the-way knowledge, without scientific system, but very available for the needs of my work. My mind is like a crowded boxroom with packets of all sorts stowed away therein – so many that I may well have but a vague perception of what was there. I had known that there was something which might bear upon this matter. It was still vague, but at least I knew how I could make it clear. It was monstrous, incredible, and yet it was always a possibility. I would test it to the full.

There is a great garret in my little house which is stuffed with books. It was into this that I plunged and rummaged for an hour. At the end of that time I emerged with a little chocolate-and-silver volume. Eagerly I turned up the chapter of which I had a dim remembrance. Yes, it was indeed a far-fetched and unlikely proposition, and yet I could not be at rest until I had made sure if it might, indeed, be so. It was late when I retired, with my mind eagerly awaiting the work of the morrow.

But that work met with an annoying interruption. I had hardly swallowed my early cup of tea and was starting for the beach when I had a call from Inspector Bardle of the Sussex Constabulary – a steady, solid, bovine man with thoughtful eyes, which looked at me now with a very troubled expression.

"I know your immense experience, sir," said he. "This is quite unofficial, of course, and need go no further. But I am fairly up against it in this McPherson case. The question is: shall I make an arrest, or shall I not?"

"Meaning Mr Ian Murdoch?"

"Yes, sir. There is really no one else when you come to think of it. That's the advantage of this solitude. We narrow it down to a very small compass. If he did not do it, then who did?"

"What have you against him?"

He had gleaned along the same furrows as I had. There was Murdoch's character and the mystery which seemed to hang round the man. His furious bursts of temper, as shown in the incident of the dog. The fact that he had quarrelled with McPherson in the past, and that there was some reason to think that he might have resented his attentions to Miss Bellamy. He had all my points, but no fresh ones, save that Murdoch seemed to be making every preparation for departure.

"What would my position be if I let him slip away with all this evidence against him?" The burly, phlegmatic man was sorely troubled in his mind.

"Consider," I said, "all the essential gaps in your case. On the morning of the crime he can surely prove an alibi. He had been with his scholars till the last moment, and within a few minutes of McPherson's appearance he came upon us from behind. Then bear in mind the absolute impossibility that he could single-handed have inflicted this outrage upon a man quite as strong as himself. Finally, there is this question of the instrument with which these injuries were inflicted."

"What could it be but a scourge or flexible whip of some sort?"

"Have you examined the marks?" I asked.

"I have seen them. So has the doctor."

"But I have examined them very carefully with a lens. They have peculiarities."

"What are they, Mr Holmes?"

I stepped to my bureau and brought out an enlarged photograph. "This is my method in such cases," I explained.

"You certainly do things thoroughly, Mr Holmes."

"I should hardly be what I am if I did not. Now, let us consider this weal which extends round the right shoulder. Do you observe nothing remarkable?"

"I can't say I do."

"Surely it is evident that it is unequal in its intensity. There is a dot of extravasated* blood here, and another there. There are similar indications in this other weal down here. What can that mean?"

"I have no idea. Have you?"

"Perhaps I have. Perhaps I haven't. I may be able to say more soon. Anything which will define what made that mark will bring us a long way towards the criminal."

"It is, of course, an absurd idea," said the policeman, "but if a red-hot net of wire had been laid across the back, then these better-marked points would represent where the meshes crossed each other."

"A most ingenious comparison. Or shall we say a very stiff cat-o'-nine-tails with small hard knots upon it?"

"By Jove, Mr Holmes, I think you have hit it."

"Or there may be some very different cause, Mr Bardle. But your case is far too weak for an arrest. Besides, we have those last words: 'lion's mane'."

"I have wondered whether Ian—"

"Yes, I have considered that. If the second word had borne any resemblance to Murdoch – but it did not. He gave it almost in a shriek. I am sure that it was 'mane'."

"Have you no alternative, Mr Holmes?"

"Perhaps I have. But I do not care to discuss it until there is something more solid to discuss."

"And when will that be?"

"In an hour – possibly less."

The inspector rubbed his chin and looked at me with dubious eyes.

"I wish I could see what was in your mind, Mr Holmes. Perhaps it's those fishing boats."

"No, no – they were too far out."

"Well, then, is it Bellamy and that big son of his? They were not too sweet upon Mr McPherson. Could they have done him a mischief?"

"No, no – you won't draw me until I am ready," said I with a smile. "Now, Inspector, we each have our own work to do. Perhaps if you were to meet me here at midday?…"

So far we had got when there came the tremendous interruption which was the beginning of the end.

My outer door was flung open – there were blundering footsteps in the passage, and Ian Murdoch staggered into the room, pallid, dishevelled, his clothes in wild disorder, clawing with his bony hands at the furniture to hold himself erect. "Brandy! Brandy!" he gasped, and fell groaning upon the sofa.

He was not alone. Behind him came Stackhurst, hatless and panting, almost as distrait as his companion.

"Yes, yes, brandy!" he cried. "The man is at his last gasp. It was all I could do to bring him here. He fainted twice upon the way."

Half a tumbler of the raw spirit brought about a wondrous change. He pushed himself up on one arm and swung his coat from off his shoulders. "For God's sake! Oil, opium, morphia!" he cried. "Anything to ease this infernal agony!"

The inspector and I cried out at the sight. There, criss-crossed upon the man's naked shoulder, was the same strange reticulated pattern of red, inflamed lines which had been the death mark of Fitzroy McPherson.

The pain was evidently terrible, and was more than local, for the sufferer's breathing would stop for a time, his face would turn black, and then with loud gasps he would clap his hand to his heart, while his brow dropped beads of sweat. At any moment he might die. More and more brandy was poured down his throat, each fresh dose bringing him back to life. Pads of cotton wool soaked in salad oil seemed to take the agony from the strange wounds.

At last his head fell heavily upon the cushion. Exhausted Nature had taken refuge in its last storehouse of vitality. It was half a sleep and half a faint, but at least it was ease from pain.

To question him had been impossible, but the moment we were assured of his condition Stackhurst turned upon me.

"My God!" he cried. "What is it, Holmes? What is it?"

"Where did you find him?"

"Down on the beach. Exactly where poor McPherson met his end. If this man's heart had been weak as McPherson's was, he would not be here now. More than once I thought he was gone as I brought him up. It was too far to the Gables, so I made for you."

"Did you see him on the beach?"

"I was walking on the cliff when I heard his cry. He was at the edge of the water, reeling about like a drunken man. I ran down, threw some clothes about him, and brought him up. For Heaven's sake, Holmes, use all the powers you have and spare no pains to lift the curse from this place, for life is becoming unendurable. Can you, with all your worldwide reputation, do nothing for us?"

"I think I can, Stackhurst. Come with me now! And you, Inspector, come along! We will see if we cannot deliver this murderer into your hands."

Leaving the unconscious man in the charge of my housekeeper, we all three went down to the deadly lagoon. On the shingle there was piled a little heap of towels and clothes, left by the stricken man. Slowly I walked round the edge of the water, my comrades in Indian file* behind me. Most of the pool was quite shallow, but under the cliff where the beach was hollowed out it was four or five feet deep. It was to this part that a swimmer would naturally go, for it formed a beautiful pellucid green pool as clear as crystal. A line of rocks lay above it at the base of the cliff, and along this I led the way, peering eagerly into the depths beneath me. I had reached the deepest and stillest pool when my eyes caught that for which they were searching, and I burst into a shout of triumph.

"*Cyanea!*" I cried. "*Cyanea!* Behold the lion's mane!"*

The strange object at which I pointed did indeed look like a tangled mass torn from the mane of a lion. It lay upon a rocky shelf some three feet under the water – a curious, waving, vibrating, hairy creature with streaks of silver among its yellow tresses. It pulsated with a slow, heavy dilation and contraction.

"It has done mischief enough. Its day is over!" I cried. "Help me, Stackhurst! Let us end the murderer for ever."

There was a big boulder just above the ledge, and we pushed it until it fell with a tremendous splash into the water. When the ripples had cleared, we saw that it had settled upon the ledge below.

One flapping edge of yellow membrane showed that our victim was beneath it. A thick oily scum oozed out from below the stone and stained the water round, rising slowly to the surface.

"Well, this gets me!" cried the inspector. "What was it, Mr Holmes? I'm born and bred in these parts, but I never saw such a thing. It don't belong to Sussex."

"Just as well for Sussex," I remarked. "It may have been the south-west gale that brought it up.* Come back to my house, both of you, and I will give you the terrible experience of one who has good reason to remember his own meeting with the same peril of the seas."

When we reached my study, we found that Murdoch was so far recovered that he could sit up. He was dazed in mind, and every now and then was shaken by a paroxysm of pain. In broken words he explained that he had no notion what had occurred to him, save that terrific pangs had suddenly shot through him, and that it had taken all his fortitude to reach the bank.

"Here is a book," I said, taking up the little volume, "which first brought light into what might have been for ever dark. It is *Out of Doors*, by the famous observer J.G. Wood.* Wood himself very nearly perished from contact with this vile creature, so he wrote with a very full knowledge. *Cyanea capillata* is the miscreant's full name, and he can be as dangerous to life as, and far more painful than, the bite of the cobra. Let me briefly give this extract.

If the bather should see a loose roundish mass of tawny membranes and fibres, something like very large handfuls of lion's mane and silver paper, let him beware, for this is the fearful stinger, *Cyanea capillata*.

"Could our sinister acquaintance be more clearly described?

"He goes on to tell his own encounter with one when swimming off the coast of Kent. He found that the creature radiated almost invisible filaments to the distance of fifty feet, and that anyone within that circumference from the deadly centre was in danger of death. Even at a distance the effect upon Wood was almost fatal.

The multitudinous threads caused light scarlet lines upon the skin which on closer examination resolved into minute dots or pustules, each dot charged as it were with a red-hot needle making its way through the nerves.

"The local pain was, as he explains, the least part of the exquisite torment.

Pangs shot through the chest, causing me to fall as if struck by a bullet. The pulsation would cease, and then the heart would give six or seven leaps as if it would force its way through the chest.

"It nearly killed him, although he had only been exposed to it in the disturbed ocean and not in the narrow calm waters of a bathing pool. He says that he could hardly recognize himself afterwards, so white, wrinkled and shrivelled was his face. He gulped down brandy, a whole bottleful, and it seems to have saved his life. There is the book, Inspector. I leave it with you, and you cannot doubt that it contains a full explanation of the tragedy of poor McPherson."

"And incidentally exonerates me," remarked Ian Murdoch with a wry smile. "I do not blame you, Inspector, nor you, Mr Holmes, for your suspicions were natural. I feel that on the very eve of my arrest I have only cleared myself by sharing the fate of my poor friend."

"No, Mr Murdoch. I was already upon the track, and had I been out as early as I intended, I might well have saved you from this terrific experience."

"But how did you know, Mr Holmes?"

"I am an omnivorous reader with a strangely retentive memory for trifles. That phrase 'lion's mane' haunted my mind. I knew that I had seen it somewhere in an unexpected context. You have seen that it does describe the creature. I have no doubt that it was floating on the water when McPherson saw it, and that this phrase was the only one by which he could convey to us a warning as to the creature which had been his death."

"Then I, at least, am cleared," said Murdoch, rising slowly to his feet. "There are one or two words of explanation which I should give, for I know the direction in which your enquiries have run. It is true that I loved this lady, but from the day when she chose my friend McPherson my one desire was to help her to happiness. I was well content to stand aside and act as their go-between. Often I carried their messages, and it was because I was in their confidence and because she was so dear to me that I hastened to tell her of my friend's death, lest someone should forestall me in a more sudden and heartless manner. She would not tell you, sir, of our relations, lest you should disapprove and I might suffer. But with your leave I must try to get back to the Gables, for my bed will be very welcome."

Stackhurst held out his hand. "Our nerves have all been at concert pitch,"* said he. "Forgive what is past, Murdoch. We shall under-stand each other better in the future." They passed out together with their arms linked in friendly fashion. The inspector remained, staring at me in silence with his ox-like eyes.

"Well, you've done it!" he cried at last. "I had read of you, but I never believed it. It's wonderful!"

I was forced to shake my head. To accept such praise was to lower one's own standards.

"I was slow at the outset – culpably slow. Had the body been found in the water, I could hardly have missed it. It was the towel which misled me. The poor fellow had never thought to dry himself, and so I in turn was led to believe that he had never been in the water. Why, then, should the attack of any water creature suggest itself to me? That was where I went astray. Well, well, Inspector, I often ventured to chaff you gentlemen of the police force, but *Cyanea capillata* very nearly avenged Scotland Yard."

THE ADVENTURE
OF THE VEILED LODGER

WHEN ONE CONSIDERS that Mr Sherlock Holmes was in active practice for twenty-three years, and that during seventeen of these* I was allowed to cooperate with him and to keep notes of his doings, it will be clear that I have a mass of material at my command. The problem has always been not to find, but to choose. There is the long row of yearbooks which fill a shelf, and there are the dispatch cases filled with documents, a perfect quarry for the student not only of crime, but of the social and official scandals of the late Victorian era. Concerning these latter, I may say that the writers of agonized letters, who beg that the honour of their families or the reputation of famous forebears may not be touched, have nothing to fear. The discretion and high sense of professional honour which have always distinguished my friend are still at work in the choice of these memoirs, and no confidence will be abused. I deprecate, however, in the strongest way the attempts which have been made lately to get at and to destroy these papers. The source of these outrages is known, and if they are repeated I have Mr Holmes's authority for saying that the whole story concerning the politician, the lighthouse and the trained cormorant* will be given to the public. There is at least one reader who will understand.

It is not reasonable to suppose that every one of these cases gave Holmes the opportunity of showing those curious gifts of instinct and observation which I have endeavoured to set forth in these memoirs. Sometimes he had with much effort to pick the fruit, sometimes it fell easily into his lap. But the most terrible human tragedies were often involved in these cases which brought him the fewest personal opportunities, and it is one of these which I now desire to record. In telling it, I have made a slight change of name and place, but otherwise the facts are as stated.

One forenoon – it was late in 1896 – I received a hurried note from Holmes asking for my attendance. When I arrived, I found him seated in a smoke-laden atmosphere, with an elderly, motherly woman of the buxom-landlady type in the corresponding chair in front of him.

"This is Mrs Merrilow, of South Brixton,"* said my friend with a wave of the hand. "Mrs Merrilow does not object to tobacco, Watson, if you wish to indulge your filthy habits. Mrs Merrilow has an interesting story to tell which may well lead to further developments in which your presence may be useful."

"Anything I can do..."

"You will understand, Mrs Merrilow, that if I come to Mrs Ronder I should prefer to have a witness. You will make her understand that before we arrive."

"Lord bless you, Mr Holmes," said our visitor, "she is that anxious to see you that you might bring the whole parish at your heels!"

"Then we shall come early in the afternoon. Let us see that we have our facts correct before we start. If we go over them, it will help Doctor Watson to understand the situation. You say that Mrs Ronder has been your lodger for seven years, and that you have only once seen her face."

"And I wish to God I had not!" said Mrs Merrilow.

"It was, I understand, terribly mutilated."

"Well, Mr Holmes, you would hardly say it was a face at all. That's how it looked. Our milkman got a glimpse of her once peeping out of the upper window, and he dropped his tin and the milk all over the front garden. That is the kind of face it is. When I saw her – I happened on her unawares – she covered up quick, and then she said, 'Now, Mrs Merrilow, you know at last why it is that I never raise my veil.'"

"Do you know anything about her history?"

"Nothing at all."

"Did she give references when she came?"

"No, sir, but she gave hard cash, and plenty of it. A quarter's rent right down on the table in advance and no arguing about terms. In these times a poor woman like me can't afford to turn down a chance like that."

"Did she give any reason for choosing your house?"

"Mine stands well back from the road and is more private than most. Then, again, I only take the one, and I have no family of my own. I reckon she had tried others and found that mine suited her best. It's privacy she is after, and she is ready to pay for it."

"You say that she never showed her face from first to last save on the one accidental occasion. Well, it is a very remarkable story, most remarkable, and I don't wonder that you want it examined."

"I don't, Mr Holmes. I am quite satisfied so long as I get my rent. You could not have a quieter lodger, or one who gives less trouble."

"Then what has brought matters to a head?"

"Her health, Mr Holmes. She seems to be wasting away. And there's something terrible on her mind. 'Murder!' she cries. 'Murder!' And once I heard her: 'You cruel beast! You monster!' she cried. It was in the night, and it fair rang through the house and sent the shivers through me. So I went to her in the morning. 'Mrs Ronder,' I says, 'if you have anything that is troubling your soul, there's the clergy,' I says, 'and there's the police. Between them you should get some help.' 'For God's sake, not the police!' says she. 'And the clergy can't change what is past. And yet,' she says, 'it would ease my mind if someone knew the truth before I died.' 'Well,' says I, 'if you won't have the regulars, there is this detective man what we read about' – beggin' your pardon, Mr Holmes. And she, she fair jumped at it. 'That's the man,' says she. 'I wonder I never thought of it before. Bring him here, Mrs Merrilow, and if he won't come, tell him I am the wife of Ronder's wild-beast show. Say that, and give him the name Abbas Parva. Here it is as she wrote it, Abbas Parva. 'That will bring him, if he's the man I think he is.'"

"And it will, too," remarked Holmes. "Very good, Mrs Merrilow. I should like to have a little chat with Doctor Watson. That will carry us till lunchtime. About three o'clock you may expect to see us at your house in Brixton."

Our visitor had no sooner waddled out of the room – no other verb can describe Mrs Merrilow's method of progression – than Sherlock Holmes threw himself with fierce energy upon the pile of commonplace books* in the corner. For a few minutes there was a constant swish of the leaves, and then with a grunt of satisfaction he came upon what he sought. So excited was he that he did not rise, but sat upon the floor like some strange Buddha, with crossed legs, the huge books all round him, and one open upon his knees.

"The case worried me at the time, Watson. Here are my marginal notes to prove it. I confess that I could make nothing of it. And yet I was convinced that the coroner was wrong. Have you no recollection of the Abbas Parva tragedy?"

"None, Holmes."

"And yet you were with me then. But certainly my own impression was very superficial, for there was nothing to go by, and none of the parties had engaged my services. Perhaps you would care to read the papers?"

"Could you not give me the points?"

"That is very easily done. It will probably come back to your memory as I talk. Ronder, of course, was a household word. He was the rival of Wombwell, and of Sanger,* one of the greatest showmen of his day. There is evidence, however, that he took to drink, and that both he and his show were on the downgrade at the time of the great tragedy. The caravan had halted for the night at Abbas Parva, which is a small village in Berkshire, when this horror occurred. They were on their way to Wimbledon, travelling by road, and they were simply camping, and not exhibiting, as the place is so small a one that it would not have paid them to open.

"They had among their exhibits a very fine North African lion. Sahara King was its name, and it was the habit, both of Ronder and his wife, to give exhibitions inside its cage. Here, you see, is a photograph of the performance, by which you will perceive that Ronder was a huge porcine person and that his wife was a very magnificent woman. It was deposed at the inquest that there had been some signs that the lion was dangerous, but, as usual, familiarity begot contempt, and no notice was taken of the fact.

"It was usual for either Ronder or his wife to feed the lion at night. Sometimes one went, sometimes both, but they never allowed anyone else to do it, for they believed that so long as they were the food carriers he would regard them as benefactors, and would never molest them. On this particular night, seven years ago, they both went, and a very terrible happening followed, the details of which have never been made clear.

"It seems that the whole camp was roused near midnight by the roars of the animal and the screams of the woman. The different grooms and *employés* rushed from their tents, carrying lanterns, and by their light an awful sight was revealed. Ronder lay, with the back of his head crushed in and deep claw marks across his scalp, some ten yards from the cage, which was open. Close to the door of the cage lay Mrs Ronder, upon her back, with the creature squatting and snarling above her. It had torn her face in such a fashion that it was never thought that she could live. Several of the circus men, headed by Leonardo, the strongman, and Griggs, the clown, drove the creature off with poles, upon which it sprang back into the cage, and was at once locked in. How it had got loose was a mystery. It was conjectured that the pair intended to enter the cage, but that when the door was loosed the creature bounded out upon them. There was no other point of interest in the evidence, save that the woman in a delirium of agony kept screaming 'Coward! Coward!' as she was carried back to the van in which they lived. It was six months before she was fit to give evidence, but the inquest was duly held, with the obvious verdict of death from misadventure."

"What alternative could be conceived?" said I.

"You may well say so. And yet there were one or two points which worried young Edmunds, of the Berkshire Constabulary. A smart lad, that! He was sent later to Allahabad.* That was how I came into the matter, for he dropped in and smoked a pipe or two over it."

"A thin, yellow-haired man?"

"Exactly. I was sure you would pick up the trail presently."

"But what worried him?"

"Well, we were both worried. It was so deucedly difficult to reconstruct the affair. Look at it from the lion's point of view. He is liberated. What does he do? He takes half a dozen bounds forward, which brings him to Ronder. Ronder turns to fly – the claw marks were on the back of his head – but the lion strikes him down. Then, instead of bounding on and escaping, he returns to the woman, who was close to the cage, and he knocks her over and chews her face up. Then, again, those cries of hers would seem to imply that her husband had in some way failed her. What could the poor devil have done to help her? You see the difficulty?"

"Quite."

"And then there was another thing. It comes back to me now as I think it over. There was some evidence that, just at the time the lion roared and the woman screamed, a man began shouting in terror."

"This man Ronder, no doubt."

"Well, if his skull was smashed in you would hardly expect to hear from him again. There were at least two witnesses who spoke of the cries of a man being mingled with those of a woman."

"I should think the whole camp was crying out by then. As to the other points, I think I could suggest a solution."

"I should be glad to consider it."

"The two were together, ten yards from the cage, when the lion got loose. The man turned and was struck down. The woman conceived the idea of getting into the cage and shutting the door. It was her only refuge. She made for it, and just as she reached it, the beast bounded after her and knocked her over. She was angry with her husband for having encouraged the beast's rage by turning. If they had faced it, they might have cowed it. Hence her cries of 'Coward!'"

"Brilliant, Watson! Only one flaw in your diamond."

"What is the flaw, Holmes?"

"If they were both ten paces from the cage, how came the beast to get loose?"

"Is it possible that they had some enemy who loosed it?"

"And why should it attack them savagely when it was in the habit of playing with them, and doing tricks with them inside the cage?"

"Possibly the same enemy had done something to enrage it."

Holmes looked thoughtful and remained in silence for some moments.

"Well, Watson, there is this to be said for your theory. Ronder was a man of many enemies. Edmunds told me that in his cups* he was horrible. A huge bully of a man, he cursed and slashed at everyone who came in his way. I expect those cries about a monster, of which our visitor has spoken, were nocturnal reminiscences of the dear departed. However, our speculations are futile until we have all the facts. There is a cold partridge on the sideboard, Watson, and a bottle of Montrachet. Let us renew our energies before we make a fresh call upon them."

When our hansom deposited us at the house of Mrs Merrilow, we found that plump lady blocking up the open door of her humble but retired abode. It was very clear that her chief preoccupation was lest she should lose a valuable lodger, and she implored us, before showing us up, to say and do nothing which could lead to so undesirable an end. Then, having reassured her, we followed her up the straight, badly carpeted staircase and were shown into the room of the mysterious lodger.

It was a close, musty, ill-ventilated place, as might be expected, since its inmate seldom left it. From keeping beasts in a cage, the woman seemed, by some retribution of Fate, to have become herself a beast in a cage. She sat now in a broken armchair in the shadowy corner of the room. Long years of inaction had coarsened the lines of her figure, but at some period it must have been beautiful, and was still full and voluptuous. A thick dark veil covered her face, but it was cut off close at her upper lip, and disclosed a perfectly shaped mouth and a delicately rounded chin. I could well conceive that she had indeed been a very remarkable woman. Her voice, too, was well modulated and pleasing.

"My name is not unfamiliar to you, Mr Holmes," said she. "I thought that it would bring you."

"That is so, madam, though I do not know how you are aware that I was interested in your case."

"I learnt it when I had recovered my health and was examined by Mr Edmunds, the county detective. I fear I lied to him. Perhaps it would have been wiser had I told the truth."

"It is usually wiser to tell the truth. But why did you lie to him?"

"Because the fate of someone else depended upon it. I know that he was a very worthless being, and yet I would not have his destruction upon my conscience. We had been so close – so close!"

"But has this impediment been removed?"

"Yes, sir. The person that I allude to is dead."

"Then why should you not now tell the police anything you know?"

"Because there is another person to be considered. That other person is myself. I could not stand the scandal and publicity which would come from a police examination. I have not long to live, but I wish to die undisturbed. And yet I wanted to find one man of judgement to whom I could tell my terrible story, so that when I am gone all might be understood."

"You compliment me, madam. At the same time, I am a responsible person. I do not promise you that when you have spoken I may not myself think it my duty to refer the case to the police."

"I think not, Mr Holmes. I know your character and methods too well, for I have followed your work for some years. Reading is the only pleasure which Fate has left me, and I miss little which passes in the world. But in any case, I will take my chance of the use which you may make of my tragedy. It will ease my mind to tell it."

"My friend and I would be glad to hear it."

The woman rose and took from a drawer the photograph of a man. He was clearly a professional acrobat, a man of magnificent physique, taken with his huge arms folded across his swollen chest and a smile breaking from under his heavy moustache – the self-satisfied smile of the man of many conquests.

"That is Leonardo," she said.

"Leonardo, the strongman, who gave evidence?"

"The same. And this – this is my husband."

It was a dreadful face – a human pig, or rather a human wild boar, for it was formidable in its bestiality. One could imagine that vile mouth champing and foaming in its rage, and one could conceive those small, vicious eyes darting pure malignancy as they looked forth upon the world. Ruffian, bully, beast – it was all written on that heavy-jowled face.

"Those two pictures will help you, gentlemen, to understand the story. I was a poor circus girl brought up on the sawdust, and doing springs through the hoop before I was ten. When I became a woman, this man loved me, if such lust as his can be called love, and in an evil moment I became his wife. From that day I was in hell, and he the devil who tormented me. There was no one in the show who did not know of his treatment. He deserted me for others. He tied me down and lashed me with his riding whip when I complained. They all pitied me, and they all loathed him, but what could they do? They feared him, one and all. For he was terrible at all times, and murderous when he was drunk. Again and again he was had for assault, and for cruelty to the beasts, but he had plenty of money, and the fines were nothing to him. The best men all left us, and the show began to go downhill. It was only Leonardo and I who kept it up – with little Jimmy Griggs, the clown. Poor devil, he had not much to be funny about, but he did what he could to hold things together.

"Then Leonardo came more and more into my life. You see what he was like. I know now the poor spirit that was hidden in that splendid body, but compared to my husband he seemed like the Angel Gabriel. He pitied me and helped me, till at last our intimacy turned to love – deep, deep, passionate love, such love as I had dreamt of but never hoped to feel. My husband suspected it, but

I think that he was a coward as well as a bully, and that Leonardo was the one man that he was afraid of. He took revenge in his own way by torturing me more than ever. One night my cries brought Leonardo to the door of our van. We were near tragedy that night, and soon my lover and I understood that it could not be avoided. My husband was not fit to live. We planned that he should die.

"Leonardo had a clever, scheming brain. It was he who planned it. I do not say that to blame him, for I was ready to go with him every inch of the way. But I should never have had the wit to think of such a plan. We made a club – Leonardo made it – and in the leaden head he fastened five long steel nails, the points outwards, with just such a spread as the lion's paw. This was to give my husband his death blow, and yet to leave the evidence that it was the lion which we would loose who had done the deed.

"It was a pitch-dark night when my husband and I went down, as was our custom, to feed the beast. We carried with us the raw meat in a zinc pail. Leonardo was waiting at the corner of the big van which we should have to pass before we reached the cage. He was too slow, and we walked past him before he could strike, but he followed us on tiptoe, and I heard the crash as the club smashed my husband's skull. My heart leapt with joy at the sound. I sprang forward, and I undid the catch which held the door of the great lion's cage.

"And then the terrible thing happened. You may have heard how quick these creatures are to scent human blood, and how it excites them. Some strange instinct had told the creature in one instant that a human being had been slain. As I slipped the bars, it bounded out, and was on me in an instant. Leonardo could have saved me. If he had rushed forward and struck the beast with his club he might have cowed it. But the man lost his nerve. I heard him shout in his terror, and then I saw him turn and fly. At the same instant the teeth of the lion met in my face. Its hot, filthy breath had already poisoned me, and I was hardly conscious of pain. With the palms of my hands I tried to push the great steaming, bloodstained jaws away from me, and I screamed for help. I was conscious that the camp was stirring, and then dimly I remember a group of men – Leonardo,

Griggs and others – dragging me from under the creature's paws. That was my last memory, Mr Holmes, for many a weary month. When I came to myself and saw myself in the mirror, I cursed that lion – oh, how I cursed him! – not because he had torn away my beauty, but because he had not torn away my life. I had but one desire, Mr Holmes, and I had enough money to gratify it. It was that I should cover myself so that my poor face should be seen by none, and that I should dwell where none whom I had ever known should find me. That was all that was left to me to do – and that is what I have done. A poor wounded beast that has crawled into its hole to die – that is the end of Eugenia Ronder."

We sat in silence for some time after the unhappy woman had told her story. Then Holmes stretched out his long arm and patted her hand with such a show of sympathy as I had seldom known him to exhibit.

"Poor girl!" he said. "Poor girl! The ways of Fate are indeed hard to understand. If there is not some compensation hereafter, then the world is a cruel jest. But what of this man Leonardo?"

"I never saw him or heard from him again. Perhaps I have been wrong to feel so bitterly against him. He might as soon have loved one of the freaks whom we carried round the country as the thing which the lion had left. But a woman's love is not so easily set aside. He had left me under the beast's claws – he had deserted me in my need, and yet I could not bring myself to give him to the gallows. For myself, I cared nothing what became of me. What could be more dreadful than my actual life? But I stood between Leonardo and his fate."

"And he is dead?"

"He was drowned last month when bathing near Margate. I saw his death in the paper."

"And what did he do with this five-clawed club, which is the most singular and ingenious part of all your story?"

"I cannot tell, Mr Holmes. There is a chalk pit by the camp, with a deep green pool at the base of it. Perhaps in the depths of that pool..."

"Well, well… it is of little consequence now. The case is closed."

"Yes," said the woman, "the case is closed."

We had risen to go, but there was something in the woman's voice which arrested Holmes's attention. He turned swiftly upon her.

"Your life is not your own," he said. "Keep your hands off it."

"What use is it to anyone?"

"How can you tell? The example of patient suffering is in itself the most precious of all lessons to an impatient world."

The woman's answer was a terrible one. She raised her veil and stepped forward into the light.

"I wonder if you would bear it," she said.

It was horrible. No words can describe the framework of a face when the face itself is gone. Two living and beautiful brown eyes looking sadly out from that grisly ruin did but make the view more awful. Holmes held up his hand in a gesture of pity and protest, and together we left the room.

Two days later, when I called upon my friend, he pointed with some pride to a small blue bottle upon his mantelpiece. I picked it up. There was a red poison label. A pleasant almondy odour rose when I opened it.

"Prussic acid?" said I.

"Exactly. It came by post. 'I send you my temptation. I will follow your advice.' That was the message. I think, Watson, we can guess the name of the brave woman who sent it."

THE ADVENTURE
OF SHOSCOMBE OLD PLACE

S HERLOCK HOLMES had been bending for a long time over a low-power microscope. Now he straightened himself up and looked round at me in triumph.

"It is glue, Watson," said he. "Unquestionably it is glue. Have a look at these scattered objects in the field!"*

I stooped to the eyepiece and focused for my vision.

"Those hairs are threads from a tweed coat. The irregular grey masses are dust. There are epithelial scales* on the left. Those brown blobs in the centre are undoubtedly glue."

"Well," I said, laughing, "I am prepared to take your word for it. Does anything depend upon it?"

"It is a very fine demonstration," he answered. "In the St Pancras case you may remember that a cap was found beside the dead policeman. The accused man denies that it is his. But he is a picture-frame maker who habitually handles glue."

"Is it one of your cases?"

"No – my friend, Merivale of the Yard, asked me to look into the case. Since I ran down that coiner* by the zinc and copper filings in the seam of his cuff, they have begun to realize the importance of the microscope." He looked impatiently at his watch. "I had a new client calling, but he is overdue. By the way, Watson, you know something of racing?"

"I ought to. I pay for it with about half my wound pension."*

"Then I'll make you my *Handy Guide to the Turf*.* What about Sir Robert Norberton? Does the name recall anything?"

"Well, I should say so. He lives at Shoscombe Old Place, and I know it well, for my summer quarters were down there once. Norberton nearly came within your province once."

"How was that?"

"It was when he horsewhipped Sam Brewer, the well-known Curzon Street moneylender, on Newmarket Heath.* He nearly killed the man."

"Ah, he sounds interesting! Does he often indulge in that way?"

"Well, he has the name of being a dangerous man. He is about the most daredevil rider in England – second in the Grand National* a few years back. He is one of those men who have overshot their true generation. He should have been a buck in the days of the Regency* – a boxer, an athlete, a plunger on the turf, a lover of fair ladies and, by all account, so far down Queer Street* that he may never find his way back again."

"Capital, Watson! A thumbnail sketch. I seem to know the man. Now, can you give me some idea of Shoscombe Old Place?"

"Only that it is in the centre of Shoscombe Park, and that the famous Shoscombe stud and training quarters are to be found there."

"And the head trainer," said Holmes, "is John Mason. You need not look surprised at my knowledge, Watson, for this is a letter from him which I am unfolding. But let us have some more about Shoscombe. I seem to have struck a rich vein."

"There are the Shoscombe spaniels," said I. "You hear of them at every dog show. The most exclusive breed in England. They are the special pride of the lady of Shoscombe Old Place."

"Sir Robert Norberton's wife, I presume!"

"Sir Robert has never married. Just as well, I think, considering his prospects. He lives with his widowed sister, Lady Beatrice Falder."

"You mean that she lives with him?"

"No, no. The place belonged to her late husband, Sir James. Norberton has no claim on it at all. It is only a life interest, and reverts to her husband's brother. Meantime, she draws the rents every year."

"And brother Robert, I suppose, spends the said rents?"

"That is about the size of it. He is a devil of a fellow, and must lead her a most uneasy life. Yet I have heard that she is devoted to him. But what is amiss at Shoscombe?"

"Ah, that is just what I want to know. And here, I expect, is the man who can tell us."

The door had opened, and the page had shown in a tall, clean-shaven man with the firm, austere expression which is only seen upon those who have to control horses or boys. Mr John Mason had many of both under his sway, and he looked equal to the task. He bowed with cold self-possession and seated himself upon the chair to which Holmes had waved him.

"You had my note, Mr Holmes?"

"Yes, but it explained nothing."

"It was too delicate a thing for me to put the details on paper. And too complicated. It was only face to face I could do it."

"Well, we are at your disposal."

"First of all, Mr Holmes, I think that my employer, Sir Robert, has gone mad."

Holmes raised his eyebrows. "This is Baker Street, not Harley Street," said he. "But why do you say so?"

"Well, sir, when a man does one queer thing, or two queer things, there may be a meaning to it, but when everything he does is queer, then you begin to wonder. I believe Shoscombe Prince and the Derby* have turned his brain."

"That is a colt you are running?"

"The best in England, Mr Holmes. I should know, if anyone does. Now, I'll be plain with you, for I know you are gentlemen of honour and that it won't go beyond the room. Sir Robert has got to win this Derby. He's up to the neck, and it's his last chance. Everything he could raise or borrow is on the horse – and at fine odds, too! You can get forties now, but it was nearer the hundred* when he began to back him."

"But how is that, if the horse is so good?"

"The public don't know how good he is. Sir Robert has been too clever for the touts. He has the Prince's half-brother out for spins. You can't tell 'em apart. But there are two lengths in a furlong between them when it comes to a gallop. He thinks of nothing but the horse and the race. His whole life is on it. He's holding off the Jews* till then. If the Prince fails him, he is done."

"It seems a rather desperate gamble, but where does the madness come in?"

"Well, first of all, you have only to look at him. I don't believe he sleeps at night. He is down at the stables at all hours. His eyes are wild. It has all been too much for his nerves. Then there is his conduct to Lady Beatrice!"

"Ah! What is that?"

"They have always been the best of friends. They had the same tastes, the two of them, and she loved the horses as much as he did. Every day at the same hour she would drive down to see them – and, above all, she loved the Prince. He would prick up his ears when he heard the wheels on the gravel, and he would trot out each morning to the carriage to get his lump of sugar. But that's all over now."

"Why?"

"Well, she seems to have lost all interest in the horses. For a week now she has driven past the stables with never so much as 'good morning'!"

"You think there has been a quarrel?"

"And a bitter, savage, spiteful quarrel at that. Why else would he give away her pet spaniel that she loved as if he were her child? He gave it a few days ago to old Barnes, what keeps the Green Dragon, three miles off, at Crendall."

"That certainly did seem strange."

"Of course, with her weak heart and dropsy one couldn't expect that she could get about with him, but he spent two hours every evening in her room. He might well do what he could, for she has been a rare good friend to him. But that's all over, too. He never goes near her. And she takes it to heart. She is brooding and sulky and drinking, Mr Holmes – drinking like a fish."

"Did she drink before this estrangement?"

"Well, she took her glass, but now it is often a whole bottle of an evening. So Stephens, the butler, told me. It's all changed, Mr Holmes, and there is something damned rotten about it. But then, again, what is Master doing down at the old church crypt at night? And who is the man that meets him there?"

Holmes rubbed his hands.

"Go on, Mr Mason. You get more and more interesting."

"It was the butler who saw him go. Twelve o'clock at night and raining hard. So next night I was up at the house – and, sure enough, Master was off again. Stephens and I went after him, but it was jumpy work, for it would have been a bad job if he had seen us. He's a terrible man with his fists if he gets started, and no respecter of persons. So we were shy of getting too near, but we marked him down all right. It was the haunted crypt that he was making for, and there was a man waiting for him there."

"What is this haunted crypt?"

"Well, sir, there is an old ruined chapel in the park. It is so old that nobody could fix its date. And under it there's a crypt which has a bad name among us. It's a dark, damp, lonely place by day, but there are few in that county that would have the nerve to go near it at night. But Master's not afraid. He never feared anything in his life. But what is he doing there in the night-time?"

"Wait a bit!" said Holmes. "You say there is another man there. It must be one of your own stablemen, or someone from the house! Surely you have only to spot who it is and question him?"

"It's no one I know."

"How can you say that?"

"Because I have seen him, Mr Holmes. It was on that second night. Sir Robert turned and passed us – me and Stephens, quaking in the bushes like two bunny rabbits, for there was a bit of moon that night. But we could hear the other moving about behind.

We were not afraid of him. So we up when Sir Robert was gone and pretended we were just having a walk like in the moonlight, and so we came right on him as casual and innocent as you please. 'Hullo, mate! Who may you be?' says I. I guess he had not heard us coming, so he looked over his shoulder with a face as if he had seen the Devil coming out of hell. He let out a yell, and away he went as hard as he could lick it in the darkness. He could run! I'll give him that. In a minute he was out of sight and hearing, and who he was, or what he was, we never found."

"But you saw him clearly in the moonlight?"

"Yes, I would swear to his yellow face – a mean dog, I should say. What could he have in common with Sir Robert?"

Holmes sat for some time lost in thought.

"Who keeps Lady Beatrice Falder company?" he asked at last.

"There is her maid, Carrie Evans. She has been with her this five years."

"And is, no doubt, devoted?"

Mr Mason shuffled uncomfortably.

"She's devoted enough," he answered at last. "But I won't say to whom."

"Ah!" said Holmes.

"I can't tell tales out of school."

"I quite understand, Mr Mason. Of course, the situation is clear enough. From Doctor Watson's description of Sir Robert I can realize that no woman is safe from him. Don't you think the quarrel between brother and sister may lie there?"

"Well, the scandal has been pretty clear for a long time."

"But she may not have seen it before. Let us suppose that she has suddenly found it out. She wants to get rid of the woman. Her brother will not permit it. The invalid, with her weak heart and inability to get about, has no means of enforcing her will. The hated maid is still tied to her. The lady refuses to speak, sulks, takes to drink. Sir Robert in his anger takes her pet spaniel away from her. Does not all this hang together?"

"Well, it might do – so far as it goes."

"Exactly! As far as it goes. How would all that bear upon the visits by night to the old crypt? We can't fit that into our plot."

"No, sir, and there is something more that I can't fit in. Why should Sir Robert want to dig up a dead body?"

Holmes sat up abruptly.

"We only found it out yesterday – after I had written to you. Yesterday Sir Robert had gone to London, so Stephens and I went down to the crypt. It was all in order, sir, except that in one corner was a bit of a human body."

"You informed the police, I suppose?"

Our visitor smiled grimly.

"Well, sir, I think it would hardly interest them. It was just the head and a few bones of a mummy. It may have been a thousand years old. But it wasn't there before. That I'll swear, and so will Stephens. It had been stowed away in a corner and covered over with a board, but that corner had always been empty before."

"What did you do with it?"

"Well, we just left it there."

"That was wise. You say Sir Robert was away yesterday. Has he returned?"

"We expect him back today."

"When did Sir Robert give away his sister's dog?"

"It was just a week ago today. The creature was howling outside the old well house, and Sir Robert was in one of his tantrums that morning. He caught it up, and I thought he would have killed it. Then he gave it to Sandy Bain, the jockey, and told him to take the dog to old Barnes at the Green Dragon, for he never wished to see it again."

Holmes sat for some time in silent thought. He had lit the oldest and foulest of his pipes.

"I am not clear yet what you want me to do in this matter, Mr Mason," he said at last. "Can't you make it more definite?"

"Perhaps this will make it more definite, Mr Holmes," said our visitor.

He took a paper from his pocket and, unwrapping it carefully, he exposed a charred fragment of bone.

Holmes examined it with interest.

"Where did you get it?"

"There is a central-heating furnace in the cellar under Lady Beatrice's room. It's been off for some time, but Sir Robert complained of cold and had it on again. Harvey runs it – he's one of my lads. This very morning he came to me with this, which he found raking out the cinders. He didn't like the look of it."

"Nor do I," said Holmes. "What do you make of it, Watson?"

It was burnt to a black cinder, but there could be no question as to its anatomical significance.

"It's the upper condyle of a human femur,"* said I.

"Exactly!" Holmes had become very serious. "When does this lad tend to the furnace?"

"He makes it up every evening and then leaves it."

"Then anyone could visit it during the night?"

"Yes, sir."

"Can you enter it from outside?"

"There is one door from outside. There is another which leads up by a stair to the passage in which Lady Beatrice's room is situated."

"These are deep waters, Mr Mason – deep and rather dirty. You say that Sir Robert was not at home last night?"

"No, sir."

"Then, whoever was burning bones, it was not he."

"That's true, sir."

"What is the name of that inn you spoke of?"

"The Green Dragon."

"Is there good fishing in that part of Berkshire?"

The honest trainer showed very clearly upon his face that he was convinced that yet another lunatic had come into his harassed life.

"Well, sir, I've heard there are trout in the mill stream and pike in the hall lake."

"That's good enough. Watson and I are famous fishermen – are we not, Watson? You may address us in future at the Green Dragon.

We should reach it tonight. I need not say that we don't want to see you, Mr Mason, but a note will reach us, and no doubt I could find you if I want you. When we have gone a little further into the matter, I will let you have a considered opinion."

Thus it was that on a bright May evening Holmes and I found ourselves alone in a first-class carriage and bound for the little "halt-on-demand" station of Shoscombe. The rack above us was covered with a formidable litter of rods, reels and baskets. On reaching our destination, a short drive took us to an old-fashioned tavern, where a sporting host, Josiah Barnes, entered eagerly into our plans for the extirpation of the fish of the neighbourhood.

"What about the hall lake and the chance of a pike?" said Holmes.

The face of the innkeeper clouded.

"That wouldn't do, sir. You might chance to find yourself in the lake before you were through."

"How's that, then?"

"It's Sir Robert, sir. He's terrible jealous of touts. If you two strangers were as near his training quarters as that, he'd be after you as sure as fate. He ain't taking no chances, Sir Robert ain't."

"I've heard he has a horse entered for the Derby."

"Yes, and a good colt, too. He carries all our money for the race, and all Sir Robert's into the bargain. By the way" – he looked at us with thoughtful eyes – "I suppose you ain't on the turf yourselves?"

"No, indeed. Just two weary Londoners who badly need some good Berkshire air."

"Well, you are in the right place for that. There is a deal of it lying about. But mind what I have told you about Sir Robert. He's the sort that strikes first and speaks afterwards. Keep clear of the park."

"Surely, Mr Barnes! We certainly shall. By the way, that was a most beautiful spaniel that was whining in the hall."

"I should say it was. That was the real Shoscombe breed. There ain't a better in England."

"I am a dog fancier myself," said Holmes. "Now, if it is a fair question, what would a prize dog like that cost?"

"More than I could pay, sir. It was Sir Robert himself who gave me this one. That's why I have to keep it on a lead. It would be off to the hall in a jiffy if I gave it its head."

"We are getting some cards in our hand, Watson," said Holmes, when the landlord had left us. "It's not an easy one to play, but we may see our way in a day or two. By the way, Sir Robert is still in London, I hear. We might, perhaps, enter the sacred domain tonight without fear of bodily assault. There are one or two points on which I should like reassurance."

"Have you any theory, Holmes?"

"Only this, Watson: that something happened a week or so ago which has cut deep into the life of the Shoscombe household. What is that something? We can only guess at it from its effects. They seem to be of a curiously mixed character. But that should surely help us. It is only the colourless, uneventful case which is hopeless.

"Let us consider our data. The brother no longer visits the beloved invalid sister. He gives away her favourite dog. Her dog, Watson! Does that suggest nothing to you?"

"Nothing but the brother's spite."

"Well, it might be so. Or… well, there is an alternative. Now to continue our review of the situation from the time that the quarrel, if there is a quarrel, began. The lady keeps her room, alters her habits, is not seen save when she drives out with her maid, refuses to stop at the stables to greet her favourite horse, and apparently takes to drink. That covers the case, does it not?"

"Save for the business in the crypt."

"That is another line of thought. There are two, and I beg you will not tangle them. Line A, which concerns Lady Beatrice, has a vaguely sinister flavour, has it not?"

"I can make nothing of it."

"Well, now, let us take up line B, which concerns Sir Robert. He is mad keen upon winning the Derby. He is in the hands of the Jews, and may at any moment be sold up and his racing stables seized by his creditors. He is a daring and desperate man. He derives his income from his sister. His sister's maid is his willing tool. So far we seem to be on fairly safe ground, do we not?"

"But the crypt?"

"Ah, yes, the crypt! Let us suppose, Watson – it is merely a scandalous supposition, a hypothesis put forward for argument's sake – that Sir Robert has done away with his sister."

"My dear Holmes, it is out of the question."

"Very possibly, Watson. Sir Robert is a man of an honourable stock. But you do occasionally find a carrion crow among the eagles. Let us for a moment argue upon this supposition. He could not fly the country until he had realized his fortune, and that fortune could only be realized by bringing off this coup with Shoscombe Prince. Therefore, he has still to stand his ground. To do this he would have to dispose of the body of his victim, and he would also have to find a substitute who would impersonate her. With the maid as his confidante, that would not be impossible. The woman's body might be conveyed to the crypt, which is a place so seldom visited, and it might be secretly destroyed at night in the furnace, leaving behind it such evidence as we have already seen. What say you to that, Watson?"

"Well, it is all possible if you grant the original monstrous supposition."

"I think that there is a small experiment which we may try tomorrow, Watson, in order to throw some light on the matter. Meanwhile, if we mean to keep up our characters, I suggest that we have our host in for a glass of his own wine and hold some high converse upon eels and dace,* which seems to be the straight road to his affections. We may chance to come upon some useful local gossip in the process."

In the morning Holmes discovered that we had come without our spoon bait for jack,* which absolved us from fishing for the day. About eleven o'clock we started for a walk, and he obtained leave to take the black spaniel with us.

"This is the place," said he as we came to two high park gates with heraldic griffins towering above them. "About midday, Mr Barnes informs me, the old lady takes a drive, and the carriage must slow down while the gates are opened. When it comes through, and before it gathers speed, I want you, Watson, to stop the coachman with some question. Never mind me. I shall stand behind this holly bush and see what I can see."

It was not a long vigil. Within a quarter of an hour we saw the big open yellow barouche* coming down the long avenue, with two splendid, high-stepping grey carriage horses in the shafts. Holmes crouched behind his bush with the dog. I stood unconcernedly swinging a cane in the roadway. A keeper ran out and the gates swung open.

The carriage had slowed to a walk, and I was able to get a good look at the occupants. A highly coloured young woman with flaxen hair and impudent eyes sat on the left. At her right was an elderly person with rounded back and a huddle of shawls about her face and shoulders which proclaimed the invalid. When the horses reached the high road, I held up my hand with an authoritative gesture, and as the coachman pulled up I enquired if Sir Robert was at Shoscombe Old Place.

At the same moment Holmes stepped out and released the spaniel. With a joyous cry it dashed forward to the carriage and sprang upon the step. Then in a moment its eager greeting changed to furious rage, and it snapped at the black skirt above it.

"Drive on! Drive on!" shrieked a harsh voice. The coachman lashed the horses, and we were left standing in the roadway.

"Well, Watson, that's done it," said Holmes as he fastened the lead to the neck of the excited spaniel. "He thought it was his mistress, and he found it was a stranger. Dogs don't make mistakes."

"But it was the voice of a man!" I cried.

"Exactly! We have added one card to our hand, Watson, but it needs careful playing, all the same."

My companion seemed to have no further plans for the day, and we did actually use our fishing tackle in the mill stream, with the result that we had a dish of trout for our supper. It was only after that meal that Holmes showed signs of renewed activity. Once more we found ourselves upon the same road as in the morning, which led us to the park gates. A tall, dark figure was awaiting us there, who proved to be our London acquaintance, Mr John Mason, the trainer.

"Good evening, gentlemen," said he. "I got your note, Mr Holmes. Sir Robert has not returned yet, but I hear that he is expected tonight."

"How far is this crypt from the house?" asked Holmes.

"A good quarter of a mile."

"Then I think we can disregard him altogether."

"I can't afford to do that, Mr Holmes. The moment he arrives he will want to see me to get the last news of Shoscombe Prince."

"I see! In that case we must work without you, Mr Mason. You can show us the crypt and then leave us."

It was pitch-dark and without a moon, but Mason led us over the grasslands until a dark mass loomed up in front of us which proved to be the ancient chapel. We entered the broken gap which was once the porch, and our guide, stumbling among heaps of loose masonry, picked his way to the corner of the building, where a steep stair led down into the crypt. Striking a match, he illuminated the melancholy place – dismal and evil-smelling, with ancient crumbling walls of rough-hewn stone and piles of coffins, some of lead and some of stone, extending upon one side right up to the arched and groined* roof, which lost itself in the shadows above our heads. Holmes had lit his lantern, which shot a tiny tunnel of vivid yellow light upon the mournful scene. Its rays were reflected back from the coffin plates, many of them adorned with the griffin and coronet of this old family which carried its honours even to the gate of death.

"You spoke of some bones, Mr Mason. Could you show them before you go?"

"They are here in this corner." The trainer strode across and then stood in silent surprise as our light was turned upon the place. "They are gone," said he.

"So I expected," said Holmes, chuckling. "I fancy the ashes of them might even now be found in that oven which had already consumed a part."

"But why in the world would anyone want to burn the bones of a man who has been dead a thousand years?" asked John Mason.

"That is what we are here to find out," said Holmes. "It may mean a long search, and we need not detain you. I fancy that we shall get our solution before morning."

When John Mason had left us, Holmes set to work making a very careful examination of the graves, ranging from a very ancient one, which appeared to be Saxon, in the centre, through a long line of Norman Hugos and Odos,* until we reached the Sir William and Sir Denis Falder of the eighteenth century. It was an hour or more before Holmes came to a leaden coffin standing on end before the entrance to the vault. I heard his little cry of satisfaction, and was aware from his hurried but purposeful movements that he had reached a goal. With his lens he was eagerly examining the edges of the heavy lid. Then he drew from his pocket a short jemmy, a box opener, which he thrust into a chink, levering back the whole front, which seemed to be secured by only a couple of clamps. There was a rending, tearing sound as it gave way, but it had hardly hinged back and partly revealed the contents before we had an unforeseen interruption.

Someone was walking in the chapel above. It was the firm, rapid step of one who came with a definite purpose and knew well the ground upon which he walked. A light streamed down the stairs, and an instant later the man who bore it was framed in the Gothic archway. He was a terrible figure, huge in stature and fierce in manner. A large stable lantern which he held in front of him shone upwards upon a strong, heavily moustached face and angry eyes, which glared round him into every recess of the vault, finally fixing themselves with a deadly stare upon my companion and myself.

"Who the devil are you?" he thundered. "And what are you doing upon my property?" Then, as Holmes returned no answer, he took a couple of steps forward and raised a heavy stick which he carried. "Do you hear me?" he cried. "Who are you? What are you doing here?" His cudgel quivered in the air.

But instead of shrinking, Holmes advanced to meet him.

"I also have a question to ask you, Sir Robert," he said in his sternest tone. "Who is this? And what is it doing here?"

He turned and tore open the coffin lid behind him. In the glare of the lantern I saw a body swathed in a sheet from head to foot, with dreadful, witch-like features, all nose and chin, projecting at one end, the dim, glazed eyes staring from a discoloured and crumbling face.

The baronet had staggered back with a cry and supported himself against a stone sarcophagus.

"How came you to know of this?" he cried. And then, with some return of his truculent manner: "What business is it of yours?"

"My name is Sherlock Holmes," said my companion. "Possibly it is familiar to you. In any case, my business is that of every other good citizen – to uphold the law. It seems to me that you have much to answer for."

Sir Robert glared for a moment, but Holmes's quiet voice and cool, assured manner had their effect.

"'Fore God, Mr Holmes, it's all right," said he. "Appearances are against me, I'll admit, but I could act no otherwise."

"I should be happy to think so, but I fear your explanations must be for the police."

Sir Robert shrugged his broad shoulders.

"Well, if it must be, it must. Come up to the house, and you can judge for yourself how the matter stands."

Quarter of an hour later we found ourselves in what I judge, from the lines of polished barrels behind glass covers, to be the gun room of the old house. It was comfortably furnished, and here Sir Robert left us for a few moments. When he returned, he had two companions with him: the one, the florid young woman whom we had seen in the carriage; the other, a small rat-faced man with a disagreeably furtive manner. These two wore an appearance of utter bewilderment, which showed that the baronet had not yet had time to explain to them the turn events had taken.

"There," said Sir Robert with a wave of his hand, "are Mr and Mrs Norlett. Mrs Norlett, under her maiden name of Evans, has for some years been my sister's confidential maid. I have brought them here because I feel that my best course is to explain the true position to you, and they are the two people upon earth who can substantiate what I say."

"Is this necessary, Sir Robert? Have you thought what you are doing?" cried the woman.

"As to me, I entirely disclaim all responsibility," said her husband.

Sir Robert gave him a glance of contempt. "I will take all responsibility," said he. "Now, Mr Holmes, listen to a plain statement of the facts.

"You have clearly gone pretty deeply into my affairs, or I should not have found you where I did. Therefore, you know already, in all probability, that I am running a dark horse for the Derby and that everything depends upon my success. If I win, all is easy. If I lose – well, I dare not think of that!"

"I understand the position," said Holmes.

"I am dependent upon my sister, Lady Beatrice, for everything. But it is well known that her interest in the estate is for her own life only. For myself, I am deeply in the hands of the Jews. I have always known that if my sister were to die, my creditors would be onto my estate like a flock of vultures. Everything would be seized: my stables, my horses – everything. Well, Mr Holmes, my sister *did* die just a week ago."

"And you told no one!"

"What could I do? Absolute ruin faced me. If I could stave things off for three weeks, all would be well. Her maid's husband – this man here – is an actor. It came into our heads – it came into my head – that he could for that short period personate my sister. It was but a case of appearing daily in the carriage, for no one need enter her room save the maid. It was not difficult to arrange. My sister died of the dropsy which had long afflicted her."

"That will be for a coroner to decide."

"Her doctor would certify that for months her symptoms have threatened such an end."

"Well, what did you do?"

"The body could not remain there. On the first night Norlett and I carried it out to the old well house, which is now never used. We were followed, however, by her pet spaniel, which yapped continually at the door, so I felt some safer place was needed. I got rid of the spaniel and we carried the body to the crypt of the church. There was no indignity or irreverence, Mr Holmes. I do not feel that I have wronged the dead."

"Your conduct seems to me inexcusable, Sir Robert."

The baronet shook his head impatiently. "It is easy to preach," said he. "Perhaps you would have felt differently if you had been in my position. One cannot see all one's hopes and all one's plans shattered at the last moment and make no effort to save them. It seemed to me that it would be no unworthy resting place if we put her for the time in one of the coffins of her husband's ancestors lying in what is still consecrated ground. We opened such a coffin, removed the contents and placed her as you have seen her. As to the old relics which we took out, we could not leave them on the floor of the crypt. Norlett and I removed them, and he descended at night and burned them in the central furnace. There is my story, Mr Holmes, though how you forced my hand so that I have to tell it is more than I can say."

Holmes sat for some time lost in thought.

"There is one flaw in your narrative, Sir Robert," he said at last. "Your bets on the race, and therefore your hopes for the future, would hold good even if your creditors seized your estate."

"The horse would be part of the estate. What do they care for my bets? As likely as not they would not run him at all. My chief creditor is, unhappily, my most bitter enemy – a rascally fellow, Sam Brewer, whom I was once compelled to horsewhip on Newmarket Heath. Do you suppose that he would try to save me?"

"Well, Sir Robert," said Holmes, rising, "this matter must, of course, be referred to the police. It was my duty to bring the facts to light, and there I must leave it. As to the morality or decency of your own conduct, it is not for me to express an opinion. It is nearly midnight, Watson, and I think we may make our way back to our humble abode."

It is generally known now that this singular episode ended upon a happier note than Sir Robert's actions deserved. Shoscombe Prince did win the Derby – the sporting owner did net eighty thousand pounds in bets, and the creditors did hold their hand until the race was over, when they were paid in full, and enough was left to re-establish Sir Robert in a fair position in life. Both police and coroner took a lenient view of the transaction, and beyond a mild censure for the delay in registering the lady's decease, the lucky owner got away scatheless from this strange incident in a career which has now outlived its shadows and promises to end in an honoured old age.

THE ADVENTURE
OF THE RETIRED COLOURMAN

S HERLOCK HOLMES was in a melancholy and philosophic mood that morning. His alert practical nature was subject to such reactions.

"Did you see him?" he asked.

"You mean the old fellow who has just gone out?"

"Precisely."

"Yes, I met him at the door."

"What did you think of him?"

"A pathetic, futile, broken creature."

"Exactly, Watson. Pathetic and futile. But is not all life pathetic and futile? Is not his story a microcosm of the whole? We reach. We grasp. And what is left in our hands at the end? A shadow. Or worse than a shadow: misery."

"Is he one of your clients?"

"Well, I suppose I may call him so. He has been sent on by the Yard. Just as medical men occasionally send their incurables to a quack. They argue that they can do nothing more, and that whatever happens the patient can be no worse than he is."

"What is the matter?"

Holmes took a rather soiled card from the table. "Josiah Amberley. He says he was junior partner of Brickfall & Amberley, who are manufacturers of artistic materials. You will see their names upon paintboxes. He made his little pile, retired from business at the age of sixty-one, bought a house at Lewisham* and settled down to rest after a life of ceaseless grind. One would think his future was tolerably assured."

"Yes, indeed."

Holmes glanced over some notes which he had scribbled upon the back of an envelope.

"Retired in 1896, Watson. Early in 1897 he married a woman twenty years younger than himself – a good-looking woman, too, if the photograph does not flatter. A competence, a wife, leisure – it seemed a straight road which lay before him. And yet within two years he is, as you have seen, as broken and miserable a creature as crawls beneath the sun."

"But what has happened?"

"The old story, Watson. A treacherous friend and a fickle wife. It would appear that Amberley has one hobby in life, and it is chess. Not far from him at Lewisham there lives a young doctor who is also a chess player. I have noted his name as Doctor Ray Ernest. Ernest was frequently in the house, and an intimacy between him and Mrs Amberley was a natural sequence, for you must admit that our unfortunate client has few outward graces, whatever his inner virtues may be. The couple went off together last week – destination untraced. What is more, the faithless spouse carried off the old man's deed box as her personal luggage with a good part of his life's savings within. Can we find the lady? Can we save the money? A common-place problem so far as it has developed, and yet a vital one for Josiah Amberley."

"What will you do about it?"

"Well, the immediate question, my dear Watson, happens to be: what will *you* do? – if you will be good enough to understudy me. You know that I am preoccupied with this case of the two Coptic patriarchs,* which should come to a head today. I really have not time to go out to Lewisham, and yet evidence taken on the spot has a special value. The old fellow was quite insistent that I should go, but I explained my difficulty. He is prepared to meet a representative."

"By all means," I answered. "I confess I don't see that I can be of much service, but I am willing to do my best."

And so it was that on a summer afternoon I set forth to Lewisham, little dreaming that within a week the affair in which I was engaging would be the eager debate of all England.

It was late that evening before I returned to Baker Street and gave an account of my mission. Holmes lay with his gaunt figure stretched in his deep chair, his pipe curling forth slow wreaths of acrid tobacco, while his eyelids drooped over his eyes so lazily that he might almost have been asleep were it not that at any halt or questionable passage of my narrative they half lifted, and two grey eyes, as bright and keen as rapiers, transfixed me with their searching glance.

"The Haven is the name of Mr Josiah Amberley's house," I explained. "I think it would interest you, Holmes. It is like some penurious patrician who has sunk into the company of his inferiors. You know that particular quarter, the monotonous brick streets, the weary suburban highways. Right in the middle of them, a little island of ancient culture and comfort, lies this old home, surrounded by a high sun-baked wall mottled with lichens and topped with moss, the sort of wall—"

"Cut out the poetry, Watson," said Holmes severely. "I note that it was a high brick wall."

"Exactly. I should not have known which was the Haven had I not asked a lounger who was smoking in the street. I have a reason for mentioning him. He was a tall, dark, heavily moustached, rather military-looking man. He nodded in answer to my enquiry, and gave me a curiously questioning glance, which came back to my memory a little later.

"I had hardly entered the gateway before I saw Mr Amberley coming down the drive. I only had a glimpse of him this morning, and he certainly gave me the impression of a strange creature, but when I saw him in full light, his appearance was even more abnormal."

"I have, of course, studied it, and yet I should be interested to have your impression," said Holmes.

"He seemed to me like a man who was literally bowed down by care. His back was curved as though he carried a heavy burden. Yet he was not the weakling that I had at first imagined, for his shoulders and chest have the framework of a giant, though his figure tapers away into a pair of spindled legs."

"Left shoe wrinkled, right one smooth."

"I did not observe that."

"No, you wouldn't. I spotted his artificial limb. But proceed."

"I was struck by the snaky locks of grizzled hair which curled from under his old straw hat, and his face with its fierce, eager expression and the deeply lined features."

"Very good, Watson. What did he say?"

"He began pouring out the story of his grievances. We walked down the drive together, and of course I took a good look round. I have never seen a worse-kept place. The garden was all running to seed, giving me an impression of wild neglect in which the plants had been allowed to find the way of nature rather than of art. How any decent woman could have tolerated such a state of things, I don't know. The house, too, was slatternly to the last degree, but the poor man seemed himself to be aware of it and to be trying to remedy it, for a great pot of green paint stood in the centre of the hall and he was carrying a thick brush in his left hand. He had been working on the woodwork.

"He took me into his dingy sanctum, and we had a long chat. Of course, he was disappointed that you had not come yourself. 'I hardly expected,' he said, 'that so humble an individual as myself, especially after my heavy financial loss, could obtain the complete attention of so famous a man as Mr Sherlock Holmes.'

"I assured him that the financial question did not arise. 'No, of course, it is art for art's sake* with him,' said he, 'but even on the artistic side of crime he might have found something here to study. And human nature, Doctor Watson – the black ingratitude of it all! When did I ever refuse one of her requests? Was ever a woman so pampered? And that young man – he might have been my own son. He had the run of my house. And yet see how they have treated me! Oh, Doctor Watson, it is a dreadful, dreadful world!'

"That was the burden of his song for an hour or more. He had, it seems, no suspicion of an intrigue. They lived alone save for a woman who comes in by the day and leaves every evening at six. On that particular evening old Amberley, wishing to give his wife a treat, had taken two upper circle seats at the Haymarket Theatre.* At the last moment she had complained of a headache and had refused to go. He had gone alone. There seemed to be no doubt about the fact, for he produced the unused ticket which he had taken for his wife."

"That is remarkable – most remarkable," said Holmes, whose interest in the case seemed to be rising. "Pray continue, Watson. I find your narrative most arresting. Did you personally examine this ticket? You did not, perchance, take the number?"

"It so happens that I did," I answered with some pride. "It chanced to be my old school number, thirty-one, and so it stuck in my head."

"Excellent, Watson! His seat, then, was either thirty or thirty-two."

"Quite so," I answered, with some mystification. "And on B row."

"That is most satisfactory. What else did he tell you?"

"He showed me his strongroom, as he called it. It really is a strongroom – like a bank – with iron door and shutter – burglar-proof, as he claimed. However, the woman seems to have had a duplicate key, and between them they had carried off some seven thousand pounds' worth of cash and securities."

"Securities! How could they dispose of those?"

"He said that he had given the police a list and that he hoped they would be unsaleable. He had got back from the theatre about midnight, and found the place plundered, the door and window open and the fugitives gone. There was no letter or message, nor has he heard a word since. He at once gave the alarm to the police."

Holmes brooded for some minutes.

"You say he was painting. What was he painting?"

"Well, he was painting the passage. But he had already painted the door and woodwork of this room I spoke of."

"Does it not strike you as a strange occupation in the circumstances?"

"'One must do something to ease an aching heart.' That was his own explanation. It was eccentric, no doubt, but he is clearly an eccentric man. He tore up one of his wife's photographs in my presence – tore it up furiously in a tempest of passion. 'I never wish to see her damned face again,' he shrieked."

"Anything more, Watson?"

"Yes, one thing which struck me more than anything else. I had driven to the Blackheath station and had caught my train there, when just as it was starting I saw a man dart into the carriage next to my own. You know that I have a quick eye for faces, Holmes. It was undoubtedly the tall, dark man whom I had addressed in the street. I saw him once more at London Bridge, and then I lost him in the crowd. But I am convinced that he was following me."

"No doubt! No doubt!" said Holmes. "A tall, dark, heavily moustached man, you say, with grey-tinted sunglasses?"

"Holmes, you are a wizard. I did not say so, but he had grey-tinted sunglasses."

"And a Masonic tiepin?"*

"Holmes!"

"Quite simple, my dear Watson. But let us get down to what is practical. I must admit to you that the case, which seemed to me to be so absurdly simple as to be hardly worth my notice, is rapidly assuming a very different aspect. It is true that though in your mission you have missed everything of importance, yet even those things which have obtruded themselves upon your notice give rise to serious thought."

"What have I missed?"

"Don't be hurt, my dear fellow. You know that I am quite impersonal. No one else would have done better. Some possibly not so well. But clearly you have missed some vital points. What is the opinion of the neighbours about this man Amberley and his wife? That surely is of importance. What of Doctor Ernest? Was he the gay Lothario* one would expect? With your natural advantages, Watson, every lady is your helper and accomplice. What about the girl at the post office, or the wife of the greengrocer? I can picture you whispering soft nothings with the young lady at the Blue Anchor and receiving hard somethings in exchange. All this you have left undone."

"It can still be done."

"It has been done. Thanks to the telephone and the help of the Yard, I can usually get my essentials without leaving this room. As a matter of fact, my information confirms the man's story. He has the local repute of being a miser as well as a harsh and exacting husband. That he had a large sum of money in that strongroom of his is certain. So also is it that young Doctor Ernest, an unmarried man, played chess with Amberley, and probably played the fool with his wife. All this seems plain sailing, and one would think that there was no more to be said – and yet!… and yet!"

"Where lies the difficulty?"

"In my imagination, perhaps. Well, leave it there, Watson. Let us escape from this weary workaday world by the side door of music. Carina sings tonight at the Albert Hall, and we still have time to dress, dine and enjoy."

In the morning I was up betimes, but some toast crumbs and two empty eggshells told me that my companion was earlier still. I found a scribbled note upon the table.

DEAR WATSON,

There are one or two points of contact which I should wish to establish with Mr Josiah Amberley. When I have done so, we can dismiss the case – or not. I would only ask you to be on hand about three o'clock, as I conceive it possible that I may want you.

S.H.

I saw nothing of Holmes all day, but at the hour named he returned, grave, preoccupied and aloof. At such times it was wiser to leave him to himself.

"Has Amberley been here yet?"

"No."

"Ah! I am expecting him."

He was not disappointed, for presently the old fellow arrived with a very worried and puzzled expression upon his austere face.

"I've had a telegram, Mr Holmes. I can make nothing of it." He handed it over, and Holmes read it aloud.

COME AT ONCE WITHOUT FAIL. CAN GIVE YOU INFORMA-
TION AS TO YOUR RECENT LOSS – ELMAN. THE VICARAGE

"Dispatched at two ten from Little Purlington," said Holmes. "Little Purlington is in Essex, I believe, not far from Frinton. Well, of course you will start at once. This is evidently from a responsible person, the vicar of the place. Where is my *Crockford*?* Yes, here we have him. J.C. Elman, MA, living of Mossmoor cum Little Purlington.* Look up the trains, Watson."

"There is one at five twenty from Liverpool Street."

"Excellent. You had best go with him, Watson. He may need help or advice. Clearly we have come to a crisis in this affair."

But our client seemed by no means eager to start.

"It's perfectly absurd, Mr Holmes," he said. "What can this man possibly know of what has occurred? It is waste of time and money."

"He would not have telegraphed to you if he did not know something. Wire at once that you are coming."

"I don't think I shall go."

Holmes assumed his sternest aspect.

"It would make the worst possible impression both on the police and upon myself, Mr Amberley, if when so obvious a clue arose you should refuse to follow it up. We should feel that you were not really in earnest in this investigation."

Our client seemed horrified at the suggestion.

"Why, of course I shall go if you look at it in that way," said he. "On the face of it, it seems absurd to suppose that this parson knows anything, but if you think—"

"I *do* think," said Holmes with emphasis, and so we were launched upon our journey. Holmes took me aside before we left the room and gave me one word of counsel which showed that he considered the matter to be of importance. "Whatever you do, see that he really *does* go," said he. "Should he break away or return, get to the nearest telephone exchange and send the single word 'Bolted'. I will arrange here that it shall reach me wherever I am."

Little Purlington is not an easy place to reach, for it is on a branch line. My remembrance of the journey is not a pleasant one, for the weather was hot, the train slow, and my companion sullen and silent, hardly talking at all, save to make an occasional sardonic remark as to the futility of our proceedings. When we at last reached the little station, it was a two-mile drive before we came to the vicarage, where a big, solemn, rather pompous clergyman received us in his study. Our telegram lay before him.

"Well, gentlemen," he asked, "what can I do for you?"

"We came," I explained, "in answer to your wire."

"My wire! I sent no wire."

"I mean the wire which you sent to Mr Josiah Amberley about his wife and his money."

"If this is a joke, sir, it is a very questionable one," said the vicar angrily. "I have never heard of the gentleman you name, and I have not sent a wire to anyone."

Our client and I looked at each other in amazement.

"Perhaps there is some mistake," said I. "Are there perhaps two vicarages? Here is the wire itself, signed Elman, and dated from the vicarage."

"There is only one vicarage, sir, and only one vicar, and this wire is a scandalous forgery, the origin of which shall certainly be investigated by the police. Meanwhile, I can see no possible object in prolonging this interview."

So Mr Amberley and I found ourselves on the roadside in what seemed to me to be the most primitive village in England. We made for the telegraph office, but it was already closed. There was a telephone, however, at the little Railway Arms, and by it I got into touch with Holmes, who shared in our amazement at the result of our journey.

"Most singular!" said the distant voice. "Most remarkable! I much fear, my dear Watson, that there is no return train tonight. I have unwittingly condemned you to the horrors of a country inn. However, there is always Nature, Watson – Nature and Josiah Amberley – you can be in close commune with both." I heard his dry chuckle as he turned away.

It was soon apparent to me that my companion's reputation as a miser was not undeserved. He had grumbled at the expense of the journey, had insisted upon travelling third-class, and was now clamorous in his objections to the hotel bill. Next morning, when we did at last arrive in London, it was hard to say which of us was in the worse humour.

"You had best take Baker Street as we pass," said I. "Mr Holmes may have some fresh instructions."

"If they are not worth more than the last ones, they are not of much use," said Amberley with a malevolent scowl. Nonetheless, he kept me company. I had already warned Holmes by telegram of the hour of our arrival, but we found a message waiting that he was at Lewisham, and would expect us there. That was a surprise, but an even greater one was to find that he was not alone in the sitting room of our client. A stern-looking, impassive man sat beside him, a dark man with grey-tinted glasses and a large Masonic pin projecting from his tie.

"This is my friend Mr Barker," said Holmes. "He has been interesting himself also in your business, Mr Josiah Amberley, though we have been working independently. But we both have the same question to ask you!"

Mr Amberley sat down heavily. He sensed impending danger. I read it in his straining eyes and his twitching features.

"What is the question, Mr Holmes?"

"Only this: what did you do with the bodies?"

The man sprang to his feet with a hoarse scream. He clawed into the air with his bony hands. His mouth was open, and for the instant he looked like some horrible bird of prey. In a flash we got a glimpse of the real Josiah Amberley, a misshapen demon with a soul as distorted as his body. As he fell back into his chair, he clapped his hand to his lips as if to stifle a cough. Holmes sprang at his throat like a tiger, and twisted his face towards the ground. A white pellet fell from between his gasping lips.

"No short cuts, Josiah Amberley. Things must be done decently and in order. What about it, Barker?"

"I have a cab at the door," said our taciturn companion.

"It is only a few hundred yards to the station. We will go together. You can stay here, Watson. I shall be back within half an hour."

The old colourman* had the strength of a lion in that great trunk of his, but he was helpless in the hands of the two experienced manhandlers. Wriggling and twisting he was dragged to the waiting cab, and I was left to my solitary vigil in the ill-omened house. In less time than he had named, however, Holmes was back, in company with a smart young police inspector.

"I've left Barker to look after the formalities," said Holmes. "You had not met Barker, Watson. He is my hated rival upon the Surrey shore. When you said a tall dark man it was not difficult for me to complete the picture. He has several good cases to his credit, has he not, Inspector?"

"He has certainly interfered several times," the inspector answered with reserve.

"His methods are irregular, no doubt, like my own. The irregulars are useful sometimes, you know. You, for example, with your compulsory warning about whatever he said being used against him, could never have bluffed this rascal into what is virtually a confession."

"Perhaps not. But we get there all the same, Mr Holmes. Don't imagine that we had not formed our own views of this case, and that we would not have laid our hands on our man. You will excuse us for feeling sore when you jump in with methods which we cannot use, and so rob us of the credit."

"There shall be no such robbery, MacKinnon. I assure you that I efface myself from now onwards – and as to Barker, he has done nothing save what I told him."

The inspector seemed considerably relieved.

"That is very handsome of you, Mr Holmes. Praise or blame can matter little to you, but it is very different to us when the newspapers begin to ask questions."

"Quite so. But they are pretty sure to ask questions anyhow, so it would be as well to have answers. What will you say, for example, when the intelligent and enterprising reporter asks you what the exact points were which aroused your suspicion, and finally gave you a certain conviction as to the real facts?"

The inspector looked puzzled.

"We don't seem to have got any real facts yet, Mr Holmes. You say that the prisoner, in the presence of three witnesses, practically confessed, by trying to commit suicide, that he had murdered his wife and her lover. What other facts have you?"

"Have you arranged for a search?"

"There are three constables on their way."

"Then you will soon get the clearest fact of all. The bodies cannot be far away. Try the cellars and the garden. It should not take long to dig up the likely places. This house is older than the water pipes. There must be a disused well somewhere. Try your luck there."

"But how did you know of it, and how was it done?"

"I'll show you first how it was done, and then I will give the explanation which is due to you, and even more to my long-suffering friend here, who has been invaluable throughout. But, first, I would give you an insight into this man's mentality. It is a very unusual one – so much so that I think his destination is more likely to be Broadmoor* than the scaffold. He has, to a high degree, the sort of mind which one associates with the medieval Italian nature rather than with the modern Briton. He was a miserable miser who made his wife so wretched by his niggardly ways that she was a ready prey for any adventurer. Such a one came upon the scene in the person of this chess-playing doctor. Amberley excelled at chess – one mark, Watson, of a scheming mind. Like all misers, he was a jealous man, and his jealousy became a frantic mania. Rightly or wrongly, he suspected an intrigue. He determined to have his revenge, and he planned it with diabolical cleverness. Come here!"

Holmes led us along the passage with as much certainty as if he had lived in the house, and halted at the open door of the strongroom.

"Pooh! What an awful smell of paint!" cried the inspector.

"That was our first clue," said Holmes. "You can thank Doctor Watson's observation for that, though he failed to draw the inference. It set my foot upon the trail. Why should this man at such a time be filling his house with strong odours? Obviously, to cover some other smell which he wished to conceal – some guilty smell which would suggest suspicions. Then came the idea of a room such as you see here with iron door and shutter – a hermetically sealed room. Put those two facts together, and whither do they lead? I could only determine that by examining the house myself. I was already certain that the case was serious, for I had examined the box-office chart at the Haymarket Theatre – another of Doctor Watson's bull's-eyes – and ascertained that neither B thirty nor thirty-two of the upper circle had been occupied that night. Therefore, Amberley had not been to the theatre, and his alibi fell to the ground. He made a bad slip when he allowed my astute friend to notice the number of the seat taken for his wife. The question now arose how I might be able to examine the house. I sent an agent to the most impossible village I could think of, and summoned my man to it at such an hour that he could not possibly get back. To prevent any miscarriage, Doctor Watson accompanied him. The good vicar's name I took, of course, out of my *Crockford*. Do I make it all clear to you?"

"It is masterly," said the inspector in an awed voice.

"There being no fear of interruption, I proceeded to burgle the house. Burglary has always been an alternative profession, had I cared to adopt it, and I have little doubt that I should have come to the front. Observe what I found. You see the gas pipe along the skirting here. Very good. It rises in the angle of the wall, and there is a tap here in the corner. The pipe runs out into the strongroom, as you can see, and ends in that plaster rose in the centre of the ceiling, where it is concealed by the ornamentation. That end is wide open. At any moment by turning the outside tap the room could be flooded with gas. With door and shutter closed and the tap full on I would not give two minutes of conscious sensation to anyone shut up in that little chamber. By what devilish device he decoyed them there I do not know, but once inside the door they were at his mercy."

The inspector examined the pipe with interest. "One of our officers mentioned the smell of gas," said he, "but, of course, the window and door were open then, and the paint – or some of it – was already about. He had begun the work of painting the day before, according to his story. But what next, Mr Holmes?"

"Well, then came an incident which was rather unexpected to myself. I was slipping through the pantry window in the early dawn when I felt a hand inside my collar, and a voice said: 'Now, you rascal, what are you doing in there?' When I could twist my head round I looked into the tinted spectacles of my friend and rival, Mr Barker. It was a curious foregathering,* and set us both smiling. It seems that he had been engaged by Doctor Ray Ernest's family to make some investigations, and had come to the same conclusion as to foul play. He had watched the house for some days, and had spotted Doctor Watson as one of the obviously suspicious characters who had called there. He could hardly arrest Watson, but when he saw a man actually climbing out of the pantry window, there came a limit to his restraint. Of course, I told him how matters stood, and we continued the case together."

"Why him? Why not us?"

"Because it was in my mind to put that little test which answered so admirably. I fear you would not have gone so far."

The inspector smiled.

"Well, maybe not. I understand that I have your word, Mr Holmes, that you step right out of the case now and that you turn all your results over to us."

"Certainly, that is always my custom."

"Well, in the name of the Force I thank you. It seems a clear case, as you put it, and there can't be much difficulty over the bodies."

"I'll show you a grim little bit of evidence," said Holmes, "and I am sure Amberley himself never observed it. You'll get results, Inspector, by always putting yourself in the other fellow's place, and thinking what you would do yourself. It takes some imagination, but it pays. Now, we will suppose that you were shut up in this little room, had not two minutes to live, but wanted to get even with the fiend who was probably mocking at you from the other side of the door. What would you do?"

"Write a message."

"Exactly. You would like to tell people how you died. No use writing on paper. That would be seen. If you wrote on the wall some eye might rest upon it. Now, look here! Just above the skirting is scribbled with a purple indelible pencil: 'We we...' That's all."

"What do you make of that?"

"Well, it's only a foot above the ground. The poor devil was on the floor and dying when he wrote it. He lost his senses before he could finish."

"He was writing, 'We were murdered.'"

"That's how I read it. If you find an indelible pencil on the body—"

"We'll look out for it, you may be sure. But those securities? Clearly there was no robbery at all. And yet he *did* possess those bonds. We verified that."

"You may be sure he has them hidden in a safe place. When the whole elopement had passed into history, he would suddenly discover them and announce that the guilty couple had relented and sent back the plunder or had dropped it on the way."

"You certainly seem to have met every difficulty," said the inspector. "Of course, he was bound to call us in, but why he should have gone to you I can't understand."

"Pure swank!"* Holmes answered. "He felt so clever and so sure of himself that he imagined no one could touch him. He could say to any suspicious neighbour, 'Look at the steps I have taken. I have consulted not only the police, but even Sherlock Holmes.'"

The inspector laughed.

"We must forgive you your 'even', Mr Holmes," said he. "It's as workmanlike a job as I can remember."

A couple of days later my friend tossed across to me a copy of the biweekly *North Surrey Observer*. Under a series of flaming headlines, which began with "The Haven Horror" and ended with "Brilliant Police Investigation", there was a packed column of print which gave the first consecutive account of the affair. The concluding paragraph is typical of the whole. It ran thus:

> The remarkable acumen by which Inspector MacKinnon deduced from the smell of paint that some other smell, that of gas, for example, might be concealed; the bold deduction that the strongroom might also be the death chamber, and the subsequent inquiry which led to the discovery of the bodies in a disused well, cleverly concealed by a dog kennel, should live in the history of crime as a standing example of the intelligence of our professional detectives.

"Well, well... MacKinnon is a good fellow," said Holmes with a tolerant smile. "You can file it in our archives, Watson. Some day the true story may be told."

NOTE ON THE TEXT

The present volume follows the text of the first British edition of *The Casebook of Sherlock Holmes*, published by John Murray in June 1927. A small number of emendations have been made to wording for the sake of logic or clarity. These changes have also been annotated. The spelling and punctuation have been standardized, modernized and made consistent throughout.

NOTES

p. 3, *the way of all flesh*: A famous phrase taken from 1 Kings 2:2 as it appears in the Douay–Rheims Bible (a seventeenth-century English translation formerly used in the Roman Catholic Church). It is also the title of a semi-autobiographical novel by Samuel Butler (1835–1902) that satirizes the mores of the Victorian period, written in the 1870s but published posthumously in 1903.

p. 3, *the beaux of Fielding... reprehensible careers*: References to some of the foremost British novelists of the eighteenth and nineteenth centuries. The picaresque works of the English author Henry Fielding (1707–54) typically comprise the bawdy escapades of lusty young male lovers (that is, "beaux"), such as the eponymous protagonists of *Joseph Andrews* (1742) and *Tom Jones* (1749). In contrast, *Pamela* (1740–41) and *Clarissa* (1747–48), epistolary novels by Fielding's contemporary and rival Samuel Richardson (1689–1761), describe the adventures of beautiful but demure young heroines (that is, "belles") who must strive to preserve their virtue against the depredations of unscrupulous male admirers. The Scottish novelist Sir Walter Scott (1771–1832) was the author of a large number of historical romances featuring heroic characters, including *Waverley* (1814) and *Ivanhoe* (1819). "Cockney" (that is, London-born) characters feature prominently in the novels of Charles Dickens (1812–70), perhaps the most celebrated example being the worldly-wise Sam Weller in *The Pickwick Papers* (1836). The most notable "worldling" with a "reprehensible career" in the works of the English writer William Makepeace Thackeray (1811–63) is Becky Sharp, an orphan who, in the satirical novel *Vanity Fair* (1847–48), is compelled to make her own way in the world, cynically exploiting the people she meets in order to climb the social ladder.

p. 3, *Valhalla*: In Norse mythology, a majestic palace in which slain heroes abide with Odin, the supreme god.

p. 3, *1889*: In fact, *The Sign of the Four* was published in 1890, first in February in *Lippincott's Monthly Magazine* and then in book form in October, under the shorter title *The Sign of Four*. Both versions of the title have been used in subsequent editions, with most favouring the four-word version.

p. 4, *the later Victorian era... feverish days*: When Queen Victoria's reign ended with her death in January 1901 – three months before the first instalment of the Sherlock Holmes novel *The Hound of the Baskervilles* appeared in the *Strand Magazine* – she was succeeded by her son, Albert Edward (1841–1910), who reigned (as Edward VII) until his death in May 1910. He was succeeded by his own son, George V (1865–1936), who reigned from 1910 until 1936.

p. 4, *I had fully determined... rash act away*: Sherlock Holmes apparently plummets to his death from the Reichenbach Falls in Switzerland during a confrontation with his arch-enemy Professor Moriarty in the short story 'The Final Problem', first published in the *Strand* and in the US magazine *McClure's* in December 1893 and subsequently as the final adventure in the collection *The Memoirs of Sherlock Holmes* (1894). Due to popular demand, however, Holmes returned in *The Hound of the Baskervilles*

(1902), a novel-length story set prior to 'The Final Problem', before being brought back on a more permanent basis in a series of adventures that were later collected as *The Return of Sherlock Holmes* (1905). In the first of these stories, 'The Adventure of the Empty House', first published in *Collier's* in the United States in September 1903 and in the *Strand* in October 1903, Holmes reappears three years after the events of 'The Final Problem' and explains to Watson that he in fact defeated Moriarty at the Reichenbach Falls, but then went into hiding in order to protect himself from the professor's confederates.

p. 4, *history... the drama*: Arthur Conan Doyle was a prolific author whose oeuvre spans a number of genres and forms. After the Sherlock Holmes stories, his best-known fictional works are those featuring the indomitable scientist Professor Challenger, notably *The Lost World* (1912), a science-fiction adventure about an expedition to a part of the Amazon basin where prehistoric animals still exist. He was also the author of a number of historical novels, including *The White Company* (1891) and *Sir Nigel* (1905–06), both of which are set in the Middle Ages, and a vast number of short stories. He also wrote three volumes of poetry – *Songs of Action* (1898), *Songs of the Road* (1911) and *The Guards Came Through* (1919) – as well as for the stage, including the plays *Waterloo* (1894), written for the famous actor-manager Henry Irving (1838–1905), and *The House of Temperley* (1909–10). His non-fiction included historical works such as *The Great Boer War* (1900), the work that – he believed – earned him his knighthood in 1902. In his later life Conan Doyle became the world's best-known proponent of spiritualism – a system of beliefs based on the notion that the spirits of the dead continue to exist in the hereafter and can be communicated with by the living – and this was reflected in his literary output. Among the many books he wrote on the subject are *The New Revelation* (1918), *The Vital Message* (1919), *The Wanderings of a Spiritualist* (1921), *The Case for Spirit Photography* (1922) and *The History of Spiritualism* (1926).

p. 5, *Carlton Club*: A private members' club in St James's, central London. It was founded in 1832 as the headquarters of the Conservative Party.

p. 6, *Sir George Lewis over the Hammerford will case*: Famous for his discretion, Sir George Lewis (1833–1911), one of the most distinguished lawyers of the day, specialized in cases from high society, and was adept at keeping his clients out of court and shielding them from adverse publicity. The "Hammerford will case" is fictitious, although whether it refers to one of Holmes's untold adventures or to a story that had featured prominently in the newspapers is unclear.

p. 6, *Queen Anne Street*: A street in Marylebone, central London, that bisects Harley Street, famously the location of the consulting rooms of many eminent physicians and surgeons.

p. 7, *the late Professor Moriarty... Colonel Sebastian Moran*: For Moriarty, see second note to p. 4. Colonel Sebastian Moran is one of Moriarty's lieutenants. He appears in 'The Adventure of the Empty House' – see second note to p. 4.

p. 7, *the Splügen Pass*: An Alpine mountain pass between Splügen in Switzerland and Chiavenna in Italy.

p. 8, *Khyber*: A mountain pass in the Hindu Kush mountain range, on the border between present-day Pakistan (then part of India) and Afghanistan. It was an essential trade route between central Asia and the subcontinent, and therefore of great strategic importance. Given his age and the year in which this story is set, it is likely that General de Merville distinguished himself there during the Second Anglo-Afghan War, a conflict that began in November 1878, when the British invaded Afghanistan from India, with the intention of thwarting Russian ambitions in the region (which were a potential threat to the British Raj). After hostilities ceased in September 1870, the country remained a British protectorate – a buffer zone between the British Raj and Russia – until 1919, after the Third Anglo-Afghan War, when Afghanistan regained its independence.

p. 10, *telephone call*: The term "telephone call" was originally used to refer to the sound made by a ringing telephone, although from the context it is clear that Colonel Damery means a telephone number.

p. 10, *Kingston*: Kingston upon Thames, a town in Surrey on the south bank of the Thames, south-west of London.

p. 10, *Hurlingham*: On the banks of the Thames near Fulham in west London, Hurlingham is the location of the Hurlingham Club, a private members' club that is regarded as the birthplace of the modern sport of polo.

p. 10, *My old friend... no mean artist*: The criminal Charles Peace (1832–79), executed for murder in 1879, became an accomplished violinist after teaching himself to play a violin with a single string. The artist and writer Thomas Griffiths Wainewright (1794–1847), who was transported to the penal colony of Van Diemen's Land (Tasmania) for fraud in 1837, was also widely suspected of being a serial poisoner following the suspicious deaths of three family members and a friend.

p. 11, *Parkhurst*: A prison on the Isle of Wight, off the south coast.

p. 11, *"nark"*: An informant.

p. 11, *entrée*: The right to enter.

p. 11, *Simpson's*: A famous restaurant on the Strand in central London.

p. 12, *breed*: Breeding.

p. 13, *Apaches*: Parisian street ruffians or thugs.

p. 14, *I disregard... less than he means*: The point being that the baron is *not* a blusterer, a class of person that Holmes usually disregards.

p. 14, *scorbutic*: Suffering from scurvy.

p. 14, *beside him on the settee... he had brought up*: In other words, Johnson has descended into the criminal underworld, here implicitly compared to hell, and returned with a piece of burning wood ("brand") in the form of Kitty Winter. See, for instance, Amos 4:11: "I have overthrown some of you, as God overthrew Sodom and Gomorrah, and ye were as a firebrand plucked out of the burning."

p. 14, *cripes*: A euphemism for "Christ".

p. 14, *to the rattle*: That is, until death. The "rattle" is the "death rattle", a gurgling sound sometimes emitted from the throat of a dying person.

p. 19, *self-complaisance*: Self-satisfaction.

p. 20, *the Café Royal*: A famous restaurant on London's Regent Street patronized over the years by many literary figures, including Oscar Wilde, Virginia Woolf and D.H. Lawrence, as well as other celebrities.

p. 21, *brougham*: A horse-drawn carriage with a roof and with the driver sitting on an open seat at the front.

p. 21, *singlestick*: A form of fencing using wooden sticks instead of swords. In the first Sherlock Holmes story, *A Study in Scarlet* (1887), Watson records that Holmes "is an expert singlestick player" on his list entitled "Sherlock Holmes – his limits" (Chapter 2).

p. 22, *tobacco slipper*: In 'The Adventure of the Musgrave Ritual', published in the *Strand* and *Harper's Weekly* in May 1893 and collected in *The Memoirs of Sherlock Holmes* (1894), Watson reveals that Holmes keeps his tobacco "in the toe end of a Persian slipper".

p. 22, *erysipelas*: An acute bacterial infection of the skin characterized by a raised bright-red rash, which often led to serious complications in the era before antibiotics.

p. 22, *Cunard boat Ruritania*: Cunard is a steamship company founded by the Canadian-born British shipowner Sir Samuel Cunard (1787–1865), originally to transport mail between Britain and Canada. The *Ruritania*, named after the imaginary central-European kingdom that is the setting for the adventure story *The Prisoner of Zenda* (1894) by the English novelist Anthony Hope (1863–1933), is fictitious.

p. 23, *By the Lord Harry*: An old-fashioned exclamation of unknown origin. "Old Harry" was a name for the Devil, although the earliest instance of "by the Lord Harry" recorded in the *OED* (1693) significantly predates that for "Old Harry" (1777).

p. 23, *the London Library*: A subscription-based lending library established in 1841.

p. 23, *cyclical dates*: In the traditional Chinese calendar, a year is referred to using two characters: one of the "Ten Heavenly Stems" followed by one of the "Twelve Earthly Branches". Of the 120 possible combinations only sixty are used, resulting in a sixty-year, or "sexagenary", cycle – that is, each combination recurs once every sixty years. It can therefore be difficult to determine in which cycle a piece of antique porcelain, which is usually marked with the two characters that correspond to a particular year, was made, although this is possible in cases in which the name of the reign is also recorded. Otherwise it is necessary to identify styles or features typical of a certain reign in order to make an accurate judgement about the year of manufacture.

p. 23, *the Hung-wu... and the Yuan*: Watson here refers to the Hongwu emperor (1328–98), who reigned 1368–98, founder of the Ming dynasty, which ruled China for nearly three centuries; the Yongle emperor (1360–1424), the third emperor of the Ming dynasty, who reigned 1402–24; Tang Ying (1682–1756), a writer and ceramist during the Qing dynasty (1644–1911) who super-intended the imperial porcelain works in the city of Jingdezhen for twenty-eight years; the Sung, a dynasty that ruled from 960 to 1279; and the Yuan, a dynasty that ruled from 1279 to 1368.

p. 24, *Christie's*: A famous London auction house.

p. 24, *Sotheby*: Another famous auction house in London.

p. 25, *the great boom*: The discovery of gold in the region of Witwatersrand in the Transvaal (now part of South Africa) in July 1886 provoked a gold rush that in turn led to the establishment of the city of Johannesburg.

p. 25, *Tang*: A dynasty that ruled China between 618 and *c*.906, a period regarded as the golden age of Chinese art.

p. 27, *the Emperor Shomu... the history of ceramics*: Shōmu (701–56) was emperor of Japan between 724 and 749. During his reign he funded the creation of a great number of Buddhist temples and artefacts, storing many of the latter in a specially

THE CASEBOOK OF SHERLOCK HOLMES

built storehouse, the Shōsō-in, part of the monumental Tōdai Temple located in the city of Nara, the Japanese capital between 710 and 784. The Northern Wei dynasty ruled northern China from 386 to 535. It was renowned for its Buddhist art, notably the cave sculptures at Yungang, but not for its ceramics.

p. 28, *vitriol*: Sulphuric acid.

p. 29, *The wages of sin*: Romans 6:23.

p. 31, *the cockaded coachman*: That is, the coachman wears a rosette or a plume in his hat as part of his uniform.

p. 31, *a loyal friend and a chivalrous gentleman*: Widely interpreted to be the king, Edward VII – see first note to p. 4.

p. 33, *worried*: Harassed, pestered.

p. 33, *write an experience of my own*: This is the first of only two stories in the Holmesian canon narrated by the detective himself (the other is 'The Adventure of the Lion's Mane', also in the *Casebook*). However, both 'The Adventure of the *Gloria Scott*' (first published in the *Strand* and in *Harper's Weekly* in April 1893 and then in the 1894 collection *The Memoirs of Sherlock Holmes*) and 'The Adventure of the Musgrave Ritual' (see first note to p. 22), which both describe events in Holmes's youth, consist largely of narratives related by the detective himself, with only brief framing narration by Watson.

p. 33, *the Boer War*: The Second Boer War (1899–1902), fought between the British Empire and the independent Boer republics of the Transvaal and the Orange Free State (in present-day South Africa). The Boers were Dutch and Huguenot colonists who settled in southern Africa in the seventeenth century.

p. 34, *deserted me for a wife*: Watson married Mary Morstan at the end of *The Sign of the Four* (1890), a story set in 1888. However, in 'The Adventure of the Empty House' (see second note to p. 4), set in 1894, Watson refers to his "sad bereavement", implying that he is now a widower. Although most likely an error on the part of the author, players of what is known as "the Great Game" – a mock-scholarly activity in which Holmesian critics, including well-known writers such as Dorothy L. Sayers, examine the canon as though Holmes and Watson were historical figures, and Conan Doyle merely Watson's agent – have interpreted this as a reference to a second marriage.

p. 34, *Throgmorton Street*: A street in the City of London (the financial district of the capital).

p. 35, *martinet*: A strict disciplinarian; one who demands total obedience.

p. 35, *the Crimean VC*: The Crimean War (1853–56) was fought against Russia by an alliance including Britain on the Crimean Peninsula. It was sparked by Russian aggression against Turkey, which provoked the latter country's European allies to intervene, leading to the destruction of Russian naval power in the Black Sea and the eventual capture of the Crimean city of Sebastopol in 1855. The military decoration known as the Victoria Cross was created for those who had shown conspicuous bravery during the conflict. It remains the highest military honour for valour a British soldier can receive.

p. 35, *near Diamond Hill outside Pretoria*: The Battle of Diamond Hill was fought on 11th–12th June 1900, during the Second Boer War – see third note to p. 33. Following the capture of Pretoria, the capital of the Transvaal, by the British on 5th June, the Boers had fallen back to Diamond Hill, twenty miles east of the city, but during the battle were driven from their positions and forced to retreat further.

p. 36, *trap*: A light, two-wheeled carriage.

p. 44, *the case... deeply involved*: Widely interpreted as a muddled reference to 'The Adventure of the Priory School' (published in *Collier's* in the United States in January 1904, and in the *Strand* in February, and subsequently in the 1905 collection *The Return of Sherlock Holmes*), in which Holmes's client was the Duke of Holdernesse, not the Duke of Greyminster. It is possible that Conan Doyle confused the title with that of another story from *The Return of Sherlock Holmes*, 'The Adventure of the Abbey Grange', which originally appeared in the *Strand* in September 1904, and in *Collier's* in December of the same year.

p. 48, *Buffelspruit, outside Pretoria*: In fact, the South African town of Buffelspruit is some 250 miles west of Pretoria.

p. 48, *stoep*: Veranda.

p. 51, *Lord Roberts*: Field Marshal Frederick Sleigh Roberts, 1st Earl Roberts (1832–1914), one of the most distinguished British military officers of the day. Among other achievements, he was awarded the Victoria Cross for his role in suppressing the Indian Mutiny of 1857–58, led British forces to a victory at the Battle of Kandahar in September 1880, thereby ending the Second Anglo-Afghan War (see note to p. 8), and, as commander-in-chief of the British forces during the Second Boer War (see third note to p. 33), took the cities of Johannesburg (on 31st May 1900) and Pretoria (on 5th June 1900).

p. 55, *The Adventure of the Mazarin Stone*: Adapted from Conan Doyle's one-act play *The Crown Diamond, or An Evening with Sherlock Holmes*, first performed on 2nd May 1921 at the Bristol Hippodrome. (The short story was published in the *Strand* in October 1921, and in *Hearst's International* in the United States in November 1921.) This accounts for the unusual use of a third-person narrator in this story, as Watson barely features in the play. The only other story in the canon to use this mode of narration is 'His Last Bow' (published in the *Strand* and *Collier's* in September 1917), although the novels *A Study in Scarlet* (1887) and *The Valley of Fear* (1915) each contain lengthy third-person flashbacks.

p. 57, *"We used something of the sort once before"*: In 'The Adventure of the Empty House' (see second note to p. 4), a wax effigy of Holmes is used to deceive the detective's enemies.

p. 57, *gasogene*: A device for producing carbonated (fizzy) water. It consists of two glass globes, one containing water and the other containing chemicals, that react together to make carbon dioxide.

p. 58, *Count Negretto Sylvius*: In *The Crown Diamond* Holmes's adversary was Colonel Sebastian Moran, the villain of 'The Adventure of the Empty House' (see second note to p. 4).

p. 58, *Mazarin stone*: The name possibly refers to the Italian-born French statesman Cardinal Jules Mazarin (1602–61), the chief minister of France from 1642 until his death.

p. 58, *gudgeon*: A small freshwater fish.

p. 59, *old Straubenzee's workshop in the Minories*: The workshop is fictitious, although the name likely refers to Major General Sir Casimir Cartwright van Straubenzee (1867–1956), a Canadian-born officer in the British army, who, among other achievements, was inspector general of the Royal Artillery in 1917–18. The Minories is a street in the City of London.

p. 64, *train-de-luxe*: A luxury train – one that consists solely of first-class carriages.

p. 64, *Crédit Lyonnais*: A French bank.

p. 64, *commissionaire*: A messenger belonging to the Corps of Commissionaires, an organization founded in 1859 by Captain Sir Edward Walter (1823–1904) in order to provide employment for veterans of the armed forces after the Crimean War (see second note to p. 35).

p. 64, *peached*: Spilt the beans, squealed.

p. 64, *I'll compound a felony*: In law, to "compound a felony" is to accept payment in return for an agreement not to prosecute, something that, historically, was punishable as a misdemeanour under English common law.

p. 66, *cove*: A slang term meaning "chap", "bloke" and so on.

p. 66, *Hoffmann 'Barcarolle'*: A song from the opera *The Tales of Hoffmann* by the German composer Jacques Offenbach (1819–80) and the French librettist Jules Barbier (1825–1901), based on the fantastical stories of the German writer E.T.A. Hoffmann (1776–1822) and first performed in 1881. A barcarolle is a song sung by Venetian gondoliers.

p. 66, *split*: Informed.

p. 66, *I'll do him down... if I swing for it*: Literally, "I will get the better of him to the value of a sovereign even if I am hanged for it." In other words, Merton is threatening to kill Sanders. "Thick 'un" was a slang term for a sovereign, a gold coin worth one pound.

p. 67, *leery*: A slang term meaning "knowing", "sly".

p. 67, *Madame Tussaud*: The famous London waxwork museum, established in 1802 by the French artist Marie Tussaud (1761–1850).

p. 74, *Harrow*: A town north-west of London, now part of Greater London.

p. 74, *I don't like the smell of you*: Some critics, notably David Martin Dakin in *A Sherlock Holmes Commentary* (1972), have pointed out that the stereotypical presentation of Steve Dixie and the uncharacteristic racism of Holmes's attitude to him are in contrast with the sympathetic treatment of the subject of interracial marriage in the earlier story 'The Adventure of the Yellow Face' – first published in the *Strand* and *Harper's Weekly* in February 1893 and then in *The Memoirs of Sherlock Holmes* (1894) – and have called into question the authorship of this story as a result.

p. 74, *the Bull Ring in Birmingham*: A large marketplace.

p. 75, *Harrow Weald*: A suburban district to the north of Harrow.

p. 75, *the Weald station*: In the early twentieth century, Harrow became the unofficial capital of "Metroland", the rapidly expanding north-western suburbs of the capital that were served by the Metropolitan Railway, which was opened in 1863 to connect the City of London in the east with the railway termini of Paddington, Euston and King's Cross, and then extended beyond central London into Middlesex, reaching Harrow in 1880.

p. 76, *attaché at Rome*: That is, he worked for the British ambassador in Rome.

p. 79, *Paregoric*: A medicine made up of opium, camphor, aniseed and benzoic acid, formerly used as a remedy for coughing, among other ailments.

p. 79, *Raphael*: the Italian Renaissance painter Raffaello Sanzio (1483–1520), known as Raphael.

p. 79, *a first folio Shakespeare*: The first collected edition of Shakespeare's plays, published in 1623.

p. 79, *Crown Derby tea set*: That is, a tea set made from bone china by the Royal Crown Derby Porcelain Company (known simply as "Crown Derby" until 1890), based in the city of Derby in the English Midlands.

p. 80, *These are from Italy*: In fact, Lucerne is a city in Switzerland.

p. 81, *Langdale Pike*: The Langdale Pikes are a group of peaks in the Lake District in the north-west of England. Since Pike is a gossip columnist, the name is likely a pseudonym.

p. 82, *a broken reed*: A weak and unreliable person. The phrase is taken from the Old Testament, where it appears a number of times, including in Isaiah 36:6: "Lo, thou trustest in the staff of this broken reed, on Egypt; whereon if a man lean, it will go into his hand, and pierce it: so is Pharaoh king of Egypt to all that trust in him."

p. 86, *conquistadors*: The Spanish conquerors of Mexico and Peru in the sixteenth century.

p. 86, *Pernambuco*: A state in north-eastern Brazil, historically a centre of sugar-cane cultivation.

p. 86, *'belle dame sans merci'*: A femme fatale. 'La Belle Dame sans Merci' (whose title means "the beautiful lady without mercy") is an 1819 poem by the Romantic poet John Keats (1795–1821) about a beautiful fairy who seduces knights and keeps them captive. Keats took the title from *La Belle Dame sans Mercy* (*c.*1424), a poem in the courtly-love tradition by the French poet Alain Chartier (*c.*1385–1430).

p. 87, *Arabian Nights*: A collection of stories taken from Middle Eastern and Indian folklore, including the tales of Aladdin, Ali Baba and Sinbad the Sailor. It was written in Arabic and compiled sometime in the Middle Ages, and first published in English in 1706.

p. 87, *overrated*: Emended from "underrated", which is also the word used in the *Strand*. "Overrated", however, makes more sense in the context.

p. 88, *calcined*: Reduced to charcoal or ash by burning.

p. 90, *compound a felony*: See fifth note to p. 64.

p. 91, *Old Jewry*: A street in the City of London. From the time of the Norman Conquest until 1290, when the Jews were expelled from England, it was a Jewish ghetto.

p. 91, *Mincing Lane*: A street in the City of London that in the late nineteenth century was the world's leading centre for tea and spice trading.

p. 91, *of even date*: Of the same date.

p. 91, *per E.J.C.*: That is, the letter has been written by an employee with the initials "E.J.C." on behalf of the firm.

p. 92, *the giant rat... not yet prepared*: One of the most famous of the more than one hundred untold stories referred to in the canon. Sumatra is one of the Sunda Islands of western Indonesia. It was a Dutch colony until 1945.

p. 92, *a Grimms' fairy tale*: A reference to the anthology of German fairy tales compiled by the brothers Jacob (1785–1863) and Wilhelm (1786–1859) Grimm, German philologists and folklorists, first published in 1812.

p. 92, *Voyage of the Gloria Scott... Hammersmith wonder*: For 'The Adventure of the *Gloria Scott*', see second note to p. 33. The rest of the references in this paragraph are to untold stories. A "Gila monster" is a large carnivorous lizard native to the south-western United States and Mexico. "Yeggman" is a US slang term for a burglar or safe-breaker.

p. 92, *Vampirism... Transylvania*: Transylvania, a mountainous region in central Europe, was part of Hungary from the end of the seventeenth century until 1918, when it became part of north-western Romania. Vampirism had come to be associated with Transylvania after it was used as the setting for the novel *Dracula* (1897) by the Irish novelist Bram Stoker (1847–1912).

p. 93, *alien religion*: Roman Catholicism.

p. 95, *played rugby... Richmond*: Blackheath is a suburban area of south-east London. Founded in 1858, Blackheath Football Club is one of the oldest rugby clubs in the world. Its name reflects the fact that the game known as rugby was originally considered a variation of football (known as "Rugby football"), as invented at Rugby School in Warwickshire in around 1845. Richmond is a suburban area in south-west London. Richmond Football Club – also in fact a rugby club – was founded in 1861. Along with

Blackheath it was one of the founding members of the Rugby Football Union in 1871.

p. 96, *Take a wire down*: Holmes is proposing to dictate a telegram to Watson.

p. 96, *Old Deer Park*: An area of open space in Richmond that contains Richmond Football Club's training grounds and pitch.

p. 99, *rebus*: An ornamental device that cryptically represents a name using pictures, symbols and so on.

p. 106, *a queen... poison from it?*: A reference to Eleanor of Castile (1241–90), who was queen of England as the first wife of Edward I (1239–1307). According to legend, she saved her husband's life by sucking the poison from his wound after a would-be assassin stabbed him in the arm with a poisoned dagger during a crusade to the Holy Land in 1272.

p. 106, *bird bow*: A small bow used for hunting birds.

p. 106, *curare*: A poisonous substance that paralyses the motor nerves and is obtained from some South American plants.

p. 109, *the same month that Holmes refused a knighthood*: Conan Doyle received his own knighthood at the same time, as part of the 1902 Coronation Honours, which were announced on 26th June of that year (the date originally set for the coronation of Edward VII).

p. 109, *the South African War*: The Second Boer War – see third note to p. 33.

p. 112, *Alexander Hamilton Garrideb*: Alexander Hamilton (c.1757–1804) was one of the Founding Fathers of the United States and the country's first secretary of the treasury (1789–95).

p. 112, *wheat pit*: Part of the floor of a stock exchange in which wheat is traded.

p. 112, *Fort Dodge*: Presumably a reference to Dodge City, a city in south-western Kansas, established in 1872. The city of Fort Dodge is in Iowa, over 500 miles away from the Arkansas River.

p. 112, *Topeka*: The state capital of Kansas.

p. 114, *covert for putting up a bird*: A bush or thicket for disturbing a game bird, thereby allowing the hunter to take a shot at it.

p. 114, *Dr Lysander Starr of Topeka*: In inventing this name Holmes appears to have adapted that of the villainous Colonel Lysander Stark (although this is itself a pseudonym), who appears in 'The Adventure of the Engineer's Thumb', a Sherlock Holmes story first published in the *Strand* in March 1892, and later republished in *The Adventures of Sherlock Holmes* (1892).

p. 114, *Tyburn Tree*: Tyburn was a village on the periphery of London (where now Marble Arch stands) and the site of public hangings. The gallows was known as "Tyburn Tree".

p. 115, *"Neanderthal", "Heidelberg", "Cro-Magnon"*: The names of three extinct species or subspecies of human being.

p. 115, *Syracusan*: From the Greek colony of Syracuse on the east coast of Sicily, a major cultural centre in the fifth and fourth centuries BC.

p. 115, *the Alexandrian school*: The ancient city of Alexandria in Egypt, founded by Alexander the Great in 332 BC, was renowned as a centre of Hellenic (Greek) culture.

p. 116, *Hans Sloane*: The Irish physician, naturalist and collector Sir Hans Sloane (1660–1753), whose collection of 71,000 items provided the foundation of the British Museum, the British Library and the Natural History Museum.

p. 118, *drills*: Seed drills, agricultural devices for sowing seeds in rows.

p. 118, *buckboards*: A buckboard is a kind of open carriage with four wheels and a plank extending between the front and rear axles, on which there are seats.

p. 118, *Artesian Wells*: An artesian well is one that makes use of subterranean water pressure and therefore does not require a pump to bring water to the surface. The name comes from the French *"artésien"*, meaning "from Artois", where such wells were first made by Carthusian monks in the Middle Ages.

p. 118, *Aston*: A suburb of Birmingham.

p. 121, *Newgate Calendar*: Newgate was a notorious prison in the City of London, on the site of today's Central Criminal Court, known as the Old Bailey. The *Newgate Calendar* was an illustrated compilation of sensational accounts of infamous crimes, originally published in five volumes in 1773. The name *Newgate Calendar* was later used for a variety of publications providing biographical information about the prison's detainees.

p. 121, *the rogues' portrait gallery*: A collection of images of wanted criminals.

p. 122, *possess our souls in patience*: "In your patience possess ye your souls" (Luke 21:19).

p. 123, *jemmy*: A crowbar.

p. 125, *bench*: Judge.

p. 127, *Cox & Co.*: A real bank, founded in 1758 as an agency for the Grenadier Guards (that is, it was responsible for distributing pay from the government to the men of the regiment), and that later specialized as a bank for active and retired officers of the armed forces. From 1888 it was based at 16–18 Charing Cross Road. It was acquired by Lloyds Bank in 1923.

p. 127, *Late Indian Army*: Watson served as an army surgeon during the Second Anglo-Afghan War (see note to p. 8), in which he was wounded – see *A Study in Scarlet* (1887).

p. 127, *cutter*: A light, speedy boat.

p. 128, *only be told as by a third person*: On the use of third-person narration in the canon, see note to p. 55.

p. 128, *Family Herald*: A magazine aimed at women published between 1842 and 1940. It contained romantic fiction.

p. 129, *some western state… in the world*: Gibson was presumably senator for California, where the discovery of gold at Sutter's Mill, Coloma, in January 1848, by the American sawmill operator James W. Marshall (1810–85), led to a famous gold rush that brought many hundreds of thousands of people to the region, and earned California the reputation of being the "golden state".

p. 129, *assizes*: A court that sat at periodic intervals in each county (in this case Hampshire).

p. 131, *reed-girt*: Encircled by reed beds.

p. 133, *booming*: Celebrating, talking up.

p. 136, *Manaos*: A city in northern Brazil.

p. 151, *At the words... into the water*: The method of the murder outlined here was inspired by the real story of a German man who weighted a revolver with a stone and then hung it over a bridge, so that when he shot himself the revolver would vanish into the water, thus allowing him to commit suicide but make it look like murder. The case was described by the Austrian criminologist Hans Gustav (1847–1915) in *Handbuch für Untersuchungsrichter als System der Kriminalistik* (1893), published in English as *Criminal Investigations: A Practical Textbook* (1907).

p. 155, *and others perhaps less excusable*: A reference to Holmes's use of the narcotics cocaine and morphine, something of which Watson vehemently disapproves. See, for instance, Watson's remonstration with Holmes over the latter's use of "a seven per cent solution" of cocaine in the first chapter of *The Sign of the Four* (1890).

p. 156, *the Copper Beeches... respectable father*: In 'The Adventure of the Copper Beeches', published in the *Strand* in June 1892 and then in *The Adventures of Sherlock Holmes* (1892), Holmes makes inferences about the character of Jephro Rucastle from what he has been told about his young son's cruelty to small animals: "My dear Watson, you as a medical man are continually gaining light as to the tendencies of a child by the study of the parents. Don't you see that the converse is equally valid? I have frequently gained my first real insight into the character of parents by studying their children. This child's disposition is abnormally cruel, merely for cruelty's sake, and whether he derives this from his smiling father, as I should suspect, or from his mother, it bodes evil for the poor girl who is in their power."

p. 157, *Camford*: A portmanteau name combining "Cambridge" and "Oxford". Oddly, Cambridge had explicitly been the setting for 'The Adventure of the Missing Three-Quarter', published in the *Strand* in August 1904 and *Collier's* in November 1904, and then in *The Return of Sherlock Holmes* (1905).

p. 159, *EC*: The "East Central" postal district of London.

p. 161, *Lumbago*: Pain in the lower back.

p. 162, *alienist*: A former term for a psychiatrist.

p. 162, *Jack*: Bennett was previously "Trevor". It is possible to interpret "Jack" as Edith's pet name for her fiancé.

p. 165, *25th August*: Changed from "26th August" here and on one other occasion, since 25th August does not occur in the nine-day pattern later described.

p. 165, *Compound of the Busy Bee and Excelsior*: The meaning of Holmes's words is somewhat obscure. The Latin "*excelsior*", meaning "higher", is often used in English to mean "Ever upwards!" or "Onwards and upwards!" This usage can be traced to the poem 'Excelsior' (1841) by Henry Wadsworth Longfellow (1807–82), in which the word is used as a refrain designed to convey a sense of aspiration: "The shades of night were falling fast, / As through an Alpine village passed / A youth, who bore, 'mid snow and ice, / A banner with the strange device, / Excelsior!" (ll. 1–5). If the terms "Busy Bee" and "Excelsior" are read in a generic sense, therefore, Holmes may be saying that Watson – or possibly their partnership – is a combination of industriousness ("Busy Bee") and a striving for something higher ("Excelsior"). The capitalization, however, suggests a specific allusion – perhaps to well-known brands or businesses bearing these names.

p. 168, *Slavonic*: Relating to the Slavonic, or Slavic, family of languages, which includes Russian, Ukrainian, Belorussian, Polish and Czech, among others.

p. 169, *Bohemian*: Here referring to the central-European kingdom of Bohemia, now part of the Czech Republic, whose capital is Prague.

p. 173, *Newfoundland*: A very large dog with a thick, coarse coat.

p. 174, *the Austrian stamp*: Bohemia was part of the Austro-Hungarian Empire.

p. 175, *serum of anthropoid*: That is, a serum (a liquid formed when blood coagulates that can be used for a therapeutic pur- poses such as inoculation) derived from one of the ape spe- cies closely related to humans, such as gorillas, orangutans or chimpanzees.

p. 177, *my withdrawal... gloom of London*: In 'The Adventure of the Second Stain', first published in the *Strand* in December 1904 and later collected in *The Return of Sherlock Holmes* (1905), Conan Doyle had made a second attempt to bring the adventures of the great detective to an end by having Watson inform his readers that Holmes had retired to the Sussex Downs to keep bees. Many more Holmes stories were to appear over the next two decades, however, all of which – with the exception of 'His Last Bow' (see note to p. 55), and 'The Adventure of the Lion's Mane' – were set before the relocation to Sussex.

p. 177, *the Downs*: The South Downs, a range of chalk hills in the south-eastern coastal counties of England, extending from Hampshire in the west to Beachy Head, a headland close to the town of Eastbourne in East Sussex.

p. 178, *rowing Blue*: That is, he has represented either Oxford or Cambridge at the sport of rowing.

p. 179, *surds and conic sections*: In mathematics, a surd is an irra- tional number – that is, any number that cannot be represented as a fraction in which both parts are integers (whole numbers) – that can be expressed as a rational number under a root sign, such as $\sqrt{2}$. A conic section is a shape formed when a plane (an imaginary flat surface) divides a circular cone, taking the form of a circle, an ellipse, a parabola or a hyperbola depending on the angle of the plane.

p. 181, *Lewes*: The county town of East Sussex.

p. 183, *bathing cots*: Otherwise known as "bathing machines", mobile huts that could be wheeled to the edge of the sea, enabling bathers to change or swim in privacy.

p. 188, *Airedale terrier*: A large terrier with a rough coat, named after the area of Yorkshire in which it was originally bred.

p. 190, *extravasated*: Blood is said to be "extravasated" when it is forced from its proper vessel into the surrounding area.

p. 193, *in Indian file*: In single file (called "Indian file" because it was believed that Native Americans marched in such a formation).

p. 193, *Cyanea!... the lion's mane!*: *Cyanea capillata*, the lion's-mane jellyfish, the largest known species of jellyfish. It is found in the waters around the British Isles in the summer months (the story is set in July).

p. 194, *It may have been the south-west gale that brought it up*: In fact, the lion's-mane jellyfish favours the colder oceans of the Northern Hemisphere.

p. 194, *Out of Doors, by the famous observer J.G. Wood*: The English writer John George Wood (1827–89) wrote prolifically on the subject of natural history. *Out of Doors: A Selection of Original Articles on Practical Natural History* was published in 1874. The quotations that follow come from the chapter entitled 'Medusa and Her Locks'.

p. 196, *at concert pitch*: Alert; in a state of readiness.

p. 197, *in active practice... seventeen of these*: Players of "the Great Game" (see first note to p. 34) generally date Holmes's retirement to late 1903 – it cannot be any earlier because 'The Adventure of the Creeping Man' (described as "one of the very last cases handled by Holmes before his retirement") takes place in September of that year, and it cannot be any later than December 1904 because that was the month in which 'The Adventure of the Second Stain', in which Holmes's withdrawal to Sussex is first revealed, was published (see first note to p. 177). Assuming that the "twenty-three years" does not include the three-year hiatus (1891–94) during which Holmes was missing, presumed dead, after his duel with Moriarty at the Reichenbach Falls (see second note to p. 4), that would place the commencement of his "active practice" in 1877 – and, certainly, it is clear from *A Study in Scarlet* (1887), set in 1881, that Holmes is already well established as a consulting detective by the time he and Watson make one another's acquaintance. Watson's claim that he was only allowed to cooperate with Holmes for seventeen years is difficult to reconcile with what can be determined about Holmes's chronology, however. Deduction of the four years between 1877 and 1881, plus the three years of the hiatus, from the inclusive twenty-six-year period (1877–1903), leaves nineteen, not seventeen years.

p. 197, *the whole story... trained cormorant*: Another of the most famous of the many untold stories referred to by Watson.

p. 198, *South Brixton*: In south London.

p. 200, *commonplace books*: A commonplace book is a notebook or scrapbook in which one transcribes interesting extracts or quotations for personal reference.

p. 200, *Wombwell, and of Sanger*: George Wombwell (1777–1850) was the owner of a famous travelling menagerie. The brothers "Lord" George Sanger (1825–1911) and John Sanger (1816–89) were well-known circus proprietors.

p. 202, *Allahabad*: A city in Uttar Pradesh, in northern India.

p. 203, *in his cups*: While drinking or during a drinking bout.

p. 209, *the field*: That which is visible from a particular viewpoint, in this case through a microscope.

p. 209, *epithelial scales*: Fragments from the epithelium, the thin layer of tissue that covers the body's surface.

p. 209, *coiner*: A person who produces counterfeit money.

p. 209, *half my wound pension*: Watson is making a joke about how much money he spends on gambling. He receives a soldier's pension from his time serving as an army surgeon during the Second Anglo-Afghan War (see note to p. 8), in which he was wounded – see *A Study in Scarlet* (1887).

p. 209, *Handy Guide to the Turf*: A reference to the annually published *Guide to the Turf* by the sports writer William Ruff (1801–56), and its imitators. "The turf" is a term used to refer to the sport of horse racing.

p. 210, *Newmarket Heath*: The site of a well-known racecourse near the town of Newmarket in Suffolk.

p. 210, *Grand National*: An annual steeplechase (a horse race with ditches and hedges) held at Aintree, Liverpool, every March or April. It was first run in 1839.

p. 210, *a buck in the days of the Regency*: That is, a fashionable young man, or dandy, during the period from 1811 to 1820, when George, Prince of Wales (1762–1830), ruled the United Kingdom in place of his father George III (1738–1820), whose bouts of mental illness made it impossible for him to discharge his royal duties. The term "Regency" is also sometimes used more broadly, to refer to a period beginning in the late eighteenth century and ending with the accession of Queen Victoria in 1837.

p. 210, *down Queer Street*: A colloquial term meaning "in financial difficulty".

p. 211, *the Derby*: An annual flat race (one with no jumps) for three-year-old horses (both colts and fillies) that takes place at Epsom Downs in Surrey in late May or early June. It was devised by a group including Edward Smith-Stanley, 12th Earl of Derby (1752–1834), who, it is said, won the honour of naming the race in a coin toss with Sir Charles Bunbury (1740–1821), another of the co-founders. It was first run in 1780.

p. 211, *You can get... the hundred*: That is, the odds have shortened from a hundred to one (or thereabouts) to forty to one (or thereabouts).

p. 212, *the Jews*: Here used to refer to moneylenders generally.

p. 216, *the upper condyle of a human femur*: A condyle is the rounded protuberance at the end of a bone that forms the joint with another bone. In fact, the femur (thigh bone) has a condyle only at the lower extremity; the upper extremity consists of the "femoral head" and "femoral neck".

p. 219, *dace*: Small freshwater fish.

p. 219, *spoon bait for jack*: A spoon bait is a fishing lure shaped like the bowl of a spoon. It is designed to wobble when pulled through the water, thereby creating turbulence and attracting fish. Jack are young pike.

p. 220, *barouche*: A kind of four-wheeled carriage.

p. 221, *groined*: In architecture, a groin is the edge formed by the intersection at right angles of two vaults (arches supported by pillars and forming a roof).

p. 222, *Saxon... Hugos and Odos*: The "Saxon" or "Anglo-Saxon" period began in the fifth and sixth centuries with the settlement in England of the Angles, the Saxons and the Jutes, Germanic peoples from what are now northern Germany and Denmark. It lasted until 1066, when England was invaded by the Normans, led by William, the Duke of Normandy, known as William the Conqueror (*c*.1027–87), who defeated the Anglo-Saxons under Harold II at the Battle of Hastings on 14th October 1066 and went on to rule as William I. "Odo" and "Hugo" are typically Norman names.

p. 227, *Lewisham*: An area in south London.

p. 228, *Coptic patriarchs*: The Coptic Orthodox Church is a Christian denomination from Egypt, traditionally founded by St Mark. Its chief bishop is known as a patriarch.

p. 230, *art for art's sake*: A slogan popular in the nineteenth century among those who did not believe that art should serve a moral or didactic purpose.

p. 231, *Haymarket Theatre*: The Theatre Royal Haymarket in London's West End, opened in 1821.

p. 232, *Masonic tiepin*: That is, the tiepin bears an emblem of the Freemasons, a powerful secret society that evolved from the medieval guild of stonemasons, and which is known for its pseudo-religious use of rituals and ancient symbols.

p. 233, *Lothario*: A womanizer or philanderer. Lothario is a character in the tragedy *The Fair Penitent* (1703) by the English dramatist Nicholas Rowe (1674–1718).

p. 234, *Crockford*: *Crockford's Clerical Directory*, the authoritative list of Anglican clergy in the United Kingdom, first issued in 1858 by the English publisher John Crockford (*c*.1823–65).

p. 234, *living of Mossmoor cum Little Purlington*: That is, Elman's living (his position as a parish priest) consists of two villages.

p. 237, *colourman*: A person who sells artist's paints.

p. 238, *Broadmoor*: A hospital for the criminally insane near Reading in Berkshire, established in 1863.

p. 240, *foregathering*: Accidental meeting.

p. 242, *swank*: Bravado.

EXTRA MATERIAL
FOR YOUNG READERS

THE WRITER

Sir Arthur Conan Doyle was born in Edinburgh on 22nd May 1859 to parents from well-off Irish families. His grandfather and two of his uncles were renowned cartoonists, socializing with the famous and the wealthy of Victorian society, but Arthur's father Charles did not succeed in his own career as an artist and draughtsman because of problems with depression and alcohol. Charles was a remote father and an unreliable earner, so the family were sometimes living in chaotic circumstances, with uncles and lodgers helping out financially. It was Arthur's mother, Mary, who provided the love, guidance and security that Arthur needed during a sometimes unstable childhood.

From an early age, Arthur devoured books. His mother used to recite the Arthurian legends to him, setting off a lifetime's interest in fiction based on myth and history. His favourite books as a child, however, were cowboy stories set in the Wild West.

When he was nine, Arthur was sent to boarding school in England – for a boy from his social background, this was usual. But boarding schools in those days could be very tough environments, with poor food and harsh discipline. However, he coped. He was already showing a flair for telling stories, and sometimes entertained the other boys with his creations.

After leaving school, Arthur studied for a degree in medicine at Edinburgh University. Medicine was seen as a reliable profession with a good income, but he found it difficult to concentrate on his studies. During his degree he encountered university lecturer

Doctor Joseph Bell – the inspiration for the fictional detective Sherlock Holmes. Bell taught his students the powers of meticulous observation in getting to the bottom of tricky medical problems, a power which Sherlock Holmes applies to criminal cases. He often tried to guess his patients' professions by making deductions from clues in their appearance – something that Sherlock Holmes is always doing.

Arthur was very adventurous. During the third year of his studies, he took the position of ship's doctor on a whaling boat travelling to Greenland and back, and at the end of his studies he became ship's surgeon on a voyage to West Africa. This adventurousness was with him most of his life. In his forties, for example, he served as volunteer army doctor in the Second Boer War (1899–1902) in what is now South Africa.

Also during his medical degree, Arthur was writing fiction, something that he continued to do after he had qualified as a doctor. It was more than just a passion – he needed the money. During his studies, he had lost his faith in Christianity, and because of this his uncles had withdrawn their financial support. He moved to Portsmouth and set up a medical practice there, and in the first half of the 1880s struggled to make a success of both his careers, doctor and writer. In 1885 he married Louisa Hawkins, the sister of a patient, and in 1886 he started writing a short mystery novel, which appeared the following year as *A Study in Scarlet*. Published in a Christmas magazine, it was a moderate success, but it was the first tale involving Sherlock Holmes.

A prolific author, Arthur was also writing historical novels and many other kinds of books, but it was when his Sherlock Holmes short stories started being published in the *Strand Magazine* from 1891 that he was catapulted into literary stardom.

Arthur's first wife died in 1906, and in 1907 he married Jean Leckie, with whom he had three children. Arthur's main interest at this time was spiritualism – the belief that the dead live on as spirits and can communicate with the living. He wrote many works about this, and in later life, after the death of his eldest son in the influenza pandemic that swept the world after the First World War, these beliefs gave him some comfort.

Arthur died of heart disease on 7th July 1930, aged seventy-one. He collapsed in his garden, and was found holding a flower in his hand.

THE BOOK

(This section contains spoilers)

The twelve short stories that make up *The Casebook of Sherlock Holmes* were originally published in London's *Strand Magazine*, as well as in an assortment of periodicals in the United States, between October 1921 and April 1927, with publication in book form occurring on both sides of the Atlantic in June 1927.

Arthur Conan Doyle's brilliant, mercurial creation had made his debut many years earlier, in November 1887, in a novel-length adventure called *A Study in Scarlet*, which told the story of the first meeting between the great detective and Doctor Watson, who would go on to become the most famous crime-fighting duo in fiction. Since then, Holmes's thrilling adventures had continued in dozens of short stories – collected as *The Adventures of Sherlock Holmes* (1892), *The Memoirs of Sherlock Holmes* (1893), *The Return of Sherlock Holmes* (1905) and *His Last Bow: Some Reminiscences of Sherlock Holmes* (1917) – and three more novels: *The Sign of the Four* (1890), *The Hound of the Baskervilles* (1902) and *The Valley of Fear* (1915).

As the years went by, not only did Holmes's preternatural powers allow him to outwit even the most dastardly and ingenious of his fictional adversaries, they also enabled him to survive the determined attempts of his creator, who grew tired of the seemingly superhuman sleuth and wished to devote himself to other forms of writing, either to kill him off – as in 'The Final Problem' (1893), in which Holmes apparently falls to his death from the Reichenbach Falls in Switzerland while struggling with the perfidious Professor

Moriarty – or to consign him to a peaceful, adventure-free retirement in the countryside as a beekeeper, as described in the opening paragraphs of 'The Adventure of the Second Stain' (1905). Such was the popularity of the character with the reading public, and so tempting were the ever-greater sums offered to Arthur by publishers for his writings, that the reluctant author was continually compelled to resurrect Baker Street's most celebrated resident – in the case of 'The Adventure of the Empty House' (1903), almost literally! – to meet the demand of hungry magazine buyers, whose appetite for more stories featuring their favourite fictional detective was apparently insatiable.

The story 'His Last Bow: The War Service of Sherlock Holmes' (later subtitled 'An Epilogue of Sherlock Holmes'), published in September 1917 and set in August 1914, on the eve of the First World War, had been Arthur's most recent attempt to provide his hero with a definitive valediction. This poignant story, which recounts the final daring feat of the now sixty-year-old detective's illustrious career, as he returns from retirement and works undercover to help the British government to entrap a German agent, ends with Holmes telling his loyal companion, "There's an east wind coming, Watson" – a reference to the imminent global conflagration.

However, although 'His Last Bow' is, chronologically speaking, the last of Holmes's adventures, in the early 1920s Arthur found himself contemplating yet another revival of the best-known of his literary progeny. As before, his motivation was primarily financial – not least because, at this stage of his life, he had become the world's best-known proponent of spiritualism, a cause to which he devoted a large amount of time and money in his later years. The success of Arthur's one-act play *The Crown Diamond, or An Evening with Sherlock Holmes*, performed in May and September 1921, first at the Bristol Hippodrome and then at London's Coliseum, had also heralded a resurgence of interest in the great detective and his exploits. Furthermore, by this time Sherlock Holmes was also a star of the silver screen in the form of the actor Eille Norwood, who, from 1921, starred in an ongoing series of silent – and highly faithful – adaptations of Arthur's stories, made by Stoll Pictures. Arthur was a great admirer of Norwood, who closely matched his own idea of what Holmes should look like. "He has that rare quality which can only be described as glamour, which compels you to watch an actor eagerly when he is doing nothing," he wrote. So impressed was Arthur with Norwood that he even gave the actor a gift of a dressing gown, which he went on to wear in many of the films. However, the author quibbled with the film-makers' decision to set the movies in the present day – that is, the early 1920s – as he felt that modern "luxuries" such as telephones and motor cars were alien to the quintessentially Victorian world of Sherlock Holmes.

So, prompted by the eagerness of Herbert Greenhough Smith (1855–1935), the editor of the *Strand*, to have new Holmes material for the magazine, Arthur adapted his own play, *The Crown Diamond*, renaming it 'The Adventure of the Mazarin Stone', which appeared in October 1921. At around this time, however, the author was forced to confess to Smith that he was stuck for ideas for new stories. Smith responded by suggesting that Arthur write a tale based on the real case of a German man who had made his suicide look like murder – he had done this by weighting a revolver with a stone and then hanging it over a bridge, so that when he shot himself the revolver would vanish into the water. Inspired, Arthur devised a story called 'The Adventure of the Second Chip', which was published in two parts under the new title 'The Problem of Thor Bridge' in February and March 1922.

Ten more stories appeared over the next five years, the final – ever – adventure being 'The Adventure of Shoscombe Old Place', which was published in the American magazine *Liberty* and the *Strand* in March and April 1927, respectively. Book versions – in which the order of the stories did not reflect that in which they had been published in the magazines – followed in both countries in June, courtesy of the publishers John Murray in the UK and George H. Doran Co. in the United States.

Interestingly, Arthur chose to set most of these tales in the latter phase of Holmes's career, with one, 'The Adventure of the Lion's Mane', even taking place after his retirement, which occurred in 1903. As a consequence, many of them have a distinctly "twentieth-century" atmosphere, particularly in their references to precisely those technological innovations whose use in the Stoll films Arthur had deplored: telephones, for instance, occur in several of the adventures.

Many readers have judged the overall quality of the stories in *The Casebook of Sherlock Holmes* to be lower than that of the previous collections and novels, something that was perhaps a reflection of Arthur's self-confessed lack of inspiration at this point in his career. (He had, after all, written no fewer than forty-four stories featuring Holmes already!) Critics of the collection point to its darker, more horrific tone compared to earlier works, citing the description of a face dissolved by acid in 'The Adventure of the Illustrious Client' or the grotesque account of the leper hospital in 'The Adventure of the Blanched Soldier' as examples, as well as the lack of the "cosiness" that was such an essential component of, say, *The Adventures* or *The Memoirs*. An explanation for the intrusion of such uncharacteristic realism into the "fairy kingdom of romance" (as Arthur himself describes it in his preface) in these stories might be that they were written in a world – and by an author – scarred by the events of the Great War. (Arthur's son, Kingsley, had died from pneumonia after being wounded in the Battle of the Somme in 1916.)

Critics have also pointed to Arthur's tendency to repeat story ideas in *The Casebook* – for instance, the plot of 'The Adventure of the Three Garridebs' bears striking similarities to that of 'The Red-Headed League', published in 1891 – as well as to inconsistencies in the characterization of Holmes himself, such as his occasional use of colloquialisms (for example, "Pure swank!" in 'The Adventure of the Retired Colourman') in a manner that is at odds with the detective's usually somewhat formal manner of speech. The Holmesian scholar D. Martin Dakin has also drawn attention to Holmes's unexpected racism in 'The Adventure of the Three Gables', something that is hard to reconcile with the gentlemanly egalitarianism typical of the character elsewhere.

Some have gone further and even argued that the solution to what Dakin called 'the problem of *The Casebook*' – that is, the difference in its tone and quality when seen alongside the rest of the canon – is that a number of the stories were not Arthur's work at all, or that he merely adapted stories that he was sent by enthusiastic readers. A candidate for exclusion from the canon on the basis of disputed authorship is 'The Adventure of the Three Gables', not least for the reason given above; doubts have also been raised about the authenticity of 'The Adventure of the Blanched Soldier' and 'The Adventure of the Retired Colourman', among others. Despite these criticisms, however, there is a consensus that some of the stories in the collection – including 'The Adventure of the Illustrious Client', 'The Adventure of the Sussex Vampire' and 'The Problem of Thor Bridge' – are as strong as any Arthur ever wrote.

In 1923, Stoll Pictures produced two silent shorts based on tales from *The Casebook* as part of *The Last Adventures of Sherlock Holmes*, their third and final film series inspired by Arthur's stories. These were *The Mystery of Thor Bridge* and *The Stone of Mazarin*. More recently, in 1991, several of the adventures in the collection appeared on the small screen in the UK as part of *The Casebook of Sherlock Holmes*, one of several series produced by Granada Television that starred Jeremy Brett – considered by many the definitive Holmes – and Edward Hardwicke. These were 'The Problem of Thor Bridge', 'Shoscombe Old Place', 'The Illustrious Client' and 'The Creeping Man' (as the titles appeared on screen). A somewhat loose and expanded adaptation of 'The Adventure of the Sussex Vampire' was transmitted in 1992 under the title 'The Last Vampyre', again with Brett and Hardwicke in the leading roles. In 1994, Brett returned in *The Memoirs of Sherlock Holmes*, a series whose episodes included 'The Three Gables' and 'The Mazarin Stone' – the latter also incorporating elements from 'The Adventure of the Three Garridebs'.

Numerous radio versions of the stories have also been produced over the years, notably by the BBC, which broadcast adaptations of every one of the sixty Sherlock Holmes adventures between 1989 and 1998, with Clive Merrison as Holmes and Michael Williams as Watson. The twelve episodes of the series *The Casebook of Sherlock Holmes* were first broadcast on Radio 4 between September 1994 and March 1995.

These adaptations and others that have been produced over the years are testament to the enduring cultural influence of Sherlock Holmes, and a demonstration of the incalculable debt owed to Arthur Conan Doyle for having created him.

THE CHARACTERS

(This section contains spoilers)

Sherlock Holmes
The main character, Holmes is an acutely observant investigator of complicated crimes, who uses his famous powers of deduction to solve baffling problems. He can come across as quite cold, but he is a good person dedicated to righting injustices.

Dr John Watson
Watson is a former army surgeon who becomes Sherlock Holmes's fellow crime-fighter after agreeing to share rooms with him at 221B Baker Street. Stolid, loyal and unfailingly courageous, he is also the chronicler of most of his friend's adventures.

Baron Adelbert Gruner
An Austrian aristocrat, womanizer and expert on Chinese pottery who is widely believed to have murdered his wife. Can Holmes and Watson save the innocent Violet de Merville, who has fallen in love with him, from the same fate? He appears in 'The Adventure of the Illustrious Client'.

Godfrey Emsworth

A young soldier who disappeared after being injured while serving in South Africa during the Second Boer War. Is it true, as his father claims, that he has gone on a voyage around the world? Could he be dead? If so, who is the deathly pale figure glimpsed by James M. Dodd, Godfrey's former comrade, at the Emsworth family home? He appears in 'The Adventure of the Blanched Soldier'.

Count Negretto Sylvius

A half-Italian big-game hunter and man about town who is responsible for stealing a priceless diamond, one of the Crown jewels. Can Holmes evade his murderous stratagems and bring him to justice? He appears in 'The Adventure of the Mazarin Stone'.

Isadora Klein

A "celebrated beauty" of Spanish origins and the richest widow on earth. But when the lurid details of her affair with the young diplomat Douglas Maberley are at risk of being made public, thereby jeopardizing her forthcoming marriage, she proves to be a formidable opponent for the great detective. She appears in 'The Adventure of the Three Gables'.

Robert Ferguson

An old rugby-playing friend of Watson's who, in 'The Adventure of the Sussex Vampire', approaches Holmes with a highly unusual and somewhat macabre problem: he suspects his new Peruvian wife of sucking the blood of their baby son. Is she a vampire, or is there another explanation?

John Garrideb

A man who, claiming to be a lawyer from Kansas in the United States, says he is searching desperately for other people with his unusual surname in order to secure a $5 million inheritance. But who is he really, and what are his true intentions? He appears in 'The Adventure of the Three Garridebs'.

Neil Gibson

A former senator from the western United States who made his fortune as a gold-mining magnate and is consequently known as "the Gold King". When his Brazilian wife is murdered, he approaches Holmes in the hope that the great detective can prove that his children's governess, Grace Dunbar, is innocent. But can Holmes get to the bottom of what really happened? He appears in 'The Problem of Thor Bridge'.

Professor Presbury

A renowned physiologist from the ancient university of Camford who is engaged to a much younger woman, Alice Morphy. But what is the cause of his recent odd behaviour and the abrupt and alarming changes in his personality, and how might it be connected to his mysterious visit to Prague? He appears in 'The Adventure of the Creeping Man'.

Harold Stackhurst

The headmaster of a coaching school in Sussex called the Gables. He befriends Holmes following the latter's retirement to the South Downs and takes Watson's place in assisting the erstwhile detective as he endeavours to solve the mystery of the death of Fitzroy McPherson in 'The Adventure of the Lion's Mane'.

Eugenia Ronder

A former circus performer who wears a veil to cover the facial disfigurement she suffered when a lion she regularly performed with savaged her and killed her husband. But why does she want to talk to Holmes now, so many years later? She appears in 'The Adventure of the Veiled Lodger'.

Sir Robert Norberton

A horse-breeder and gambler with a volcanic temper. He hopes to pay off his extensive debts by running a horse, Shoscombe Prince, in the Derby, an important race. But what can explain his recent erratic behaviour? Why did he give his sister's dog away to a local innkeeper? And what is the purpose of his mysterious nocturnal visits to the old crypt? He appears in 'The Adventure of Shoscombe Old Place'.

Josiah Amberley

A retired art-supply dealer who hires Holmes to investigate the disappearance of his wife and her lover. But why has he chosen this time to paint his house? He appears in 'The Adventure of the Retired Colourman'.

GREAT FICTIONAL DETECTIVES

Sherlock Holmes is almost universally believed to be the greatest fictional detective of them all, but authors have created countless other investigators over the years, and many of them are almost as famous. Sometimes they work within the police, and sometimes they work independently of the police – in either case, they generally possess, like Sherlock Holmes, peculiar traits and eccentric quirks which define their characters and influence their way of working. Many of them appeared in the 1920s and 1930s – this is often called the "Golden Age" of detective fiction, because the genre gained many of its features and much of its popularity in that time.

C. Auguste Dupin

The creation of the American writer Edgar Allan Poe (1809–49), the French detective Le Chevalier ("the knight") C. Auguste Dupin is often identified as the first of the great fictional sleuths. He makes his appearance in 1841, in a story called 'The Murders in the Rue Morgue'. Dupin only appears in three stories in total, but he is the prototype of all the investigators that follow, including Sherlock Holmes, and the tales that feature him establish many of the elements of detective fiction: the unconventional investigator, the first-person narration by a close friend and the inadequate official police officer. Arthur Conan Doyle wrote that the stories are "a root from which a whole literature has developed... Where was the detective story until Poe breathed the breath of life into it?" Dupin was raised in upper-class, wealthy circles, but now contents himself with a humbler lifestyle, investigating crimes with his companion, the narrator of the stories (who is never named). His method is based on putting himself into the minds of criminals so that he can understand and deduce their actions.

Miss Marple

Miss Marple was the creation of the English author Agatha Christie (1890–1976). Like Dupin, she is an amateur detective – even more so, given that she is an elderly lady living in a little English village. The first Miss Marple novel is one of the most famous – *The Murder at the Vicarage* (1930). There were a further eleven Miss Marple novels, and twenty short stories. Agatha Christie invented at least half a dozen detectives in her fiction, and has the distinction of creating two of the greatest of all time: not just Miss Marple, but also Hercule Poirot, a fastidious Belgian, who starred in thirty-three novels and more than fifty short stories.

Lord Peter Wimsey

Dorothy L. Sayers (1893–1957) was an English writer and intellectual. She invented Lord Peter Wimsey as the vehicle for her detective fiction, and wrote eleven novels about him. He is the archetypal English upper-class gent: he enjoyed a wealthy upbringing and an Oxford education; he has a glamorous lifestyle and is an expert on cars, wine and classical music. Lord Peter Wimsey is assisted in his investigation by his valet, Bunter, whom he met while fighting in the First World War.

TEST YOURSELF

Can you apply the same forensic powers of logic and reasoning to the stories in *The Casebook of Sherlock Holmes* that Sherlock Holmes uses to solve his cases? Try this multiple-choice quiz to find out. The answers are on p. 284.

1. One of the stories in *The Casebook of Sherlock Holmes* was originally going to be called 'The Adventure of the Black Spaniel'. Which do you think it was?
   A) 'The Adventure of the Creeping Man'
   B) 'The Adventure of the Illustrious Client'
   C) 'The Adventure of the Blanched Soldier'
   D) 'The Adventure of Shoscombe Old Place'

2. In 'The Adventure of the Illustrious Client', how does Kitty Winter take her revenge on Baron Adelbert Gruner?
   A) She throws acid in his face
   B) She sets a specially trained mastiff on him
   C) She shoots him
   D) She deliberately infects him with leprosy

3. In 'The Adventure of the Mazarin Stone', how does Holmes trick Count Negretto Sylvius and Sam Merton into believing he is in the bedroom next door?
   A) He plays a wax-cylinder recording of a violin on the phonograph
   B) He plays a disc recording of a violin on the gramophone

 C) He asks Watson to hide in the room and smoke his (Holmes's) favourite tobacco so that they will think it is him

 D) He places a wax dummy in the bed, leaving the door ajar and dimming the lights to make it look as though he is asleep

4. In 'The Adventure of the Three Gables', what alerts Holmes to the possibility that the stolen manuscript provides the key to the mystery?

 A) It is written in code

 B) It is written in Spanish

 C) The narration changes from the third person to the first person on the final page

 D) The narration changes from the first person to the third person on the final page

5. In 'The Adventure of the Three Garridebs', what is hidden beneath the trapdoor in Nathan Garrideb's house?

 A) The body of the forger Rodger Prescott

 B) A collection of the skulls of extinct species of human being

 C) A gambling den

 D) A printing press for producing counterfeit banknotes

6. In 'The Problem of Thor Bridge', what is Maria Gibson clutching in her hand when she dies?

 A) A note from the governess, Grace Dunbar

 B) A note from her husband, Neil Gibson

 C) A golden pince-nez

 D) The last page of a stolen manuscript

7. At the beginning of 'The Adventure of the Creeping Man', Holmes asks the question: "Why does Professor Presbury's faithful wolfhound, Roy, endeavour to bite him?" What is the answer?

 A) He has been trained to do so by the professor's secretary, Trevor Bennett

 B) He has been trained to do so by Professor Morphy, Presbury's professional rival

C) He has been driven mad by a faulty serum created by the quack Lowenstein
D) He thinks that the professor has turned into a monkey

8. In 'The Adventure of the Lion's Mane', what fools Holmes into believing that Fitzroy McPherson had not entered the water?
A) His skin is dry
B) His towel is dry
C) The tide is too far out
D) He is still fully dressed when he dies

ANSWERS

1—D
2—A
3—B
4—C
5—D
6—A
7—D
8—B

SCORES

1 to 3 correct: You deserve to be apprehended at once…
4 to 6 correct: Lestrade could just about get this many…
7 to 8 correct: Sherlock Holmes has found his successor!